"A too-bright, too-observant girl with a withered hand and her single mother, who dispenses as much magic as mayhem. The town homosexual, magnificent but beleaguered in the Mississippi of 1953. The beautiful hustler who comes into their lives. Families disappoint and families betray, and wisdom comes at a price in the edenic coastal village of Belle Cote. Gwin one more time proves her mastery of the Delta landscape, human and geographic, in prose as rich as a New Orleans praline and a story that would have raised the eyebrows of Tennessee Williams."

—**Wilton Barnhardt, author of** *Western Alliances* **and** *Lookaway, Lookaway*

"Minrose Gwin's *Beautiful Dreamers* was a dream from which I didn't want to wake, a novel set in the vivid world of 1950s Gulf Coast Mississippi, peopled with complex and charismatic characters who together redefine family. Gwin is a skillful, compassionate, wise storyteller, one who finds hope in the antidotes to violence and hate: family and love, truth and justice. I have been a fan of Minrose Gwin's work for years, and *Beautiful Dreamers* is, hands down, my favorite: a book that I couldn't put down and didn't want to end."

—**Lori Ostlund, author of** *After the Parade* **and** *The Bigness of the World*

"Through the compelling characters of Memory Feather, Virginia, and Mac McFadden, Gwin weaves a narrative that is as poignant as it is powerful. The many challenges that are faced by these characters are portrayed with sensitivity and depth. Gwin's prose is nothing short of breathtaking, painting vivid portraits of love and resilience underneath the backdrop of the south during a tumultuous time in history. This book is truly one for the ages."

—**Angela Jackson-Brown, author of** *Untethered* **and** *Homeward*

"Poignant, unsettling, wise. By turns hilarious and profound, this rich insightful novel explores the bravery of Deep Southerners who cannot bear cruelty, who will not tolerate prejudice. Gwin's unforgettable characters navigate a brutal world ever-so-slowly bending toward justice, where billy clubs mercifully are no match for a majorette's baton."

—**John Howard, author of** *Men Like That* **and** *Truths Up His Sleeve*

BEAUTIFUL DREAMERS

BEAUTIFUL DREAMERS

MINROSE GWIN

HUB CITY PRESS
SPARTANBURG, SC

Library of Congress Cataloging-in-
Publication Data

Names: Gwin, Minrose, author.
Title: Beautiful dreamers / Minrose Gwin.
Description: Spartanburg, SC : Hub City Press, 2024.
Identifiers:
    LCCN 2024011626 (print)
    LCCN 2024011627 (ebook)
    ISBN 9798885740364 (hardback)
    ISBN 9798885740418 (epub)
Subjects: LCGFT: Novels.
Classification:
LCC PS3607.W56 B43 2024 (print)
LCC PS3607.W56 (ebook)
DDC 813/.6—dc23/eng/20240322

LC record available at https://lccn.loc.gov/2024011626

This book is a work of fiction. References to real people, events, establishments, organizations,
or locales are intended only to provide a sense of authenticity, and are used fictitiously. All other characters,
and all incidents and dialogue, are drawn from the author's imagination and are not to be construed as real.

Epigraph from *Dream Work* copyright © 1986 by Mary Oliver.
Used by permission of Grove/Atlantic, Inc.
Any third-party use of this material, outside of this publication, is prohibited.

HUB CITY PRESS
200 Ezell Street
Spartanburg, SC 29306
864.577.9349 | www.hubcity.org

In memory of Lynn Kincannon Holland,
who taught me and so many others to love the Mississippi Sound.

Beautiful dreamer, wake unto me,
Starlight and dewdrops are waiting for thee.

  Stephen Foster, "Beautiful Dreamer"

Did I actually reach out my arms
toward it, toward paradise falling, like
the fading of the dearest, wildest hope—
the dark heart of the story that is all
the reason for its telling?

  Mary Oliver, "The Chance to Love Everything"

I.

———

CERTAIN STORIES ARE WILLFUL children; they run in circles without rhyme or reason. They are fierce and wild in their desires, wanting the future as much as the past.

Suffice it to say that in the beginning there were three of us: my father, my mother, and myself. And then, without warning, there were two.

IN THE LATE SUMMER of 1953 when we returned to Belle Cote, my mother had reached the dismal old age of thirty-one. She was sad and mad and lately divorced, my father, a decorated air force pilot turned spy, having flown off into the wild blue yonder of a French woman's arms—the Frog hussy, my mother called her. His desertion of us had soured her on M-E-N, so much so that she spelled the word rather than uttered it, as if it were a curse or referred to some unnameable body part. There were, in fact, only three members of the opposite sex she could tolerate: my grandfather the lawyer, who pursued my father across the Atlantic Ocean and returned with a settlement that supported me in the rousing amount of fifty dollars a month; Dr. Milton Campbell of Colorado Springs, Colorado, who'd ushered me into the world, a baby girl born blue and missing two fingers on my left hand, the tiny hand itself as withered and twisted as an old grapevine; and, finally, my mother's favorite, her childhood friend Mac McFadden.

My mother had adored Mac since the moment he wet through his diapers while sitting on her father's lap at her second birthday party, an event she celebrated by clapping her little hands together and laughing merrily. Mac's mother had named him Milton, after the poet. She was a well-read woman, a teacher of British literature, highfalutin, some said. She admired John Milton, the way he saw Satan as a tortured soul, whose brand of evil flowed from passion and struggle and a love of beauty. It was enough to make you prefer him to God. Mac's mother was struck by her first male child's mane of gold, prettier by a country mile than his older sister's thin rim. By the second day of the baby's hitherto brief life, though, Mac's father, a no-nonsense shopkeeper, put an end to the Milton business and gave Mac his plebeian nickname, Milton being for sissies and English teachers. The name Mac, his father said, in excusing himself to his wife, would lend emphasis to his own family's ancient Scottish roots, baked to a crisp in the Georgia sun, then transported to the Mississippi Gulf Coast in 1804, a year after the Louisiana Purchase.

Mac, my mother explained to me, was an *unusual* human male. Now we would simply call Mac McFadden gay, one of the countless gay men who flourish in small southern communities. Back then, he was referred to as being light in the wing tips—a fairy or a flit, or worse—though actually the locals of Belle Cote didn't talk much about Mac, preferring instead to observe him and roll their eyes.

There was, in fact, something magically buoyant about Mac in his heyday. He was a large man, a substantial man, yet so blond and light-skinned that parts of him seemed translucent as he poured tea for my mother and me and offered us cold biscuits with apple butter and great chunks of sharp cheddar in the weeks following our homecoming. He lived in a sprawling house with floor-to-ceiling windows and twenty-foot ceilings, where sunlight splashed the splintery pine floors and shone through the vegetation outside to make leafy patterns against the white-washed walls.

Mac's house sat squarely in the center of town, behind the First Baptist Church. In a previous life, the place had been an eighteenth-century French school for boys and had a wraparound porch he used for entertaining; for what Mac lacked in visitors from Belle Cote, he made up in lavish parties with dozens of guests from New Orleans: seersuckered men in panama hats with long, delicate fingers that held glowing cigarillos in pearl-tipped mouthpieces. *Beautiful men,* said my mother, her breath catching in her throat. On Saturday nights, they cavorted until all hours as the sounds of Benny Goodman and Ella Fitzgerald mingled with the moans and groans of the Holy Rollers on the edge of town. Some Sunday mornings, the guests' cars were still there to shock the prim-faced Baptists on their way to Sunday school.

Mac was brilliant, my mother said, a physicist by training, a Harvard PhD. He'd been stationed at the Pentagon during the war, ferrying top-secret equations, many his own, back and forth between Los Alamos National Labs in New Mexico and the Pentagon. Afterward, when the war turned cold, Hiroshima and Nagasaki weighed heavily on his conscience, and he returned to Belle Cote and went to work for Ingalls Shipbuilding, which built nuclear-powered submarines. This eased his conscience only minimally; and in 1951, he quit, just two years before he would have been fired anyhow, given that Eisenhower would soon sign Executive Order 10450 that prohibited those practicing "sexual perversion" from working for the government or its defense contractors. Fortunately for Mac, art was his second love after physics. This was as it should be, he was fond of saying, the two being obverse reflections of each other. An art gallery in his Mississippi Gulf Coast hometown seemed just the ticket and, if not redemptive, at least relatively harmless.

Some of this information I learned from Mac himself. Ever since I was little, his letters, addressed in a bold, almost indecipherable script, had followed my mother from pillar to post like a pack of playful puppies. Depending on where we were currently living, she stashed them in different places, which became more challenging as time went on, given their growing abundance and our shrinking domiciles. At the El Camino Motor Hotel, where we lived for the better part of a year in

Room 37, she situated them on sheets of newspaper and stowed them under the bed alongside the upturned remains of dead roaches. She told me never to touch her "Mac letters," as she called them, but of course I did. They were full of news about his parties—*Papa's old moth-eaten kilt was a big hit last night!*—and hometown people I didn't know, especially local boys who had died in the war. The letters always closed with an earnest entreaty to hasten home. My mother wrote Mac back; she spent what I considered an inordinate amount of time on her letters to him, posting one every Monday morning, refusing to do another thing on Sunday until she had accomplished that task. She was secretive about these letters, scribbling like a madwoman, her non-writing hand shielding the pages from my prying eyes.

Of my mother's old high school crowd, only Mac remained lively and active in Belle Cote, her girlfriends having been scattered across the globe by the winds of war and most of the unmarried men under forty-five having lost noteworthy parts of their anatomy—or, worse yet, their minds—in the fighting. My mother was an anomaly; there were a few young war widows in town but no divorcées and certainly none with an offspring in tow, in my case a curly-haired blond child with an unfortunate deformity and the round freckled face of her Irish father, who was fondly remembered about town as a jokester, daredevil, prize-winning dancer, and speaker of gibberish from a multitude of foreign countries.

My mother's name was Virginia Feather. She was the beloved only child of Martha and Memory Feather, having been born late in her parents' lives. In truth, my grandparents, who were third cousins, both bearing the name Feather before they married, and my mother, who'd taken back her maiden name against all convention, looked a bit like wetland birds. Each of them had a long, narrow neck and spindly legs, coupled, oddly, with a certain muscularity at the shoulder and thickness in the chest (my grandmother quite busty), as if their torsos were composed of folded wings. They walked with a forward thrust of the head and a backward trending of the buttocks, which in my grandparents seemed to grow more pronounced and pigeon-like as the years passed, at least so it seemed in the photographs they sent. In my mother, the effect was more delicate and graceful. Sometimes, when she leaned forward to read Mac's scribblings, her neck elongated, she resembled an egret bent to the water at the edge of a marsh.

In the course of a life, it can be hard to tell beginnings from endings, and in this case, they converged. After the war, my father returned to his first love, which was not my mother but language. At Ole Miss he'd been known as a whiz kid, mastering French, Spanish, and Russian in short order. After the war he'd gone back to school on the government's dime, studying German at the University of New Mexico, just a few blocks from his posting at Kirkland Air Force Base in Albuquerque, and then was deployed to Paris to listen in on East German and Russian communications. "Words, words, words," my mother complained as he walked around the house muttering to himself in a variety of foreign tongues. "You talk all the time but you don't say anything I can understand."

When he absconded with the French hussy, leaving us quite literally high and dry in Albuquerque, she packed up two suitcases with our belongings, three paper sacks filled with Mac McFadden's letters, and me, also named Memory Feather, after my grandfather. Struggling with these meager worldly possessions, we took three buses across town to the El Camino up on North Fourth Street. There she settled into her new job of cleaning rooms, which were used mostly for short-term purposes and stunk of old dust, body odor, and whiskey. In a matter of weeks, her small pink hands had flamed into red mittens, her dark hair dulled to blacktop on the road.

The El Camino sign, which hung directly over the office, boasted neon lights in all colors of the rainbow. The yellow VACANCY sign was always flashing. SINGLE, a designation someone had taken as a selling point, was a sickly green. EL CAMINO a radiant royal blue, GOOD NIGHT'S REST a lurid red. In small letters was the promise of A QUIET COMFORTABLE STAY, which only lit up after dark. At night my mother fell exhausted into the lumpy bed we shared as I lay there watching the VACANCY sign flicker on and off through the threadbare drapery that hung over our one small window.

Soon after we moved into the El Camino, something in my bony chest clicked shut. That fall, when the chamisa bloomed yellow and buzzed with bees and the cottonwoods chattered expectantly, odd spells of breathlessness and disorientation left me unable to follow the lines in my schoolbooks. Some afternoons when the winds kicked up, I'd come in from school squeaking like a rusty hinge. My mother would have to put down her mop or broom to draw a bath as hot as I could stand. As I sat in the tub gasping for breath, she instructed me to count the small black and white tiles on the bathroom floor to determine whether there were more of one or the other, as if such a calculation somehow mattered. When I complained about the dust along my route to the local library, my mother replied, "Lucky you. Every Saturday you walk the Old Camino Real that ran from Mexico City to Santa Fe centuries ago. *Four* centuries ago. Not many children have history right under their feet."

My morning walk to Taft Primary School where I attended fourth grade was dusty too, the road overhung with desert willows and Russian olives with their small silvery leaves. A flock of rotund guinea hens with their chicks kept me company, clucking companionably. The school itself was surrounded by a swath of farms. The farmers flooded their acreages of orchards and field crops of chile, corn, and alfalfa with the precious water that flowed from the Rio Grande into centuries-old irrigation ditches.On the way home in the afternoons, I often strolled along the ancient acequias that ran full to the top in growing season and dry as a bone from October to April. Massive, gnarled cottonwoods with their muscled trunks lined the ditches, glistening and rattling in the early fall breezes.

I should mention here, at the risk of being thought odd, that after our move to the El Camino, I began to hear things other people could not. To be precise, nonhuman creatures and sometimes even plants conversed with me. It was as if, upon his departure from our lives, my father had left a door ajar. I slipped through it unawares, becoming, like him, a translator in the process.

One night over supper, I told my mother that the school hamster had entreated me to free it—it wanted to eat fresh grass, feel the fall breezes ruffle its fur. She emphatically urged me not to reveal to anyone else the questionable fact that my ears had been set to a different pitch from all the other human ears of the world. "Our silly little secret," she said, a smile playing at her lips. "You'll outgrow it."

Never mind. The world sang to me. When the golden cottonwoods rattled, I heard the sound of subterranean breathing—a whoosh and then the sharp intake of air, as if the trees were expressing some barely restrained desire. *Wanting, wanting,* they sighed, thinking, I imagined, of water. When the water was flowing in the acequias, I would sit on the banks and watch giant crayfish nibble at the frogs, making them sing out *Oops!* and skitter across the water's brown surface. Sometimes I would sit there until dark, listening to the murmuring world. Sometimes, in this attitude of listening, I would look down at my hand, so curled in upon itself, my own paw, and understand that I, too, was an animal, albeit a misshapen one.

VIRGINIA FEATHER HAD CHOSEN, pridefully, not to inform my father or my grandparents of our precarious financial situation or our new mailing address at the El Camino. The monthly checks from my father stopped abruptly. Months went by without word from my grandparents. Only Mac knew of our whereabouts, and my mother tore up the checks that fell out of his letters.

One August afternoon, my mother's plan to disappear from the face of the earth bit the dust when an old friend of my grandparents, a man with salt-and-pepper hair and warm eyes, arrived at the El Camino and happened upon my mother scrubbing the toilet in his room. She was on her knees, intent on her task, wet half moons blossoming under her arms. I was standing beside her and in the act of handing her some cleanser when his key turned the lock and he entered the room. Behind him, Fourth Street bustled with cars and a few tractors; above Fourth Street the Sandia Mountains loomed, white clouds at their tips.

My mother turned her head to look, clearing her throat to announce her presence and murmur, as was her custom, that she'd have the room ready in just a few minutes; she was almost done.

Then she froze.

The man peered down at her. "Virginia?" he said. "Little Virginia Feather?"

She leapt to her feet and raised one hand, as if preparing to salute. She tried to smile and failed. A wistful lock of hair had fallen over her left eye. Her eyes were bloodshot. The night before, she'd thrown herself across the bed and wept inconsolably for Ethel Rosenberg, who'd been electrocuted three times, the third apparently the charm that finally stopped her intractable heart and sent a puff of smoke emanating from her head. Ethel, my mother maintained, was a *mother*; her only crime was marrying that horrible Julius Rosenberg, and that really wasn't a crime since she apparently loved him enough to go to the electric chair for him. If any so-called high crime of treason had been committed, it was Julius alone who was the perpetrator. Joe McCarthy and Roy Cohn and their red-baiting, homosexual-hating cronies—they were the ones who ought to be executed, not the mother of two little boys, bless their hearts.

"VIRGINIA." THE MAN SAID her name more firmly now. "What in heaven's name are you doing in this place?" His arm swept the room, then fell to his side.

My mother glanced down at me. "Making a living."

"My heavens," he said, his jaw dropping, "What would your mother and daddy think? Virginia Feather cleaning commodes."

My mother put her hand on my shoulder. "We're doing just fine here," she said. "Just fine."

"I have asthma," I said. "I have to breathe in steam."

The man knelt down and took the cleanser from my hand and set it on the floor. "I'm so sorry," he said. "I bet the salt air in Belle Cote would make it better."

I looked up at my mother, who was glaring at me. "Mr. O'Brien," she said. "We're really just fine here. Memory is doing well in school, aren't you, Mem?" She nudged me.

"I've always wanted to see the Sound," I said, ignoring my mother's question. I was a child of the Mississippi Sound before I ever encountered it. Wandering the dusty streets and paths in the north valley of Albuquerque, I spent most of my waking hours yearning for the ninety-mile-long body of water I'd never seen but that my namesake grandfather had written long letters describing, letters that came with military regularity before my mother decided to disappear off the face of the earth.

"Memory," Mr. O'Brien said. "Named after your grandfather. A fine man."

I wanted to tell Mr. O'Brien about how, just the last Tuesday, my mother had lost her balance and slipped while cleaning out a bathtub in Room 56 and chipped her front tooth on the tub's faucet, how she'd cried inconsolably after smiling into the cracked mirror in our tiny bathroom. How this past Christmas she decorated our room with cutout paper angels made from napkins pilfered from the motel restaurant. We cut out rows and rows of the little white angel shapes, glued the rows together, then marched them across the top of our chest of drawers and around the bulb of the only lamp in the room, which had the unfortunate effect of catching the paper angels on fire. It was a pretty sight, the fiery angels, until my mother filled a glass and put out the flames, leaving a soggy mess of gray ash to clean up. I wanted to tell Mr. O'Brien how, when I needed school supplies or had an aching tooth, my mother would work nights. She'd put her hair up in a French twist and pull out a scuffed pair of red patent-leather high heels and her one pair of stockings. She wore the same dress, a little black number with a wide patent leather belt, which she pulled so tight one hole had stretched into another. After she dressed, she turned her back to me and asked if her stocking seams were straight. She made me go to bed early and turn out the lights. She kept the key to let herself back in and, before leaving, waited until she heard me click the lock into place. Barring a fire, I was not to unlock the door for anybody but her. She returned in the early morning hours and ran herself a bath. Some mornings I'd find her asleep in the tub, the water gone cold.

A few weeks previous to our encounter with Mr. O'Brien, my mother had gone out in the black dress, locking the door behind her. I was just dozing off when the doorknob began to turn as if it had a mind of its own. I sat up in bed, mesmerized, the hotel VACANCY sign flickering across the room. The knob began to shake and rattle. On the other side of the door, someone was breathing hard. This was not the first time such a thing had happened. My mother, who kept a baseball bat under her side of the bed, would whisper it was just a drunk trying to get into the wrong room, be quiet and he'd go away.

The door wasn't substantial; the knob was loose in its screws. The hair rose on the back of my neck. The quiet insistence of the doorknob man seemed more sinister than the confused ramblings of a regular drunk. I crawled over to my mother's side of the bed and reached under the bed for the bat; then, thinking the better of a direct confrontation with whoever was on the other side of the door, I slid to the floor and under the bed, pushing aside our suitcases and piles of Mac McFadden's letters. Roach corpses crunched under my back and legs. I lay there clutching the bat, fighting the urge to cough as I inhaled the dust in the carpet. After more knob jiggling, the man whapped the door and shouted, "Hey!" Just that, nothing more. My chest tightened up and seized, once, twice, three times. I stuffed my hand into my mouth to keep from coughing.

I woke up in the bathtub, my mother splashing hot water over my chest. "Wake up, Mem. For god's sake, wake up."

My chest rattled and squeaked as if a small animal were trapped inside. "Don't you ever go leaving me again," I gasped. "Don't you do it."

She stood up. One of her stockings had broken open at the knee. Her eyes were wet and wild, her hair frizzed by the steam in the bathroom. "Do you think I *like* going out at night? I *hate* it. I *hate* leaving you."

"Why do you go then? Why do you go out partying?"

Her face sagged. "I'm not partying, honey. I'm trying to make a living for us. For *you.*"

"Make a living doing what?"

She sat on the commode and loosened her stockings from her garter belt. The torn one she yanked off and threw in the wastebasket, the good one she rolled up and laid on the back of the toilet. Then she said she planned parties for the El Camino guests, parties for gentlemen to have a good time so they'd come again. For this service, she said, the management paid her extra. She would never have left me otherwise.

I wanted to tell Mr. O'Brien this story in particular because he seemed like a nice man who might rescue us in some unforeseen way, but my mother shot me a look to kill. "She's just fine," she said. "Mem is an exceptional student."

"I'd do better if I didn't have to walk a mile each way," I said.

"It's not a mile and you know it." My mother gathered her cleansers and moved toward the bathroom doorway where Mr. O'Brien stood.

He looked puzzled. "Virginia, honey, why on earth would you rather clean toilets in this godforsaken place than come home where you belong?"

She squared her shoulders and proceeded to tell him everything that was wrong with Belle Cote. It was too small. Everybody was into everybody else's business. There were white water fountains and colored water fountains, which was height of absurdity. People had judged her when I came too soon, even her own mother and daddy. People made fun of her good friend Mac McFadden. The list went on.

She stopped abruptly. "And what brings you to our crummy little hotel in the middle of nowhere? You're certainly a long way from Belle Cote, Mr. O'Brien."

He studied the tiles on the floor. "Business."

"Business? What kind of business?"

"Real estate."

"And how, may I ask, is *Mrs.* O'Brien?"

Mr. O'Brien's face turned pink. He pulled a handkerchief from his pocket and wiped his brow. "She's doing fine."

My mother juggled her cleaning supplies. "Too bad she's not here to enjoy our lovely hotel. Give her my regards," she said and pushed me out the door.

I came in from school a week later, my saddle oxfords, white socks, and bare legs covered in dust. The door to our room was open to the parking lot. Sitting in the one rickety chair in our room was a large man with the little pointed teeth of a possum. My mother paced back and forth in front of him, her hands on her hips. He was a private detective, as it turned out, sent by my grandparents. He was explaining that my grandfather had retained him to find us; moreover, the first Memory planned to go to court for custody if my mother wouldn't bring me home. The El Camino Motor Hotel was no environment for a young girl. The jig was up; my mother's determined run at a poverty-stricken life as a motel maid was over.

In EFFECTING MY RESCUE, my grandfather purchased my mother and me tickets on the CSX Rail Line. Over the long days and nights of the train trip home, I pressed my face to the window of our double berth and watched the high desert with its red mesas and long vistas give way to lush green valleys and prairie, then to flat delta country where men, women, and children bent over weary rows of cotton as far as the eye could see. In the reflection of the glass, my own small skull a ghostly imprint on the face of a vast landscape.

Over the drowsy miles, my mother told me stories about the Mississippi Sound: how it carried memory and history in its slosh and swirl; how archaeologists had unearthed great burial mounds and towering oyster and clam middens in the Sound's adjacent estuaries where Indians had harvested shellfish; how, thousands of years later, women from Santo Domingo had been brought in for French explorers to take for their selfish pleasure; how Bienville's men had fished from the Sound's teeming waters with their bare hands.

When I finally tumbled off the train at the Belle Cote depot that muggy September night and fell into my grandparents' unfamiliar arms, a warm wet breeze slapped me awake. My sinuses popped gloriously open at the scent of salt, and I took my first deep breath in a year.

It was as if I'd been given a set of gills.

THE NEXT MORNING A basket full of oranges, lemons, and kumquats appeared on my grandparents' upper deck, along with an engraved card bearing Mac McFadden's name and the message WELCOME HOME, DEAR FEATHER, his pet name for my mother. The following day Mac himself came calling. He looked like a Viking with his electric blue eyes and full mane of hair the color of the sun. "Little Feather," he proclaimed, thrusting a box of Russell Stover chocolates at me, then sweeping me up into his muscular arms as if I were his own long-lost child. He took my withered hand in his and, of all things, touched it to his lips and kissed it. Then he whispered, "We're going to have a ball, sweetheart, just you wait and see!" His lips tickled my earlobe, sending a chill down my spine. I buried my face in the lionly ruff that sprouted from his open collar and hugged him the way I'd seen daughters on the newsreels hug their soldier-fathers coming back from the war, the way I would have hugged my own father had he not gotten lost in the arms of the French hussy.

My mother appeared in the doorway. "Oh, Mac," she cried out, reaching for him. "What a disaster!" Her face crumpled.

He put me down. "Feather, darling," he said and pressed her chapped hands to his cheek. "Think of the *fun* we're going to have now that you're home. You must come to supper *chez Mac* this very night." He stepped back and eyed her. "You look a bit bedraggled, my dear. We need to fatten you up. Oysters and shrimp remoulade and an eight-layer coconut cake. That's the ticket. Six o'clock sharp, ladies. My friend Oliver will have the champagne chilled."

"I don't have any friends here," I said, wanting him to linger, pay attention.

Mac squatted, put his hand on my shoulder. "You have me, Little Feather." He glanced up at my mother, who was wiping her eyes on her sleeve. "Sweetheart, you had me before you were ever born."

II.

———

THAT AFTERNOON, MY GRANDPARENTS took me on a tour of Belle Cote in their giant toadstool of a car, a gray Plymouth. My mother stayed home. She needed a swim and then a nap; the train trip had been interminable.

In as far as I could tell, the Belle Cote we'd come home to was a cozy little place—a magical place, said my grandfather—with a few large houses on stilts and a dozen grand hotels sprinkled on a slight rise across Beach Boulevard from the Sound. Smaller homes with docks dotted the Bay of St. Louis, which separated Belle Cote from Pass Christian, where well-off upstate planters summered, and, a few miles east, from Gulfport and Biloxi with their glitz and gambling crowds.

The town itself rested on a thick thumb of land, surrounded on three sides by water: the Bay of St. Louis to the northeast, the Jourdan River to the north, Lake Bourne to the southwest. Due south lay the Sound, which threaded its way through several barrier islands to the Gulf of Mexico. Belle Cote's Main Street dead-ended into the Sound as if the street itself were an estuary. Main Street offered eight restaurants and Frapini's Knock Knock Bar; Phillipe's Grocery with its canned goods piled floor to ceiling and giant window fans that roared year round; a shoe repair shop; Lance's Pharmacy that boasted two impressive cases of lipsticks under a Barq's Root Beer sign; Mac's art and antique gallery whimsically called Beautiful Dreamer; and the A&G Theatre, which featured Sunday afternoon musicales, after which the New Orleans crowd headed back into the City. Scalio Brothers Gas Station, a small octagonal building with giant aluminum extensions like bat wings, was the place to go with a flat tire or failing engine, and the Yacht Club hosted sailboat regattas in the Bay every weekend, weather permitting.

At the A&G, there was a billboard advertising *On the Waterfront*. On the side of the building, a set of rickety stairs led to a door at the top that read COLORED, which I then took to mean that the film was in color, not black and white.

This was before the high-rise casinos that served buffets of Alaskan king crab and small suckling pigs with apples in their mouths, before Hurricanes Betsy and Camille, before DuPont appropriated the upper end of the Bay and began to manufacture the whitening agent in everything from toilet paper to paint, before oil spills mucked up the swamps and pelicans and coastal oyster reefs. It was before the ancient live oaks became so rare that they were given names like Lucius Cassius and Serendipity. The Bay and Sound teemed with life. Wading in the water, children giggled and shrieked when shrimp and tiny bay anchovies invaded their swimsuits. Even the poorest of the poor had small fishing boats, and many lived off seafood and what their sandy gardens produced during the long growing season. Ship Island was still whole, and the stacks of Chiquita bananas on the docks in Gulfport had yet to harbor the poisonous brown spiders that could take the flesh off your bones.

MY GRANDFATHER PARKED THE car on Beach Boulevard and we began to walk. Above us the giant oaks dripped Spanish moss as we made our way through the sea oats and saw grass. My grandfather pulled a thatch of the gray moss off one of the tree limbs, let me touch it, then piled it onto my grandmother's head. She shrieked, making us laugh. Over the water, pelicans with their white-tipped heads glided by in flocks of hundreds. Under it all, the Sound murmured and lapped against the seawall, punctuated by the train's whistle as it shimmied along on its trestle across the Bay.

I spotted my mother, a dot on the horizon, slowly plowing back and forth in the brown water. I worried she'd ventured too far out, but my grandfather said she had grown up in that water; she could swim to Mexico if she took a mind to. Besides, the Sound had a long shallow shelf; she was closer to land than it appeared. I waved, but, intent on her swim, she didn't see.

As we walked along the seawall, my grandfather took my hand and began to relate the origin of the Mississippi Sound and the animals that roamed there during the Paleo-Indian Age, his gravelly voice becoming theatrical.

In the beginning, he said, when the earth was young, there were only the one great landmass called Pangaea and the one great ocean called Panthalassa. Then the earthquakes heaved and the volcanoes roared and spewed and the land cracked and cleaved, and the one great ocean poured salt water into the bowl the land's parting had made, and a Gulf was born, sloshing and teeming, tracking the pull of the moon, hungry—*ravenous*, he said—for the touch of the land.

But in the millennia to come, the river called Mississippi would send its seep and ooze south and an afterthought of barrier islands would emerge from the Gulf, thwarting its desire for land, and the ninety-mile finger of salt water between the islands and the land would quieten and flourish with mullet and porpoises and oyster beds. A beautiful coast rose up from this Sound, fresh and green and new. Animals walked upon it and flew above it: mastodons and saber-toothed tigers, camels and white pelicans, the whitest of white, and the pelicans made their rookeries in the ancient oaks and the mammals grazed upon the green plains and rested under the boughs that sheltered them and their young.

"And it was good," pronounced my grandfather. "It was Paradise."

"Oh, Memory," my grandmother said to him. "You do go on."

We came upon a bench at the water's edge and sat down, she on one side of me and my grandfather on the other. "Now then," said my grand-mother, patting my knee, "tell us about yourself, Miss Memory Feather. What do you like to do? What are your *enthusiasms*?"

The latter question I considered odd, or at least oddly phrased. Perhaps that's why, fortified by my grandfather's grandiose tales of saber-toothed tigers and mastodons, I forgot my mother's injunction and proceeded to tell my grandparents about my enthusiasm for chatting with nonhumans.

"You have imaginary friends," murmured my grandmother encouragingly.

I said no, these were real animals, real plants and trees, with whom I enjoyed holding conversations. They were in no way imaginary. To make my point, I told them about my daily conversations with the ditch frogs and cottonwoods and guinea hens, less frequent ones with Phyllostomatidae, the ghost-faced bats that made their homes under the rafters at the El Camino; Heteromyidae, the leaf-nosed mice that chewed their way under our bathroom sink until my mother stoppered it with steel wool; Viperidae, the western diamondback rattlesnakes, from which I kept my distance, not knowing how close a person could get without their taking umbrage. "I suppose it depends on the snake's particular personality," I said.

"I suppose," said my grandfather.

Encouraged, I launched into a story about how, the previous winter, I'd become entranced by the untidy formations of migrating sandhill and whooping cranes, who'd swooped down on the field across from my school. The cranes all talked at once. When they weren't feed-ing, they flew about in circles above the field, emitting excited spurts of gargling and hooting, a cacophonous chorus of celebration, a party. On the ground they stood around in clumps, with one quietly watching me while the others drilled the ground with their needle-sharp beaks, dredging for the grains and bugs and worms they relished. One of the sandhill watchers, larger than the other cranes in his group, with more distinct burnt orange stripes on his side, ruffled his lacy under-feathers and asked me politely not to come any closer. *Stay*, he instructed me, as if I were a dog in training. That's all he said, but he was quite stern about it, I told my grandmother.

"How unusual," she murmured.

"Hard being an only child," said the first Memory.

"And living in that *place*," my grandmother said.

A flock of gulls landed in front of us, squawking and preening. My grandfather pulled some bread from his pocket and threw it at them. *Mine*, they screamed at one another. *No mine.*

THAT NIGHT MY MOTHER and I walked to Mac's. My grandparents hadn't wanted us to go. We'd been in town less than forty-eight hours. We needed to rest and settle; my grandmother had a good supper planned: deviled eggs and ham. My mother waved aside their objections. Mac was her best friend in the world. He'd gone to trouble; we couldn't disappoint him.

Mac's French schoolhouse had two stairways of fifteen steps each, divided into three groups of fives, leading up to the porch. My mother said he'd taken the schoolhouse in a trade for the beach house of his parents, who, along with his sister, had drowned in a sailboat accident when he was in his first year at Harvard. There were three doors across the front, and the back and side yards were shaded by four giant live oaks whose serpentine limbs were sheathed in resurrection moss. The tree limbs pushed like anxious lovers against the porch railings, tempting me to climb from the porch directly onto their branches, though my mother took one look and forbade it.

"Remember your table manners," she said, as we started up the second flight of steps. My mother was big on table manners. At the El Camino, she'd pocketed the nicked flatware from the café for my lessons. We'd had imaginary meals that made my mouth water—first, second, third, and even fourth courses with utensils for each. She described foods I'd never even imagined: icy cold raw oysters with lemon and horseradish on big scalloped plates, watercress salads with mustard and relish-stuffed eggs, flounder amandine with asparagus, caramel pie with high-as-a-kite mcringuc as a grand finale. My mother arranged the forks and spoons and knives just so on the bed, and then showed me how to work from the outside in when picking them up. "Don't forget to wipe your mouth from time to time," she instructed. "You tend to pick up crumbs." By the time she'd finished with me, I felt quite accomplished as an eater of delicacies I could scarcely conjure up. In real life, we chose our one free meal in the evenings at the El Camino restaurant. The rest of the time we opened cans of beans and potted meat for sandwiches and for breakfast ate bowls of Rice Krispies, sometimes with the plums, grapes, and peaches I pilfered from the bushes that leaned out over the paths along the acequias.

Mac must have been watching us mount the steps; the middle of the three front doors opened before we could knock.

"How wonderful you're here! 'What a lark, what a plunge,' as Mrs. Woolf would say!" He stepped aside and made a sweeping gesture for us to enter. His hair shone gold as a crown in the late-day sun.

My jaw dropped as I looked around. Mac's sweeping living room had floor-to-ceiling windows on two sides so that we seemed to be walking into the treehouse of a giant. The other two walls were covered in enormous oil paintings of monkeys and vine-laden trees and ocean vistas. The colors leapt out from the whitewashed walls: the bluest of blues, the emerald greens of jungles and women washing clothes in rivers amid splatters of violet and mustard here and there in landscapes that seemed so vividly alive you could walk right into them.

Among all these, one painting stood out. It was of a man, a young man, his skin carrying the look and texture of velvet. I was struck by the painting, not because of the model's nakedness (though that would certainly have been enough since I'd never laid eyes on a man's private parts, which looked as vulnerable as bread dough in contrast to the rest of the young man's tightly packed anatomy) but because of his sheer beauty. He gazed directly out of his gilded frame at us and seemed to be about to give an order or issue a summons, as if he were a prince.

Yet there was something about him that was unsettling. A certain curl of the lip, the way his eyes seemed to mock my paw. I was drawn to him, yet repelled, as if he were a beautiful but poisonous snake.

"My beautiful dreamer, I couldn't resist him," Mac said with a twinkle in his eye. "I picked him up in the City years ago. I thought I'd take him down to the gallery, but I couldn't bear to live without him. The painting, that is. So I named the gallery Beautiful Dreamer after him." He looked down at me and winked, then turned back to my mother. "Actually, I spotted him in the flesh coming out of a bar on Chartres a few weeks ago. He had a lady on each arm. He was considerably prettier than they were. I told him he was barking up the wrong tree. 'They're just window dressing,' he said, 'ladies of the street I'm helping home.'"

My mother eyed me. "Mac, you behave now. You have company."

"And I expect my company would like some libations." He knelt down. "How does a Shirley Temple sound, Little Feather? Mind if I call you Little for short?"

I nodded, impatient to learn what kind of beverage a Shirley Temple was.

My mother poked me.

"Please," I added.

"And you, Feather? Oliver has a bottle of champagne chilling. We can celebrate."

"Not much to celebrate," my mother said. "Here I am back where I started. Here's where I'll live out the rest of my dreary little life and die."

"Buck up, Feather. If I fell to pieces every time someone absconded on me, I'd be dead and buried a dozen times over. Besides, *look* at you, my dear! Those eyes. That heart of a face. Darling, you're going to have all the able-bodied men up and down the whole Gulf Coast drooling over you the minute you get some skin on those bones and a decent wash and set."

"*I* like it here," I said. "I think it's swell."

I gazed up at the portrait of the man. His eyes had followed me to the center of the room.

My mother sighed and sank into a leather chair that dwarfed her. Mac sat down on the arm of the chair and began to rub her bony shoulders. She looked like a drab mouse nestled in Mac's lionly mane, her eyes strangely unfocused, as if she were on the verge of falling asleep. A single tear slid down her right cheek.

He pulled a strand of her hair back behind her ear and leaned over her. "Feather, I have a splendid idea. How'd you like to come work for me? The gallery's doing well with the New Orleans crowd on the weekends and some locals too. It's running me ragged; I could use an assistant. We could take buying trips into the City and have martini lunches at Antoine's. We could go to Maison Blanche to get you something respectable to wear. My god, darling, it's not like we're in the Arctic wilderness down here in Belle Cote. There are *options*."

"I don't know anything about art," said my mother.

"I'll teach you," Mac said. "It's settled. Now where's that Oliver with the champagne?" He gave my mother a final pat and headed for the kitchen.

I took his place on the arm of the chair next to my mother's thin little arm. "You're going to be all right, you'll see."

She glared at me. "What do *you* know about *me?*"

Actually I knew a truckload, two or three truckloads. Indeed, I considered myself the world's living expert on Virginia Feather. I knew that my mother had once been happy. She'd grown up in a spacious house, windows flung open to the salt breezes, sheer curtains billowing peacefully, her own room a wallpapered garden of pink and white roses. I'd just seen these things with my very own eyes. She'd grown up with a mother who fried country ham and eggs for breakfast, who put away pickled peaches in a crock. Once, Virginia Feather had laughed out loud and busied herself in the world. After my father had gone off to war, she'd taken his absence as an opportunity to do her part for the war effort, finding a job at the base typing and filing and answering the phone. Each morning she'd set me down in a big room with toys and other children and smiling young women who spoke English to us and Spanish to one another. When the Sandia Mountains turned watermelon pink in the late afternoon, she'd return and pluck me up and we'd walk home together to our little flat-roofed stucco house across from the base. She'd pour us some lemonade and we'd go out onto our porch stoop to watch the mountains turn from pink to blue as the sun went down. Sometimes after supper we made cutout sugar cookies in the shapes of stars and half moons and eat them warm at the kitchen table. Afterward, my mother washed the dishes and I wiped crumbs from the oilcloth of grape clusters and leaves. Then we would sit down to a game of Old Maids.

After the war, letters had arrived from my father in France. He'd quit the service. He was teaching three languages at the Sorbonne to make more money for us. He'd be home at the end of the term. By the time his letters slowed to a trickle and finally stopped except for that one last terrible one, a deep vertical trench had wormed its way between my mother's eyebrows. Her hazel eyes had become as faded and empty as a cloudless sky.

When the last letter from my father arrived in the mailbox, my mother snatched it out and rubbed it against her cheek. "It's about damn time," she said.

"Read it." I was as excited about my father's letters as she was. Although they were always written to her alone, she always read me sections of them, especially the last lines when he inquired about my health and told her to give me a hug for him.

She ripped it open and stood on the sidewalk to read. It was summer, the sun high in the sky. A hot wind blew a tumbleweed back and forth across the street. I shaded my eyes and looked up at her, eager to hear the latest from my father, whose letters usually were filled with reports of gay Paree: how people sat at little tables in the streets sipping wine with their midday meal, how the trees bent over their tables and apple blossoms floated down into their glasses.

The letter was disappointingly short, only one page. My mother's hungry face turned to stone as she scanned the words. The letter was on onionskin stationery. The words were smaller and neater than my father's usual script, as if what he were saying had to be said quietly. There were only a few lines on the one page. After a moment my mother dropped the letter and envelope on the sidewalk and walked into the house.

I reached down and picked up the letter. It began, *Virgina, dear, I am so sorry, but…* No mention of me, the daughter. I tore it into a million shreds and watched the wind blow them down the street, some catching in the restless tumbleweed.

But. Such a small word. I followed my mother inside to start our whole new life.

In the months that followed, it was as if time itself had gone haywire, the days and weeks hardening across my mother's face. It wasn't just the trench between her eyebrows or the terrible emptiness of her eyes; it was in her new way of walking with a slight stoop and a nervous habit of clenching and unclenching her hands. Her hair thinned and grew long. I had to remind her to wash it. It was as if she'd forgotten there was something called hair on her head.

Under these circumstances, my grooming, such as it was, suffered. As I grew older, I attended to it on my own as best I could, spurred on by an increasingly urgent desire to fit in at school, which was nigh unto impossible if you lived in the El Camino Motor Hotel and had a hand like mine. I swiped a pair of dull paper scissors from school and made my mother cut my hair every so often. I acquired three bobby pins from various motel rooms, which I used to tack the loose strands back from my face. Once I snagged a blue ribbon someone had left out on the bed in one of the rooms I was helping my mother clean. My mismatched clothes came from a big box at the Church of the Nativity of the Blessed Virgin Mary, which was set out on the steps between its twin steeples the second Saturday morning of each month. So it had been an immense relief when, that very morning, my grandmother rummaged through my suitcase and pronounced my odd wardrobe a disgrace; she'd take me over to Biloxi and buy me some outfits the very next morning.

THERE WAS A COMMOTION in Mac's kitchen. Something had fallen and was clattering about on the floor, followed by a short exclamation and a burst of laughter. A monster black cat came careening around the corner, skidded across the floor, and leapt up onto a massive buffet next to the dining room table, where she then arranged herself on a large platter, as if preparing herself to be served for supper.

In a moment a man with red hair and freckles burst through the opening between kitchen and living room. He bore a large silver tray with a bottle in a bucket of ice and three goblets. Mac trailed behind, carrying a tall glass filled with a pink liquid and a handful of maraschino cherries and orange twists, which he handed to me with a bow. Both of them seemed in high spirits, enjoying a private joke.

Mac frowned at the cat. "Get down from there, Minerva."

The cat ignored him, turning her attention to chewing the tip of her tail.

"We can't do a thing with that cat. She's a force of nature. Your drink, Little," Mac said. Then he turned and put his hand on the man's shoulder. "And this is Oliver. Oliver, these are the marvelous Feather girls."

My mother smiled and waved a little wave at Oliver, who grinned so broadly you could see his gums.

"Honored," he said. Still grinning, he took the bottle, untwisted the wire on the top, and began to push at the cork with his thumb.

"Where on earth did you get the champagne?" my mother asked.

Oliver winked. "The City, where else?"

The champagne cork popped, making me jump, and Oliver began to pour from the foaming bottle, moving quickly from glass to glass.

The cat lifted her head and looked straight at me, her yellow eyes wide as an owl's. She seemed to be asking me a question. My name? *Memory Feather,* I answered, without speaking aloud. *Call me Mem.* She stood up and turned around on the platter and repositioned herself, not taking her eyes off me. Minerva, I could tell, was something of a cynic.

Oliver, Mac told us, was a writer of stories. He'd just had one published in the *New Yorker*. He was almost finished with his first novel. He was the new Steinbeck—actually, in Mac's humble opinion, a cross between Steinbeck and Tennessee Williams. His novel was going to take the literary world by storm. Just you wait and see.

Oliver blushed and grinned that gummy grin of his. "Don't listen to him."

Mac held up his hand. "Wait. We need a toast," he pronounced, looking first at my mother, then at me, his face torched by a sunbeam thrown, in just that moment, from the westward-facing window. "Here's to my two beautiful Feathers. Welcome home."

We all lifted our glasses and drank. As we did, the sunbeam on Mac's face reached over and tickled my mother's cheek. She touched her cheek as if brushing it away and smiled at me, revealing the chip in her front tooth. A flawed smile, but now, miraculously, charged with something that looked like joy. Outside, a little breeze whipped up and the oak leaves began to quake. The shadow from a small forked branch appeared like the lines of a map across my mother's face. The leafy patterns danced across her cheeks and forehead, as if her features were gathering themselves to embark on a journey.

In that moment of quickening, I saw my mother, Virginia Feather, as she had been before my devil of a father had gone and broken her heart. It was as though I'd been seeing her face underwater. I'd forgotten how beautiful she was.

III.

———

It was well past midnight when my mother and I made our unsteady way down Mac's porch steps.

"We're just getting started," Mac said as he ushered us out.

We all agreed to meet again soon. Oliver wanted to take us sailing the following weekend.

"I'll begin at the gallery on Wednesday," my mother called out, "once I get Mem settled at Our Mother."

It had been decided that I'd attend Our Mother of the Sound Academy, a Catholic school for girls, despite the fact that my own mother and I were the furthest thing from Catholic you could imagine, if you didn't count my wardrobe of Catholic hand-me-downs. It was my grandmother who had insisted on Our Mother. She herself had gone there, though Virginia, unfortunately, had not, insisting instead on going to the inferior county schools. There'd been no problem getting me in; I was a *legacy*. Although I'd already started fourth grade in Albuquerque earlier that September, Our Mother was just that week opening for the school year. I would begin Wednesday along with all the other girls. It was a good thing my mother and I had come home when we did. I would fit right in.

My grandmother was being wildly optimistic. Children my age were sadists, my clenched fist and missing digits irresistible targets. The whispered rhymes always began with some combination of *paw, saw,* and *claw,* one of the more memorable: "I turned the corner / and here's what I saw / a girl named Feather / with a scary bear claw." I looked forward to my first day at Our Mother the way the Christians must have looked forward to entering the Colosseum in Rome when it was full of starving lions.

ON THE WAY BACK from our evening at Mac's, my mother and I strolled along Beach Boulevard; or rather, I strolled and she staggered, her arm around my shoulder, not as a gesture of motherly affection but out of an urgent need for physical support. The three of them had downed the bottle of champagne in short order and, after that, a bottle of white Bordeaux with the shrimp remoulade. After the meal, we'd gone outside to do a bit of porch sitting, whereupon they polished off a half bottle of Grand Marnier.

The combination of two Shirley Temples and the coconut cake had sugared me up. My heart galloped like a racehorse as I held on to the waistband of my mother's skirt to prevent her from toppling over on our way back to my grandparents'. She lurched along, humming a tune that had no discernable beginning or end, then muttering something about the brothers Iberville and Bienville, who'd come looking for the Father of Waters in 1699 but had come upon Belle Cote instead. "You don't always find what you're looking for," she said. "Life is a disappointment."

Beyond the grassy slope leading down to the seawall, the Sound shimmered under a crescent moon, the water as speckled as a quail egg from the stars overhead. *Oh my,* the little waves said as they licked the seawall. *Oh, joy!*

The lights at my grandparents' were blazing. Perched on stilts on a slight bank, the house soared and swaggered in the distance.

"Damn," muttered my mother.

A few moments later we began to climb the long flight of stairs to the first floor. My mother went first, with me pushing at her behind from the step below. As we got about halfway up, a curtain moved at the window and my grandmother's face appeared.

My mother lurched backward, stumbled, then righted herself.

The front door opened and my grandfather stepped out onto the porch. He was wearing pajamas, and what little hair he had was sticking straight up. "Virginia?" he called out. "Is that you?"

"Who else?" my mother said.

"We were worried." He leaned over the banister to peer down at us.

"I'm not in high school, Daddy." The assertion mismatched with the childish name.

My grandmother stepped out of the shadows behind him. "Worried sick, we've been worried sick." She came toward me, clucking. "You poor child. You should have been in bed hours ago."

Around us, the cicadas revved up, applauding my grandmother's scolding. My mother managed the last two steps to the porch. "For god's sake, Mother, she had a wonderful time. *We* had a wonderful time. It was the best time we've had in *years*." She staggered again. I took her elbow, righting her.

My grandfather peered at her. "Virginia, have you been drinking *spirits*?"

"No child should be subjected to this," said my grandmother. "No wonder the poor thing talks to wild animals."

I moved closer to my mother. "I talk to domestic animals too," I said. "And Mac was *nice*. He and Oliver made us feel right at home."

"Is that one of his *house boys*? Really, Virginia. This is disgraceful. How are you ever going to find *nice* friends if you fraternize with the likes of Mac McFadden?"

I turned to my mother. "What's a house boy?"

"Merciful Jesus!" said my grandmother.

My mother opened her mouth to answer, then began to pant. She lurched over to the rail and began to vomit raw oysters off the side of the porch.

"You're *drunk*," my grandfather thundered.

"It's the oysters." I stepped between him and my mother, who continued to heave and gag. "I'm feeling kind of sick myself." Which, I realized, was truer than not.

My grandmother peered at me under the porch light. "Feeding raw oysters to a *child*."

"I need to go to bed," I said.

"Of course, you do. It's almost one in the morning. What's your mother *thinking*?" She took my arm and maneuvered me through the front door.

WHEN I CAME DOWNSTAIRS the next morning, all was quiet. Hot too, despite the open windows. I walked out onto the porch, my head throbbing and my mouth as dry as if I'd chewed a box of chalk. All I wanted to do was throw myself into the Sound, despite the fact that no one had seen fit to explain to me the science of swimming. Watching other children from my grandparents' porch, it seemed an inexact undertaking at best, one which involved a great deal of thrashing about until a person got the hang of it.

Just then my grandparents drove up. My grandfather got out and went around and opened my grandmother's door. From above, she looked like a great egret emerging from the Plymouth, the top of her hat covered in snowy plumes, a fashion, I'd later learn, that almost sent the *Ardea alba* into extinction.

She tilted her head upward, her hat slipping toward the left side of her head. "Mercy, Memory. What are you doing wandering around in your nightgown for all the world to see? It's bad enough, not going to church."

I looked around. Except for the children swimming, there was no one in sight. Just the water below, high tide, and I must say it was something of a disappointment. No crashing waves, no sugar sand, only water splashing the top step of the seawall. There was, though, a mesmerizing quality, an undercurrent, to the Sound. It whispered of drumbeats and dance; of spear hunts for large, fierce animals; the decorating of pottery with a human eye weeping in the palm of an open hand. Choctaw, Pascagoula, Biloxi, Bayougoula: all living their lives just as we were living ours, though larger and, I imagined, more heroic.

After the previous night, I'd begun to understand why my mother had resisted leaving our cozy nest at the El Camino. I yearned for our dinghy little room, the curve of my mother's exhausted body in the bed beside me at day's end, the taste of dust on my tongue. She'd slept on her side facing the wall, and some winter nights, I curled myself around her back like a snake seeking heat on warm pavement. Sometimes she turned over and held me close, her warm breath purring in my ear.

I ran upstairs to dress, almost colliding with her in the hallway. The hair on one side of her head was standing straight out, mascara splattered across her cheeks. She still had on the dress she'd worn the night before, her scrawny arms bare, her collarbone a long thin line bisecting her upper chest. She held on to the top of her head as if she were afraid it was going to fly off.

She glared at me, her right eye open much wider than her left. "Go get dressed and make up your bed, Mem."

I went back to my room. Truth be told, I myself was still jittery and out of sorts. My paw ached and burned, which it sometimes did when I was tired or sick. Sometimes when it hurt like that, it felt as if it had been caught in a trap. I'd grown accustomed to my clenched hand. I took painstaking care of it the way my mother had taught me, gently pulling the three remaining fingers back slightly to wash my palm with soap, then holding them out while I dried it. The night before, Mac had reached over the supper table and touched it lightly. "I know a doctor over in the City who can take a look at this, maybe operate." He winked at me, then my mother.

She leaned over her plate of shrimp. "Are you sure?"

"Worth a try," he said, leaving me to wonder if the doctor could indeed fix my paw and, if so, what life would be like without it. I'd come to think of it as an indelible mark left by my father's departure. When I looked at it, gnarled and tangled as an old cottonwood, I saw that one lock of hair over his eyes, which were blue as a February sky. I saw his long, tidy feet, remembering how he liked to go around the house bare-footed, the way his toes marched downward in length with remarkable regularity. I saw my father in pieces, not the whole, as if he were a jigsaw puzzle I could never quite complete. When we still lived near the base and my mother received that final letter, she'd gathered all his things and photographs of the three of us together, and tossed them into our garbage can in the side alleyway. She rolled up a piece of newspaper, struck a match to it, and tossed it into the can. Ten minutes later, my father was nothing but dust and ashes.

But my paw, even as it stained me with my father's absence, also placed me anew in the world of other living creatures, so much so that, now, I can barely remember a time when I didn't believe it had magical properties. It welcomed me into another whole world—the buzzing, chattering, you-come-you-go world of creature-life. It was the aperture into another way of being.

THAT MORNING I MADE up my bed the way my mother had taught me to make the beds at the El Camino, with tight sheets, symmetrical sides, and a sharp crease under the pillows, and then headed downstairs to the kitchen, where I found my grandmother in a flowered brunch coat and my grandfather still in his Sunday shirt and tie. They were eating sandwiches and pickled peaches at the kitchen table. My grandmother's top lip was sprinkled in crumbs, her hair flattened from the hat.

My grandfather saw me first and got to his feet. "Well, here she is," he said heartily. "Come take a seat, my child. Let's get you something to eat."

"She looks like death warmed over. Up until all hours," said my grandmother.

"Now Martha." He turned to me. "What kind of sandwich can we fix you, my dear? We have ham and chicken salad."

My stomach growled. My grandfather smiled. "Sounds like you could use one of each."

I ate my sandwiches while my grandmother washed dishes and my

grandfather dried, whistling under his breath. There was a dear familiarity to their motions, my grandfather reaching for the dripping dish a
split second before my grandmother finished washing it.

Just as I took the last bite, my mother called out from upstairs, "Mem,
come here."

At the sound of her voice, my grandmother paused in her washing,
my grandfather's hand left waiting in midair.

In the bedroom, my mother was throwing clothes into her suitcase.
She smelled like vomit and stale smoke.

"Go pack," she said.

I was accustomed to talking my mother down from various ledges.
"Why don't you take a swim?" I suggested. "That would be refreshing,
maybe calm you down."

"Don't *you* start telling me what to do."

Logic sometimes worked. "Where will we go?" I asked. Surely a
reasonable question, though reason wasn't my mother's strong suit.

She looked at me scornfully. "To Mac's. Where else?"

"Does he know we're coming?" The idea of appearing on Mac's doorstep with suitcases in tow and being turned away, kindly but firmly,
the way you'd turn away Jehovah's Witnesses, made my chest close up.
Where would we go then? What would we do? I knew that if my mother
marched out of my grandparents' house, there would be no returning,
my mother being among the most prideful and stubborn of human
creatures.

She swept the question aside with an impatient gesture. "Don't be
silly. He'll love having us. Now go pack."

I went back into my room and got my suitcase out of the closet and
my things out of the drawers I'd just filled. In the fewer than three days
I'd been in Belle Cote, I'd already amassed a collection of shells, which
I'd lined up on the dresser. I gathered them carefully and wrapped them
in my underwear. When I clicked my suitcase shut, the sound frightened
me in some deep way, as if it were a portent of doom, a closing off of
some as-yet-unknown possibility.

Across the hall, my mother and grandfather were arguing. There were standards of behavior in his house; my mother could abide by them or leave. She selected option number two. She was no longer a child and wasn't going to be treated like one; she could go wherever she damn well wanted and do whatever she damn well wanted. And she would not allow her child to grow up in a *prejudiced* household.

I lugged my suitcase out into the hall. In my mother's room, the two of them glared at each other across the bed, my grandfather's twinkling eyes gone cold.

"If you're going to play the fool, Virginia, at least leave the child here with us," my grandfather said. "Don't go dragging *her* into that den of iniquity."

My mother spotted me. "Memory, have I ever mistreated you?"

I stopped in the doorway. My mother never used my full name. We'd been so close physically in that one small room at the El Camino, with so few normal distractions—in her case a husband and other children, in mine a father and brothers and sisters—that names seemed redundant. When she ate enchiladas, I tasted green chile. When I savored the flan at the El Camino restaurant, I imagined her tongue relaxing to the smooth texture of the watery custard. We'd breathed the air from each other's lungs, our speaking and hearing becoming their own echo chambers.

"Answer me, Memory."

"No."

"No, *ma'am*," said my grandmother, who'd just appeared at the door.

My mother ignored her. "Have you ever gone hungry, Memory?"

I thought of all the cheese enchiladas we'd consumed since we moved into the El Camino and grinned, trying to lighten the tone. "Enchiladas, tortillas, flautas. Mucho gusto!"

"She doesn't even speak decent English," said my grandmother.

"Memory," said my mother. "What's the past participle of *lie*?"

"*Lain.*"

"How do you spell *malevolent*?"

"*M-a-l-e-v-o-l-e-n-t.*"

"What's a synonym for *prejudice*?" she asked with a covert glance at my grandmother.

"Bigotry," I said.

"Oh, Virginia, stop it. She's not a trained parrot," said my grandmother.

My mother ignored her. "Mem, do you want to stay here or go with me?"

The question surprised me. Normally, my mother told me what to do in no uncertain terms. If I stated a preference for one course of action or another, her usual response was to ignore me.

My grandfather turned to my mother. "How can you make her choose between her life and yours?"

My mother ignored him. "Mem?"

I looked down at the floor, avoiding the safety of my grandfather's eyes. I took a deep breath. "I want to go with you," I said to my mother.

"All right then."

She picked up her suitcase. I hesitated a moment, then picked up mine. It was heavier than I remembered.

My grandfather put a hand on my shoulder. "We'll be right here. Come on back when your mother gets over this fool idea."

"Mem can visit whenever she wants," said my mother.

As we were lugging our suitcases down the outside stairs, my grandmother appeared on the porch above. "Virginia," she called out to my mother. "Ginny. Don't do this."

My mother continued her descent.

As we walked along, the sky turned gray and the Sound choppy. My mother looked up at the gathering clouds. "It's getting ready to rain," she said. "We need to hurry."

We labored along, salt grass whipping up around our ankles. Sweat poured down my forehead and stung my eyes. I stopped in my tracks. "This suitcase is heavy as lead."

"Give it to me," my mother said. "Now come on. There's a storm moving in."

When we turned left and away from the water onto Bienville Street where Mac lived, the air went still and my mother stopped to wipe her face. Her hair had gone limp and frizzy. Her breath smelled of rotten apples. When we got to Mac's house, she dropped the suitcases and told me to wait on the lawn. I sat down under one of Mac's oaks, causing consternation, then delight, among the resident chiggers.

My mother was inside a good long time. At long last, she appeared at the top of the stairs, a glass of iced tea in her hand. I ran up the steps, leaving the suitcases in the yard.

The house was blessedly cool. All the windows were open and huge ceiling fans were plowing the air. Mac and Oliver sat together on the sofa, looking grave and a bit under the weather, whiskery shadows on their cheeks and chins. Oliver wasn't giving out any gummy grins.

"I hear you've had quite a morning, Little," said Mac. "Maybe you'd like a cool bath and a lie-down."

"Yes, thank you. I would," I said, clawing at my chigger bites.

Mac rose and Oliver after him. "Feather," Mac said, "why don't you get her situated, and we'll get your suitcases. You two can use the back bedroom." His words carefully measured.

Oliver looked at Mac, then at the floor. "I'll have to move my typewriter out of there. Get some other things."

"Come on, Mem," said my mother, heading toward the back of the house. Her tone was muted, and I followed her uncertainly. There was a bathroom on the left as we went back. My mother stopped at the door. "Go on in and draw your bath," she said. "I'll bring you some clothes when I get your suitcase unpacked."

I hadn't realized how tired I was until I sank into the warm water. My eyes closed and then I was out on the Sound, floating along in a sailboat, or what I imagined to be a sailboat—I'd never been on one—so far out I couldn't see land. A monster wave, then another, swamped the boat, and I fell overboard. Down and down I went until I was surrounded by fish and octopuses and giant eels, the octopuses spewing blue ink to welcome me to the world below. Ribbons of light streamed all around me, and it was peaceful and still.

Someone was yelling at me, pulling at me. I woke up sputtering and coughing, slipping and sliding.

"Mem! Wake up! Are you trying to drown your fool self?" My mother leaned over me, her breath sour and hot. "Get up out of there. The water's gone cold."

And so it had. I was covered in goose bumps and shivering.

She held out the towel. "Come on."

I thrashed about in the water and stood, embarrassed by the bumps on my chest. I snatched the towel from her and wrapped myself in it. She leaned over and pulled the plug in the tub. There was a gray ring around the sides.

"Clean the tub," she commanded. "The sun's come out. I'm going for a swim. I'll be back after a while. Just go on into the bedroom and take a nap. Don't bother anybody."

Then she was gone.

I tiptoed toward the back of the house, not sure where I should go. There was a door ajar at the end of the hall, which I assumed was the bedroom my mother and I would be occupying. The room was painted a deep blue-green, what we now call teal, on two walls, and a clay color, terracotta, on the other two. Over the bed was a painting of two men walking on the beach; a dazzling sunset stretched out before them, splashes of purple and rose with a touch of yellow. On the dresser sat a framed picture of a family: a boy, Oliver, flashing his gummy grin; a sister, older, with her arm flung around his shoulder; a mother leaning into the side of a father. The father wore overalls, the mother a dress made of what looked like sackcloth, the girl a smaller version of the same dress. Oliver's pants ended between his bare ankles and his knees. A farm family, poor as dirt, yet something about their mouths suggested a certain amount of satisfaction, even pride. From the knobs of the dresser hung bangles of Mardi Gras beads in green and purple and gold. Pushed into the corner of the mirror on the dresser was a snapshot of Oliver and Mac bare-chested and knee-deep in the Sound, looking for all the world like they were starring in a picture show.

Under the window was a small desk with a typewriter on it and a stack of papers beside the typewriter. I sat in the chair in front of the desk. A palmetto bush rustled at the window above. *Hello there.* I picked up the first page in the stack of papers, which read THE SOUND: A NOVEL by Oliver Knight. Just as I was picking up the second page, there was a knock at the door. After a moment, Oliver stuck his head in. "I need to get my writing things."

I pulled the towel tight. He came in quickly, not looking at me, and picked up the typewriter, balancing the stack of paper on top. Then he was gone, shutting the door silently behind him.

The bed was so high off the floor I had to make a flying leap to get onto it. I lay back on the pillow, which smelled pleasantly of sun and salt air, and pulled the bedspread over me. I tried to go to sleep again, tossing from side to side, eyeing the sun as it moved from one window to the next and then started down through the leaves of a huge oak that shadowed the back window. The window was open, and I could hear the oak leaves tittering among themselves like a crowd of girls. If this were my room, I thought, I'd come and go on that limb. On warm nights, I'd perch there like a bird.

I lay there a good long time. The house was quiet. Then the front door creaked open and I heard footsteps. Minerva cried out a greeting, then began meowing for food. Over the sound of her cries, voices:

"I didn't sign up for this."

"It's temporary, Ollie. It won't be for long."

"How long?"

"Until I can find them another place. For Christ's sake, Ollie, have a heart."

"I have my work, Mac. I'm at a crucial point. Now, I have nowhere to go in this house."

"What am I supposed to do? Kick them out?"

"It's not like you'll be kicking them out on the street. They have a perfectly nice place to live, with *family*."

"Feather and I *are* family," said Mac then. "She's always stood by me, she's always been my best friend."

"I thought *I* was family, I thought *I* was your best friend. Mac, things are hard enough as it is."

There was a long silence. Then Mac said wearily, "I love you to pieces, Ollie. Please just hold on a little while."

"How long?"

A pause. The creak of a chair.

"As long as it takes."

Silence again. Then Minerva turned baritone in expressing her desire for food.

"Feed your goddamn cat, Mac," said Oliver.

Barely a breath, then the front door slammed shut.

There were footsteps, then the rattle of cat food being poured and Minerva went quiet.

IV.

———

THE NEXT MORNING THE pictures on the dresser had disappeared, the drawers left open and empty. I'd slept through Oliver's packing up, slept in fact all that afternoon and night, straight through to the next morning. I stumbled out to find Mac and my mother sitting shoulder to shoulder at the kitchen table, Mac's head buried in his arms, my mother patting him on the back.

"Now, Mac, you listen to me," she said. "It's not too late to track him down and bring him back. Go on now. Go get him back." She gestured at me. "Mem, start packing your suitcase."

He looked up, his face crumpled as paper. "He made me choose and I chose you."

"Oh, Mac, why in heaven's name did you do that?"

"You've always stood by me, Feather. Remember third grade? It was you and me against the world."

"Oh, Mac, honey, you know I'll always love you," my mother said. Then they both teared up and fell into each other's arms. "This isn't permanent," my mother murmured into his neck. "Just long enough to get us on our feet."

"Don't be silly," he said, pushing his hair out of his eyes. "You'll always have a home here."

Then they turned and looked up at me and smiled the exact same smile, as if they'd choreographed it.

"And now we have Little," said Mac.

SO MY MOTHER AND I settled in with Mac, nesting in our poached household the way wrens move into flower pots or other unlikely spots, messily and in fits and spurts, making more and more of Mac's house ours in small ways and large. A month after I'd begun classes at Our Mother, Sister Helena, the principal, called on my mother at the gallery to inform her I was no longer welcome. Through no fault of my own—I was but an unfortunate child with no control over my circumstances— my living situation had become morally repugnant, quote unquote, and would most surely impinge on my innocent character and spread like a malignancy throughout the school. My mother had a week to enroll me elsewhere. That night my mother draped her napkin over her head in some semblance of a nun's habit and recited the principal's words, mocking her lisp.

Mac was not amused. "See if I ever contribute any more art to their spring auction," he said.

I, on the other hand, roared with laughter, relieved beyond measure that I'd been released from the chants and prayers and girly whispers, the starched white shirts buttoned to the chin and the itchy plaid pleated skirts that made me look like a checkerboard turkey.

I suggested to my mother and Mac that I eschew school altogether and study on my own. I'd always been a loner. Our residence at the El Camino, coupled with my hand, had precluded what you'd call normal social interchange with the other children; in truth, I much preferred the company of animals to that of children, most of whom I found shallow and malicious. I was quite sure I could, in my infinite wisdom, design my own education plan.

"Don't be ridiculous," said my mother. "You're blue-blazes smart, Mem. You need to learn everything you can in this podunk place."

"You don't even know what you don't know," Mac added. He'd come up through public high school in Belle Cote. It wouldn't be so bad, if you weren't, well, *different*, like him.

I said I felt different enough, thank you very much; but a week later I found myself trudging up the treacherously uneven concrete steps of Harris County Elementary, my mother nipping at my heels like a collie dog. It was unseasonably cool that morning, and I had on a new dress Mac had bought me at Maison Blanche. Navy blue, all the rage back then, with a white Peter Pan collar and white stitching at the waist. I felt crisp as an autumn leaf, breezy as a walk along the Sound. I had armed myself with my own pencil box, retrieved from Our Mother, and a purple loose-leaf notebook full of clean paper.

Harris Elementary turned out to be a vast improvement over Our Mother. I had the good luck to be placed in Miss Muldoon's homeroom class, which in those days meant she taught us all our subjects except chorus, singing not being one of her many talents. Miss M, as she was called, was a large, jolly woman with a bouncing bosom, a welcome relief after the solemn-faced Sister Theodora of Our Mother, who'd always seemed on the brink of tears each morning as she looked out over the sea of us squirming girls. In contrast, Miss M boomed and jiggled, clapping her hands in delight whenever one of us gave the right answer to a question and sometimes when we didn't. I felt buoyed by her enthusiasm, as did my classmates, a sunburned, mostly pleasant sort. My classmates were all white; Black children attended school in a small rickety building with peeling paint out on the northeastern edge of the county. (Mac had, in fact, the week before ordered a truckload of paint for the school, which he said was a disgrace to the state of Mississippi. He and some of the children's parents were to start painting that very weekend.)

In the mornings, my classmates from outside Belle Cote tumbled off the one school bus that lurched around the county roads, plucking them from frame houses, gray with mildew and so covered over by the gnarled branches of oaks that they appeared to be part of the trees themselves. At recess we gathered around Miss M like puppies, awaiting her cheerful instructions as to how we might best exercise our bodies. The county children who'd already done a half day's farm chores she allowed to nap in the shade of the giant mulberry tree that sat in the middle of the playground.

Best of all, Harris Elementary, not being burdened by the necessity of prayer and moral instruction, let out a full hour earlier than Our Mother. My mode of transportation to and from school was my own two feet, which in the afternoons landed me either at Beautiful Dreamer gallery, where my mother now worked, or on Mac's front porch. At the gallery, Minerva would be stretched out in the front window, the sun toasting her black coat to a rich chocolate. I'd become attached to Minerva. I'd say hello, ask how her day had gone. She'd eye me sternly, then stretch and purr.

TWO MONTHS AFTER MY mother and I moved in with Mac, I became a woman, an event for which my mother had ill-prepared me, thinking she had more time. When I rushed in from school, bow-legged from the dirty gym sock stuffed in my underwear, Mac stood outside the bath-room door and instructed me as to how to proceed. "A perfectly normal bodily function, Little," he pronounced. "It just means you must not under any circumstances let a boy put his penis inside your vagina. You might end up pregnant and get left holding the bag. Then where would we be?"

He spoke calmly, even casually, as if instructing me on how to make gumbo. Mac was direct like that, always calling body parts by their proper names, not mincing words about bodily functions. A few weeks before, when we'd first moved in with him, he had instructed me to defecate and urinate in the mornings before heading off to school because, as he put it, who knew when another opportunity would present itself?

One Friday afternoon I came straight home (yes, I thought of Mac's as home now) instead of going to the gallery, not from any womanly emergency but simply because it was a fine day and I didn't have to have my homework done until Monday. When I came in the front door, Mac was sitting on the sofa reading the *Saturday Evening Post* and sipping a glass of iced tea. He wore a flowered woman's blouse with pleats at the chest and a black patent-leather belt similar to my mother's, clinched tight around his trousers. To this ensemble he'd added the lime green scarf I'd given my mother the previous Christmas. I'd paid a quarter for it at a secondhand shop on Fourth Street. She liked to wear it when it was windy, as it so often was in Albuquerque, especially in the spring. It turned her hazel eyes green. Mac had tied it around his neck, flaring the edges at jaunty angles.

He looked up from his magazine. "Would you like a glass of tea, Little? How was your day, sweetheart?"

"That's my mother's scarf."

He touched his neck and looked at me gravely. "It is. She offered to let me try it. It really makes the outfit, don't you think?"

I said he needed to be careful with the scarf; I'd paid good money for it. I then added that it did indeed bring out the greenery in the background of the blouse. He thanked me for noticing. Maybe I'd like a brownie with my tea? He'd just baked a batch. And a walk along the beach later, after I'd done my homework? Did I have much homework? Had I done some of it in study hall? I could do the rest at the kitchen table; he'd clear a space while I changed out of my school clothes. Better to get it done and over with on Friday afternoon, not have it hanging over my head all weekend. And what a glorious weekend it promised to be! A touch of fall in the air at long last.

In our year at the El Camino, my mother had kept a box of Oreos on the chest of drawers for me. I was to eat no more than two when I came in from school. She never inquired about the status of my homework. School, she told me, was my own little red wagon. On my first day, she'd squatted down in the schoolyard and explained that I was a very *unusual* child, emphasizing the *you* in *unusual*. I could do anything I wanted if I just applied myself. It was up to me and me alone as to how I'd wear the mantle of being *unusual*. It was an odd conversation for a mother to have with a nervous little girl whose one good hand clutched a ream of construction paper, a box of crayons, and a dented second-hand lunch box with the Lone Ranger on the front—but my mother's eyes were fierce and her tone serious. It was before we left the base, and my mother's face was framed by the Sandia Mountains behind her. The peaks were already tipped in a pinkish snow, and lower down, the aspens flared in a wash of yellow. It was as if a veil had been lifted. I saw myself reflected in my mother's hazel eyes, her beauty making me beautiful too.

Later that afternoon, Mac changed from the blouse to a plain white men's shirt, but he kept on the scarf. The two of us walked along the seawall and collected shells. I asked him why some were chipped and broken and some remained whole.

"Some are older or from very faraway places or more fragile to begin with," he said. "Or maybe some are just more determined to hold on to their essence. They're hardheaded like me, or I should say hard-shelled." He chuckled at his own joke.

That night, when we got into bed, I asked my mother why Mac wore women's things.

She turned over to face me. "Everybody needs a change every now and then."

"I just don't want him making off with your green scarf."

She raised herself onto her elbow. "Don't worry, he won't. But listen to me, Mem. We're a family now and some things are kept private, within the family. Our business, nobody else's. This is important. In fact, don't mention Mac at all, to anybody. You understand? Especially not to Mother and Daddy."

I giggled at how the idea of any talk of Mac's affection for scarves and blouses would send my grandparents straight through the roof. I'd settled into a routine of seeing my grandparents every Sunday, which I found on the whole a dull undertaking. In the morning I would walk to their house in my Sunday dress and we would go to the First Presbyterian Church. (Although my grandmother had attended Our Mother Academy, the Feathers on both of my grandparents' sides were staunch Calvinists.) After church, the three of us went out for Sunday buffet at Boudreaux's Seafood Shack in Pass Christian, an old white house with a porch overlooking the Bay, on the back side of which Black people in their Sunday clothes stood out in the hot sun waiting to order at a small window, their children playing in the dusty parking lot.

After my grandparents and I filled up on fried fish and potato salad and pie, we went back to their house and had a chat. They would ask about school, and I would say it was fine. They asked if I needed anything, anything at all. I'd tell them some small thing, a pair of sandals or a jacket or just a new notebook, and the following Sunday they'd produce it triumphantly. They asked how my mother was doing, and I said she liked working at Beautiful Dreamer. "Beautiful Dreamer," my grandmother said. "What a ridiculous name."

As the conversation progressed, their eyes glazed over and they started to yawn. I'd take the hint, say my goodbyes, get a peck on the cheek from my grandmother and a hug from my grandfather, and head on back to Mac's, tearing off my white lace socks and patent leather shoes as soon as I got down to the water's edge.

Walking along the water, I thought about my father across the ocean. Thanks to Miss Muldoon, I knew by then that the Mississippi Sound and Gulf of Mexico don't end up in Europe unless you take the long way around, but being at the water's edge brought him to mind. I'd read up on Paris. Was my father sitting at a sidewalk café drinking wine and wearing a beret? Was he strolling along the Champs-Élysées with the French hussy on his arm? Or was she pushing a baby stroller? Did I have a little brother or sister with my nose or eyes? At that point in my girlhood, I looked nothing like my mother. My face was round rather than oval, my hair ash rather than auburn. I had freckles instead of her flawless complexion, and my eyes were green to her hazel. Nor did I favor my grandparents. I wondered what it would be like to look at another face and find something recognizable. How might my life have turned out had my father sent for my mother and me? Would we be strolling alongside him now, me on one side, my mother on the other? Would there be a cool fall breeze? The oak leaves (were there oaks in Paris?) a burnished *vert*. The state tree of France was the yew. What did it look like? Would it speak to me in French? Would the animals? I pictured myself wearing a beret to match my father's, looking cocky and smart.

In bed with my mother that night, I listened to the humming of the crickets and the croaking of the swamp frogs. A frond of the giant palmetto scratched at the window on my side of the bed. *Let me in,* it whispered. Mac in his green blouse and scarf called to mind my father in his air force dress blues, the navy fabric so stiff it almost stood up by itself, with brass buttons on the lapels and some brightly colored stripes on the left shoulder. His face shining from a fresh shave, he'd pace the living room waiting for my mother to get dressed for whatever official function they were attending. Finally, she would fling open the door of their bedroom and emerge, trailing clouds of "Forbidden" cologne. "Do I look all right?" she'd asked my father, a self-conscious little smile playing at her lips. She looked better than all right, and she knew it. For such occasions, she always put her hair up in a French twist, lacquered with spray, and wore one of two dresses—an emerald green number with a voile wrap or the rose-colored evening suit she'd worn when she married my father. Before I understood the implications of what she was saying, she told me they'd gotten married at the Harris County Courthouse on Main Street because I was on the way. Later, when I understood that she'd been forced by my imminent presence to leave college as well as marry, I asked whether she would have married my father anyway. "I wanted you to have a decent life," she said, after a moment of silence. "I didn't know he was going to break my heart."

That night, after our conversation about Mac, my mother seemed uneasy in her sleep, tossing and turning as if someone were prodding her again and again. At the El Camino, she'd fallen into bed and slept like the dead until the pop music from our radio alarm jolted us awake at 6:30. After we moved in with Mac, though, she was not as bone-tired after a day of less strenuous work at the gallery and had become a restless bedmate, some part of her more awake than asleep, busily plotting and planning and pacing the floor in her busy dreams. Some nights, when she moaned and thrashed more than usual, I'd grab my pillow and head for the living room sofa.

The next Monday morning, I came into the kitchen to find her and Mac sitting at far ends of the kitchen table, glaring at each other. Minerva sat like a referee in the middle of the table, pulling at her claws with her teeth.

"Honestly now, Mac. Don't you think it's for the best?" my mother was saying.

"No, I absolutely do *not* think it's for the best." He slammed his hand down and Minerva skittered away. "You need to get your feet on the ground. You need to save money. Enough of this living hand-to-mouth. It's not fair to you or Little. You're being selfish, Feather."

She rose from her chair. "How dare you say I'm selfish! Every single thing I've done I've done for her, including moving in with you."

"Maybe she'd have been better off with your parents."

"Being raised by people who call *you* names? Not on your life. They're Mem's grandparents, but they're small-minded, Mac. Worse than small-minded. You, of all people, should understand that."

"Don't go, Feather. I can't bear it."

"Mac, you need to have a *life*."

He looked up at her. "Don't you *see*, Feather? Don't you *know*?"

"See what? Know what?"

He opened his mouth to answer just as I rounded the corner. "Look, here comes the sleepyhead."

I looked from one to the other. "What are you two fighting about?"

"Nothing," they said in unison.

"Doesn't sound like nothing," I said.

My mother sighed. "I was just telling Mac that you and I should get our own place, now that he's been kind enough to give me a job." She looked back at him. "You need your privacy back, Mac. We've imposed on you long enough."

Mac smiled at her. A tense, quick smile, almost a grimace. "I'll bar the door if you try to escape. You're stuck with me."

"You're too kind, Mac," my mother said quietly. "You need to have yourself some fun."

"Feather, what do you think I'm doing every day of the week? I'm having a ball, sweetheart. I'm deliriously happy." He beckoned to me and when I went over to his end of the table, he grabbed my good hand. "What about you, Little? Aren't you deliriously happy too?"

I nodded vigorously.

Mac turned back to my mother. "See? She's happy as a clam. Let's keep it that way."

She looked at me, then at Mac. "You two are ganging up on me. All right then. For a while longer. Then we'll see."

THE FOLLOWING WEEK MAC built me a tree house in one of the giant oaks out back. I spent hours up there writing little sketches that I read aloud to my classmates. Minerva threw herself at the massive trunk and clawed her way up so that she was waiting for me at the top, her brush of a tail flicking the leaves. Still silent, she nonetheless seemed to encourage me as I climbed, a slow process because of my clenched hand.

Once I made it up to our little roost, she settled herself on a branch, tucking her front paws under her chest and watching me lazily as I wrote in my notebook. By then I'd read all the Charles Dickens books in Mac's library, and my own scribblings had always had a destitute orphan or two wandering around getting into scrapes and having harrowing adventures; one of them was a boy named Joshua who wore girl's clothes. After I turned that one in to Miss Muldoon, she asked me to stay after class. "You have a very vivid imagination, Memory Feather," she crooned, leaning over her desk and revealing her cavernous cleavage. "Here's the thing, though, dear one. Some people might not understand a male in female clothing. You don't want to make a fuss, now, do you? Let's keep this one between the two of us, dear."

One Saturday morning Mac stood at the foot of the oak tree and called up to me. "You can't be reading and writing every minute, Little. What you need is a productive hobby. You need to learn to use your hands." I looked down at my paw when he said it, but he added, "You can use them both. I've seen you do it."

That afternoon he led me over to the underside of the house. In the coolness of the shade, we lined the sandy soil with old newspapers and began to refinish an old pedestal table he'd picked up at an auction in Gulfport. Over the next few weeks he showed me how to apply and remove the stripper and then sand with the finest of sandpapers so that the wood surface felt like glass, apply boiled linseed oil, wipe it off a day later, and apply layers of lacquer with a good brush and a light hand, sanding between applications. The process could not be rushed. The oil needed to soak in; each coat of lacquer had to dry thoroughly.

Over time, we moved from old furniture to antiques, scouring the Gulf Coast auctions and warehouses for damaged and discolored bargains. "Diamonds in the rough," Mac said, "like you and Feather were when you first came to Belle Cote." We rode eastward on Highway 90, the Sound gently lapping at the seawall, punctuated every now and then by sandy beaches. Mac had an old beat-up Ford Ranchero, a minotaur-like vehicle that was half car, half truck, which sufficed to transport our breakfronts, tea tables, bed frames, and other sundry pieces. As time went on, Mac had the underside of the house closed in, so we had a snug place to work. It was hot in the summer and cold in the winter, but it was dry and that's what counted. When the lacquer fumes made me cough and wheeze, Mac installed an exhaust fan in one window. Meanwhile, my mother rearranged the gallery so that the back corner became a show place for our growing assortment of gleaming wood pieces, while Mac put up a sign in the front window that read, ANTIQUES, BEAUTIFULLY REFINISHED.

Mac and my mother sat me down one night to discuss my hand. "I made an appointment for you next Wednesday with a doctor in the City," Mac began. "He's an orthopedic surgeon. We're hoping he can fix things."

I shook my head and tucked my paw under my shirttail. My paw was a sign I'd once had a father; it immersed me in the murmuring world around me. Like a wild creature, I was a survivor of a trap that wounded but didn't kill. I could see that my mother understood. Her own wound wasn't visible in a physical deformity like mine. She was like a burned tree after a forest fire, sap-hardened on the outside, the inside hollowed out.

She put a hand on my knee. "All right, Mem, we'll cancel for now. Let us know when you're ready."

THE SCHOOL YEAR PASSED uneventfully, Miss Muldoon's good cheer buoying me along in my studies. As the fourth grade grew to a close, she spoke to my mother and the principal, and before anyone saw fit to ask my opinion, I'd been pole-vaulted over the fifth grade into the sixth. Mac marked my height on the kitchen door and announced I'd shot up a foot in the nine months since I'd come to him—a tribute, he said, to his good cooking. Meanwhile, the hard, tender buds on my chest had swollen to the size of demitasse cups. When the moon was full, something deep inside my belly thrashed about restlessly, the way my mother did in her sleep.

Mac kept me too busy to worry about my peculiar internal workings. When he and I weren't out buying furniture or refinishing it, he taught me the twist of wrist it takes to shuck an oyster, the art of deveining and butterflying shrimp, the torturous business of dismantling blue crab. He laughed at me when I told him my arm was going to fall off if I had to stir a gumbo roux one more minute. "Use the other hand, Little," he said, taking the spoon and gently pulling the three clenched fingers on my paw outward, then putting the spoon handle in my palm. "A decent roux demands perseverance."

When my mother came in from work, all she had to do was put her feet up. Mac and I would sit on either side of her. We'd tell each other about our days, what items from Beautiful Dreamer had been sold, what furniture acquired, my school-day pleasures and trials.

One afternoon Mac wasn't there when I got home. I changed out of my school clothes and ate some leftover cake on the kitchen table. I was washing my plate when I noticed a snapshot propped on the windowsill. The picture seemed to have been taken at night. Mac's golden mane jumped out at me. He stood beside another man, both of them grinning and leaning against a streetlight, in front of an open door. I peered at the other man, who looked familiar, then realized I was looking at Mac's beautiful dreamer, his shirt hanging loose, a lock of hair over one eye: the man in the painting. Holding the snapshot in my hand, I walked into the living room to compare it with the painting. Yes, the grin was the same, the eyes, the hair. And yes, the effect still strangely unsettling.

I stepped out onto the back porch. It was spring, my first in Belle Cote, the cloudless sky the color of bluebird eggs. I decided to head down to the gallery. I walked down to the water and followed the shoreline for three blocks, Minerva at my heels. A line of brown pelicans cruised right above the water line. A great blue heron stood motionless in the shallows. *Go*, it commanded when I paused to look. The Sound was still as a lake. A regular spring day in Belle Cote, but somehow extraordinary. As the afternoon sun's rays flared across the water, something within me, a weight, shifted: I always thought about my father when I walked along the water's edge, but for the first time, I felt *glad* he'd left us without a backward glance. Mac, not my father, had claimed my mother and me. Mac would never leave us, never allow us to leave him.

That was not to say he didn't have other interests. The previous month he'd gone to a training camp up in Tennessee called the Highlander Folk School.

"Training for what?" my mother asked when he told us of his plans.

"For Revolution with a capital *R*," he said. "The fight's coming to Mississippi, and we need to be ready. Ask a man to fight for this country and not let him vote? Run him off land that's rightfully his? String him up when he doesn't toe the line? It's not right."

"Many things aren't right in this damn place," my mother said. "That's one reason I didn't want to come home. That's why I didn't want Mem living with her grandparents."

"Some things get under my skin more than others," said Mac.

AFTER A FEW BLOCKS, Minerva and I reached Main Street and turned inland. As we approached the gallery, I spotted Mac and my mother scrubbing the front windows, dipping their cleaning cloths into a large bucket of suds. At first I thought they were spring cleaning, but as I drew closer I saw the look on their faces. People walked back and forth on the sidewalk, taking quick looks and whispering behind their hands to one another. My mother looked up and saw me. She put down her bucket and came striding down the block, motioning me to turn around.

There was writing on the front window. I picked up my pace to get a better look, my mother bearing down on me. She waved her arms. "Go on home, Mem. It's a mess here. Go on now." I took another step and the window came into view. It read, HOMOS = PINKOS.

By then I knew what homosexuals were and I knew what pinkos were, but I didn't see the connection, though I'd read in Sunday's *Times-Picayune* that government people were being fired left and right because somebody said they were homosexual and could therefore be blackmailed by the Communists. People called them "the lavender lads," though what my favorite color had to do with homosexuals and Communists I failed to grasp. Mac's big brain had helped us win the war; he was no more a Communist than I was.

"Get on home, Mem. I mean it," said my mother, turning me around and giving me a push. "I'll explain later. We'll be home in a little while."

They came dragging in hours later. My mother's hair was in tangles, her lipstick lodged in the corners of her mouth. Mac's hands, usually so lively, dangled at his sides. They glanced at me stone-faced, then at each other.

Mac walked over to the windowsill and put the snapshot of him and the man in the portrait in his pocket.

The telephone, which was on a little desk in the hall, rang.

"Let it ring," said my mother.

He shook his head, walked into the hall, and answered it.

"Yes," he said, "she's here." He handed the phone to me. "It's a girl."

I shrank from it. No one from school ever called me. Mac pushed the receiver toward me, impatient.

WHEN I ANSWERED, THERE was a burst of giggling on the other end. Then a chorus of girls' voices: "Memory Feather is a house boy. Memory Feather is a house boy."

Something slithered in and around their words.

"Shut up. You shut up." I threw the phone to the floor.

My mother picked up the receiver and held it to her ear. Then, her voice clotted with fury, she said, "Go to hell, you stupid little bigots." She slammed down the receiver.

I burst into tears and ran for the bedroom.

Later, when Mac knocked on my door and said it was time for supper, I pretended to be asleep.

He came in and sat on the edge of my bed. I rolled over and looked up at him. It was dusk. The shadow of the palmetto outside the window made a dark pattern of spears across his face.

"Little," he said, "sometimes the human species is abominable. The trick is to let it roll off your back. Now you need to get up and eat supper. I made chicken and dumplings."

I lay there a while longer, until it was deep dark. Mac sat beside me, still as glass. Outside my window, a mockingbird sounded its last call; in the distance another answered. I sat up and swung my legs toward the floor, and he took me by my good hand and led me into the kitchen where my mother waited at the kitchen table, and they sat with me, watching as I ate.

"What's a house boy?" I asked.

My mother glanced at Mac and then cleared her throat. "It's an ugly way of saying that Mac is homosexual."

Mac got up, took my plate, and began to wash it at the sink.

"But why were those girls calling *me* a house boy?"

"They were just talking, Little," Mac said. He didn't turn around.

Then my mother sighed and rose from the table. "It's been a long day, I'm off to bed." She beckoned me. "You too, honey."

My mother had never in her life called me honey.

"Not until somebody tells me what a house boy is. I'm not even a boy."

"Oh good grief, Mem, you're like a dog after a bone," said my mother. "People are just being mean when they say things like that about Mac because he likes men."

I turned to Mac. "Was Oliver your house boy?"

My mother whirled around. "*Never* use that term again. It's demeaning. It's not kind. Not to Mac and not to Oliver or anyone else. It's one of those words we don't use...ever, under any circumstances. Do you understand me? Now go get in bed. Enough of this. Thank Mac for the good supper." She gave me a little push toward Mac, who was still busy at the sink.

"Thank you for supper," I whispered.

He didn't turn around.

Later that night, I heard him under the house dragging furniture around, then the sounds of scraping and sanding. I tossed and turned, jerking the covers up, then throwing them off. Hours went by, and still he kept on with the scraping and sanding, so loud at times that it seemed to be coming up through the floorboards. Minerva had parked herself on my chest. Her breath smelled like fish.

Finally, I put my pillow over my head and fell into an uneasy sleep, though it didn't feel like sleep because I was journeying around the house (Was I walking or floating?), looking out windows at the shadowy oaks, touching Mac's books and my own shells on the windowsills. In the living room, the beautiful naked man in the painting shook himself like a dog rising from water and climbed out of his gilded frame. At first I was afraid, afraid of the shame that beauty casts upon ugliness. My paw throbbed, the palm sweaty.

But then the young man in the painting walked toward me, smiling as if he knew me. I reached for him with my good hand, wanting his touch. Wanting it to burn me, mark me as his.

I woke up to Minerva digging her claws into my neck, her eyes round and anxious.

"What?" I said.

She didn't answer.

V.

AFTER SUPPER THE NEXT night, Mac and my mother called me into the living room. They were sitting on the couch together, but not leaning back into the cushions the way they usually did at the end of the day, their feet propped companionably on the coffee table. Now, they looked like two blackbirds perched on a wire, precarious and watchful.

My mother spoke first. "Wonderful news, Mem. I've found us a nice little house to rent. We'll have the whole thing to ourselves, and it's right down the street."

"We've got *this* whole house," I said, looking over at Mac, who sat with his arms crossed.

"This is for best for everyone," said my mother. "Mac?"

Mac ran his fingers through his hair. "I can't do this." He got up and headed for his room.

"Mem," my mother said. "This is the best thing. You've got to trust me."

I didn't trust her as far as I could throw her. My mother did her best, I knew that, but sometimes her best (a prime example being the El Camino Motor Hotel) simply wasn't good enough.

"Mac agrees," said my mother. "He's just too sad to say it."

"Well, let him say it. I don't believe you."

My mother got up from the sofa and went down the hall to Mac's bedroom. She knocked on the door, then went inside. After that I could hear only murmurs, her voice rising and falling.

The talking went on and on; then Mac came out. "Little," he began, studying the floor, "you've got to trust us on this. There's not a good *atmosphere* out there right now. That vile Joe McCarthy has stirred up *feelings*. Your mother and I want you to be safe and untroubled. These people mean business." His words came out in small explosions of breath, as if he were singing.

"It's not like we're going to the moon. Our little place isn't far from here," my mother said brightly, popping out from behind Mac's left shoulder, taking his hand as if to seal their collusion against me. "You can visit Mac any time you feel like it. Things won't be all that different." She smiled an insincere smile. "And Mac will have some space to pursue his own *interests.*"

What those interests were besides Revolution with a capital *R* I didn't know. On occasion, Mac drove over to the City or up to Jackson for "a night or two out with the boys." Otherwise, he seemed happy as a clam with my mother and me as sole companions.

BUT THE DIE WAS cast. Several days later, on a Monday when the gallery was normally closed and I was in school, the two of them moved my things. The house they'd selected was a buttery yellow shotgun with gingerbread trim and a long screen porch down the left side. Picturesque and quaint with a little mossy picket fence, which had once been white, it peeped out from behind giant camellia bushes and palms like a shy exotic bird. Over a hundred years old, my mother said. "Think of it, Mem, think of all the people who've lived here!" She clapped her hands like a little girl.

Inside, the house was tiny and dark. The floors were pine plank, blackened by decades of shellac and, I was soon to find out, riven with splinters. The walls were whitewashed pine paneling, which had turned dingy. Except for the sofa, my mother and Mac had furnished the place in old furniture, large gloomy pieces in cherry and mahogany, so dark they almost didn't show up against the floor. Over the ancient fireplace, which I was sure would burn the place down if ever lit, was an oil painting in somber gray and purple tones, a mother combing her daughter's hair, the only light in the picture from their blonder–than–blond hair. "Don't you think it's perfect, the mother and daughter?" said Mac. "I found it in the back corner of a gallery on Magazine on my last trip into the City." At the back of the house, behind the living room and dining nook were the kitchen, two tiny bedrooms, and a bathroom the size of Mac's pantry, not even a tub just a ratty little shower jammed into a corner.

There was a musty smell to the place, as if it hadn't been used for a while. I coughed once, then twice.

"It's dismal," I pronounced. "It's going to give me asthma."

"No worries, Little," said Mac. "We'll clean it from top to bottom, give it some pizazz. Give us time. You can help paint."

Then he said he'd better take off. He'd see me soon.

"When?" I asked, following him to the door.

"Let's give it a few days," he said, slipping out the door. "Let you two get settled. Then we'll see. Maybe you can come for supper this weekend."

My mother put her hands on my shoulders. "Maybe you'd like to think of inviting a friend home from school later in the week."

The truth was, I'd moved quickly to ingratiate myself with my class-mates at Harris Elementary by freely sharing the lavish lunches Mac packed for me, especially the deserts: brownies so gooey they stuck to your teeth, chocolate chip and peanut butter squares, lemon drop cook-ies, lukewarm slices of pecan and caramel pie. The deal I struck was that the recipient of my largesse had to sit with me at lunch and make some semblance of conversation. At morning recess, I circulated through the grapevine a list of the mouthwatering items in my lunch box; by noon, I had a line of contenders salivating beside my table. I coldheartedly chose the most popular girls and they usually drew a crowd of followers. There were two results of this exchange: first, many of my classmates—some of the prettiest girls especially—put on pounds, becoming in some cases quite chubby, while I became willowy and tall; second, I never ate alone. Now that we'd moved, I suddenly realized, my mother would be packing my lunches. Dreary peanut butter and jelly, bologna, and the most disgusting of all—liver cheese, one of my mother's favorites—would be my fate.

As summer came and went and I found myself in junior high, I devised other methods for rendering myself acceptable to the sixth-grade lunch crowd. I told tall tales about my father. I made him into a famous scientist. Currently, he was in the Arctic studying the mating habits of polar bears. He wore a fur coat with a hood and pole-fished on ice floes. He lived with an Eskimo family in an igloo and ate seal and fish the size of boats, rode in a sled pulled by huskies. My tall tales were big hits; I was asked how he stayed warm, whether he spoke Eskimo, when I had seen him last.

On Halloween afternoon, I spotted a cluster of girls huddled in the corner of the hallway leading out the front door. There was going to be a party at school that night. I was eager to get home and change into my costume, a fairy godmother get-up Mac and my mother had fashioned out of tulle and net. I stopped at the edge of the huddle, hoping to catch part of a conversation I presumed to be about plans for the night. They were talking about Miss Muldoon, who'd moved—much to my delight—from fifth grade to sixth, ("You can't get rid of me, Memory Feather," she'd said when I walked into my classroom to find her sitting there), and Miss Madison, our chorus teacher, an exacting but pleasant woman with the voice of an angel, as tall and lanky as Miss Muldoon was short and round. Miss Madison was already rehearsing us on all the verses of every carol imaginable in preparation for our Christmas concert. The girls called them M&M, like the candy. It seemed the two of them shared a house.

As I drew close, a girl named Normagene McGuire leaned over to me. "Let's roll M&M's place tonight," she whispered in my ear. The other girls quieted and leaned in to hear what she was saying, the result being that I became pleasantly enclosed by their circle.

"Let's show them we know what they are," said Normagene. "They live just on the other side of the railroad tracks, not far from here."

I wasn't sure what Miss Muldoon and Miss Madison, collectively, *were* (Or was I? Looking back, I'm not entirely convinced of my innocence), but the circle of girls, now that I was inside, felt playful and friendly.

"We can sneak out of the Halloween party," I said, seizing the moment.

"Yes," said Normagene. "Let's go tonight. Trick or trick." She grinned at me and winked.

Like puppets controlled by the same set of strings, we all nodded vigorously.

That night I showed up in my fairy godmother outfit, complete with tiara and wand, both of which Mac had picked up in New Orleans. The outfit was pink and puffy. It made me feel pretty and powerful, as if whatever I did, whomever I touched, would be magically transformed. I even had pink slippers to match. Leaving the house, I grabbed a sack and got three rolls of toilet paper from the bathroom cupboard.

"What's the toilet paper for?" Mac asked as he fluffed my costume on my way out the door. He had come over to our place to help me get ready and taken a whole roll of film on his Polaroid, critiquing each picture as it came sliding through. One didn't show my wand, one cut off the slippers, in one my eyes were closed.

"We're doing crafts," I said.

"Come straight home," my mother said. "We'll be right here."

"I'll be late," I said. "I'm on the cleanup committee."

MY SLIPPERS CRUNCHED ON the fallen acorns as I set out. It was perfect Halloween weather, crisp and cool and witchy. My slippers were several sizes too large, and I kept having to stop and slide my feet back into them.

At the party, I was surrounded again by the circle of girls, swept along in the planning of our trick on Miss Muldoon and Miss Madison. At nine o'clock we slipped out individually, met on the corner, and set out, laden with our sacks of toilet paper. We crossed the railroad tracks and turned down one little dirt street, then another until the houses thinned and there were open fields on either side. Then Normagene stopped cold and threw out her right arm. "Ssssh," she said, "there it is." There were no streetlights, but the half-pie moon shone down on the small white house, now dark inside, surrounded by live oaks whose branches dipped to the ground. There was a mimosa tree out front too, now brown and covered in pods. "Perfect," Normagene said, pointing to the lower branches of the oaks and mimosa within easy reach.

So we began. Working in pairs, we rolled the toilet paper branch by branch, even connecting the trees by throwing rolls from the branch of one to the branch of another. It was a beautiful sight in the silent moonlight, those ghostly white strips looping from tree to tree, swaying just a bit in the slight breeze. A work of art.

A train came through. Then just the fulsome buzz of night.

We were being girls together; we whispered and giggled. We stood back and admired our handiwork. I volunteered to climb the mimosa and put the finishing touches on the top. Just as I reached the top with my half roll on the wrist of my paw, the tree began to sway and groan. *No. Don't.*

At that moment a light in the little white house came on, then the porch light.

The front door opened and a female figure in a robe, buxom and large so it must have been Miss Muldoon, came out on the front porch. "Who's out there? Who are you?" Her voice was shrill and afraid.

The girls scattered, some flying up the street, others diving under shrubbery. The mimosa reached out and snatched at the tulle on my outfit, stole first one slipper then the other as I scrambled down.

When the police car pulled up, its spotlight found me straddling the lowest branch of the mimosa, trailing the last of my toilet paper. I loosened my grip on the roll, and it bounced tiredly on the ground beneath.

And that was how I came to be taken to Harris County Jail and had to endure my mother's fury and, worse, Mac's refusal to speak to me at all after he said, "How could you be so *cruel*, Little? Haven't I taught you *anything*?" Which made me realize, at least in part, that what I'd gone and done had been darker than a prank, had been something else altogether. When I walked into the gallery the next afternoon, he left without a word. My mother said to give it time, let him be. She forbade me to go by his house. I had deeply disappointed them both, she said, but particularly Mac. He could not bear cruelty; he would not tolerate prejudice. Nor would she.

I withered under Mac's condemnation. I stopped eating breakfast and my midday sandwich; I slept at my desk at school. My hair grew dull and dingy, my lips cracked and burned. At night I cried silently so my mother couldn't hear from her room next door.

An old grief made new.

After a month of this, my mother sized me up as I headed off to school. "Have you lost weight?" she asked, frowning.

That afternoon I came home to find Mac bustling around the kitchen. He glanced up at me and frowned, "My god, Little, you look perfectly dreadful." Then he opened the oven door and out came a pan of brownies.

I began to cry. "Why were you so mean to me?"

He turned, the pan still in his hand. "Why were you so mean to those poor women?"

"It was just a prank. I didn't think it up."

"You did it. You played along with those little monsters."

"It was a joke."

"No it wasn't. It was much more than that. One day you'll know what you did, and it will haunt you the rest of your life. I hope it does. It was cruel, it was *prejudiced*. You have deeply disappointed me, Little, and I don't say that lightly."

He set the pan of brownies on top of the stove.

"I'm sorry," I whispered.

"You don't know how sorry you should be," he said. "You have no idea. You have wrecked two people's lives."

—

AFTER THE TOILET PAPER incident I steered clear of Normagene and her crowd. I ate alone at lunch, my paw curled in my lap. One afternoon on my way home, I noticed the drum majorettes in their tasseled boots practicing their moves on the playing field, their batons flying skyward, shining like swords in the afternoon sun.

There was a beauty to the way the batons caught the light, the grace, the naturalness of the girls' throwing and catching, as if that was what they'd been born to do. Mac's beautiful dreamer in the portrait would have smiled at the sight of them, though their beauty was different from his, theirs not in their features but in the motion of their reach, the curve of their arms against the sky.

That afternoon, as we were lacquering a chest of drawers, I asked Mac to get me a baton.

"I'll do you one better, Little," he said. "Did you know I was head drum major at Harris High? I have a *full selection* of batons in the attic."

Later that night he showed me his high school album with a picture of him, slim and smiling, marching backward, his baton raised high, a grin covering the bottom half of his face.

"Aren't I something?" he asked.

I nodded. "You look like a king."

I SET UPON BATON twirling with a vengeance. I practiced for hours in Mac's yard, my feet crunching through the acorns and leaves, aggravating the squirrels, who retaliated by chattering obscenities at me. Minerva expressed her excitement by chasing them up into the oaks. Mac shouted orders and blew on his old drum major whistle, calibrating to my one good hand. He put me through my high-stepping paces every afternoon after school. I went from Flat Spin to Vertical Spin to Vertical Spin-Toss in the space of two weeks, once giving myself a black eye and almost knocking out my front teeth. After practice, Mac and I sat together in the leaves, cross-legged while he critiqued my form. After a month of this, he pronounced me ready for the big time; I should go talk to the junior high band leader, a Mr. Willard Fann, who would surely want a girl of my talent for the halftime shows at football games.

As it turned out, Mr. Fann was only too happy to have me after I showed him my repertoire. "Just think. A one-handed twirler," he murmured, eyeing the good long fingers on my working hand. The only thing that was holding me back was a uniform, which could be quickly made by Mrs. Fann for a cost of five dollars. And so it was that the following Friday night, I made my debut as a majorette, my outfit a short black skirt and white top, long sleeved, with a Nehru collar, the front clotted with sequins and tassels—majorettes dressed modestly in those days. My boots had been discarded by a girl who'd had to drop out of school that fall for reasons undisclosed. They were a size too small, but the pain of jamming my toes into them was a small price to pay for glory. When I strapped on my tasseled white helmet that Friday night, I felt downright faint from excitement.

The Harris County Pelicans were up against the Ocean Springs Dolphins and leading 21 to 7 at the half. Excitement ran high in the stands. As the band lined up behind the goalpost, I scanned the bleachers, hoping to get an encouraging nod or wave from Mac and my mother, who were sitting about halfway up. Mac had been hesitant about coming. Football games were rough affairs in those days, with fistfights erupting in the stands when a referee's call went against the grain. Roughnecks came into town on Friday nights looking for trouble. I'd begged him to come; in the end, he agreed.

What I saw instead of Mac and my mother was a group of men, large men in khakis, standing where they'd been sitting. Something was off. People were scattering. One of the men raised his arm. In his hand was a billy club. Just as he brought it down, Mac burst up from the melee, flailing, then crumpled beneath the blow.

The band started to play; the majorettes around me held their batons straight up, the way Mr. Fann had taught us. I shot a look up into the stands again. The billy club was going down and down. Mac hadn't emerged again. Then my mother popped up, waving her hands, shouting something I couldn't hear.

I set out in a sprint across the field, jumping the barricade and racing for the stands. I took the steps two, three at a time, the lapels on my majorette outfit swinging from side to side. When I got to the men, I whapped the one wielding the billy club over the head with my baton. My mother popped up again and kicked another man in the face. The first one turned on me, his club in the air, then stopped and backed away when he saw me. I must have been a sight. My tasseled hat had slid down over my eyes. I pushed it up, striking out wildly with my baton.

The men turned and spat, one by one. There were four of them in all. One said *fag* and one said *homo*. My mother reached over and grabbed those two up by the hair. I poked another between the legs with my baton, knocking him to his knees. Then they began to back away, leaving the hole in their middle that was Mac. He was folded over like a box, the top of his head bloodied. A trickle of blood from his ear ran down into his collar. He didn't stir.

"They came up from behind. They surprised him," said my mother. "He was watching you." It sounded like an accusation.

She began to scream for help, somebody help. People in the seats around us had scattered; others nearby ignored her. The band was marching down the field, the majorettes were twirling, the drum major conducting. There was an empty space in the line of majorettes where I should have been. I thrust my baton at my mother in case of more trouble and ran down the steps, then across the front of the bleachers, all eyes on me, the recalcitrant baton-less majorette, legs plowing the dust. At one point my hat slid down again, and I flung it into the dust. When I got to the entrance of the stadium, I saw a policeman and told him to radio for an ambulance. Then I ran back to where my mother stood over Mac, shielding him from view.

Mac was in the same position I'd left him in. The policeman had followed me, and he and my mother slid Mac to the aisle, just as the band finished up. Then the announcer said, "Ladies and gentlemen, a short break. Someone in the bleachers has been hurt. An ambulance is on the way."

Dead silence and hundreds of eyes. Then Mr. Fann, bless his heart, motioned for the band, which had scattered to the edge of the field, to play. They began with "Dixie" and everyone stood and began to sing because this was, after all, Mississippi. Under it all, the siren. Then the men from the ambulance trooped out in front of what seemed in that moment like the whole wide world. They took Mac's pulse, then put him on the stretcher. My mother and I walked on opposite sides of him, our hands on his shoulders, my mother still looking fiercely right and left and brandishing my baton.

THE NEXT FEW DAYS were a blur. I skipped school and stayed by Mac's side in the hospital in Gulfport during the day while my mother kept the gallery going. She came in the late afternoons to pick me up and stayed awhile. Mac was awake, but not prone to conversation. He had a concussion and stitches across the top of his scalp. His chest was bound; three ribs had been broken. Someone had had a knife; his arm had been sliced in multiple places, requiring more stitches. Worst of all, his ankle had been caught under the seat in front of him and broken in the struggle—a bad break, said the doctor who casted it.

Mac told me to take care of Minerva. Her food was in the cupboard; make sure she had enough water. Maybe take her home with us for a while. We told him we'd already done that.

No arrests were made. No one knew the men who had hurt Mac; no one knew anything at all. They were said to be roughnecks from out in the county, not anybody decent.

This was when I came to understand what could happen to people like Mac.

I also came to understand what my classmates and I had done to Miss Muldoon and Miss Madison. What I haven't told is that the day after Halloween, a Tuesday, neither of them showed up at school.

And again, on Wednesday, neither of them came. And the next day and the next.

The following Monday morning, the principal called an assembly during which he announced that Miss Muldoon and Miss Madison would not be returning to Harris County Junior High.

Sometimes Minerva and I would walk by their little white house. A handsome man and his pretty wife had moved in. They had two little children, a girl and a boy. The perfect family. Some nights at dusk the mother and father sat together on the porch and watched their children play as dark came on.

VI.

———————

My mother and I brought Mac home to our little shotgun. My bedroom looked out on a restful grove of cypress trees so we decided to put him up there. I would sleep on the sofa.

We didn't tell him our plan until we picked him up at the hospital.

"You don't have room for me," he said when we turned onto our street.

"Oh, Mac, it'll be fun," said my mother, pulling the car into the driveway. "It'll be a house party. No one knows where we live. You'll be safe."

"The place is bigger than you think," I added. I'd actually come to like our little place, its cool silence at the end of a long day at school, its welcoming side porch, my own room, now painted eggshell blue, with three windowsills for my shells.

In his first few days with us, Mac slept like the dead. Each afternoon when I came home from school, I'd wake him up and we would plan our supper. If special ingredients were needed, I'd walk down to Phillipe's Grocery and pick them up so as to have a meal on the table when my mother came home from work. I'd not wanted to go back to twirling, but Mac laid down the law. "We must not let a few redneck pecker-woods stop us from living our lives. We must be brave," he intoned from his prone position on my bed.

His recovery was sluggish; one week his arm and ankle seemed to improve, the next the ankle swelled to the size of a ham, requiring another trip to the doctor, the old cast cut off, a new one put on. My mother was working hard to keep Beautiful Dreamer going and the books up to date. Mac insisted on doubling her salary. When she protested, he said, "You deserve sainthood, Feather. Putting me up and burning the midnight oil at the shop. Don't you dare turn me down."

When she didn't tell him is that, since his attack, sales at the gallery had gone down the toilet. The only people buying art and antiques were tourists from New Orleans who didn't know which way the wind was blowing in Belle Cote.

"Seems to me people would feel sorry for Mac," I said. "Seems to me they'd want to help him out. What's wrong with people?"

My mother's mouth tightened. "The human species is worse than you think."

At long last, though, Mac began to heal and started spending several hours a day at the gallery, driving my mother crazy with his "bright ideas," as she called them, insisting that she move the refinished furniture here and there, rearrange items on the shelves. When he began to alphabetize the cans in our home pantry, my mother gently broached the subject of his returning home. Things had quieted down, she said; the peckerwoods had gone back under their rocks. Mac, to her relief, agreed; he was ready to get back to his own kitchen, his own bed, not that he wasn't grateful for everything we'd done. He'd be eternally grateful.

"That's what family's for," said my mother. "You'd do the same for us."

Mac's house had become musty from disuse. One rainy Wednesday, my mother closed the shop early, and the two of us swept and dusted and mopped until it smelled of furniture polish and vinegar.

After Mac settled back in, Minerva roamed in her queenly way between our two houses, and we each fed her secret treats to keep her close. She grew fat and sleek. As time went on, Mac spent more time in New Orleans, sometimes the better part of a week, returning, a smile playing at his lips, bearing special trinkets for my mother and me, new paintings, old furniture in need of restoring. Now that he was back on his feet, the pace of his and my mother's lives revved up. She began to come and go from the City too, attending gallery openings and buying art. He reinstated his Saturday night house parties, and the next Sunday, when my mother opened the gallery, a troop of men would be clustered at the door like a flock of impatient gulls. When she was gone overnight, Mac came over and stayed with me. His hair had grown over the places in his head and the scars on his arm had begun to fade, though every so often he had dizzy spells, a lingering effect of the head injury. He walked with a limp, which disappeared after a time.

By then it was summer again, and I'd turned twelve. Mac and I spent more and more time out on the water. He still had his parents' ill-begotten sailboat moored at the Yacht Club but kept it only for friends, preferring his small fishing boat. Several afternoons a week we motored up into the Bay to do some serious fishing. We didn't talk much on these excursions, just enjoyed the warm weather and each other's silent presence. Sometimes, though, Mac's sunny disposition turned dark and, as we threw our lines into the shore, he took on the troubles of the world—the low-life bigots who took the lives of Black people, even children like that Chicago boy up in Money, barely older than I was. He'd just sent the *Delta Democrat* a piece on the occasion of Emmett Till's birthday. Emmett would have turned sixteen, *his whole life unfolding like a flower*, wrote Mac, *a beautiful flower*. Mac also worried about the space race and the pitiful animals—dogs, cats, monkeys—that would soon be circling the earth in capsules the size of rural mailboxes. "How'd *you* like to be shot into outer darkness?" he asked me, staring morosely at the water.

While I pulled in mullet and catfish, he worried and stewed. He marched in from these fishing trips and headed straight for the kitchen table, grabbing paper and pen on the way. He wrote his first letter slowly, then picked up the pace as he copied it again and again to send to newspapers across the country. Sometimes he enlisted me in copying the letters, which always began with "Dear Sir," and were peppered with adjectives like *cruel, outrageous,* and *unjust.*

Meanwhile, the furniture side of the business, the name of which he'd changed to Little Feather Antiques, was thriving. He rented a well-ventilated warehouse and hired two men to do the stripping. I still did the sanding and was looking forward to a particular challenge, a walnut breakfront with a zillion scrapes and scratches, four drawers, and a six-shelved cabinet with leaded glass doors. Redone properly, it would bring a pretty penny. Mac had started giving me half the profits of whatever pieces I refinished. He took me down to Belle Cote Bank and Trust and showed me how to deposit my money and get the teller to mark the amount in my bank book. I grew fond of my bank book. The smell of the leather cover, the way the figures lined up just so.

At school I'd been named head majorette for the following year, with a new twirling routine for each game, choreographed by Mac. Returning to school that fall, I missed Miss Muldoon and Miss Madison. Where had they gone? What had they done? To this day, I imagine them begging out in front of the Cabildo in New Orleans, sandwiched between the fortune tellers and street artists, holding their cups out to passersby, telling their sad story of the girls who turned against them, one Memory Feather in particular. I see them lying in twin coffins after drinking poison like Romeo and Juliet. In my dreams, they still come to me in tattered black dresses, their faces green with death. I wake up in a sweat, furious with myself for seeing them like that, forcing myself to remember Miss Muldoon's neon smile and Miss Madison's willowy arms raised high in the air as she pulled sweet sounds from our unworthy throats. Surely they made their way in the world; surely they survived the maliciousness of children. Or so I hope.

So TIME PASSED, THE summers flowing into the school years and returning like the Sound's slow tides. I polished off my last year in junior high with all As. To celebrate, my mother said she would take me on her next buying trip. She'd gotten herself a snappy bob on her last trip into the city and treated herself to some new outfits; she wanted to do the same for me. At night she, Mac, and I took up cards—hearts, gin rummy, and bridge when we could find a fourth, usually Miss Bess Bailey, who lived in the house next door to Mac. Miss Bess, a retired teacher who'd grown more crippled over the years, was always up for a game of bridge. Miss Bess was pretty for an old lady. Her hair a dandelion fluff of white, her face round and rosy, her lips naturally red. When she smiled, her teeth were surprisingly white and even for a woman her age.

Winter or summer, Miss Bess carried a pleated Japanese fan with her, shoving it down the front of her shapeless dresses. The fan, covered in butterflies, fluttered up from between her breasts, which hung like pears from her chest. You could always tell when Miss Bess had a good hand because she'd whip out her fan and start fanning herself like it was a hundred degrees inside. Whoever was lucky enough to be her bridge partner knew to bid high; the other two of us sank in our seats.

ONE SUNDAY MY MOTHER drove up in Boudreaux's parking lot just as my grandparents and I piled out of their Plymouth for our after-church fish fry. "Mind if I join you?" she asked, as if we were casual acquaintances who'd just happened to meet up. She directed her question at my grandfather, whose eyes brightened at the sight of her. Before he could answer, my grandmother said the fish was good and so was the company, which made us all laugh. The four of us climbed the rickety steps to Boudreaux's, my grandmother leading the way in a straw hat topped with daisies, my grandfather in his shirt sleeves and tie, having discarded his suit coat in the car, my mother wearing a blue voile dress, as if she too had gone to church. At the table we talked of the humidity, the predicted hurricane season, the rumor that a Piggly Wiggly was coming to Biloxi.

As we gathered ourselves to go, my mother asked me if I wanted to ride home with her. I glanced at my grandparents. "I'll go with them so we can have our visit. See you in a while."

"That's good," she said quickly. "That's just fine."

From then on, until Memory and Martha Feather perished, my mother—their daughter—met us at Boudreaux's at the dot of 12:15 p.m. every Sunday.

When I returned home that first Sunday, I asked her why she'd decided to end her quarrel with my grandparents. She looked at me over the newspaper she was reading. "They're not bad people, Mem. They're just *limited*. And they love you. You know if anything happened to me, you'd end up with them."

"I'd want to stay with Mac."

"You wouldn't be allowed to. He's not a blood relation."

"Nothing's going to happen to you," I said.

She winked. "Not if I can help it. Let's see if the two of us can't drag these old fogeys kicking and screaming into the twentieth century."

As July moved into August, the Sound beckoned each morning. My mother had taught me to swim years before. With its long shelf and gentle tides, the Sound was ideal for swimming lessons. We waded out until the shelf gave way, pools of tiny fish tickling first my calves, then my thighs and chest. *Oh and oh and oh.* My mother taught me to trust the Sound. "Salt water will always hold you up if you let it, but you have to relax and let it," she said when teaching me to float. "There's nothing here to harm you."

Every morning that summer of my thirteenth year, my mother and I swam side by side across the horizon. The water rested me in a deep way. When we tired of swimming, we flopped over on our backs and bobbed in the slight waves, holding hands to stay together. In the water, there was a gentleness to my mother. She always floated on my right side, where my good hand was. If it slipped out of hers, she'd reclaim it, laughing. "Come here, you."

In those moments, I thought all was right with the world. I thought the rest of my life had opened up. An oyster shell, a pearl.

—

SOMETIMES, THOUGH, A STORY can hit a riptide. A moment of inattention, and down you go, thrashing, fighting for breath, into the murky darkness below.

The morning that Mac called and invited my mother and me for a celebratory supper, he didn't say what he was celebrating or that he was expecting a visitor. I made potato salad with lots of Zatarain's mustard and dill pickle, the way he'd taught me. My mother snagged some fresh strawberries at a fruit stand on the side of Highway 90.

Mac met us out on the porch. "I've got a surprise, Feathers." He hustled us through the front door. "Meet the man in the portrait. Our beautiful dreamer."

As I came through the door, my jaw dropped. There, before us, sat the man in the painting that hung in Mac's living room. He was older than his likeness and even more beautiful. His full name dreamily alliterative: Antonio Alessandro Amato. He was sitting on the sofa, his arms flung wide across the back, the sleeves of his yellow shirt draped like butterfly wings. He leapt to his feet, teeth flashing white, a shock of dark hair picking up the glow of the lamplight. He was *delighted* to meet us *finally.* He'd heard so much about us from Mac, and weren't the two of us knockouts? Please, we must call him Tony.

There was an inflection in his way of speaking, something of a lilt, that seemed exotic. He took my mother's hand and kissed it an unnecessarily long time. Then he snatched up mine—the good one—and kissed it not once but twice. Each time his lips hovered. I could feel the tip of his tongue, the moisture from his mouth. I snatched my hand away, then rubbed it on the back of my shorts. At that point, I'd never been kissed by anyone except my mother, who still kissed me goodnight, a dry whisper of a peck on the cheek, and Mac, who in moments of exuberance, might see fit to kiss the top of my head. Nor did I have a boyfriend. Boys took one look and saw my clenched hand. A few seemed fascinated by it, but not in a good sort of way.

Over supper that first night, Tony told stories. Once, when he was a boy, he had ridden an elephant. Its skin, he said, stroking the circular edge of his dinner plate with wandering fingers, had felt like a dirt road, edge of his dinner plate with wandering fingers, had felt like a dirt road, hard and dusty and full of ridges and ruts. His father paid a man at the circus to hold the elephant and situate a ladder for him to climb up its side. They walked around the ring, the man encouraging the elephant with a long curved prod. It was like being atop a swaying building.

Tony's father's father had come from the old country to work in the steel mills in Bessemer, Alabama. When Tony's father was twenty, he'd hitched a ride down to New Orleans and started cutting hair in the Ninth Ward. Now he owned four barbershops in the City. Tony had a talent for hair too, if he did say so himself. He managed one of his father's shops on Frenchmen Street, where he *personally* trimmed the balding Mayor Schiro's rim, along with his little mustache, sometimes even going to the mayor's office when he was busy. Oh, the tales he could tell of famous men! They were scoundrels, every single one.

That first evening Tony Amato's tales went on for hours, dripping from his lips like honey from the comb. My mother and I sat mesmerized. That summer I was deep into Homer's *Odyssey* and suddenly imagined us sitting around a fire in ancient times listening to the spine-tingling sagas of the gods and goddesses. My mother's lips slightly parted as she listened. She seemed suddenly fired by an inner glow. Her chest swelled perceptibly. If she'd been a courting peacock, she would have fluffed her tail feathers and shuddered all over.

Mac didn't notice her transformation. He only had eyes for Tony, who, I noticed, kept a hand on Mac's knee as he spoke.

Minerva crept into the dining room, leapt up onto the buffet, and hissed, her tail transformed to a plume, her back a ridge.

"I've just had a wonderful thought," Mac said. He scooted his chair toward Tony. "Belle Cote needs a barbershop. I have to drive over to Biloxi to get a decent haircut."

Tony flashed a grin. "I'll talk to Papa about it. He's been looking for another place to expand, somewhere the rent isn't so high."

"I know just the place," said my mother. "There's an old shoe-repair shop on Main Street for sale, right next to the gallery. It'd be a perfect spot, Tony. You'd get all the men who work downtown. The lawyers and bankers."

Mac stood up from the table. "Wonderful idea. Let's walk over there now. I need a stroll after that meal."

The three of them sprang up from the table like the house was on fire. I began to gather the dishes.

"Don't worry about those, Little," said Mac. "Come along with us."

"I'd rather do the dishes," I said.

"Be sure to bring a pencil and paper," my mother said to Mac. "We need to get the number on the sign."

Then the three of them sallied forth into the night, laughing and talking among themselves, plotting and planning.

After that first night, Tony entered our lives in bits and pieces, casually, as if he were a neighbor stopping by to borrow a cup of sugar. Just suppers with Mac at first, with my mother and me invited some, though not every time. It was silly, Mac said one night as the four of us were eating our dessert chocolates, for Tony to drive back to the City so late. Tony's old Chevy was a rattletrap; it could break down on the causeway over the Rigolets and then where would he be?

"I'd be stranded," Tony said, popping a chocolate-covered cherry into his mouth.

"It's decided then," said Mac. "Wonderful."

My mother looked back and forth between the two of them. She rose from the table. "Well, tomorrow's a workday."

I reached for another chocolate.

"Time to go, Mem," she said.

"I'll be along. I can help with the dishes," I said.

She poked me in the shoulder blade. "Come on."

Mac got up and began to clear the table.

Tony sat, his eyes on his plate, his fingers tapping the tabletop.

"Let's go, Mem," my mother said again. "Thanks, Mac, it was wonderful as always. Tony, you take care now."

On the way home, my mother stopped and turned to me in the dark. "Mac needs to live his own life, you know."

I kept walking. The night was unusually quiet for a summer evening. Normally the frogs and katydids were in a contest to see who could make the most racket.

She caught up and put her hand on my arm. "Do you hear me, Mem? Let it be. We have to let them be." Her voice unnecessarily loud against the silence.

The next day as I walked along the Sound, I saw Mac's fishing boat out on the water, two figures sitting face to face, still as herons on the hunt.

As things turned out, Tony said his father wasn't interested in expanding his fiefdom of barbershops beyond the New Orleans city limits, which was no problem whatsoever, Mac said, because he himself had been looking for just such an investment opportunity in real estate. *He* would buy the old shoe-repair shop, and *they* (meaning he and Tony) would renovate it for Tony's barbershop. Tony could get out from under his father's thumb and start his own business right here in Belle Cote. He could do things exactly the way he wanted, nobody looking over his shoulder, nobody telling him what to do. Once the business got rolling, Tony could pay rent and Mac make back his investment. It would work out swimmingly for all concerned.

These plans unfolded over a course of several weeks. Renovations on the old shoe-repair shop began. Tony moved in with Mac, lock, stock, and barrel. Now, when I showed up at Mac's, I had to knock. I couldn't stay overnight because the back room was now Tony's, his clothes were hung in the closet and folded neatly in drawers, replacing the jumble of pajamas and underwear and shorts I kept there, all of which had been put in a paper sack by the front door.

Tony was like a frenzy of sharks—here, there, and everywhere. He mowed the grass at Mac's every Tuesday; he did all the grocery shopping, and went on buying trips with Mac. One day I came into our downstairs refinishing shop and found him rubbing linseed oil into my breakfront.

"I wasn't finished sanding that," I said.

He looked up from his work. "Mac told me to finish up this piece."

"It's not smooth yet."

"It's smooth enough." He poured more linseed oil on his rag. "He wants it on the floor by the end of this week."

"He should have told me himself. I'd have gotten it ready."

Tony tossed me the rag. "Okay, then, get it ready. You think I'm getting a kick out of this?"

Later, I asked my mother if Tony was Mac's boyfriend, though I sensed that Tony Amato was in a different category from Oliver. Mac and Oliver had been easy together, laughing about everything, rough-housing with each other. With Tony, Mac seemed jittery, always asking where Tony wanted to go, what he wanted to do. There was a self-assurance about Tony, the quiet way he talked to Mac that drew an invisible circle around them, the way he touched Mac's arm to get his attention.

My mother said yes, the two of them definitely liked each other.

On monday i showed up at Mac's front door bright and early. My plan was to snag him for the day before Tony could get his clutches into him.

It promised to be a fine morning. It had rained overnight and the resurrection fern was perky and green against the dark branches of the oaks. There was a buzzing in the clover below the porch, the bees gossiping among themselves. Raindrops still glistened on the tips of the palmettos that lined the front steps.

I knocked. No one came to the door, so I knocked again, louder.

Still no one. I sat in the swing on the porch and pushed off, swinging higher and higher. Mac's swing needed oiling. It squeaked to high heaven, making a racket to wake up the dead.

Finally Mac opened the door. He was still in his pajamas and bleary-eyed. "What're you doing here at the crack of dawn, Little?"

"It's not the crack of dawn. How about we take a ride over to Ocean Springs today?" I took a step forward onto the doorsill.

"Not today. Tony and I have work to do. Another time." He moved to close the door.

"When precisely will that other time be?"

"Oh, heavens, Little, I don't know. Don't be a bother."

I spun on my heel and marched across the porch and down the front steps, expecting to be called back.

The door clicked shut.

On the street, I looked up at Mac's house. There, in the full-length bedroom window on the far left, stood Tony, his legs locked and spread. He was dressed only in his briefs, and the slant of the morning sun struck him full on. The top of the window cut off his head so that, in the morning light, his torso looked like a statue of a Greek god, chopped and sheared. There was an otherworldliness that radiated from him, as if he'd been dropped from the sky or had risen from the depths of the ocean. Zeus or Poseidon.

Then he abruptly turned from the window, as if someone had entered the room.

Over supper that night, I complained to my mother. "Mac acts like he doesn't give a flip about us anymore."

"Mac's in love," she said.

"I thought he loved *us*."

"Being *in* love and loving—they're two different things. Let him have his fun."

After that, I stayed away from Mac and his house.

BUT THEN ONE LATE afternoon, as I was boiling some shrimp for my mother and me to have for supper, Tony breezed in, ending up in the kitchen before I knew he was there.

"Hey, Birdy, look what I snagged down at the dock," he said, holding up a sack of oysters. "I thought we could eat them while they're fresh." He looked hopeful and innocent and new.

"Don't call me Birdy," I said. "I already made supper."

He leaned over and peered into the pot on the stove, then looked up at me and winked. "What say you share some of your shrimp with me, and I'll fry up some of these oysters? Come on, be a sport now. Mac's up in Hattiesburg tonight, and I'm lonesome. Have mercy on a fellow."

"These shrimp are almost ready and my mother's going to come in from work hungry," I said. "You'll have to shuck all those oysters. It'll take forever."

He held up the sack. "Bet you supper it'll take me ten minutes tops to shuck them. You can time me." He leaned around me to pick up a knife on the counter. "Did I ever tell you I shucked oysters at Acme down on Iberville when I was a boy?" He plopped a shell on the counter and opened it in one flip of the wrist. "Get me a bowl. And some cornmeal and salt. You made cocktail sauce yet?"

"No."

"Well then, you can do that while I tackle these oysters. Then we'll have a feast ready for your hard-working mother when she gets home." In the time it took to give me directions, he'd popped three more shells. "Where's your skillet?"

I opened the drawer under the stove and pulled out the iron skillet Mac had given us as a housewarming present when we moved into our little place, declaring no self-respecting kitchen should be without one. I plunked it down on the stove eye.

"Mind if I get a beer?" He pulled a can of Jax from the icebox. "You're the best, Birdy Feather," he said with a wink. "Maybe after supper we can play some cards."

"I said don't call me that."

He reached around me, brushing my bare shoulder with the little spider hairs on the top of his hand, opened the drawer to the left of the stove and took out the church key.

"How'd you know where that was?" To my knowledge, he'd never darkened our door.

"Where else would it be? This is the perfect spot," he said.

He punctured the top of the can. One side a little, then the other all the way, so the beer didn't foam.

Tony finished with the oysters in nine minutes, not ten, and tossed them in a bowl with the cornmeal and salt. "Oil?" he asked, and I pointed to the back of the stove. "How about you set the table?" he said, turning on the burner.

By the time my mother opened the door, the oysters were sizzling, the table set, and my cocktail sauce, pinkened by enough horseradish to take the fur off a bear, sat waiting.

"Mem," she called out as she walked through the living room. "How many times have I told you not to fry anything when I'm not here. You could start a fire."

Tony poked his head around the corner of the kitchen. "Don't worry, little mama," he said. "We're having a feast tonight, just me and the two lovely Feather ladies."

"Oh!" my mother said, and her hand flew to her bob, fluffing it, then smoothing it down, then fluffing it again. "What a nice surprise, Tony. Let me freshen up."

She went into the bedroom and came out a few minutes later smelling to high heaven of Forbidden cologne. She'd darkened her brows and put on lipstick. Her bob was freshly brushed and she'd put on a blue shirt that brought out the blue in her hazel eyes.

"Going somewhere?" I asked.

She glared at me. Tony winked at her.

We sat down at the table to eat. The oysters melted in my mouth.

"Tony, these are wonderful," proclaimed my mother, her redder-than-they-should-have-been lips glistening with grease.

He leaned across the table. "Did I tell you about the time I worked at Acme?"

"Less than half an hour ago," I said.

"Really?" said my mother. "My goodness, Tony, you've certainly been around. Is there anything you *haven't* done?"

"I haven't fallen in love."

"Really?" my mother said.

"Not until now," he said. He tilted his chair back and looked at her.

It was as if he'd thrown a dead fish on the table. My mother's mouth opened and stayed that way. I froze in the process of standing up and reaching for the plates to clear the table. Then my mother's mouth snapped shut, like a mullet hitting on a bread ball.

Tony took her hand. "Let's take a walk and shake down these oysters." He turned to me. "Miss Birdy Feather, you're nominated to wash the dishes while your mother and I take a walk. Then I'll let you beat me at gin rummy." He tugged on her hand, pulling her up from the table. "We'll be back in a bit."

My mother, struck dumb, followed him out the door.

I washed the dishes and dried the dishes and put up the dishes. I got out some ice cream and ate it. Then I washed my bowl and spoon, dried and put them up too. Still they hadn't returned.

I turned on *Father Knows Best* and watched it all the way through. I got up and washed my face and brushed my teeth for bed. Then I got out the cards and played two games of solitaire. Minerva appeared in the open window above the kitchen sink and jumped up on the table beside me. In the middle of the third game, my mother and Tony tumbled in the door, both of them flushed and laughing full out.

Minerva hissed, leapt for the window, and disappeared into the night.

Tony stopped short, his eyes narrowed. "That cat doesn't like me," he said.

We played gin rummy late into the night. I won two dollars and seventy-five cents off Tony, who, it seemed to me at the time, was a terrible player. Maybe it was the liquor he tossed down, the better part of a pint of Jack Daniels my mother had been saving for a Christmas fruitcake. After several hours, he said, "Okay, I'm done. Let me stagger on home, pretty ladies."

He walked over and opened the screen door. My mother followed him. They stood there for a moment murmuring to each other, letting in the mosquitoes and June bugs and at least two flying roaches.

I went back into the kitchen and came out with his sack of oyster shells. "Here," I said to Tony, "get rid of these before they stink up the house."

"Yes, ma'am," he said, taking the sack with a grin.

Then, with a tip of an imaginary hat, he disappeared into the buzzing dark.

VII.

———

THE NEXT MORNING WHEN I was taking my beach walk, I spotted Mac's sailboat skimming across the Sound with Tony at the tiller. I decided to use the opportunity of Tony's absence to head over to Mac's for some books. Mac's overflowing floor-to-ceiling bookcases ranged down the whole left wall of the dining room. The shelves contained a wealth of riches.

Thanks to my grandfather's dramatic recitation of local history dating back to the Paleo-Indian period, I had planned a report in school about the area's deep past. I was hoping to dig out some books on the subject among Mac's collection. That morning, as I walked along the Sound, I squinted my eyes and imagined a mastodon mother the size of an elephant lumbering toward me, her massive tusks carving a path through the brush, her wooly wonder of a baby trailing along through the tall grasses. The landmass we stood on stretched all the way to Mexico back then, so there was no escape into the water. Was that a saber-toothed tiger peeking from around a giant oak?

The stories I used to tell myself!

Since Mac was supposed to be at an auction in Hattiesburg, I didn't knock. The living room was dark; the drapes still covered the windows.

I'd never been in the house during the daylight hours when the sun, filtered by the giant oaks, wasn't dancing along the pine floor, making leafy patterns. Even at night, Mac kept his windows uncovered so that when my mother and I came up the front walk for our suppers together, the glow of the lamps inside cast a light all the way down to the street, welcoming us in advance of our arrival.

I was thirsty after my walk so I went into the kitchen to get a glass of water, then stopped short. Dirty dishes were piled sky high; the garbage can was running over. The kitchen stunk with rancid meat. By the door, Minerva's water bowl was empty, her food bowl nowhere in sight. I filled up her water bowl, then drew my own water and headed back into the living room. It was too dark to see the bookshelves, so I opened the drapes. The bookcase was dusty, the coffee table littered with overflowing ashtrays. Sheets of newspaper lay scattered about. There were no fresh roses on the coffee table. Mac was particular about his roses. He had a garden out back that was lined with exotic varieties of hybrid teas with names like Ebb Tide and Double Delight.

Mac's latest haul from New Orleans was piled up on the dining room table. A few weeks ago he'd scolded me about my reading habits. "You always have your nose in a novel," he declared. "You need to branch out, test the waters. Short stories, poetry, that's the ticket." I knew he'd selected these with me in mind, that by some hook or crook, he'd insist I sample them, so I resignedly gathered up Kate Chopin, Anton Chekhov, and Emily Dickinson. After I made my selections, I went back into the kitchen to put down some food for Minerva. The smell made me gag. I decided to take out the trash; then one thing led to another. I tackled the mounds of dishes, wiped down the counter, and put a new sack in the garbage can, which needed hosing out, but I decided someone else could take on that chore, though I wondered who, given the sad state of the house.

I headed back into the dining room to search for books on local history when I heard it. It was slight, but it was a sound, a creak actually. I froze, books in hand. A bedspring?

"Hello?" I said. "Is anyone here?"

Another creak, a shifting of weight, a sigh.

"Mac?" I said. "Is that you?"

Another shifting, then a deep groan. The hair rose on the back of my neck.

I dropped the books onto the table and headed for Mac's room. The door was shut. I knocked. "Go away." The voice of an old man, tired and peevish. I turned the knob. The door opened onto shadows. As in the living room, the curtains were drawn. The room hot and airless, suffocating. Mac's back was to me, the bedcovers pulled up over his head. Only his golden mane of hair was discernable in the gloom, disheveled and tangled.

"Mac. What's the matter? Are you sick?"

He turned onto his back, groaning as he moved.

"What's wrong with you? Why are you in bed? It's boiling in here."

I went over and opened the curtains. The windows were shut and locked. I unlatched them and raised them high. I turned on the rotating fan that sat on a chair across the room. In the light, I could see Mac's flushed cheeks, his glittery eyes, the bucket by the side of the bed.

"Go away," he said again, panting a little. "I'm not fit for human consumption."

"I'm not going to *eat* you, Mac," I said with as much of a laugh as I could muster. I went into the bathroom and wet a washcloth. The bathroom stunk to high heaven too, with badly soiled underwear and undershirts soaked in sweat scattered about. I threw open the window beside the commode, picked up the clothes and put them in the laundry hamper. I carried the hamper out onto the back porch, just to get the smell out of the house.

I took the washcloth back into the bedroom and wiped Mac's face.

"Thirsty," he said, throwing off the covers. His breath smelled like garbage. His lips were split and salted over.

I headed into the kitchen and filled up the glass I'd just put in the drain. I popped some ice cubes out of a tray in the freezer and dropped them in the water.

When I brought the water, Mac seemed to have gone back to sleep. I pushed on his shoulder and his eyes flew open again. He looked around wildly. "What?" His voice gravelly.

"Let's get you up on the pillow so you can drink."

He struggled to push himself up, his eyes on the glass of water. "Thirsty," he said again, then fell back on his pillow. I ran back into the kitchen and opened the pantry, searching for the straws he used for my Shirley Temples. I found them at the back of the third shelf, snatched one out of the box, and carried it into the bedroom. Mac's teeth were chattering. He'd pulled the sheet and bedspread up around his chin. "Cold," he said.

I put the straw down in the water and then into his mouth. He began to draw up the water, stopping only to catch his breath. When he drained the glass, he fell back on the pillow, panting.

I went into the hall and dialed up my mother at the gallery. When she answered, I opened my mouth to tell her about Mac. My throat closed and nothing came out. "Who is this? Stop this harassment right this minute," she said, her voice tinged with fear.

"Mac's really sick," I finally managed to gasp.

"Is that you, Mem? What's the matter?"

"Mac's shaking and sweating. He's been sick to his stomach."

"I thought he was in Hattiesburg. Where's Tony?"

"He's out on the water."

"I'll be there in five minutes. Keep him hydrated. A cold cloth on his face."

"I did all that."

"Do it again."

When she hung up, I went back into Mac's room. He'd thrown off the sheet, turned to the wall, away from the light.

His feet were tangled in the sheet. As I unwrapped it and it loosened, I let it billow over him like a sail, thinking it would cool him off. I saw then that his pajama bottoms were soiled. Blood spots bloomed on the bottom sheet.

"Stop that," he said sharply, batting the sheet down.

I tucked the sheet around him, patting it in place around his torso.

My mother came in and took one look.

"He has diarrhea," I said. "And blood."

She lifted the sheet and took one long look.

He groaned. "Oh, Feather, get out of here."

"Don't be silly." She put her hand on his brow. "Where's the thermometer?"

His eyes rolled back into his head.

She turned to me, her eyes two points of fire. "Look in the medicine cabinet."

When I brought it to her, she stuck it between his lips. She stood there, tapping her toe against the floor, holding the thermometer in his mouth.

Then she whipped it out and took it over to the window. One look, and something changed in her face, as if all her features had been erased and nothing but one central purpose remained. "Stay with him," she said and went into the hall.

She dialed. "A hundred and four point five," she said into the phone. "Dehydrated and delirious. Diarrhea. Bloody diarrhea. No, I don't know how long he's been like this, but from the looks of things a while. Please hurry."

When she hung up the phone, she turned to me. "Go home now, Mem. I'll take care of this."

"No," I said.

She didn't argue, just headed back into the bedroom. Mac was trying to pull himself up in bed, his eyes wide with fear.

"Lie down, Mac," said my mother.

"You're all right, Mac," I said.

We both moved toward him and he snatched at us. I took his hand.

"Don't touch him," my mother said. "You might catch this."

I ignored her. His hand, hot as a poker, squeezed my paw until I had to pull away.

"Don't leave me," he said. Then he sat up and looked around wildly. "Where's Minerva? Where's my cat?"

"Minerva's fine," my mother said. "Now you lie back down and rest."

He sank back onto the pillow, then began to twitch and thrash about like a madman, to the point that we had to stand back for fear he'd strike us.

When we heard the ambulance down the street, my mother took in a shaky breath. "Run out and show them in. Tell them he's having a seizure. Tell them to hurry."

The siren ended in a burp, and gravel scattered. I ran down the steps and out onto the driveway, motioning the driver to pull closer. Heads up and down the street popped out of windows. Several women stepped out onto their porches, wiping their hands on their aprons and squinting in the midday sun.

Miss Bess hobbled out onto her front stoop. "What's the matter? What's happening over there?" she shouted, her voice frail and fearful.

The two men in the ambulance took out a stretcher and moved up the steps in one fluid motion. When they brought him down, Mac opened his eyes and looked at me. "Minerva," he whispered. "Find her." In the bright sun, his face looked as if it had been scraped raw.

"I'll find her," I said. "Don't worry."

My mother climbed into the ambulance with him. "Go on home," she told me. "Go on now. Don't touch anything in that house. Don't go back in that house."

The ambulance headed down the street, sirens blaring.

I collapsed on the steps and thought how best to find Minerva. Before Mac got her fixed, he said she used to gallivant around town playing the fool. The only way to get her home was to open a can of tuna and go out into the streets hollering *tuna* at the top of your lungs. I went back into Mac's house and got a can from the pantry.

I walked around the yard brandishing the can and calling out. I was just getting ready to walk down the street when I heard a thin wail. It was the sound a baby makes when it's been crying too long. I stopped and listened. Nothing. Then it started up again, this time sounding more like the mewing of a newborn kitten. I peered under some camellia bushes and an overgrown date palm. Nothing. Then here it came again, and again, trailing off into a throbbing silence. "Minerva?" I called out. Then one long cry, ending abruptly, as if it had been cut by scissors.

I slipped into the cool dark under the house, then to its center, the little workshop Mac had enclosed for our refinishing projects. The door to the shop was shut tight, which was strange—normally it was left open for the lacquer fumes to evaporate. The ventilation fan that Mac kept running day and night had been turned off.

One more faint cry.

I opened the door and turned on the light. There, on the concrete floor, lay Minerva next to an oily pool of lacquer thinner and a stained rag. She stared up at me, her eyes rheumy and slitted. Her coat was matted and dull. She raised her head, then dropped it back to the floor. I lifted her up, and it was as if I were holding nothing but a shred of skin. Her heart fluttered like the pulsing of hummingbird wings.

"Oh, Minerva," I said. "Oh, sweet baby." I struggled to stand up with her, the fumes having made me lightheaded.

I brought her upstairs and laid her in front of her water bowl, but she didn't lift her head. I got a teaspoon from the drawer and dipped it into the water and put it down by her mouth. She lifted her head, but the effort seemed too much for her and she shut her eyes. I stroked her, then got some milk out of the icebox and put it into a saucer and dipped the teaspoon into it. I put it beside her mouth, but she didn't take any. Then I remembered the box of straws in the pantry. I got one and sucked some milk into it and put a drop into her mouth, which, oddly, was partly open. She swallowed, and so I put another and another. After a while her mouth closed and she went to sleep, purring hard.

I put the straw in my pocket and gathered Minerva in a dish towel. "You're coming home with me," I told her. In the towel she seemed more substantial, and when I walked into our front door, she lifted her head for a moment. I took her back to my bedroom and laid her on the bed and went into the kitchen to open another can of the tuna I'd promised her.

I was removing the lid when I heard *you you you* from the bedroom. When I went in, Minerva's head was down and her eyes closed, but again I heard *you you you* and I knew then that some membrane between us had been breached. Minerva had decided to speak.

Over the course of the afternoon she lifted her head and took some oil from the tuna through the straw, then water, then oil again. After several hours, she yawned and began to stretch.

I covered her and lay down beside her. She curled herself in the crook of my arm and began to lick my paw.

I was jolted awake by the phone. It was late afternoon, judging by the cast of light playing across the bedspread. Minerva lifted her head and stared toward the kitchen where the phone was. I jumped up and ran for it.

It was my mother. "He's going to be all right," she said quickly. "He has a dysentery called shigella. They've put him on an IV drip and anti-biotics. He should be all right. Mem, did you find Minerva? That's all he's been talking about."

I told her where I'd found Minerva and what condition she was in.

"That's odd," she said. "That door always stays open. Maybe the wind the other night with that rainstorm. I'll tell Mac we have her and we'll hold on to her until he gets out. How Tony could leave Mac in that condition and go out on the water I don't know. I'm going to stop by on the way home and give him a piece of my mind. The house was a horrible mess too."

"I cleaned up the kitchen."

"You handled Mac's dirty dishes? I told you not to touch anything, Mem."

"And I took out the garbage. It was running over." I didn't tell her about the soiled laundry.

"Oh, Mem. I just hope you don't catch this. The doctor said it's been going around in the City like wildfire."

"When are you coming home?"

"I'm going to wait until he goes to sleep. Now you keep Minerva inside. Get that old litter box of hers from the garage. We don't want her trying to go back to Mac's."

"When you see that Tony, ask him why he told us Mac was in Hattiesburg."

"Believe me, I will. I don't understand any of this." She hesitated.

"Mem, I want you to take a good hot shower and stay home the rest of the day. Lock the front door, not just the screen."

Her tone surprised me. What was she afraid of? I checked the door, which wasn't locked, and locked it.

Minerva followed me to the door and pawed at it. *Out.*

"No way," I said. "Look where your wandering got you. I saved your fool life. Don't push your luck."

I went out to the garage and got out her litter box, an old turkey roaster Mac had scavenged. I poured in some sawdust shavings we kept for that purpose. We hardly ever needed to keep Minerva in, but we kept the box ready during hurricane season.

I put the box in the bathroom and picked up Minerva and put her down in it to let her know her needs were taken care of. She glared at me as if I'd insulted her and strolled haughtily into the kitchen, where she let out an angry yawl. *Give me.*

I pulled out a can of cat food. *Yes yes.* She pawed at my leg as I got out the opener.

As I was putting the food into a dish and setting it on the floor, there was a knock at the door.

I opened it a crack and peered out. It was growing dark and had begun to drizzle. Although the porch was covered, a wind had come up and raindrops matted the screen door. My grandmother and grandfather stood hunched outside in the rain. My grandfather held a casserole dish covered with waxed paper.

"Lord, Memory, you're locked up like Fort Knox. Let us in," said my grandmother.

I unlatched the door and she came bustling in, fluttering about like a wet hen, my grandfather bringing up the rear. Minerva rounded the corner and made a beeline for the door, which I slammed before she made her escape.

My grandmother jumped. "Great sakes alive, Memory. You don't have to slam the door."

"I didn't want to let the cat out."

"You keep that cat inside? Isn't that unsanitary?"

I ignored the question. "This is a surprise, to see you two."

Soon after my mother had shown up for Sunday dinner at Boudreaux's, my grandparents had started coming over for supper every Wednesday night. My mother had instigated these events, saying I needed to know my own flesh and blood. On her own turf, she made peace by offering up simple one-dish meals like shrimp creole or boiled seafood. My grandmother always brought pineapple, carrot, and cottage cheese Jell-O salad, which my mother and I did not care for but dutifully ate. Conversation ran to topics like the weather or the state of the Presbyterian Church, now split between southern and northern branches because of segregation, or my school activities. There was never a cross word spoken over our little kitchen table; nor did my mother ever darken her parents' door.

It was Friday, not Wednesday, so I was surprised they'd shown up unannounced and uninvited, there being a kind of unwritten code that they didn't just drop in. For one thing, they might have run into Mac, which would have quickly broken their fragile truce with my mother.

My grandfather set the dish down on the table. "Macaroni and cheese," he announced.

"I have some gumbo I can heat up."

My grandmother clapped her hands. "A smorgasbord! I'll slice the tomatoes."

"We don't have any," I said.

"*Voila!*" She whipped two tomatoes out of her purse like rabbits out of a hat.

When we sat down at the table, a quiet came over us as we began to eat.

I looked at my grandparents and caught them beaming at each other. "What made you decide to come by tonight?"

"Delicious gumbo," said my grandmother. "Your mother follows my recipe. There's nothing like a good seafood gumbo. None of that turkey or sausage business. Just pure seafood."

"Well, that's one thing you taught her," said my grandfather.

I put down my fork and waited.

My grandmother took a sip of water and cleared her throat. "Your mother called and said she was going to be late. She said you might be wanting some company. She didn't say where she was."

I took another slice of tomato. They were creole tomatoes, large and meaty and sweet. "I don't mind being by myself."

My grandfather reached into his pocket and brought out a sack of marbles and put it on the table. "Well, you'll just have to put up with us tonight. I've got my Chinese checkerboard out in the car."

My grandfather loved Chinese checkers. If he could corral a partner, which was usually me, he'd play nonstop until heaven and earth froze over. I preferred card games, and after the day I'd had, all I wanted (and needed) were a hot shower and some TV. *Alfred Hitchcock* was coming on at seven.

But I smiled at my grandparents, who seemed bound and determined to babysit me until my mother got home. "Let's save some macaroni and cheese for my mother."

"I'll put some aside and do the dishes," my grandmother said. "You two play some checkers."

My grandfather got up from the table. "Memory, would you go out to the car and get my checkerboard? It's in the back seat."

I headed out to the car. When I opened the screen door, Minerva, who'd been stretched out on the back of the sofa, headed for the door, then stopped short. *No no no.*

Outside, the rain had stopped, but the air was thick. Clouds covered the moon. I opened the back door of my grandparents' Plymouth and leaned in to pull out the checkerboard.

As I turned to go inside, I sensed a presence blocking my way.

I peered through the thicket of dark. Then the presence cleared its throat.

"Who's there?" I whispered.

"It's me, Tony."

I shut the car door. "About time you showed up."

"Where's Mac?" he asked.

"What do you care?"

"Where is he?"

"The question is where have *you* been? He was sick as a dog, and you left him there while you took *his* sailboat out on the water and had yourself a fine old day."

A sliver of moon pushed through the clouds, illuminating his face for a moment. What I saw there surprised me, a look of something between concern and worry.

"He *told* me to go. He said he was feeling better."

"Any fool could see he wasn't."

"I'm not a doctor, Birdy."

"Don't call me Birdy. Why didn't you tell us he was sick? Why'd you tell us he was in Hattiesburg?"

A cloud covered the moon again. Gravel crunched underfoot. I sensed him move toward me. Instinctively, I raised my grandfather's checkerboard.

"Listen, he *made* me lie. I didn't want to. I *told* him he needed to go to the doctor. I told him to call your mother. He didn't want her to see him like that. You know Mac. He's always doing for somebody else, never wants anybody to help him. He *told* me to get out, he needed to rest. He's a pretty stubborn guy, you know, when it comes right down to it. We all love him, but he can be hardheaded. You don't really think I'd *abandon* him, do you?"

"Why'd you leave the place such a pigsty?"

He took hold of my arm, his fingers encircling it. But his touch was light. There is a kind of crab with long legs, a hermit. It crawls into the homes of other shellfish and takes up residence there.

"You're going to fault a fellow for being a little messy? I've been running myself ragged taking care of that guy."

"And what about Minerva? She was shut up downstairs with fumes enough to start a fire. She was half-dead when I found her."

A pause. "Jeez, Birdy, how was I supposed to know that's where she was? You think I'm responsible for messing up the whole world? Next thing I know you're going to say I got Mac sick?"

"He's in the hospital, in case you're interested."

"Hospital? What's wrong with him?"

"Something called shigella."

"Shigella, you say?"

"Yes, it's a dysentery."

Another pause.

"I know."

"Very contagious."

"Yes."

"Well, if you want to see him, go," I said.

"Are we square?" The moon broke through the clouds again. I could see it in his eyes.

"I don't know," I said. "I'll think about it."

My grandfather came to the screen door. "Memory, are you out there? Is somebody there?"

Tony slipped into the shadows.

"Just a friend passing by," I called back to my grandfather.

When I stepped inside the door, my grandmother was peeking out of the window. "Isn't that Mac McFadden's house boy?" she said. "The one with the barbershop?"

"Mac doesn't have 'house boys,'" I said. "He has *friends*."

My grandfather put his hand on my shoulder. "Don't talk to your grandmother in that tone of voice."

"It's true," I said. "*House boy* isn't a nice word, and I won't stand for anybody to use it about Mac's friends." When I said the words, I knew I'd cut the thin thread that connected me to these two old people, who lived in a world completely alien to the one I inhabited with Mac and my mother. The world of feathered hats and Our Mother uniforms and Sunday buffets and sweet afternoon naps under lazy ceiling fans: everything my mother had fled.

I knew which world I wanted to live in.

In the kitchen, my grandmother turned off the water in the sink. She walked into the living room where my grandfather and I faced each other.

"Memory," my grandmother said. We both turned to her, but she was addressing not me but my grandfather. "I think it's time to go."

"No, Martha," said my grandfather, holding up his sack. "It's time to play Chinese checkers."

She turned away then, wiping her hands on my mother's apron, over and over, as if some bit of food had stuck to them, as if the fate of the planet depended on her removing it. Like all of her gestures, it was small and just shy of frantic. And then she was gone and the water in the kitchen sink started again, as if nothing of consequence had happened.

At what moment, I wonder now, did the mastodons strip the last bark off the trees with their massive tusks and lumber away into oblivion and the Sound come in? The heavy footsteps laboring off in the distance, the first trickle of water. One story ending and another beginning. Family: Mammutidae. Order: Proboscidea. Extinct.

VIII.

————

FOUR DAYS LATER, MAC returned home from the hospital and I came down with shigella. When my mother got sick too, he collected us both, half-dragging, half-carrying us to his car and up those three flights of steps to his house. He deposited us in the double bed in his back bedroom that we'd occupied before moving out. We thrashed, feverish, kicking off the sheets, pulling them back up. Occasionally, one of us leapt from the bed and ran for the bathroom, sometimes making it, sometimes not. Mac administered our medicine, cleaned our nightclothes, applied cold washcloths to our heads, fed us saltines and ginger ale.

My mother and I slept through our regular Sunday dinner with my grandparents, and when the two old people didn't call—if they did, we weren't at home to answer—we took no notice as we tossed and turned feverishly.

It was the milkman who finally alerted the police after a week's worth of milk bottles lay untouched on my grandparents' front porch. They must have lain about for days without medicine or someone to give them so much as an ice chip. They were pronounced dead from dehydration, plain and simple. In the haze of fever, it never occurred to me to call or send word, and for that I blame myself, just as I fault myself that my last words to my grandmother had been delivered in anger, and even worse—scorn—even as I was infecting her with the budding microbes that would kill her.

At the funeral, no one but the pastor said a single word of comfort to my mother and me, both of us pale and gaunt from our physical ordeal. No one put a kind hand on our shoulders at the pretty cemetery on the bluff above the Sound. The afternoon the two of them were lowered into their side-by-side plots, a warm rain fell steadily, punctuated by the screech of seagulls. A phalanx of pelicans flew low over the open graves. Getting out of the car, I stepped into a puddle up to my ankles and sat through the burial service with water pooled inside my patent leathers.

Despite the weather, most of Belle Cote came to see my grandparents off, except for Mac, who stayed away because my mother asked him to. There were audible whispers about how my mother and I had broken my grandparents' hearts, how we'd ignored them in their final days on this earth, let them die like dogs in their sickbed, uncared for, unloved. In the days that followed, not a kind word was offered, not a single ham or cake or casserole. People glared at my mother on the street. The business at the gallery dwindled even further, to the degree that she offered to quit her job there, an offer Mac met with an impatient wave of his hand. "Don't be ridiculous, Feather," he said. "I'm more of a pariah in this town than you'll ever be."

IN THE WEEKS THAT followed, I tried my best to feel sorrowful. My grandparents' blood pumped through my veins: they had made my mother and my mother had made me. Surely they must have had more substance and complexity than I gave them credit for. Surely they had beating hearts that loved and hated and felt saddened at their only grandchild's blatant indifference to the culture they'd grown up in, a culture as alien to me as that of the Paleo-Indians who hunted and fished along the lush riverbanks and plains of the land that would become coastal

Mississippi. Even now, Martha and Memory Feather remain in death, as in life, stick figures to me, though the indisputable fact that I was the instrument of their passing has settled like a heavy cloak on my shoulders.

Minerva followed me everywhere, an ever-present reminder that I'd managed to save her, a cat, but not my own flesh and blood.

Aside from my obvious shortcomings as a loving grandchild, complicating things even further was the fact that my grandparents had left me a tidy sum of money and their house on the Sound. The inheritance came in the form of a trust fund to be administered by Belle Cote Bank and Trust, specifically a Mr. Jameson Wadlington, Esquire, until I was eighteen. Mr. Wadlington informed me of this change in my fiscal prospects via an official-looking letter, which began with the salutation "Dear Mistress Feather," making me sound like a stripper. My mother called and made the appointment for us to come in and have him inform us as to the particulars. As she was preparing to hang up, her eyes narrowed. "Oh?" she said, her voice suddenly cool. "I *am* her mother." She listened some more. "Yes, I understand *perfectly*." She hung up without saying goodbye and turned to me. "It's only you he wants to see. He said that was their *directive*."

"I don't want to go by myself," I said. "I'm thirteen years old. What do I know about money?"

"You'll be fourteen soon," said my mother, turning from me to take up a dish towel and rub an invisible speck from the kitchen counter. "You're no fool, Mem. Just walk over to the bank tomorrow afternoon. He'll fill in the details."

Then she began to cry.

"I'll give you the money. I don't give a flip about it," I said, taking her hand.

"It's not that," she said. "I just thought…" She dabbed her eyes, then turned around and put her hands on my shoulders. "Everything will be taken care of. Just take some notes and bring them back to me. I don't know how much money there is, but I have a feeling it's enough to change your life, kiddo. So get ready. Be smart. You'll need to decide what to do with their house."

"We could go live in it," I offered, looking around at our tiny kitchen. "I like our little place."

I thought of the spacious sunny rooms of my grandparents' house, the sheer window curtains billowing in the ocean breezes. The Sound itself, right under the windows, murmuring and singing. "I'd like to have more room, maybe a bigger bathroom, one with a bathtub."

"I can't live in that house, Mem," she said, and that was the end of it.

MR. WADLINGTON GREETED ME with a flourish. He lived up to his name, a round man whose belly protruded over and under his belt. His bulbous nose became redder and redder as he told me I'd inherited what in those days was a small fortune: my grandparents' house on the Sound, their well-maintained Plymouth, and as an added surprise, an apartment in the French Quarter that currently housed tenants. "It's all yours when you turn eighteen," he said. "Between now and then, you'll get three hundred dollars a month, and you'll have to put up with me. If you have any special needs—if you decide you want to make a large purchase, a musical instrument, a trip or some such—come to me and I'll release the additional funds. On your direction, I am authorized to sell any pieces of property and place the funds acquired thereby into your account. And let me be clear, Miss Feather, this is *your* money, not your mother's. Those were your grandparents' wishes."

I rose from my seat. "My mother makes her own way."

Even as I spoke, I knew my monthly allowance alone—not to speak of the rest of it—changed everything.

That night I sat out on our front stoop, watching the moon rise. The palmettos in the front yard rustled in the breeze. Minerva slunk by, casting me a sideways look. *Shame shame.* Here I hadn't even mourned for the grandparents I'd unknowingly killed. Through their industry and thrift, they'd made me rich as Croesus, and I couldn't even muster one measly tear for them. Nor was I taking what was rightfully mine. My mother was my grandparents' true heir. It was their small-mindedness that had made them generous.

At the gallery, Mac greeted the news of my inheritance with good cheer. "Fabulous news! Little, you're now among the nouveau riche," he proclaimed. "We must celebrate."

"My grandparents just died," I said.

My mother looked up from dusting the countertops. "It's too soon."

"Of course. I'm sorry, I wasn't thinking. But do come over for supper on Saturday. I'll go over to Gulfport and get the oysters and some bananas and ice cream for this new dessert I had at Brennan's the last time I was in the City. Bananas Foster."

Mac himself needed cheering up. Tony had been gone two weeks without a word. He hadn't even gone by the hospital on his way out of town.

When the bell on the front door jingled, none of us looked up, thinking a tourist had come in to browse. It was midafternoon on a Friday, a time when people took off work early to drive over from the City for a little salt breeze, perhaps an ice cream cone and a browse about town, maybe a seafood supper. Judging by the uptick in traffic on Main Street heading toward the Pelican Inn, the well-off were arriving to spend the weekend.

But our visitor was no tourist.

His newly acquired tan was accentuated by a white shirt, unbuttoned to mid-chest. A lock of curly hair hung over one eye. His eyes were briskly earnest.

"Well, well, he lives," said my mother. "Where've you been keeping yourself, Tony?"

"Nothing like disappearing into thin air," I said.

I looked up at Mac, who'd burst into a dazed grin. Some mice, I've observed, seem mesmerized by the cat that stalks them.

Tony came up to Mac and touched his shoulder. "All better?"

Mac nodded.

"We both caught it," my mother said.

"Caught what?" asked Tony.

"I told you. Shigella." I said impatiently.

"Did you have it?" my mother asked him.

"Nope. My madre had it, though. I had to go back and nurse her. It hits old people hard. It's all over the City. Three people sick one minute and then hundreds the next."

Outside, a sudden wind came up and acorns peppered the tin roof of the gallery. Minerva slunk out the door Tony had left ajar, her belly dragging the ground.

My mother put her hand on Tony's wrist. "Is your mother all right now?"

He nodded.

"I wish you'd told us," said Mac. "We were worried."

"I went without thinking, with just the clothes on my back. It was my *mother*."

"Of course," Mac said. He took a breath. "And you're back just in time for our little supper celebration."

"No celebration," my mother said.

"What are we not celebrating?" asked Tony.

"Little's rich. Her grandparents left her a fortune."

"They died. Of the shigella," I said.

The gold flecks in Tony's eyes flickered. "How much did they leave you?"

Mac turned away and touched a small table I'd just refinished. Even he knew it was a rude question.

"Mem is grateful that they remembered her so generously," my mother said quietly.

"But I'm sorry they're dead," I added quickly. "They died because I gave them shigella."

"You say you had it too?"

"We both did," said my mother, "from nursing Mac while you were out on the water."

"I told him to go," Mac said quickly. "I didn't want him to see me like that."

Tony turned to me. "Did you get your grandparents' house too? That's a nice place, right on the Sound."

"Yes, and their apartment in New Orleans. And their car."

"An apartment in the City?"

"In the Quarter."

Tony flashed his perfect teeth at Mac. "Maybe later we can throw a party there."

"We'll have a nice supper tomorrow night for sure," said Mac. He threw an arm around Tony's shoulders. "Let's go home." He turned to my mother. "Feather, can you close up?"

"I always close up," she said. Just as the two of them turned to go, the bell on the door jingled again, and in walked Leticia Powell. Leticia was my age. She'd worked at Beautiful Dreamer for almost a month. She came in after school every afternoon during the week and all day on Saturdays and Sundays, cleaning and hanging pictures. She knew how to place paintings to show them to full advantage, which one would complement another, how to catch the light with a crystal bowl or mirror. A pretty girl with lustrous brown eyes and teeth that matched Tony's in sparkle and whiteness, Leticia was friendly but strangely guarded as if she might be accused of doing something illicit by pushing a mop around or placing a painting just so at a time of day when other girls our age were doing their lessons or watching *American Bandstand*.

I liked hanging new paintings under her direction, standing on the ladder, nails in my mouth, a hammer in my good hand. "There, up a little; no that's too far," Leticia would squint her eyes and say, directing the placement of the picture with a certainty I envied. But she wouldn't let me help her with the drudge work, the dusting and mopping, worried, I suspect now, that I'd try to claim some of her pay. I should have wondered how she got her schoolwork done, how she managed to get enough rest. I should have asked her what subjects she was taking, where her enthusiasms lay. She was afraid, I see now—afraid she would be let go for some slight oversight, afraid she would lose her small wage and have to go home empty-handed to her brothers and sisters (she came from a family of eight, my mother told me).

Leticia was smart in a way I was not. She and Mac met in the gallery at ten on Sunday mornings before it opened at noon. They labored over numbers and signs that were indecipherable to me, Leticia every now and then exclaiming over an equation, as if it were the greatest thing since sliced bread. I admit I was jealous. Mac had never offered to tutor me in math, and when I asked him one night after supper to show me what he was teaching Leticia, he said certain people possessed talents that others did not; mine most definitely wasn't advanced mathematics.

"You wouldn't even know what you were looking at," he said.

"What are they, then, *my* talents?" I asked.

"You know how to watch and listen; you write stories. You have an innate connection to the world around you."

"Teach me more of that, then."

"Little, I've been teaching you since the day you showed up on my doorstep. Plus, you don't need teaching," he said, a tinge of impatience in his voice, "unless it's about the advantages some people have over others. Look at Leticia. She's working her fingers to the bone to put bread on her family's table. She's so busy she doesn't even have time to think. And yet, she's got the mind of a physicist. The school for her race doesn't even teach algebra, for god's sake. For her, I'm the only game in town. Surely, Little, you don't begrudge her that."

"Well, you might have explained that before now," I said. "How am I supposed to know this sort of thing if you don't explain it to me?"

"Use your powers of observation, Little. Use them on people, not just on animals and plants."

Now LETICIA STOPPED SHORT and looked at us uncertainly. "Hey, Miss Virginia. Hey, Mr. Mac," she said softly, then turned to me. "Hey, Mem."

"Hello, Leticia," said my mother. "This is our friend Tony."

Leticia smiled and nodded.

"You're a pretty little thing," said Tony. "You from around here?"

Her smile vanished. "Up the road a ways. Not a far piece."

"Over near the mill?"

"Round about."

"Round about what?"

Instead of answering, Leticia turned to my mother. "What needs doing today, Miss Virginia? The usual?"

My mother nodded. "But first, I've got some new paintings to hang. Maybe, if Tony'll stop giving you the third degree, you and Mem could tackle those."

Tony's face darkened. "Just a friendly conversation, Virginia. Come on, Mac, let's go home."

And off they went down Main Street, Tony walking slightly behind, touching Mac's waist as if to guide him on the path ahead. They shimmered as they moved away from us, the late afternoon rays catching their hair, dark and light, as if they were archangels walking back up into heaven. Beyond them the Sound, beyond the water the horizon and setting sun.

I looked up at my mother. She was eyeing them oddly. "That Tony." She took a deep shudder of a breath, as if she'd been underwater a long time.

BEFORE I KNEW IT, summer leached over into fall and high school started in the midst of a September heat wave. Two weeks later, the house one door down from Mac and next door to Miss Bess Bailey on Bienville Street came up for sale. I got the down payment from Mr. Wadlington at the bank. He'd handled the sale of my grandparents' house, and so was amenable to the relatively small amount I asked for as a down payment, as long as my mother paid the mortgage, which he also arranged at the bank. "Property is a good investment," he pronounced. "You're starting off wisely, my dear."

The house was double the size of our little rental and the sun streamed in from all four directions. It was a Sears craft bungalow, the kind that was sold in the 1920s and would have arrived in large sections on flatbed trucks, each room flowing into the next with no hallways between. The pine floor was uneven at the seams where it had been put together. In certain spots you could see through to the ground. I feared the gaping fissures one day might give way and we would fall through to the dark underneath. Who knew what creatures came and went from that dark?

Tony was at loose ends. The barbershop had been a dismal failure, the men of Belle Cote having decided to continue driving to Biloxi rather than letting Mac McFadden's latest house boy give them a cut and shave. (Not to speak of the fact that Tony closed the place whenever he felt like leaving town.) Faced with a long list of tasks to prepare our new place for habitation, my mother hired Tony to caulk the holes in the floor, whitewash the walls, and paint the outside a dusky green with beige trim. In preparation, he slashed back the sumac vine that had taken over the front and sides of the house. The hummingbirds it had sheltered over the years screamed and dive-bombed him as their cup-sized nests and the two white eggs in each one fell to the ground. *Lost.*

As the work neared completion, the slower and more meticulous Tony became. My mother was growing impatient, given that we needed to vacate our little rental by the first of October. I offered to help finish off the inside trim. The Saturday morning of the last weekend in September, Minerva and I walked over to the bungalow for a day of painting. She settled on the kitchen counter while I opened all the doors and windows. I'd just taken up my brush when Tony's head appeared in the window. Minerva leaped up, hissing. Startled, I jumped back, splattering paint into the kitchen sink.

A cigarette hung lazily from his mouth, the flattened pack of Camels rolled up in the sleeve of his t-shirt. His hair was oiled, as if he'd just been to the barbershop. His paint-stained t-shirt hung damp and limp.

"Mind if I come in and cool off?" he asked. Without waiting for an answer, he got down from his ladder and came through the back door.

Minerva, meanwhile, had jumped onto another windowsill, tracking paint from my spill. She leaped to the ground outside, then hightailed it across the grass, leaving a trail of paw prints in her wake.

It was midmorning and already blazing hot. Tony wiped the sweat from his face with his shirt, then took it off and hung it around his neck. His shoulders were tipped in red peeling skin.

He splashed some water from the faucet on his face, then put his mouth under the faucet and drank.

"Birdy, can you help me outside?" he asked, wiping his face again.

"Don't call me Birdy," I said automatically, knowing he wouldn't listen.

With only one working hand, I found it hard to hold on to the ladder and paint at the same time, so he took the high spots and I took the low. I brought my transistor outside, and we sang along to the Top Forty, Tony in his fake bass, me in my thin soprano. We were singing about who wrote the book about love.

Who indeed, I wondered, love being so mysterious to me then.

Below him I danced around singing backup and waving my paintbrush, splattering paint down the side of the house.

"Now look what you've gone and done, Birdy Feather," Tony sang out. "Tell me, tell me, tell me, tell me who: who's going to clean that up?"

That was the thing about Tony. It wasn't just his beauty, although that was certainly enough. (Anyone seeing his portrait on Mac's living room wall would nod and say, "Oh yes, I see now. *Now* I understand what you mean.") He also had a certain alchemy. How do I explain the way I hated and distrusted him one minute and adored him the next? How his smile turned me to putty? How that one lock of hair kept falling into his eyes? How he pushed it back the way a little boy would, an impatient yet endearing gesture? There was something about Tony that *compelled*. Back then, we all had a finger in that socket, sizzling, electric.

Around noon he said, "Let's go down to the water and get a dog and a Nehi, Birdy. My treat."

"Sure," I said.

Pete's Hot Dogs, a beach shack with a neon dachshund flashing day and night, was one of the hangouts for the high school crowd, who usually clustered on beach towels between it and the water. We walked the two blocks to the beach still singing and laughing. It was a cloudless day. The Sound looked like a giant lake, the waves only slight disturbances along its smooth surface.

Outside Pete's, we sat down in the sandy grass, sipped our Nehis, and waited for our hot dogs.

Tony looked out over the water. "Sometimes," he said, "the waves tell me things."

"What things?" I asked, secretly thrilled.

"Depends. Sometimes, when I'm feeling sorry for myself, they tell me to buck up."

I laughed. "They say, 'Buck up, Tony'?"

He ran his fingers through his hair, still looking out to sea. Then he turned back to me, his eyes serious. "Yeah. They say I don't have it so bad. They tell me to quit complaining."

"Animals and plants talk to me." I was surprised by my own words, my limited exchanges with my mother and grandparents on the subject having been met with skepticism bordering on amusement and, in my grandmother's case, alarm.

"I know."

"You *know*?"

"People like us just know each other. It takes one to know one."

"My mother told me not to tell anyone."

"So did mine. We have a lot in common, Birdy."

Over his shoulder, Pete waved in our direction.

"I think our hot dogs are ready."

He patted his back pocket. "Damn," he said, "got off this morning without my wallet. You got any money, rich girl?"

I had a dollar and a quarter in my shorts pocket, left over from some grocery money my mother had given me the day before.

I counted the money over to Tony. "Hope that's enough." Tony had ordered three chili dogs; I'd ordered one.

Tony got up. "Let me handle this."

He walked up to the window where Pete had the four hot dogs lined up. I turned back to the water. After a moment I heard Pete's voice rising. Then I heard Tony call my name.

I turned and he beckoned me. "Your mama's good for this extra hot dog, right?"

"You're thirty-five cents short," Pete said, his voice gravelly. "I got to make a living here. This ain't the first time you've pulled this stunt."

"You don't have to make a federal case out of it," said Tony.

"I'll bring it to you this afternoon," I said. I could feel my face flush. Even in our El Camino days, my mother and I had never shorted anyone.

"Come on, Birdy." Tony gathered the hot dogs in one sweeping motion and headed back toward the water.

I lingered. "I'll be back," I told Pete. "You don't need to worry."

His eyes were hard and glittery in the sun. "I got a girl your age," he said. "I watch over her like a hawk. I watch over all my girls. Tell your mother she should do the same."

"I said I'll be back with your money."

He leaned further out the pickup window. "Tell your mother to keep her eyes wide open. I could tell you stories."

"My mother takes good care of me, don't you worry," I said curtly.

"She ought to if she don't," Pete came back.

I shoved my hot dog back at him. "Here, take your damn hot dog."

"You ordered it. You bought it."

"Fine. You'll have my money within the hour."

By the time I caught up with Tony, he was halfway through his second hot dog.

"You shouldn't order things you can't pay for," I said.

"Hot dogs remind me of my sister," he said, ignoring my comment.

"Why's that?"

"She loved hot dogs. She would have been about your age."

"Would have been?"

He waved away a gull. "She died when we were kids."

"What happened to her?"

"She drowned at Pontchartrain Beach."

I'd been to Lake Pontchartrain in New Orleans once with my mother and Mac, soon after she and I had arrived on the coast. I remembered a Ferris wheel and cotton candy and children running everywhere. The brackish water seemed murky. My mother let me wade, but said I needed to learn to swim before I could venture out farther.

"Your sister couldn't swim?"

He waved off a gull. "Everybody blamed me. I was supposed to be watching her, but she had to have a hot dog. She was only six years old."

"How awful."

"I just turned and she was gone."

I thought of Mac's family, going under. "I'm so sorry. You and Mac have that in common."

He took another bite and looked out at the water.

I shut my eyes. I could see a little girl sink beneath the murky surface, gasping for breath, her mouth filling up with brackish water, the terror she must have felt. Tony racing into the water, splashing about for his beloved little sister: his horror, his guilt.

I opened my eyes. "Oh, Tony. That must have been terrible." I touched his hand.

Pete, I noticed, was peering at us from his order window. "I need to go to the gallery and get that stupid thirty-five cents," I said. "I'll meet you back at the house."

I took what was left of my hot dog and, glaring at Pete, fed it to a waiting seagull.

My mother scowled at me when I walked in. Several customers were browsing the shop, but she took me by the arm and pulled me back into the storage room.

"What's this about not paying for a hot dog?" She whispered, pulling at my arm. "You know better than that."

"Did Pete call you for his stupid thirty-five cents?" I asked. "How petty is that?"

"How could you stiff a man like Pete? He works out there day and night in all kinds of weather trying to make a living. Just because *you* have plenty of money now doesn't mean that everybody in the world got a fortune handed to them on a silver platter."

"I told Pete I was good for it."

"Do you know how many times a day he hears that? Pete has to support his family. He has six children and an old mother. My god, Mem, what is *wrong* with you?"

An ancient wagon wheel hung over the shelf above her. I willed it to topple over.

"Well, give me the money so I can *rush* it over before his whole family starves to death."

A visitor in the gallery called out for her. My mother glanced over at the door. "He sent one of his girls over to collect it. She looked *thin*, Mem." Her hand tightened on my arm until I squirmed. "Don't *ever* buy something you can't pay for. Remember where we came from, how we counted out every nickel. I want you to go home and consider your blessings. Think about your callousness to the hardships of others. Remember how it felt to be hungry."

"I was never hungry," I said.

"Well, *I* was, my dear. *I* was hungry a great deal of the time. You ate because I went without. I *did* things because of you. Things I'm not proud of. People struggle, Mem. We need to help as much as we can, now that we have the means. Now get on home and start packing for the move."

With that, she let go of me suddenly, so that I almost fell backward. She opened the storage room door. "Be right there," she called out to the customer, then turned and looked back at me. Her eyes swept mine once over, then again, and then a third time, as if she were seining for some missing fleck of color and not finding it. Then she turned and was gone.

At home I began to pack my clothes in readiness for our move, nice clothes, nothing patched or threadbare or from the Blessed Virgin charity bin. I packed carefully, as if these things were as breakable as fine china. Some I'd outgrown I put in a pile on the bed. Maybe, I thought with a twinge of guilt, one of Pete's girls could use them.

When my mother came home and I told her about my plans for the now-towering pile of old clothes, she smiled. "Now you're cooking. Take them over to the Baptist church, that's where Pete's people go."

In the years ahead, I would catch, out of the corner of my eye, a swatch of fabric, a skirt with a certain swing, a bright blouse, quick-silver in the hall at school. The girls who wore them all looked alike: thin, ponytailed, wiry and fast-moving. They reminded me of myself in our El Camino days, darting up and down the acequia banks where the cottonwoods crowned the ditch's edge, rustling and calling out their unquenchable thirst in a dry land.

IX.

———

MOVING DAY DAWNED STIFLING and overcast.

"Hurry up and get going now, Mem," my mother called out from the kitchen. "And strip your bed. Mac and Tony'll be here in a few minutes. The least we can do is be ready when they come. Oh my, look at that sky. I hope it isn't going to rain."

As I headed for the bathroom, I stopped short. In the kitchen my mother stood at the window in a color-coordinated getup of lavender shorts and a sleeveless shirt of pink and lavender flowers tucked into her shorts, which were belted—*belted*—with a beige tie. Her hair, which she'd let grow, was drawn up in a perky ponytail, her bangs perfectly rolled under, her eyes deeply charcoaled. My father had faded from my features as much as he had from my memory (and as he's continued to fade, decades hence—his face now a mystery to me). I'd grown to look more like my mother. Now, she looked like a prettier version of me.

"Why are you all gussied up? We're *moving*, not going to the picture show." Despite Mac's efforts, I'd never known my mother to fuss much with her appearance. Her usual attire for work consisted of a loose dress in the summer, sweater and pants in the winter, nothing to jump up and down about.

She blushed. "Well, that's no reason not to look one's best, Mem."

An hour later, we heard the clatter of Mac's Ranchero.

"They're here," my mother sang out.

She opened the door and Mac strode in.

"Where's Tony?" she asked, peering out the door.

"He went up to Money this weekend to help out some friends of his, but he's heading back soon. Let's get going. It's already hot as hell warmed over."

Tony's friend in Money was named Jesse Murray. The afternoon before, as I was shelling butter beans in the porch swing at Mac's, I'd overheard him telling Tony he wished he wouldn't associate with "that Murray devil" and his cronies. They were mixed up with that murderer Roy Bryant. Nothing but white trash in sheets, every last one of them.

"He's my friend. Not a bad sort. Besides, he's Roy's cousin," said Tony.

"Nobody deserves what that boy got," Mac said, "and you know it."

"Jesse told me he didn't have anything to do with that business. He said I could take that to the bank. He can't help who he's kin to."

"You're a fool if you think anybody palling around with Roy Bryant isn't a bigot."

"Don't call me a fool."

They were in the kitchen, and Mac was cooking. He started slamming pots around, making a racket.

Tony ended it by saying Mac couldn't tell him what to do, who to associate with. If he tried, Tony said, there would be *consequences*. After he said that, there was silence. A while later, Tony came outside carrying a dufflebag. He did a double take, as though he'd forgotten I was there.

"See you tomorrow, Birdy. Don't pay any attention to us," he said and galloped down the three flights of steps and got into Mac's newly-acquired Mustang.

"WHEN'S TONY COMING?" ASKED my mother, fretfully. "We need him." A wisp of hair had escaped her ponytail. She threaded it back behind her ear.

"Calm down, Feather. You've got me," said Mac. "Why are you all dressed up?"

"I wish people would quit telling me what to wear," she said.

Mac looked at me and raised an eyebrow.

I rolled my eyes and shrugged.

"Let's take the light stuff first," he said, grabbing two kitchen chairs. "We can wait for Tony to help us with the sofa and beds and table." He looked around. "Where's Minerva?"

"She's sitting in that box by the sofa," I said, pointing. Minerva had become mine by choice. After her ordeal, she gave Mac's house wide berth, although when he came to our place, she settled companionably on his lap as soon as he sat down. Several times he'd taken her home with him. A few minutes later, I'd find her back on our doorstep.

"We need to make sure we take her to the new place so she'll understand where to go," he said.

I'd already thought of that. "I'll walk her over later."

After we loaded up and my mother and Mac headed out, I found Minerva asleep in her box. I woke her up by stroking her back. Ever since her ordeal, Minerva didn't like to be disturbed while she was sleeping. She'd growl and hiss. Once she bit me. "Come on, old girl," I said. "We're going to take a walk."

Normally, Minerva followed me when I went out. Sometimes she said things as we walked along—*bird* or *hush* or *see*, sometimes something unexpected like *lizard* or *sneeze*—but usually we walked along in a companionable silence. We started out just fine, but we had to go by Mac's to get to the new place, and when we drew close, Minerva hightailed it back in the direction of our little shotgun.

When I got back, she was in the process of clawing our screen door. "Okay, okay," I said and let her back in. She did a victory circle around the kitchen table and then plopped herself down on the floor underneath.

Tony didn't show up until four that afternoon. By then my mother and Mac and I had moved everything the three of us could carry. Mac had even put up the regrettable picture of the mother and daughter on our new living room wall. My mother's fancy outfit was filthy, her shirttail was out and most of her hair had slipped from her ponytail. There was a long smear of something brown on her cheek. Tony looked even worse. His shirt was filthy with mud. He stunk of old sweat and something burnt. By the time he showed up, the three of us were back in the old house collapsed in a row on the living room couch, since it, along with the kitchen table, a heavy bookcase, and the dressers in the bedrooms, was the only stick of furniture left in the place.

We all leapt to our feet when he walked through the front door, as if he were the president.

"Where the hell have you been?" said Mac, picking up one end of the couch. "We could have finished in half the time."

Tony took the other end, not answering. The two of them crab-walked the couch through the door, my mother giving directions. I ran ahead and lowered the back of the Ranchero.

After he and Mac had unloaded the remaining furniture at our new place, I walked back over to the empty shotgun to find Minerva. It was dark by then. The electricity to the place had been cut off earlier in the day. Once inside, I could hear Minerva purring loudly, the way she did when she was anxious. I felt my way through the house. Groping around in my closet, I found her hunched up in a corner.

Where? Where?

I picked her up and put her over my shoulder like a baby. I took the long way around the block behind our new place. Then I doubled back so as not to pass Mac's house. Minerva rode along like a sack of meal, not complaining. When I got her into the bungalow, she went straight for the kitchen, hopped onto the table, and demanded her supper, as if she'd lived there forever.

Later that night I couldn't sleep. My mother's bedroom on the other side of the living room seemed to be in another county. I remembered our nights at the El Camino, lying beside her, comforted by her soft snores, the way she flung her arm across my chest as she slept. Now there was only a deep quiet, the kind of quiet that holds its breath. Minerva had chosen to sleep on the couch. Outside my open window, nothing whispered or rustled or spoke to me. I tossed and turned, pondering what would happen next in my up-and-down life. The previous year my teachers, much to my dismay, seemed bound and determined to send me leapfrogging over the ninth *and* tenth grades into my junior year in high school, which they said would get me off to college sooner.

The thought of college made my paw throb. After four years in Belle Cote, I was just getting my feet on the ground. One of my hobbies the previous summer was learning German, and I'd run across the words heimlich and unheimlich. I'd moved throughout my early years, from pillar to post, military base to base, feeling unheimlich, literally unhomelike. Now I was finally home. I liked the feeling and wasn't in any hurry for it to end. Nor did I feel especially smart. True, there was a part of me that ticked along, faster and faster sometimes; but when it came to the world around me, the world of you come and you go, I felt dumb as a bucket of sand. There was a part of me still unfinished. It was as if I were a cake in the making, and some essential ingredient awaited adding, something that made the cake a cake. I was awaiting that ingredient, though I didn't know yet what it was.

After the school IQ tests had come in and my mother had met with my teachers, she called a family meeting around our kitchen table. "Not in my wildest dreams," she said, ignoring me and passing a piece of paper with the results across our kitchen table to Mac. "I knew she was unusual, but my god, if these scores are right, she's a damn genius." Then the two of them began discussing my imminent departure from Belle Cote.

"Why are you pushing me so?" I said. "I'm not a piece of meat going bad."

"You are *unusual*, Mem," said my mother. "You have an IQ up in the stratosphere. They don't think they can teach you anything else in high school."

"We should be looking at Radcliffe," Mac murmured, "money being no object."

I rolled my eyes at him.

"Sophie Newcomb to start, then," said Mac, "just over in the City. You can come home on the weekends. Your teachers say you can go to college next year if you want."

"I'm not going anywhere. You can't make me."

And so I stayed.

Sometimes a terrible thought leaps into my head. Would things have ended differently if I'd left? What I know now is that everything hinges on place and time: where a person is and when. If and if and if. And how's anyone supposed to know how one thing leads to another? Cause and effect. It makes you not want to get up in the morning. Not move your one good hand in any direction, for fear that it might brush some unknown fabric, unravel some invisible thread.

A WEEK OR SO after my mother and I moved, I asked her to teach me to drive, my argument being that if she were so bound and determined I grow up before my time, I should at least be armed with some basic life skills.

It was a Sunday afternoon when I brought up the subject. Tony was driving the three of us home from brunch at Brennan's in the City. Mac's new Mustang was humming along. We were pleasantly full and in good spirits. We were crossing the Rigolets. Below us, sailboats skimmed along the gleaming water. A formation of hungry pelicans glided above the swells. Gulls dipped and swooped against a cloudless sky. *Ahoy ahoy.* After brunch, we'd roamed the riverfront, slurping our snowballs, and counting ships from foreign lands coming into port. Tony entranced us with depictions of each country: China, Brazil, France, claiming to have visited them all. We knew him well enough by then to know that wasn't true, but no one was in the mood to say so. We had followed him up Royal Street, dipping in and out of antique stores with their gleaming chandeliers and brass doorknobs. He had cajoled Mac into buying my mother and me matching silver and turquoise bracelets.

"I'm too nervous," my mother said. "Don't they have a class in driving?"

"*Parents* are supposed to do that," I said. "I can get a permit when I turn fifteen. It's my right to learn how to drive and it's your job to teach me." Lately I'd become argumentative and litigious.

Mac chuckled. "Our girl's going to be a lawyer. Probably end up on the Supreme Court."

Tony glanced in the rearview mirror at my mother, who was riding directly behind him. "I can teach her. I taught my sister."

"I thought she died," I said.

"That was another sister," he said.

My mother leaned forward and put a hand on his shoulder. "Would you, Tony? Are you sure you don't mind?"

"Somebody's got to do it," said Mac. "We're going to need her to chauffeur us around in our old age."

A WEEK LATER, TONY knocked on our door. My mother invited him in for a cup of coffee. She'd dressed up again; this time it was a sundress that showed off her shoulders and upper arms, slightly muscled from moving furniture around the gallery.

He shook his head. "If I come back in one piece, I'll be asking for a beer." He winked at me, then her.

Of course my mother blushed. My mother's blushes were unfortunate. She blushed in patches, giving her the appearance of a reticulated giraffe.

I must admit I'd dressed for the occasion too. I had on a yellow crop top and some navy shorts. I had on my best sneakers with some yellow polka-dotted socks. The night before, I'd washed my hair and put lemon juice on it to bring out the sun streaks.

My mother handed Tony the car keys to our inherited Plymouth. "The brakes are tight," she said. "Go easy on them. And remember," she said, lowering her voice, "she's got only one fully functioning hand."

Tony doffed an imaginary hat. "Yes, your majesty."

My mother's patches turned a deep purple.

"Come on, Birdy," he said, and waved me out the front door in one grand gesture.

Tony pulled the Plymouth out onto the street, my grandparents turning over in their graves at the spectacle of him at the wheel of their beloved vehicle. "I'm going to take you off the beaten track, where you won't do any damage."

He turned out onto Highway 90 and then took the first side road away from the beach. Then he took another and another until I finally lost count. We were in piney woods now, on dirt and gravel, weaving deeper and deeper inland. It was still overcast, and as the overhanging pines became denser, it grew dark. I wondered how Tony knew such a place.

I let my good hand hang out the window and touched the pine needles as they scraped the side of the car. *Watch out now*, they whispered as we jounced along, the air filled with their scent.

Finally Tony stopped the car. He got out, came around to the passenger side, and leaned in. "Scoot over, Birdy."

He said it soft as a lullaby, kind as the kindest grandfather. Tony, I'd come to realize, was something of a ventriloquist. He could affect a cultured tone when ordering at Brennan's, his subjects and verbs dancing a perfect waltz. He could talk trash when arguing with Pete or the service station boy who left streaks on the windshield. He could speak like a New Yorker or a shrimper. His voice an instrument he played at will.

I scooted over. My feet couldn't reach the pedals.

"Pardon my reach," he said. He leaned over, put his hand between my knees and brought up the seat.

"The first thing you do is put your foot on the clutch. No, that's the brake. The clutch is on the far left. Use your left foot." He leaned over and pointed, his breath lingering on my face. "Now here's what you're going to do. Once you get it cranked, you put it into first, and let out the clutch real slow."

He sat close, his left thigh touching my right, his arm behind me on the back of the seat as if I were his girlfriend. "Now you're going to have to steer with this hand," he said, pointing to my paw. "Pull those fingers open and put them around the wheel. Keep them there. You're going to have to shift with your right hand." As he took me through the gears, his body heat made me sweat. After a few tries, I managed to get the car lurching down the little road. Tony showed me how to make the clutch and accelerator work together. "It's like a man and a woman," he said, his voice a melody. "Give and take, back and forth, keep it going just right," which at the time I didn't understand. Everything he said, he said carefully and quietly, not making a fuss, never raising his voice, not even when I ran off the road and almost clipped a tree. He was the perfect teacher.

"You ought to do this for a living," I said.

He laughed easily. "I only do this for pretty women who'll support me in my old age."

I shot him a quick glance. He was looking at the road not at me. Then he turned and smiled at me and I forgot I was driving.

"Watch the road!" he shouted.

Up ahead a sharp curve.

I hit the accelerator and we careened toward the turn.

"No! Brake!"

I was too busy trying to steer with one hand to worry with the brake. We hit the curve hard, kicking up gravel and dust. I made the turn but then the car veered toward the opposite side of the road, toward a stand of dark pines. *Watch, watch, watch,* they screamed in unison.

He leaned over and pulled the key from the ignition and the car jerked to a halt just short of the trees.

I opened the car door and got out. "You drive," I said. Sweat crept through my hair like fire ants, burning and stinging. My paw hummed with alarm.

He slid through to the driver's seat, and I thought he was going to take the wheel, but then he got out too and came and put his arms around me. His body a furnace. He held me like that for a moment, the way a father would.

Then he said, "Get back in the car, Birdy."

I obeyed without a word. There was something in his tone that made me do what he told me to do, the way the smallest child will obey when the parent speaks in a certain way.

"Try it again," he said quietly.

And so I did, and somehow I managed to get the car back onto the little road and we bounced along for a while longer until we came to a little clearing cluttered with felled tree trunks and he told me to pull over and stop. "Clutch and brake together," he instructed. "Never brake without the clutch."

As if by magic, the car came to a halt without stalling out. I turned to Tony, smiling now.

"Turn it off," he said.

I looked out over the clearing. There were squirrels everywhere, scampering up and down the trees, lolling about on limbs with their little legs hanging over the sides, chasing one another around the giant trunks. *Who?* they chattered, then froze.

"I've never seen so many squirrels," I said.

"Ever gone hunting?"

"Why would I want to do that?" The squirrels were plump and sassy now, chattering again, darting here and there. One approached, then raised itself on its haunches and looked at us, its mouth twitching. *Quick now,* it said, then scurried up a tree.

"This is the day for lessons," said Tony. "Let's stretch our legs."

We got out of the car. Then he unbuttoned his shirt two buttons and I saw the leather holster strapped across his chest. He pulled out the gun.

"Meet my best girlfriend. She's one pretty lady," he said. He walked out ahead of me. A pine branch slapped his throat, then flopped back in my face. "We're going to get us some squirrel," he said and took aim.

"Let the poor things alone," I said, giggling. I thought he was joking.

He laughed a quick hard laugh; then, before I could take another breath, he fired.

The bullet was a hummingbird. *Zip, zip,* and the squirrel fell from a low branch of a pine on the other side of the clearing. Its blood bright against the carpet of needles.

In the moment after, not a pine needle rustled, not a twig moved.

Then the bloodied squirrel twitched.

"It's still alive, poor thing," I said.

Tony raised the gun and shot again. The squirrel flew into a million pieces.

After a moment, a second squirrel scurried out from behind a tree and began to nose a bloody piece of the dead one's fur.

Tony moved toward me, the gun now dangling by his forefinger. "A lady needs to know how to protect herself. Dangerous world out there. Like that boy up in Money, he was after my friend Roy's wife, Carolyn. Sweetest lady you'd ever meet." His voice smooth as a baby's cheek.

He moved in behind me, his chest fitting against my upper back and neck, a furnace against my shoulder blades. His vinegar sweat, a cedar bush in August.

He reached around and took my good hand and pulled it up so that it was pointing straight ahead. "This little lady packs a kick. I'm going to hold you steady until you get the feel of it." He slipped his arm around my waist and drew me backward. My hip sockets loosened and my thighs melted. I let him take me against him. I felt a knot form at the small of my back.

"Now then, Birdy Feather," he said, "I'm going to teach you how to shoot a gun. Don't be afraid."

"I don't want to."

He hummed in my ear. "This is something you need to learn, Birdy. You need to be able to defend yourself."

He put the gun in my hand. It was hot, hot.

"Now," he said, "point it at something. That squirrel there, by the dead one." He raised my arm into place, his hand over my wrist. It was as if I were welded to him, the spoke to his wheel, an extension of his will.

"No. Not a squirrel."

"You have to practice on a moving target." His voice was quiet and patient as if he were still teaching me to drive. "A man won't stand still for you to shoot him, Birdy."

The forest around us chattered and rustled, swimming in the pool of its own sweet innocence.

So I let him guide my good hand and point the thing at the squirrel who was still trying to puzzle out the scattered remains of the dead one. *What?*

My paw began to sweat and sting and throb, as if it too were gripping the gun.

"Hold it steady," said Tony. He moved his hand from my wrist and put it around my waist so that he held me with both arms.

Sweat crept down from my scalp and rolled into my eyes.

"Stand firm, aim, and *shoot.*"

The last word he breathed into my ear. When the shiver the *sh* produced ran down my arm through the vast network of nerves and tendons and muscles on down into my wrist and from there out to my forefinger, calloused from the baton, I pulled the trigger.

I was expecting the impact to knock me backward, but it didn't. Perhaps because Tony shored me up, at least so I thought at the time. In the moment I shot the gun, he moved hard against me once, then twice, then a third time. Something in me, a tension, collapsed in stages, the way a bridge or a large building collapses, and then it was over and the squirrel I'd just shot looked at me and said *oh* and then folded itself into the leaves, its little limbs twisted, its back end and hind legs blown clear away.

Tony released me in one quick motion. I staggered to keep my balance.

"Look at that. You're a natural," he said.

The gun was too hot. I dropped it. "Take me home. I want to go home now."

"Never drop a gun like that," Tony said. "It could go off." He picked it up off the forest floor and put it back into its holster. "You drive," he said.

I went around to the driver's side of my gentle grandparents' car and started the engine, not forgetting the clutch.

I turned the car in a circle, then shifted into second, then third, smooth as silk, and we took off down the road. Tony leaned over and whispered in my ear, "Next time we'll get us a deer."

X.

———

THE NEXT DAY I stayed in bed. I felt hollow, as if the shot I'd fired into the unlucky squirrel were an expulsion of my very self, the me of me.

Oh, it had said.

My mother came in at noon and put a hand on my brow. "What's the matter? Are you sick?"

Minerva, who normally slept next to me, was nowhere in sight. When Tony and I had walked into the house the afternoon before, she'd crawled under my bed. When he left after sitting at the kitchen table with my mother until dark, she'd come out, sniffed my foot, and disappeared into the night. *You. No.*

Outside my window, there was the thud of the ladder being moved against the house, then the clang of the paint bucket. Tony had decided the place needed a second coat.

"It's Sunday. Leave me alone."

My mother left the room, then came back in with the thermometer. "Open your mouth," she said.

"Can't a person sleep late around here?"

"Open, and don't speak to me that way. It's a nice day outside. Look."

I glanced out the window. A squirrel sat on a branch of a big gum tree, watching me. *Blood.*

"No temperature," my mother pronounced. "Get out of that bed. It's already afternoon."

I turned my face to the wall. "I'm tired. Leave me alone."

The next day, Monday, I still didn't feel like getting out of bed.

"Cramps?" my mother asked, opening the curtains.

"Can't a person just be sick once in a while?"

A few minutes later I heard her on the phone.

I turned over and went back to sleep. When I woke again, it was midmorning and Mac was sitting on my bed gazing down at me.

I turned back to the wall. "Can't people just leave me alone and let me sleep?"

"What's really the matter, Little?"

"I just don't feel like going to school."

"Well, I don't feel like going to work. Let's you and me plot our escape. I need to look at some furniture in the City anyhow. We can make an overnighter of it. Feather and Tony can hold down the fort here."

I rolled over. "My mother's not going to like me missing school."

"You let me handle your mother. I'll be back to pick you up in thirty minutes. Pack a decent outfit."

I leapt up and headed for the bathroom. In the kitchen I heard Mac. "The child is *depressed*, Feather."

"Why on earth would she be?" asked my mother. "She has *us*."

"Maybe we're not enough," Mac said. "Does she ever bring friends home?"

There was a long silence. Then my mother cleared her throat. "I don't like her playing hooky."

"Feather, haven't you ever felt so low you didn't want to get out of bed in the morning?"

"But I *did*," she said. "I *did* get out of bed. I got up for *her*."

"This is different," said Mac. "This is a child, Feather; she's so smart we forget that she's still just a child. A child with a *handicap*. She makes straight As. Let her have a day or two off."

When I emerged, he was gone and my mother stood by the bathroom door, her arms folded. "Mem, you know you can talk to me about anything, don't you?"

I nodded, though I could no more talk to her about what happened with Tony than I could fly to the moon. I couldn't even articulate it to myself. People hunted. People taught other people to shoot guns. Tony was right to brace me against the recoil of the gun. Squirrels died every day. They fell from trees, got diseases, got eaten. One less squirrel was just a ripple in the Sound.

But there was a bad smell to it. Even then, I knew that much.

MAC AND I STARTED out around noon. Tony was painting the back side of the house and didn't make an appearance at our leave-taking. The sun was hot and directly overhead, the swampland on either side of Highway 90 teeming with hidden life, bubbles in the green scum. Dragonflies skimmed the surface, resting on the cattails and saw grass. A great egret stood at the water's edge, perfectly still but leaning well forward in hunting posture, its neck and head outstretched, its yellow eye glittering with resolve. Egrets and herons let their prey come to them, relying on stillness; their beaks do the rest. I admired their unflappable patience, their resiliency.

As we rode along, Mac and I made plans. We would enjoy the rest of the afternoon and evening, then visit some antique shops on Royal the following morning. Usually they had some pieces in the back they were willing to sell for next to nothing. It was a pleasure to watch Mac bargain for them, eyeing a damaged bookcase, a desk with a cracked leg, telling the shop owner he should pay *him*, Mac McFadden, for taking the piece off his hands. We would stay at the Monteleone and have a sit at the rotating bar. After supper we'd find some good music, maybe meet up with some of Mac's friends.

"Just what the doctor ordered," he said, glancing over at me.

It was the first time in a long time I'd been alone with Mac, and I found it restful. I believe he felt the same. Mac was a sensitive soul. He hated unhappiness in anyone. Once he'd confided in me that he sometimes felt like one giant antenna, attuned to everyone else's static, the noise of all the world. Tony, I'd noticed, kept Mac hungrily watchful.

"Mac, would *you* teach me to drive?" We'd just turned off St. Charles and were heading up Canal toward Iberville and the Monteleone.

"I thought Tony was teaching you," he said.

A heavyset woman was lumbering across the tracks, the streetcar fast approaching, jangling its bell. The woman wore royal-blue pedal pushers and a skintight shirt. Her breasts bobbed and wobbled as if she'd stuffed a litter of puppies inside her shirt. She was red-faced in her determination to outrun the streetcar.

Would she make it? The conductor was laying on the brakes, the car was screeching to a halt.

"I just think you might make a better job of it."

He shot me a sharp glance, and I turned my head to look out of the window. "Why's that? I'm nervous as a dog with fleas, Little. I'd be a wreck. Probably make you have one."

"You're a better driver. I want to learn from the best. See? You're waiting for that streetcar. Tony would have turned right in front of it. He's...unsafe."

"Don't cast aspersions."

The woman had made it across the tracks. The streetcar passed. Cars honked behind us.

"I'm not casting aspersions. I just want *you* to teach me to drive. I know the basics. I just need practice."

"All right, all right, I'll teach you, but not in the City."

"Well, I should hope not." The din outside was deafening. Taxis, buses, cars, and trucks—they all seemed to be threading their way up Iberville.

When Mac pulled the car over at the hotel, a valet leapt into action and we were whisked inside and up the lobby stairs. Behind the desk, a man with a handlebar mustache smiled from ear to ear, his teeth flashing in the light from above. "Mr. McFadden! How lovely to see you again." The man leaned over the counter and peered at me. "And who is the young lady?"

"This is Miss Memory Feather," said Mac, "my dear niece." When Mac needed a label for me, niece was one he often used, along with

varying adjectives. Sometimes I was his brilliant niece, others his beautiful niece. *Dear* was an old staple. "We're so hoping we're in time to snag
the Royalty Rooms."

The man reached into two cubbyholes and picked up two massive key
holders. "King, Queen," he said. "I saved them for you."

"You're a dear, dear man, James," said Mac, slipping a crisp ten-
dollar bill across the counter.

The four walls of the elevator were covered with mirrors. Mac put his
hand on my shoulder. It was the first time I'd seen us as one image that
spoke to the world. The two of us did look as if we could be related, I
a faded replica, his blond hair a few shades lighter than mine, even his
clothing brighter, fresher. My skin lackluster while his glowed, two pink
spots on his cheeks. It was as if I were the ancient grandmother and he
the young man. I pushed a lock of hair out of my eyes, straightened my
shirt.

"You're going to love the Queen's Room," Mac said, his eyes twinkling. "And if it isn't to your taste, you can have the King's. Your wish
is my command."

The rooms were at the end of a long corridor. When the valet unlocked
the door to the Queen's Room, a delicious smell wafted out into the hall.

"Ahh," said Mac. "These rooms always smell like eucalyptus."

We followed the valet in. With a flourish, he opened the red velvet
drapes and the early afternoon sun flooded the room. I gasped. The
room buzzed with color, beads, and bangles. Golden cords hung from
the canopied bed of another century. The walls were flocked in gold and
red paper. The dresser held a massive vase filled with dried eucalyptus.

"Oh my," I said.

"I demand a trade," said Mac.

I giggled. "I'm the queen, not you."

Mac laughed. "Some might beg to differ, my dear. Let me show you
the King's Room and you may change your mind."

The King's Room was a bit much, the bedposts the size of tree trunks,
the mahogany chifforobe a small cottage. A family of bears could have
hibernated in the bed. I counted eight lamps, one that resembled a
Tiffany.

Mac turned to me. "Little, before I forget, I want to show you something." There was a door between the two rooms. He opened his side. "Go around to the Queen and open yours."

When I opened the door from my side, he said, "Now, we'll keep these shut but unlocked on both sides at night. If you hear something or feel nervous or worried, all you have to do is let me know and I'll be at your side in two shakes."

I nodded happily. I'd read of rich people who got "a suite of rooms," and now I knew what they meant.

"Get out of those dreadful clothes and have a bath. Thirty minutes. We must hurry if we're going to get everything in. The City awaits!" He shut his door.

I shut mine, and threw myself onto my bed, gazing up at the underside of the red canopy, imagining myself inside the belly of Jonah's whale. Money, I'd begun to realize, bought escape. One could remove oneself from whatever seemed troubling. I thought it was that simple.

There were bath salts on the edge of the tub. I ran the water and poured them in; the scent of lavender filled the bathroom. I shampooed my hair. I scrubbed every inch. I had the blood of an innocent creature on my hands. I couldn't get clean enough.

Mac banged on the door between us. "What are you doing in there? It's time to go. Carpe diem."

The afternoon passed in a whirl. That evening we strolled over to Frenchmen Street. It was a warm night but uncharacteristically dry, a touch of fall in the air. Music floated from the bars onto the balmy night air. We stopped in the open doorways and listened. At the Spotted Cat, Mac spied a group of his friends and pulled me in their direction. There were hugs and introductions all around as we settled at a round table in front of the window.

"Isn't it a school night?" one of them asked.

"Memory," said Mac, abandoning my nickname, "is indeed playing hooky today."

"And tomorrow," I said with a grin.

"Here, here," the men said in unison, clicking their glasses. "Here's to hooky and Uncle Mac."

"She can afford to miss a couple of days," Mac said. "She's very serious about school. We are looking at Radcliffe."

"Newcomb," I said.

Everyone cheered again and clicked their glasses in my direction.

While Mac was at the bar getting our drinks, his friends began asking me questions. What year was I in school? What was my favorite subject? What were my hobbies? When I mentioned that I was head majorette at Harris County High School, their eyes flew to my withered hand. "I watch birds too," I said quickly, careful not to mention that they spoke to me on occasion.

"I like to watch birds," said the gray-haired man siting next to me. "What are your favorites?"

"*Ardea alba* and *Ardea herodias*," I said, showing off.

"*Ardea* what?"

"Egrets and herons, " I said.

He smiled. "Ah, the wading birds! Those beautiful necks. They take my breath away."

At that moment, the long-lost Oliver walked through the door. He caught sight of us and waved. The men waved back and so did I. Such a rush of pleasure it was to see him recognize me and his gummy smile break into a grin. He shook hands all around, then took me by the shoulders. "Just look at you, Memory Feather. Oh, what a perfect name," he said. "You are simply gorgeous." He looked around expectantly. "Where's Mac?"

I pointed to the bar. "My mother and I moved out. You can come back."

"Not what I hear," said Oliver.

"Tony," one of the fellows said. "His name's Tony."

"I heard his name was the devil," another said.

The men looked down at their drinks.

One leaned across the table. "Hey, Ollie, congratulations on your book. It's so brave. Better watch out for the Hooverites, my friend."

"Somebody's got to tell our story," said Oliver.

Mac came back to the table with a pink drink for me and a gin and tonic for himself. Both drinks were full to the top, and his eyes were on them. When he looked up and saw Oliver, he stopped in midstride.

There was a terrible moment when the two of them simply stared at each other. Then Mac smiled. "Ollie, oh my. I thought you were living in New York now."

"I'm back and forth. Can't get New Orleans out of my blood," said Oliver. "And of course Belle Cote." He extended his hand. Mac laughed and in an awkward shuffle set down the drinks.

Their hands met over my head. It was as if something electric had happened, the flash of lightning seen in pictures of the Greek gods touching. At that moment, the band stopped playing, and there was, for just the briefest second, total quiet in the bar.

Mac broke the silence. "I've got all your books," he said quietly.

Oliver looked at him for a long moment. Then he shook his head, turned, and walked out the door.

I turned to Mac. There was a look on his face I'd never seen before: regret and something else, something beyond regret.

One of the men said, "No use crying over spilt milk."

That broke the spell, and Mac sat down. But a slight pucker lingered around his mouth as he looked around the table at his friends.

The conversation flew around the table. Tennessee was back in town; someone had spotted him at the Voodoo down on Rampart. Had anyone seen his *Cat on a Hot Tin Roof*? Someone had a new job at the museum. Another hated his at the shipyards. The gray-haired man sitting on the other side of me was having a big party the following weekend; we must all come.

It went on like that for a while. Having not slept much the night before, I found myself struggling to keep my eyes open, especially when the talk turned to a trip to Key West someone had recently made.

I was doing my best not to doze off when the gray-haired man leaned behind my back to speak to Mac. "I saw Tony in the Quarter a couple of weeks ago," he said. "Seemed to be having a good time of it."

"Oh?" said Mac, his voice cool. Then he said, "I sent him over to pick up some furniture."

Which was a bald-faced lie. I knew every piece that went in and out of the shop. No new pieces had come in within the past month. My mother had been scrambling to sell the ones we had, marking them down left and right.

I darted a look at Mac. He gave me the stink eye, his lips tight as a purse string.

The gray-haired man pushed closer, breathing down the back of my neck. "He was dancing. Slow dancing. With a girl."

"Tony has his friends, I have mine," Mac said.

"Mac," said the gray-haired man. That was all he said.

We were packed in around the table, my shoulder companionably pressed up against Mac's arm. He'd been leaning forward, his elbows on the table, catching up with his friends. I'd been leaning on him, half-asleep. When he stood up in one quick motion, I fell over into his chair. He took me by the arm. "Come on, Little."

"Mac, we've been friends for a long time. You know I'm not a gossip," said the gray-haired man, reaching across me to touch Mac's elbow.

Mac pulled away.

One of the men called out, "We'll walk you back!"

Another said, "Bottoms up!"

We headed down Frenchmen, everyone laughing and joking, except for Mac and the gray-haired man. When we got to Esplanade, we all stopped before crossing over onto the neutral ground in the middle of the street.

I glanced up at Mac as we crossed. Overhead, the oak limbs threaded their way through the electric lines and made feverish patterns on his face. He looked sad and furious at the same time, his features under the branches coiled into tortured shapes, his head tilted at a stern angle.

As the group of us stopped to look before crossing again, a black sedan came racing up Esplanade toward the river. The car was loaded with men, three in the front, three in the back. Two of Mac's friends who'd already started into the street jumped back onto the neutral ground, knocking into the rest of us.

"What the fuck?" said one of the men. Immediately the others chastised him and he apologized to me. "But *really*," he said. "What do they think they're doing? They almost ran us down."

Just as the words came out of his mouth, the black sedan stopped short. The driver gunned it and the sedan hopped the curb directly in front of us, threading its way between two oak trees on the neutral ground, bumping over the exposed roots and coming down on the other side of the street.

We all froze. As if they were the limbs of one body, Mac's friends moved in to encircle me. Mac's hand closed on my wrist. On the other side, the gray-haired man took my upper arm, his grip tight enough to cut off circulation. Everyone moved in closer until we were one cell, with me as the uneasy nucleus. The car bounced up onto the curb, circled around, and sat waiting in the street on the side we were attempting to cross.

"Back," shouted Mac. "Let's go back."

We turned to retrace our steps across Esplanade, but here it came again, hopping the curb a second time and skimming the two oaks and sitting now on the *other* side of the street from which we'd just come. Down Frenchmen there were neon lights and bars and music, people coming and going as if they hadn't a care in the world. Some college students strolled along singing. A man and a woman walked along the street, followed by a dog. A boy squatted on the corner hawking copies of the *Times-Picayune*. Between us and all of that was the black sedan.

"Careful now," the gray-haired man said quietly.

"Make a run for it," said another man.

"More of them than us," a third observed.

"The girl," someone said, and the men drew closer.

Mac and the gray-haired man tightened their grips on me, their odor suddenly tart and acrid. A window was coming down in the car. The muzzle of a gun emerged, then a face, weasel-like, the nose and chin pointing at us, the eyes hooded and small and close together.

Around me, the sharp intake of breath.

The oak leaves rustled uneasily above us. A squirrel. *Your turn now.*

"What's a bunch of fags like you doing with a sweet little lady like that?" said the face. "Maybe she better come with us."

"Go!" Mac shouted and jerked my arm. The gray-haired man jerked too. My feet left the ground. Around us, Mac's other friends closed in behind us, shielding us from the black sedan, which was again crashing over the curb of the neutral ground and swerving to turn and come at us.

There was a bar on the other side of Esplanade. Mac and his friends shoved me through the door, then piled in after me.

I turned to them. "Call the police! We need to call the police!" My voice a squeaky hinge.

Mac's friends just looked at me. Then Mac shook his head. His hair, usually so carefully combed, hung in his eyes. "Better to call a cab," he said.

The men nodded.

Mac went up to the bartender and asked for two cabs, one for him and me and one for the rest of our group. "And give us all a shot of whiskey," he added.

"Her too?" asked the bartender.

"Yes," I said. "Her too."

Mac shook his head. "You can have a sip of mine."

BACK AT THE MONTELEONE, Mac and I sat together for a good long time at the bar. He had another whiskey and ordered me a lemonade. All the freshness from my bath had long since bitten the dust. My hair felt clammy against my neck.

Finally, he looked at me and said, "Well, Little, you ready for bed?" I nodded and we got up. In the elevator mirror, we gave each other a rueful smile.

"Nothing like this has ever happened before," Mac said.

The elevator pinged and the doors opened. We headed down the hall to the King's and Queen's Rooms, which had been spoiled now but still awaited us.

THE NEXT MORNING AS we headed up Royal, I broached the subject of Oliver. Would Mac lend me Oliver's books? Not yet, they were mature subject matter. Would Mac consider taking him back? No, what's done was done. Pushing it, I asked if Mac didn't prefer Oliver over Tony, only to become the recipient of a withering glare as Mac threaded his way through the hubbub of the Quarter.

"Of course, that's your personal business," I said hastily.

"It most certainly is," said Mac. And that was that.

I'd been taught by Mac to sniff around in antique shops for bargains, so when we walked into the first shop we came to, he made a beeline for the back storage room and I for the back corners of the main exhibition area, scanning quickly left and right for items that might interest us. At first I didn't see anything and was going to join Mac in the back, when I saw a shadowy shape beside an ancient dresser. Something about its lines caught my interest. The piece was solid and forthright, as if to announce a certain no-nonsense functionality. It was an upright rectangle with one door, which I opened. Propped inside was a set of movable shelves and some dusty sheet music. When I wiped the piece off, I could see that it was handmade with various kinds of wood—scraps, I assumed, that the craftsman had salvaged, then put together. There were inlays of what appeared to be maple, framed with mahogany and chestnut. Even the round handle was a different piece of wood from the door it opened. The piece was arresting, a testament to ingenuity and perseverance in the face of limitation. I pictured the labor that had gone into it, the care in cutting and fitting and gluing, the finishing and sanding, the paper-thin delicacy of the sheets of music as they lay safeguarded on the shallow shelves. For a moment, I was acutely aware of the outer shell of my body: how it shielded the beating heart, the slosh of organs, the detritus of blood and bone and connective tissue, the incessant whir of the brain—that filament I call Memory Feather, created out of spare parts and glue.

When Mac came out from the storeroom, I called him over. "This," I said. "I'd like to work on this."

"It's a mess," he said. "What is it?"

"Look," I said and opened the door.

"Sheet music?" said Mac. "I've never seen anything like this."

We snagged the music cabinet for eighteen dollars, knocked off the dust and cobwebs, and later that afternoon loaded it into the Ranchero. It was heavier than I'd imagined.

On the ride home, Mac turned to me. "I don't think…"

"…we ought tell my mother about last night."

He nodded and then was silent. We were halfway across the Rigolets. A single raindrop spit on the car windshield. Below us, the water was choppy and dark. The buoys bounced and dipped. I was glad we'd wrapped the music cabinet in a tarp.

"At least you were queen for a day."

I tried to smile. "And you were king."

XI.

WHEN MAC PULLED UP in front of the bungalow, Tony was plastered up against the left side of the house like an overgrown vine. He stuck the handle of his paintbrush into his mouth and waved, then started down. Mac reached for the door handle.

"Would you mind taking me down to the gallery?" I said quickly. "I'd like to see my mother first."

"Why didn't you say so?"

Mac leaned out the window. "See you at home," he called to Tony.

Tony stopped on his way down the ladder and nodded, giving me a lazy glance.

Minerva lay asleep on the window ledge directly under the gallery sign, as if she herself, and not the shop, were the Beautiful Dreamer. When we walked up, she jumped down, running out the open door to greet us. Inside the gallery, my mother was down on her knees making a half-price sign for the furniture.

"The prodigals have returned," said Mac.

My mother turned, a large crayon in her hand. Her face was flushed, her hair a dust storm around her face.

She jumped to her feet and came over and hugged me, which was surprising; my mother was not a hugger. "Oh good, you're back. Are you feeling better? Did you have fun?"

"Yes and yes," I said.

"I went by school and got your homework," she said. "You've got some catching up to do."

Mac took the crayon from her hand. "I'll do this. Why don't you two run on home and enjoy the rest of the afternoon? Little, I'll bring your suitcase by on my way home."

My mother smiled. "You can tell me about all the mischief you and Mac got into. Let's stop at Phillipe's on the way home and get some shrimp. I'll make you a welcome-home supper."

Her voice was strangely musical, lighter somehow, as if a weight had been lifted. I was struck, too, by her sudden turn toward domesticity. My mother was a perfunctory cook at best. I, on the other hand, had adopted Mac's enthusiasm for good coastal meals. Over our years in Belle Cote, I'd become the one who planned our suppers, shopped for food, and, when Tony wasn't around, prepared what we ate.

She walked along the narrow sidewalk ahead of me. Something about her was different. It was in the way she carried herself, swaying a bit more as she moved along, bearing her head carefully, as if it were a platter of food. She wore a summer dress I hadn't seen before, flowery and thin. It clung to her breasts and hips, swished as she walked along. Her backside jiggled, as if she weren't wearing underwear.

We took Beach Boulevard, and the Sound stretched out before us, scalloping the green coast.

My mother turned to me, walking backward, the sea breeze blowing her hair into her face. "Boiled shrimp for supper?"

"Something simple," I said. "I ate too much in New Orleans."

"Shrimp and tomato salad?"

"Let's see what looks good at Phillipe's."

Sh . . . . The sound came from behind me. I glanced back. Minerva was following us, walking in the grass beside the sidewalk. *Sh, sh* . . . she said again.

The problem with having animals speak to you is that it sometimes can be impossible to discern their meaning; I could usually get the gist of Minerva's cryptic remarks, but the *sh* eluded me. Just to be further aggravating, she leapt on a butterfly, then devoured it.

Phillipe's Grocery on Beach Boulevard specialized in seafood of all kinds, depending on what the shrimpers and fishermen brought in. Phillipe himself, a forty-year-old bachelor with finger-length earlobes, had had a crush on my mother from the first moment he'd laid eyes on her, to the degree that she disliked going into the store.

"Go see what the tomatoes look like," she said, heading back to the seafood counter, which again surprised me. Phillipe husbanded the seafood counter, seldom leaving it.

I picked up a head of lettuce and two tomatoes, then walked back to the rear of the store. Much to my surprise, I found her flirting with Phillipe over the seafood counter. *Ha, ha, this* and *ha, ha, that* kind of flirting. He couldn't get enough of her. Flinging off his white apron in a gesture that reminded me of a matador flinging his cape at a bull, he came around to our side of the counter. Something clearly had changed in the two days I'd been gone.

Minerva, who'd trailed us into the store, made her way around behind the counter. Balancing on her back feet, she eased up, stretched, and put her paws on its edge, carefully assessing the fish on ice, whiskers twitching. She stuck out a tentative paw and lovingly patted a hillock of flounder.

Instead of chasing her off, Phillipe went around and cut off a hefty piece, put it on a piece of wrap, and offered it to Minerva, who let out a delighted yowl, and dragged it behind the over-sized ice box.

"Now you have a friend for life," said my mother, laughing. Her teeth sparkled as if they'd been varnished. The little chip in her front tooth made her look like a snaggled-toothed girl. Even her dark hair, tousled from the wind coming off the water, seemed to take on new life, a bit of curl, a deep wave that ran from crown to tips.

"Maybe I could bring her some scraps sometime?" Phillipe asked hopefully.

"Oh, I don't think so," said my mother. "We don't want to spoil her, do we, Mem?"

"I wouldn't mind," I said.

My mother shook her head. "A pound of shrimp, no heads," she said. Phillipe sighed and put his apron back on. He went back behind the counter and piled shrimp on the scale until it reached two pounds.

"That's too much, Phillipe," said my mother.

He tore off some oil paper and plopped the shrimp on top. "We're loaded in shrimp, Virginia. They're going to go bad on me."

"Just a pound, Phillipe, that's all we need."

He took a few shrimp off the scale.

"Still too much," she said.

"You never let me do anything for you, Virginia."

"I don't need anything done for me, Phillipe. We're perfectly fine. Aren't we, Mem?"

I shrugged.

My mother frowned at both of us.

Phillipe stole a glance at my mother and took two more shrimp off the scale. He quickly wrapped the rest, handing over the package before she could protest. He peered over the scale at her, crestfallen.

Minerva emerged from behind the refrigerator. She sat down at Phillipe's feet and began to clean her face.

"Thank you," said my mother.

On the way to the checkout I whispered to my mother, "You know, you could be nicer to Phillipe. He'd be a good one to go around with."

She laughed. "Oh, Mem, he's not my type."

I put the lettuce and tomatoes on the checkout counter. "And why the hell not?"

"Don't curse, Mem." She looked around, then leaned over and whispered, as if we were girls together, "He's too nice. He *fawns* on me. And those *ears*."

"And that's why you don't like him? That's crazy."

"He's not *appealing* to me. One day you'll know what I mean." My mother shook her head slightly, eyeing the cashier, who happened to be Phillipe's mother.

"A dollar twenty-seven," Phillipe's mother said. Then she cleared her throat. "Beggars can't be choosers is what I think."

"No beggars here," my mother said curtly.

I hastily pulled two dollars from my pocket and planted it on the counter.

My mother snatched up the bag of shrimp and gestured for me to grab the vegetables. "Keep the change," she said and walked out, leaving me to balance the lettuce and tomatoes in my arms and make my escape while holding the door for the reluctant Minerva.

The three of us continued along Beach Boulevard, the late-day sun beating down. Beside the Belle Cote Bank and Trust building were the town's two water fountains.

"I'm thirsty," I said.

"Drink from the colored," my mother said automatically. From the time we'd moved to Belle Cote, she'd told me to always drink from the fountain marked colored. Separate facilities, she said, were ridiculous.

"It's dry," I said. "Look." I turned the handle and nothing came out.

"Damn it," she said. "I've called the mayor twice. I'm going to call the plumber myself."

"I'm dying of thirst," I said, moving over to the white fountain.

"Nobody's dying of thirst," she said. "You can wait."

BIENVILLE STREET RAN BEHIND an old monastery where the monks still lived, though we seldom saw them. A small cemetery, where deceased members of the order were buried under giant date palms and live oaks, was situated between our house and the monastery itself. Our street was narrow and our bungalow overhung in pines instead of the live oaks that clustered around Mac's place. Unlike Mac's, most of the houses on our street were modest shotguns and bungalows, though the yards were deep and filled with azaleas and crepe myrtle and oleander.

Nestled under some overgrown bottle palms, our house looked small and quaint. Tony was nowhere in sight, though his efforts were on full display. In my short absence, he had put the finishing touches on the porch railings, painting the diamond shapes in the corners terra-cotta, which set off the dusky green of the house and its cream trim. Someone had planted red geraniums in the giant concrete containers on each side of the steps, and four ladder-back rocking chairs with red pads sat invitingly on the long front porch. The house looked as welcoming and fresh as a magazine cover.

"Hasn't Tony done a wonderful job on the place?" said my mother, stopping on the sidewalk.

"I like the rocking chairs. They make it look homey."

"Tony and I found those over in Ocean Springs yesterday," said my mother, all in a happy little rush. "A bargain."

"You went to Ocean Springs?"

"There was an auction over there. We needed porch chairs. It was a nice day."

"Tony went with you?"

"He drove the Plymouth."

"You went together?"

"Well, of course, we did, Mem. I can't move furniture by myself. I was glad to have Tony help me."

"You can't move a rocking chair?"

"How was I to know what I was going to find?"

"Did you get anything else?"

"No, we didn't. There wasn't anything else I wanted. Why the third degree? Tony and I worked really hard to get the house ready for you."

I sat down in one of the chairs and began to rock harder and harder until the chair almost tipped over backward. My mother grabbed the back and righted it.

"No wonder they were a bargain," I said. "They're going to break somebody's neck."

"You just have to remember to rock gently," she said. "Don't take everything so seriously."

That last admonition ironic, coming from my mother, who was the queen of taking life seriously. As she headed inside, I opened my mouth to tell her so, following her into the living room and then the kitchen at the back of the house. I didn't get a chance. There at the kitchen table sat Tony. He held a carton of ice cream and was digging into it. On the table a can of Jax. His back was to us when we came into the room. He scooped out another spoonful of ice cream and shoved it into his mouth before he turned.

"Cheers," he said, a white trickle running down to his chin. His threadbare t-shirt, stained with the colors of our house, revealed the way his torso tucked and tumbled into his pants.

The first thing that came into my mind was that he was putting his spit into our ice cream—chocolate ripple, to be precise. My favorite.

My mother beamed down at him.

Tony held up the ice cream carton in one hand and the beer in the other. "Couldn't decide which I needed the most after painting the whole damn day." He smiled.

Tony Amato had a smile like no one else I've ever known. It wasn't just the white-white teeth or the way his eyes flickered like candles. Tony's smile was the struck match in a dark room, illuminating the thrill, the tumble of life. With Tony, color turned to neon, ice cream to an urgent hunger. In that moment at the kitchen table, when he smiled that Tony smile, all I wanted was to lick that dribble of chocolate ripple right off his chin.

My mother walked over to him so that his face was at breast level. Then she leaned down and opened her mouth. Her breasts in the summery dress loosened and threatened to spill. He took a good long look, spoon in midair, then chuckled in the way that only Tony could chuckle, a low growl in his throat. He dug into the carton and brought out a heaping spoonful. He fed it to her with tenderness, as if she were a baby eating Pablum, leaving traces of it around her mouth; then carefully, ever so carefully, he went around her lips with the spoon, drawing the traces up into her mouth. The gesture, the scraping clean of my mother's full lips, the pink tip of her tongue, unbearably intimate.

He shot a quick look at me, then turned back to her. "Watch out now, Virginia. You're about to lose your shirt and get indecent on me." He covered his eyes in a mock gesture and laughed a little when my mother flushed and pulled up her blouse. Then he dipped the spoon into the ice cream and waved it at me. "How about you, Miss Birdy?"

I put the vegetables one by one on the kitchen counter; then I turned and walked out, their laughter trailing me out the door.

On my way out, I heard my mother say, "I'll take it if she won't."

Minerva was perched in the pine tree out front. She shimmied down when she spotted me. I headed for Mac's and she followed behind. *See?*

"I've seen enough," I said, exasperated at her cryptic remarks.

Watch now, she said.

WHEN I GOT TO Mac's, I didn't knock, just went right in as if I still lived there. He was in the kitchen stirring a pot of red sauce and singing "The Battle Hymn of the Republic" at the top of his lungs. When he came to the part about trampling out the vintage where the grapes of wrath are stored, he stamped his foot for emphasis.

"Oh hell," he said. "I forgot to bring your bag by. I closed early and ran home to get this sauce ready. It's Tony's favorite. He says it reminds him of his mother. The trick's in the anchovies."

"Mac," I began, then began to cough. My childhood asthma had been acting up lately, a giant thumb that sometimes appeared out of nowhere and pressed down on my throat.

"Come over here," he said and put his spoon down. "Put your head over the pot and breathe."

I leaned over the pot. Tomatoes, garlic, oregano, basil. Mac had taught me how to make what he called authentic red sauce. Tony, he said, had taught him. The same Tony who was sitting at my kitchen table like he owned the place. The same Tony who was feeding my mother ice cream, then scraping her sweet lips clean. Was the Tony of the authentic red sauce the same Tony who shot the squirrel, who made me shoot the second squirrel, who clutched me to him as I killed an innocent animal? The same Tony who just wanted to please, his hand on Mac's knee?

Even then, when I was just a girl, I saw Tony not as a man but as a multiplication of men cut out like the paper angels my mother and I made that one Christmas we spent at the El Camino, all visually identical in shape but, in Tony's case, each different from the other in subtle but invisible ways. A cutout figure, a facade. A function of some impulse we all shared.

"Let's go down to the water," I said to Mac.

I had suggested a walk along the shore because it was an activity, something Mac and I could do together while my silence gathered itself. I couldn't say to him what I thought I should, which was that Tony, and perhaps my mother too, might deceive him, were perhaps already deceiving him and that their game, if it were that, was a sinister thing that would break his heart, not so much through Tony's betrayal as through my mother's. She and she alone had been Mac's home in this world of J. Edgar Hoover, Roy Cohn, clucking Baptists, midnight phone calls, hoods with headache sticks, vigilantes in black sedans. Long before I was born, she had been his respite, his home, the one place where he could breathe easy. How could she betray him?

My thoughts in the moment were actually not that precise, more a sense of inexpressible doom, sensation rather than analysis. I still wasn't sure what I'd seen in that gesture, the wiping of my mother's mouth. What did I know of the world of adults? With my withered hand as an obstacle, everything I'd learned about flirtation I'd learned by observation. So I didn't speak, for fear of being wrong.

At least that's my excuse for not telling Mac what I'd seen in the kitchen. If I had, this story might have ended another way. I could have ended it that very day in September with a single sentence. I could have struck the match to the paper angel and burned down the house. Tony would have hightailed it back to the City, crawling back under the rock he'd slithered out from under; my mother and Mac would have been furious with each other for months, maybe years. Then maybe my mother would have apologized and Mac would have gotten another true-blue boyfriend like Oliver, maybe even Oliver himself, and forgiven her. Everyone might have walked away wounded but still whole.

Or I could have ended it by knocking that spoon right out of Tony's hand. I could have slapped that grin right off his face. I could have turned on my mother and made her ashamed.

Although I sometimes wonder whether Mac—by no means a fool— knew more than he let on. Did he know and, assessing what was between them as a harmless flirtation, not wanting to lose either of them, chose not to speak? Did he think we could survive this? Did he see and not see? Did he know and not know?

Each day now my mother wraps herself around me like a fur cape. Each morning when I rise she comes up behind me, flings her arms wide, and leaps onto my shoulders, buttoning herself around my throat and chest, heavy and hot and wild.

Sometimes, now, decades later, I walk the Quarter from the French Market to Jackson Square and back. I favor busy weekends, when the Quarter is teeming with tourists. I zigzag up and down the narrow cobbled streets and look at the people. Sometimes I see a woman with dark hair walking up ahead. Sometimes I rush to catch up with her, shoving my way through the crowd. But then the woman turns and looks at me, curious, her eyes questioning and a little afraid. Other times, I find a seat at a sidewalk table at Café du Monde and watch the people go by. There are apparitions in the distance, slender tall women who carry their heads in a careful way. I watch them approach. Before I can discern their features, the blood throbs in my neck. I find my mother's face at the bottom of my coffee cup.

WHEN I ASKED MAC to take a walk with me, he reached out and took my chin, turning my head toward him. His touch brought tears to my eyes.

"Hey, you're crying in my sauce." Then, there were no lines on his face, but two formed between his brows as he looked down at me.

I jerked aside my chin.

He leaned down and looked into my eyes. Mac had a way of looking that burrowed right down into my chest and made a nest there. He turned off the stove and untied his apron. "All right, Little. A walk it is."

The Sound was quiet except for the shushing of the waves and a few men netting mullet and talking among themselves. It was suppertime, and we were the only ones walking along the seawall. Minerva came out from under her step and trailed us, then ran ahead, then trailed us again, pouncing on tiny crabs that poked their heads up through the sandy grass. We walked along in silence, Mac bending down every now and then to pick up a shell.

Then he stopped at a covered pier and looked out over the water. The setting sun, framed by the cover over the pier, flared red across the water. "Little, I'm going to tell you a story," he said. "Back in high school I had a friend. He was a lovely friend, just like your mother, except that he was sad all the time and he made everyone around him sad—sad for him, and, after a while, sad for ourselves. So we began to stay away from him; no one likes to be sad for too long. Sometimes being sad is the only thing to be, the way I was when my whole family drowned, but sadness has to end sometime, or it just gets hungrier and hungrier. It gobbles you up, bit by bit. Sadness needs to be a temporary condition, Little, like the measles. You catch it for good reasons, but then it fades a little, then a little more, and you feel better. You need to keep yourself above water. You need to remember to *breathe*. You hear me, sweetheart?"

"What happened to your friend?"

"He was sent away."

"Sent where?"

"He's in Whitfield."

"I fail to see how being sad can land you in the state asylum. That's for raving lunatics. He wasn't mental, he was just sad."

"Greg wasn't a lunatic," said Mac. "He just wouldn't get out of bed, wouldn't eat. Wouldn't even turn over when you walked into the room. He'd swum out too far; the tide had taken him out. He couldn't get back. Honey, I know you're sad about that bastard of a father of yours, but the hell with him is what I say. The hell with him. Let it go."

When Mac said that, I realized with something of a start that it had been months—maybe a whole year—since I'd even thought about my father.

I wanted to tell Mac I was sad about one specific squirrel, my mother eating ice cream like a baby, Oliver's gummy grin.

I said, "I'm not sad anymore about my father. You're my father now."

He flung an arm around my shoulder. "No," he said. "But I'll have to do, won't I?"

We walked until the sun unrolled across the water like a net; then we picked our way home, barefooted in the growing dark.

When we returned to Mac's, Tony was sitting in the porch swing.

Mac turned to me. "I'll drive you and your suitcase home," he said. "Let me get the keys."

I got into the Ranchero. On his way into the house, Mac leaned down and touched Tony on the shoulder, letting his hand linger. Tony pushed off, and the swing began to creak and groan.

By the time Mac drove me home, Minerva was sitting in one of the flowerpots on the front porch, right on top of my mother's geraniums.

"That cat sure gets around," said Mac.

"Yes, she does," I said.

XII.

———

As the days and weeks passed into early fall, Tony succeeded in making our house into his number one project. He was everywhere, inside and out: sanding, painting, hammering, sawing. He installed built-in bookcases in the living room, a medicine cabinet in the bathroom, a mantel over the fireplace, gingerbread gables on the front porch. He painted the shed out back, poisoned the colony of rats that lived in it.

His man-sweat, a Brylcreem tang to it, saturated the fabric of our furniture, the curtains, the clothes in our closets. I tasted it when I chewed the ends of my hair. It caught in my throat like a strand of wool yarn.

My paw grew more clenched by the day, fingernails cutting into my palm.

"That Tony," my mother would say at the completion of each of his accomplishments. "How in the world did we ever manage without him?"

I could think of nothing else but how to stay away from him, thinking that if I made myself scarce enough, small enough, he'd forget about me; he'd leave me alone, having chosen my mother instead. I still felt the gun's heat, smelled the splattered blood. Afternoons, I stayed late after band practice and helped Mr. Fann clean the instruments. "Get on out of here. Don't you have better things to do, Memory Feather?" he said once, but when I looked up from polishing a tuba and he saw my face, he brushed the words away with his hand as if they were flies.

I took a page from Minerva's playbook. When Tony was at work on the bungalow, I'd find her perched up in the big pine tree out front when I returned from school. *No no no*, she would report, and off we'd go, heading for the Sound. It was a pleasant thing to walk in the brisk fall breezes, the afternoon sun cutting diamonds across the tops of the little whitecaps. Fall was my favorite time of the year because of the Friday night football games. I loved throwing my baton up and up into the air at halftime and listening to the crowd's intake of breath as it twirled high above my head. My right arm grew muscular and strong. Sometimes I caught a flash of myself in the brass of the French horn or tuba, shoulders thrust back, head held high, capped and tasseled and bold. Memory Feather at her best. No matter that after the game, when my classmates would break off into groups and walk arm in arm out of the stadium, chattering about their plans for the rest of the evening, I would be left alone with Mr. Fann putting away the instruments. Never mind that my mother and Mac never came to another home game. Once, as the band was getting ready to take the field, I looked up into the stands and thought I saw Tony.

As I walked up the shoreline all the way to Waveland and back, up and back again, Minerva trailing along behind me, I felt fully alive, truly myself. I believed nothing could hurt me as long as I put one foot in front of the other.

At home, I became catlike in my motions. I imagined myself with a tail.

FALL TURNED TO WINTER, bringing cold squalls of rain. One Saturday afternoon, my mother came home dripping wet, her face as stormy as the outdoors. She slammed the front door behind her and threw her umbrella on the floor, where a puddle collected around it.

"Damn that Leticia! Damn her hide," she exploded. "No reason.

No notice. No nothing. Just sashaying through the door first thing this morning to announce she's quitting, this job isn't suiting her 'needs.' What 'needs'? I'd like to know," said my mother, kicking the wet umbrella back toward the door so that it left a long wet trail along the floor. Leticia had been fine the night before, when my mother had left her to do a deep cleaning of the gallery. Tony had been there retouching a china cabinet when my mother left; he could testify to the fact that Leticia had been just fine.

"Tony?" I said. "He was there when you left?"

My mother paused, but only for a second. "This isn't Tony's fault, Mem. That girl left me hanging. No notice, no good reason."

"Maybe she wanted more money."

"I offered her more. She just shook her head like the Queen of Sheba and said there were more important things in life than money."

After she left the gallery, I didn't see Leticia for several weeks.

Nor did Mac. She'd quit him too, it seemed, just as decisively as she'd quit Beautiful Dreamer. He worried about her, went by her house, where her mother told him she was up in Clarksdale maiding. She'd dropped out of school. Mac called his friend Aaron Henry to see if he could find out Leticia's whereabouts and situation. Aaron Henry was what people called a race man. He was chairman of the Mississippi NAACP, all the time getting into hot water with his sit-ins and voter drives and boycotts. The police up in Clarksdale hated him so much they'd chained him to the back of a garbage truck and paraded him through the streets on the way to jail, the way the Romans used to parade their captives, chained and bloody, behind their chariots when they returned from battle. Exactly like that, Mac said; Aaron Henry was the bravest of men.

He was also kind, reporting back that not only had he found Leticia staying with an aunt; he'd talked her into returning to school and brought her into his own household, where she had room and board in return for helping with his little girl and a few light chores. So Persistence being his middle name when it came to Leticia, Mac began driving up to Clarksdale on Sunday mornings to continue tutoring her, saying it would be a tragedy if a girl of her talents fell by the wayside.

WINTER HUNG ON. THE water in the Sound became gray and uneasy. Minerva relinquished her guard post in the pine tree for the sunny front window at the gallery, and when Tony was at the gallery, for parts unknown. Without her to warn me of Tony's whereabouts, I didn't bother to stop by the house on the way home from school. I memorized my lessons in study hall and over the sandwich I ate one-handed at lunch. As time went on, I dumped my lunchtime sandwich in the trash, enjoying the cleansing giddiness of hunger, the way I could encircle my upper arm with the fingers of my good hand. My schoolwork dispensed with by the end of the school day, I'd leave my books under my desk in homeroom and head straight for the water. I grew brown and lean. Drivers along Beach Boulevard slowed as they passed me walking along the shore.

As they passed, I saw myself as they saw me, as gaunt and bent against the wind as the hungry great blue heron I passed every afternoon hunched on a ramshackle fishing pier. He cast a shadow, a ghostly figure floating on the water.

My presence irritated the heron. He *krack*ed at me, told me to move along, let him fish in peace.

Why didn't I go sit in the gallery, cozy up to the wall heater to warm my cold chapped hands, then pull up an old chair to an old desk (everything in the gallery being old) and do my homework after school like a regular girl? For one thing, I was quietly fuming at my mother. She'd taken care of me from the time I was born; now I could feel her turn her attentions to a more engaging enterprise. It was as if she'd given birth to another child. Then, too, I feared Tony would come calling. He had a way of popping up when least expected. I'd have to see him and my mother together again, breathe the thickness in the air between them that sucked all the oxygen out of whatever space they were in. The Sound, cold and desolate as it was, seemed preferable.

To Mac, who actually asked where I went after school, what I did and with whom, I lied, vaguely mentioning clubs and band. I was busy, I told him; I had projects, I had friends.

Which was loosely true. I'd become quite attached to the pelicans that perched in rows on the ragged pilings of abandoned piers, and, I liked to think, they to me. Brown pelicans, members of the ancient Pelecanidae family, thirty million years old, associated in ancient Egypt with death and the afterlife. Phalanxes of them skimming the dark winter waters, plunge-diving for fish, an indecorous splat, then success: the full pouch and the climb. For the most part, friendly birds, rich in gossip, playfully sword-fighting with their beaks as they roosted.

There is a myth about pelican mothers, that in times of hardship they will stab their own breasts with their beaks so that their nestlings may eat from their flesh. In reality, the mothers are not that self-sacrificing; they are simply pressing on their breasts to fully empty their pouches.

I liked to walk along the water's edge when the setting sun flung a variegated bruise across the horizon. In the water, the bruise possessed motion, a secret life.

Some afternoons, I came upon my old friend, a pelican on a single piling, shard of the old pier, black against the pink water. If I stood and watched long enough, she would take to the sky on long cold wings. One deep dive, and she'd surface, carrying her secret deep within her pouch.

MY MOTHER, MEANWHILE, BROUGHT an ornate full-length mirror home from the gallery and studied her face and figure from all angles, holding up a hand mirror and turning this way and that. I found this behavior at once amusing and disturbing. My mother had never been vain or shallow. Naturally slender and small-breasted, she eschewed the pointy brassieres of the day, wearing only a full slip under her dresses. The last time I'd seen her in stockings was when she went out at night at the El Camino. In the time I'd known her, she'd never owned a girdle.

Now, she brought home dresses from the City in tropical shades of pink and green and yellow. She lingered over them as she hung them in her closet, flowered numbers that swished and fluttered, tight cardigan twin sets, detachable white collars rimmed in lace to place at her neck.

The heels and platforms of her shoes grew higher, she taller and more willowy. She let her hair grow to her shoulders and wore it down.

In all these machinations, she seemed to be getting lighter somehow, as if she were filled with nothing but air, not a beating heart and lively red organs going about their secret business. It was as if she were nothing but the facade of skin. The woman I'd known as *mother*, that dense viscous one whose body weighed down the bed we'd shared at the El Camino, had vanished. The woman who admired herself in the mirror seemed all motion, no substance—my mother, Virginia Feather, only a memory.

One school-day morning, as I was putting on an old skirt, she came into my room, stood for a moment and looked me up and down.

"Mem, you need some new things," she said. "Some nice things. Besides, you've lost some weight. Your clothes are starting to hang on you."

I reached into my closet and pulled out a white shirt. "I don't need anything new." Lately, I'd turned to the oldest clothes in my closet, some of them as worn as my Catholic castoffs; I relished their softness against my skin, the comforting familiarity in the way they clung to my body like fur.

My mother snatched the shirt out of my hands. "Look," she said triumphantly, holding it up, "the sleeves are frayed." She flung it on the bed. "Wait," she said. Then she left the room and returned bearing a blouse with red poppies splattered over it. The blouse trailed a long attached tie. "Now this," she said, "would dress up that old skirt, bring out the color in your cheeks. You're a pretty girl, Mem; surely you must know that."

"I wouldn't be caught dead in that thing."

"I'll have you know I've gotten compliments on this blouse."

"Who from? *Tony?*"

My mother stopped in her tracks, her face weary, weary. Something wounded there, something veiled.

"Oh, Mem," she said. "Don't you think I deserve a little fun? Something more than *this?*" She flung out her arm.

I looked around the room. "What's wrong with *this*?"

"Oh, honey, nothing. But there's more to this world than going to work every day, coming home every night, day in and day out."

"What then?" I asked. It was a sincere question.

"Laughter, music, dancing, floating on air. *Passion*, Mem."

"I liked things the way they were before." I didn't say before Tony, but we both knew that's what I meant.

"Do you know how sad I've been since your father left, Mem? How lonely? Each day just marching along, nothing to look forward to?" Her eyes filled. "Soon you'll be gone too. Soon I'll be six feet under."

As she spoke, the tie on the blouse slid to the floor. As if on cue, Minerva rounded the corner, batted at it for a moment, then snatched it up and took off with it, blouse trailing. "Damn you, cat," said my mother, running after her. "I don't know why I put up with you."

IN THE WEEKS AHEAD, the salt breeze from the Sound warmed. The new leaves on the oaks up and down the shoreline pushed out what was left of the old. I hung my jacket in the back of my closet. My mother pulled out her spring finery and went to work every day looking like she was going to the Easter parade. One bright Friday morning, Minerva began rummaging through my hair as I was sleeping. *Get up, get out.* I pushed her aside and tried to go back to sleep. Around midnight I'd awoken and found myself sitting straight up in bed, my throat a drum. I'd turned on the lamp beside my bed and looked around the room. My sense of dread, of impending doom, floated like a speck of dust in the corner of my eye. The fact that there was no rhyme or reason to my fear convinced me that I was fast becoming Whitfield material. There wasn't a moment, even when Tony was away, that I didn't plot and plan and expect some unimaginable catastrophe to befall us at his hands.

The previous afternoon I'd run into him as I walked along the Sound. He stood on the steps of the seawall, casting off his line. The water was choppy; a wind was whipping up. Minerva did a U-turn and slunk off in the other direction.

Before I could follow her, Tony spotted me, waved, and reeled in his line, his face open and eager. "Hey, Birdy," he called out, lifting the bucket beside him. "Want to take some of these home for supper?"

I shook my head and turned to go. "No thanks, we're all set."

He picked up the bucket and came toward me. "Don't worry. I'll clean them."

I pretended not to hear and broke into a run.

When I glanced behind me, he was still standing there. He looked puzzled, the bucket dangling forlornly from his hand, his shadow in the setting sun extending three times his size.

The next morning, Minerva purred in my ear, reminding me that Fridays were our best times—Tony would be either heading into the City for the weekend or helping Mac with some errand or other. He would not be back to our house until Monday. I sat up and yawned. Then I remembered that today was a teacher workday and I was looking at a three-day weekend.

I straggled into the kitchen where my mother was standing at the kitchen counter slurping a cup of coffee and reading the *Times-Picayune*. My mother always slurped her coffee from the edge because she filled her cup too full, as if someone had ordained that this would be the one and only cup of coffee she was ever going to get in her entire life.

I poured myself some milk and coffee, then took a portion of the newspaper and sat down at the table. Just then Mac burst through the front door.

My mother jumped, sloshing her coffee all over her section of the paper. "Damn, Mac," she said, "whatever happened to knocking?"

Lately, she'd been avoiding Mac, speaking with him on the phone about gallery business, whether to buy this or that piece of art, how to place the refinished furniture, what kind of advertising was most effective in light of dwindling sales, but not much more. Several times he'd invited us to supper, but she'd made excuses.

Mac paused in the doorway, a hint of reproach in his eyes. "I didn't know I needed to knock, Feather."

"Never mind," said my mother, turning to swipe at the newspaper with a sponge. "You just surprised me, bursting in on us like that. What?"

"Aaron Henry is coming down here. He's bringing a bunch of his people to help that doctor over in Biloxi, Gilbert Mason, and his group do a wade-in on Sunday in Biloxi. They're going to stay with me Saturday night. Do you two have any extra bedding and towels? I need everything you've got."

The beaches along the Sound had long infuriated Mac. Like everything else in those days, most of the shoreline along the Sound was segregated. There was a short stretch west of Belle Cote and Waveland where the shallow water jutted out onto rock and several large runoff culverts poured into the water, dredging deep holes into the shelf so that one minute you were up to your knees and the next thrashing about underwater. No telling when the culverts would drain either, and each season someone, usually a child, was swept under in the runoff. This was the place Black people could bring their picnic lunches and swim. In Biloxi and Gulfport, whites claimed the sand beaches for themselves.

My mother put down her newspaper. "Good for you for wanting to help, Mac, but wouldn't it be better if they stayed with some of their own people?"

Mac frowned. "Why *not* me? Aaron and I are friends from way back."

In the time I'd known him, Mac had talked up a storm about Aaron Henry, the two having become friends at Little Joe's Juke Joint up in Jackson, where men like them liked to go, Black and white together. Mac called these Jackson trips his "little vacations." Once I asked him what he did up there, and my mother had shushed me. "Mac has his private business, everybody has their private business," she said, and Mac laughed: "No big secret, Little. The fellows just get together and drink some beer, eat some catfish."

My mother took a sip of coffee. "Friends or not…."

Mac cut her off. "He asked me because he knows they'll be safe with me. God knows what'll happen to them come Sunday morning."

"Safe? How're you going to make a bunch of demonstrators *safe*?"

"I've got protection."

My mother's eyebrows shot up. "A gun? *You*?"

"It's loaded and in my nightstand, right next to me every night."

"I bet Tony showed you how to use it," I said.

"He most certainly did," said Mac. "He bought it for me. For the two of us. You can't be too careful."

"Oh, Mac," my mother said, shaking her head. "*You* shooting somebody."

"Only in self-defense, Feather. Now, will you help me out?"

"Of course I will, Mac, but it's against my better judgment."

Listening to Mac and my mother, I saw how history was playing out all around me. My mother always moved the COLORED sign forward on the streetcars in New Orleans, and we'd drink from the colored water fountain if it worked, which it often didn't. I read the newspapers: the columnist in the Jackson *Clarion Ledger* who likened Black people to apes, the cartoons, the lynchings, the poverty all around me. The whole state of Mississippi was exploding: churches firebombed, Aaron Henry chained to a stinking garbage truck; people strung up, thrown in paddy wagons; boys and girls my age and younger locked up in livestock pens at the state fairgrounds, half-eaten alive by dogs; merchants, doctors, lawyers, teachers, farmers put out of business and run out of town on a rail, their land and livelihoods stolen because they'd tried to register to vote. Until that morning such happenings had seemed far removed from my own life. In New Mexico, I'd gone to school with children named Erlinda and Manuel, language being the only division between us, and one easily bridged by familiarity. In Belle Cote, neither my mother nor Mac had ever hired a maid or a cook, so I'd lived in a white world without giving it a second thought. I saw but didn't see. A necessary blindness, a studied innocence.

The only Black person I'd known, and only briefly, was Leticia.

What I know now: I should have warned her. I should have lifted my eyes from the gray sand, the uneasy water. Then, though, there were no words precise enough to explain the hair that rose on the back of my neck, the sudden queasiness. The way my underarms poured when I felt Tony's careless eye fall on me. There was all that and more, but not language, not the words to tell a defenseless girl: *Be vigilant.*

"I WANT TO HELP get ready for the waders," I told Mac as he turned to go.

"You'll stay out of it," said my mother.

"Feather, I'll count on you for that bedding," said Mac, heading out the door. "I'll be back for it tomorrow morning."

"They'll find out. They'll come after you," said my mother, her voice trailing off, unexpectedly frail.

"*They* are after me anyhow, they're after me six days a week and twice on Sunday." Mac threw the words over his shoulder, letting the screen door slam behind him.

Then he said through the screen, as if it were an afterthought, "Oh, and Tony's going to be up in Money this weekend. Maybe for the best."

"Why?" I asked, glancing at my mother, who stood frozen at the door, the newspaper dangling from her hand.

Mac cleared his throat. "Tony doesn't think the way I do about such things."

I followed Mac onto the porch, out of earshot of my mother. "I can help cook supper for them," I said.

He grinned. "Now I can't help it if you happen to come by after Feather goes to work, can I? I can't help it if you decide to pitch in with the cooking while you're there. I'm on my way to the store now. We'll make gumbo. Two o'clock."

WHEN I ARRIVED AT Mac's that afternoon, opera was pouring out of the open windows—his favorite duet from Bizet's *The Pearl Fishers*, two men singing to each other of undying friendship. (Mac insisted it was passion, despite the fact, I later learned, that they end up fighting over a woman). He was humming along and pulverizing anchovies for a red sauce already bubbling on the stove in a monstrous vat.

"Spaghetti *and* gumbo?" I said. "Aren't you going a bit overboard?"

"No telling what's going to happen come Sunday morning. Least I can do is offer them a decent supper."

He pointed to the kitchen table where five stalks of celery, four onions, and a bulb of garlic sat waiting. I groaned. I knew my role in making the gumbo, and that was chopping all that lay before me into the most minuscule of pieces, to spread the flavor evenly through the roux.

He handed me his chopping knife. "I sharpened it for you."

"How kind of you."

"Least I could do," he said, grinning. "This is like old times."

BT, I thought. Before Tony.

I chopped and Mac stirred until we'd added all the vegetables to the roux, then water and bay leaves.

Mac pulled out two slices of white bread and put them on plates, then ladled some of the red sauce over them. "Let's eat a bite," he said, passing one plate to me. "We need to keep up our strength."

We ate standing at the kitchen counter, checking the pots every few minutes. Minerva, who'd been sleeping in the window, demanded bread, which she preferred to almost anything else in the world, so I broke up a half piece for her, using the other half to mop up the last of my sauce. She dragged her half back up onto the windowsill and polished it off.

Mac put his plate in the sink and said he was heading down to Phillipe's for the seafood. I was to stay with the pots and stir until Mac returned. I was to use separate spoons so as not to contaminate the gumbo with red sauce, or vice versa. We'd add the seafood tomorrow night, right before the group arrived. They'd be coming right after dark, for obvious reasons, he said. In the morning we'd make cornbread and a big dish of bread pudding. He needed cornmeal and white bread and cinnamon.

"You'll need somebody to help you serve."

Mac shook his head. "Your mother'll be home by the time they get here. She won't want you here."

I'd already thought of that. "You could send her into the City. Make up an errand. Pick something up for you."

Mac paused. "Well, it might be edifying for you to meet some committed young people. The consignment shops are open until six. I guess I could send her over in the afternoon to look around."

"You could."

He grinned. "The infamous consignment shop plot."

I giggled. "The *notorious* consignment shop plot."

After Mac left for Phillipe's, I turned off the record player and switched on the radio, changing the channel from Mac's classical music. The Top Forty was playing, and I sang along, happily stirring the pots, remembering when my mother and I had just come home to Belle Cote, that first supper with Oliver. How I wished for his gummy smile, his easy ways. How I wished my mother had insisted he stay, had moved us back with my grandparents until we could afford our own place. Then Tony would have stayed locked inside his portrait, barely worth a passing mention.

I'd been struggling to figure out what Tony was up to, what kind of man he was. Back then, I thought that there were men who liked men and men who liked women, period, no seesawing back and forth between the two. For me, Tony was a whole new species, and I didn't know what to make of him. Perhaps, I thought, that was why I found him frightening; perhaps the poor thing was just genuinely mixed up about who he liked. Maybe, I thought then, I was just being small-minded, maybe even *prejudiced*, the worst of all sins in Mac's playbook.

I began to dance around the kitchen, more to let off steam than out of any desire to dance. Surely I was making a mountain out of a molehill; Tony and my mother were just friends, nothing more. *Come on-a my house, my house a-come on.*

What I didn't know then is how one person can *use* another. The economics of sex, let's call it, but I don't just mean prostitution, which is all about money, at least on the prostitute's end. Tony wanted money for sure—he perceived us all as rich beyond his wildest dreams, and he was right about that—but even then, I sensed that there was something more than money he wanted, something I still don't have a name for. What he had to give in return: not just beauty, but the headiness he brought into the room, a sweaty exhilaration, which translated into an odd kind of joy. He wanted us to dance to his tune—a mindless dance, like a young boy click-clacking his way along the Quarter streets, hoping for nickels and dimes instead of pennies.

When the front door clicked open, it was as if my thoughts had summoned him. Without a word of warning, Minerva leapt from the windowsill and darted behind the icebox, her twitching tail still visible. Not having her powers of perception, I turned to wave at Mac, thinking he was returning.

And then, there *he* was, dancing into the kitchen, a tweed cap pulled rakishly down over one eye, heading straight for me.

"Birdy Feather," he called out. "Long time no see. *Come on-a my house, my house a-come on.*"

Coming toward me, his shoulders and hips shimmying, he sang out, "*I'm gonna give you candy.*" At first I shrank from him, measuring the distance to the back door, when, eureka, he actually reached in his pocket and brought out a Milky Way and waved it at me.

Everything seemed safe and funny then, as if we were in a musical. My dread, my fear: all of it dropped to the floor as if I were shucking my dirty clothes. How ridiculous I'd been, how downright silly. I laughed and reached for the candy bar. He held it high, out of my grasp, still dancing and singing and flashing his Rock Hudson teeth at me. He was wearing a brown shirt with gold flecks in it that brought out his eyes. It was open to the third button. Around his neck a cross on a gold necklace. A cross of gold. Oh, my, I thought, Tony's religious! His cap slipped farther down over his eye, glossy brown hair escaping on one side of his head. Bless his heart, the poor thing needed a haircut.

My head stopped saying danger, my feet kept dancing. I'd never been to a dance at school, but I'd danced along to *American Bandstand* and knew all the new moves.

"The girl can *dance*," Tony sang out. He took my good hand and snaked me around his waist. I circled him once, twice, three times. Close in, Tony smelled like Beech-Nut gum and Aqua Velva lotion; he smelled like a man on his way to church.

The music stopped and he came closer. "What's cooking?" he asked. He had a glittery famished look.

I said, "Your favorite. Red sauce. And we've started some gumbo."

He picked up two potholders and took off the lids, both at the same time, a grand gesture, and looked down at the vats of bubbling liquid. "You and Mac planning on feeding an army?"

"Better than that," I said eagerly. And then I told him about the people coming, the wade-in on Sunday and Aaron Henry, the need for extra bedding. All in a rush of gossipy excitement and *come-a come on*, I told Tony every single thing.

XIII.

———

AS THE WORDS OF Mac's plans tumbled from my mouth like a pod of playful porpoises, Mac himself walked through the door, carrying two large brown paper sacks, one soaked through and dripping—Phillippe always put his seafood on ice—and one with four loaves of Sunbeam bread poking out of the top. Looking from me to Tony and back to me, Mac slid the sacks on the table.

I stopped in midsentence.

"So, Mac, I hear you're having company," said Tony.

"Just a few friends from the City."

"Not what I hear from Miss Birdy here."

Mac looked at me again. His mouth moved a little, then froze.

"Aaron Henry and his band of—" said Tony.

"Don't say it," Mac said.

"In *this* house. Sleeping and eating in *this* house. And here you are cooking for him, for *them*, like some kind of goddamn mammy."

"That's right, Tony. *My* house. *My* houseguests."

"No skin off my nose then."

"I thought you'd be up in Money this weekend with your questionable friends."

"You're a fine one to talk about *my* friends. I forgot something."

"Oh? What was that?"

"Just a jacket. It's still cool at night." Tony turned on his heel and went back into Mac's bedroom and came back out a few minutes later with his flight jacket on. It was brown leather, weathered, with a fuzzy collar. My father had had a jacket like that.

Tony turned to me, ignoring Mac. "You're a good dancer, Birdy Feather. We need to go juking sometime."

"Over my dead body," said Mac.

Tony pulled the Milky Way out of his pocket and took my good hand and pressed it into my palm. Then he was gone.

When the front door clicked shut, Mac pulled the shrimp and oysters out of the sack and went out on the back porch to put them into the small icebox he'd bought. I grabbed a dish rag and followed him, wiping the drips up from the floor in his wake.

When he came back into the kitchen, he didn't look at me. The commercial for Maison Blanche was blaring from the radio. *Jingle jangle jingle, here comes Mr. Bingle.*

"I'm sorry," I said. "I didn't mean to tell."

"I didn't know you couldn't keep a secret, Little. I didn't know that about you. Remind me not to tell you anything I don't want broadcast to the whole damn world." He spoke softly, eyeing Minerva as she slunk out from behind the refrigerator, her whiskers trailing spiderwebs.

"I said I was sorry. He asked me about the food, why there was so much. You didn't say not to tell."

He cleared his throat. "There are ways to be circumspect, Little. You could have said I was having a little supper gathering."

"I didn't think of that," I said, genuinely miserable.

Appropriately, Brenda Lee came on the radio, louder even than the commercial, singing that she was sorry, so sorry; please accept her apology.

"I hate this music. Why is it blaring like that?" Mac muttered. He stalked into the living room and turned off the radio.

At that moment both the roux and the red sauce boiled over. I scrambled for the spoons, dropping one on the floor.

Mac rounded the corner. "Oh, good grief. I told you to stir the damn stuff. Can't I count on you for anything? Take the lids off! Turn down the flame! Don't you have good sense, girl?"

Then I dropped the second spoon and reached to take the lid off the gumbo pot, forgetting a potholder. The handle scorched my good hand. I burst into tears.

Mac reached over me to turn down the two flames. "Run it under cold water." He leaned over me and turned on the cold water faucet in the sink. "Put your hand under there." Then he looked down at the two spoons on the kitchen floor, which was splattered red and brown from one end to the other, and began to laugh. "Oh, Little, what would we do without each other? What would we *do*?"

I sputtered, "We'd go jump in the Sound and drown ourselves, that's what we'd do."

He laughed harder. "Maybe we'd better do that right now and get it over with. Let somebody else clean up this mess."

He picked up the spoons and lids and rinsed them. I wiped up the floor.

I was still sniffling. Mac pulled a handkerchief out of his back pocket and handed it to me. "Here, blow your nose. I need a drink."

"Not five yet," I said. Mac's rule for himself was never to drink before five unless it was Thanksgiving, Christmas, New Year's Day, or somebody's birthday.

"It's five somewhere," he said.

"It's somebody's birthday," I said.

He went over to the breakfront in the dining room and brought back a bottle of vodka. "Screwdriver," he said. "A perfectly respectable drink for this time of the day."

"If you get a screwdriver, I get a tonic," I said. I'd graduated from Shirley Temples to tonic water and lime.

"I'll make the drinks. You check the pots and stir everything. Make sure nothing's sticking on the bottom. And try not to throw the spoons all over the kitchen. They're not batons."

So Mac made the drinks and we sat together at the kitchen table and downed them, both of us disheveled and breathing hard. I tilted my chair back and began to twist my ponytail. My hair needed washing.

Mac studied me, then leaned over the table. "Little, one thing you have to learn. When I tell you a secret, it's because I trust you. We have to trust each other." He tapped his finger on the table, punctuating each statement as if I were three years old.

I yanked at my ponytail. "You expect me to read your mind? You didn't say all this was a secret."

He considered. "Well, maybe not *explicitly*, but I trusted you to be discreet."

"Tell me. Do you trust Tony?"

Mac's eyes scurried around the kitchen, bright and busy, surveying the pots, the bread piled up on the table, the dishes in the sink, Minerva back on her windowsill above the sink. "There are different kinds of trust," he said finally. "I'd trust you and your mother with my life." He started to say something else, but then he stopped and looked around again. "That's why it's important for you to keep what I tell you in confidence, just like I don't tell your mother everything you tell me. I'd never do that."

He clinked the ice in his drink, marking a period to the conversation. "Speaking of your mother, I need to call her. Tell her about that important errand tomorrow. You keep on stirring and lay out the bread on the table so it'll be stale by tonight when we make the bread pudding. Don't let Minerva get to it."

He went to the phone and dialed. He told my mother that he'd been thinking: Beautiful Dreamer needed more decorative items; she was to head into the City tomorrow morning—yes, close the gallery—and browse the consignment shops down on Magazine and out on Veterans Highway. Yes, they were open until six on Saturday. No, he'd take care of the gallery, not to worry. Yes, she'd get home after dark, but she didn't have to open up until noon on Sunday, so she could sleep late, couldn't she? Just take the checkbook and go crazy, it'll be a lark. Maybe she could go by Maison Blanche and pick herself up something nice. Eat a decent po'boy. Have herself a good time. Yes, he'd check on me, no worries.

And so it was arranged. When I got home late that afternoon, my mother was buzzing around, ironing herself a nice dress. Surprisingly, she'd put a meat loaf in the oven, along with some potatoes and carrots. "We can eat on this all weekend," she said, explaining to me about Mac's strange request that she shop for decorative items. "Decorative items. I'm not even sure what he means by that. Will you be all right if I get in after dark?"

I pointed out that in the winter she got in after dark every day when she was working.

She put down the iron. "You probably wish I were more like a regular mother."

"I know you like working at the gallery."

She smiled. "I like meeting people from all over. Sometimes, when they talk about where they come from, it almost feels like I've been there too. Maybe someday we can take a trip."

"Where to?"

"Anywhere but France," she said.

THE NEXT MORNING I woke early, disturbing Minerva, who was curled up against my stomach. She growled under her breath, then hissed when I pushed her away. "Oh shut up," I muttered. She jumped off the bed and vanished in a huff.

I'd dreamed about the waders. One by one they'd walked into the Sound, far, far out on the shelf, dots against the vast horizon, until their shoulders, then their whole heads, went under. *No no no,* I'd shouted from the shore, you're only supposed to *wade*; but one by one they walked out until the last one, a girl my age (*Leticia, come back,* I scream-whispered), vanished, and the water folded over them like molten glass and all was as it had been, calm and pretty and peaceful, with little milky scallops of waves lapping like a thousand tongues at the sand beach of Biloxi. I woke up shivering, as if I'd been in the water too. I'd bitten my tongue in my sleep, and by the time I'd gotten up to perk myself some coffee, one of the many canker sores I suffered from had taken up residence at the site of the wound and was beginning to sting and throb.

I peeled off my pajamas and put on some shorts and a torn t-shirt. It was chilly for April, but I knew the day would warm quickly. I went into the kitchen and started the flame under the percolator. After I'd had my coffee and Rice Krispies, I walked out into the front yard. There was dew on the grass and the palmetto fronds floated in the slight breeze. The air was crisp. Not a cloud in the sky. A perfect spring day.

Behind me, the front door opened and my mother peered out, her hair tangled from sleep. "Look at you in that torn shirt and scraggly shorts. Why don't you come into the City with me? We could do a little shopping. Get you some decent things."

I didn't turn around to face her. "Nope, I've got plans."

"We could have a nice supper."

I shook my head.

"What are you going to do all day then?"

"School stuff. I have a lot of homework for Monday."

"Well, all right," she said. "It would have been nice to spend some time with you. You seem so distant these days. I *miss* you."

Well, I thought, if you'd put Tony Amato out of my house, *our* house, we could have plenty of fun. We could play bridge with Miss Bess and have oyster suppers with Mac again if he'd give Tony his walking papers too. Then Minerva and I wouldn't be running from pillar to post and I wouldn't be dancing with Tony one minute and hating him for the bigot he is the next, and I could be your daughter again.

I didn't say any of that. I stood in silence, my back still turned. After a while she sighed. It was a sigh that lifted off into the blue, blue sky and made lazy circles above us. Out of the corner of my eye, I could see her shadow. Then the shadow disappeared and the door clicked shut.

I looked back at our little bungalow. There was Tony's discarded paint can on the front porch, the brushes in it soaking in turpentine for him to take up on Monday; there was the door he'd rescreened; there the tortured tracings of the ivy he'd pulled away from a front window.

Inside, I got the bedding Mac needed and piled some blankets and our two extra pillows on the sofa. Then I got back into bed and pulled the sheet over my head. I didn't move when my mother came into my room to tell me goodbye. After she left, I got up and went into the kitchen. On the counter was a plate of eggs and grits with a note. *See you tonight. Don't work too hard!* I ate a bit of the eggs and then put the plate on the floor for Minerva. She gobbled them up, then started on the grits, first daintily licking the melted butter on top, and finally cleaning her face with her paw.

"Let's go," I said, and we set off for Mac's.

The morning had turned warm. I cut across Miss Bess's front yard, which had a bare track through the St. Augustine grass that Mac, my mother, and I had made as we went from one house to the other. Miss Bess's arthritis had gotten worse, and she spent most of her time at her picture window looking out to see what she could see. I waved and she waved back.

As I approached Mac's yard, I heard a loud hum, as if from a powerful electric current, coming up behind me. I turned and there they were, about twenty of them, church ladies waving palm fronds, coming up the street like one giant prehistoric creature with forty eyes and a swish of green feathers. I'd forgotten it was Palm Sunday weekend. They were going to decorate the church.

Minerva took one look and bolted into a camellia bush.

One lady, an appendage of the creature, pulled away from the larger body. She looked me up and down, taking note of my torn shirt and old shorts. "Let Jesus into your heart, sweet child," she called out, extending her arm toward me, appendage of the appendage. Her voice seemed to come from underwater.

I picked up my pace and made it to the middle of Mac's yard. When I turned to climb the stairs to his porch, the creature followed me into the yard, then, in one tumbling, groaning motion (some of the ladies quite old) fell to its knees and began to cry out. It was a terrible sound. A cloud passed overhead, and the creature looked up. The sky darkened, and the appendage shouted, "Into the arms of the beast. A precious child lost to Satan!"

The hair rose on my arms and the back of my neck. The woman came closer and made a grab for my paw. "Jesus will heal this, he makes all things whole." Her voice rang out up and down the street.

Miss Bess banged on her front window with her cane, causing the creature to turn its head. In the second her distraction afforded me, I ran up the steps onto Mac's front porch and tried to get in. The door was locked.

The creature rose on its forty feet and milled about below me in Mac's yard, then bellowed its outrage and pain, as though it had been stabbed to the heart.

I banged on the door, then kicked it. "Mac, let me in!"

The door swung open suddenly, as if blown by a gust of wind. "Get in here," said Mac.

He pulled me in and kicked the door shut.

"For crying out loud, Little, all I need right now is a bunch of crazies in my front yard. Can't you use a little discretion?"

"Apparently, discretion isn't my long suit," I said.

He peered out the front window. "Damn. They're camping out in the front yard."

The creature's moan began to climb the musical scale, sounding more like a sustained shriek.

"Now you just turn right around and go back home. Tell them you needed to use the phone—yours is on the blink. No, wait a minute—now you're using the phone. Wait a minute or two." He paused, listening.

"Afraid of a bunch of church ladies." I ventured a smile.

"Not afraid for myself, Little. I'm afraid for my guests. They're coming in a few hours and here you go dragging the whole damn town into my front yard." He turned me around and pushed me toward the door. "Now you get back out there and tell them you had to borrow my phone. Make them go away. You brought them, get rid of them."

"But I want to help you get ready."

"I'll call you later." He opened the door and motioned for me to go through it.

I stepped outside and the sound stopped. Everything dead quiet except for the twittering of sparrows in the wisteria that hung from the underside of Mac's porch. In that moment the sun emerged and struck me squarely in the eyes.

I stood there, shading my eyes with my good hand, trying to accustom myself to the glare. The creature below began to move stealthily toward me, as if I were prey.

I raised my hand in the air, saluting the monster and began to speak. I started off soft so that the creature drew closer; then I shouted, my voice pushing, pushing it back. I told it how I needed to use the phone, how ours was on the blink, how my neighbor had lent me his so that (ah, the lie grew and grew) I could call my mother, who (fat chance) was helping decorate *our* church, to tell her about the phone, how I was just heading home to change so I could help too. "An emergency," I said.

A sigh, a shuffle, and the creature now just twenty silly women, out of sorts in the heat of the sun, their hair plastered to the sides of their faces like rain-splashed weeds, fanning themselves with palm fronds, in their flowery dresses and cruel shoes.

I took off running across Miss Bess's yard. She was standing on her porch, leaning on a rickety chair. "You, Memory Feather," she cried out, hoarsely, as if she hadn't spoken to anyone in a good long time. "Are you all right?"

I nodded and waved to her and kept running until I got home and locked the door, almost slamming it on Minerva, who'd lunged out from behind the camellia bush and was hot on my trail.

WHILE I WAITED FOR Mac to call me to come back, I began to clean the house. First, I opened the windows and then all the bedroom and closet doors to try to rid the house of Tony's smell. I swept and then ran the carpet sweeper over the rugs. I knocked the cobwebs off the ceiling fans, which hadn't been used since the previous summer. I wrapped the dust mop in a damp cloth and wiped the blades clean, something my mother never in a million years would have done—would never have even thought to do before turning on the fans full speed and sending dust and spiders and the leavings of the spiders' winter feasts drifting down into our hair.

When Mac still hadn't called, I filled a bucket with water and vinegar, and started mopping the kitchen floor. When I finished, I went outside and dumped the water from the bucket and considered what to do next. The weather was fine; I would have liked to have gone for a walk along the Sound, but I didn't want to miss Mac's call. I got out the carpet sweeper and headed for my mother's bedroom. The door was closed and when I opened it, the smell of Tony about knocked me down, but not the same Tony I'd danced with. Stale sweat and hair oil. Underneath all that, something glandular that smelled like cheese. Tony, I saw, had been putting up shelves in my mother's closet. His stepladder still stood in the center of the room; a hammer, a box half full of nails, the others treacherously scattered about on the floor, as if he'd dropped them and forgotten to pick them up.

My mother's bed hadn't been made, not an unusual occurrence; she was busy from daylight to dark. After a long day in the City, after being led on a fool's errand, she deserved a clean bed to come home to. I felt a pang of guilt for lying to her. Now I could do something nice; I could change her sheets.

I took the spread and blanket off the bed and threw them on a chair. When I yanked at the sheets, something fell to the floor. It was small and flaccid and translucent. I bent down to pick it up and then stopped in midreach. The thing looked repugnant, like a half-dead snail, white and pulpy. As I peered at it, baffled, Minerva sauntered into the room. She stopped short, then slunk over to the thing, her belly low to the floor. She stopped about a foot from it, her tail twitching. Then she wiggled, preparing to pounce.

Then she too froze, her forepaw in midair. She shook her head, as if to clear her thoughts, then sniffed it. *Dead,* she said. She looked at me and it, and, without warning, began to growl. It was not her playful growl, the one she used when trying to pull one of her mouse toys from my hand. Not even the menacing growl she used when chasing a roach around the house. This growl moved up and down the scale like an opera singer warming up.

I picked the thing up with a piece of toilet paper. It seemed to belong in the toilet, so that's where I put it. When I flushed the toilet, it didn't go down, just circled lazily, as if it had something to tell me. I flushed it again, holding down the handle, and finally it disappeared.

It was as if it had never been. In the moment, an odd figment of the imagination.

The phone rang on the wall in the kitchen. I ran to answer it.

"You can come on over now," Mac said, without so much as a hello. "Bring the bedding. Some towels too."

"I'll have to make two trips," I said, suddenly breathless.

"Just don't bring any crazies with you. Try to be discreet for once in your life, Little."

"I don't know how to be discreet when I'm carrying a stack of sheets and towels and pillows," I said. "It looks like I'm moving in for life."

"I don't have time for jokes." He hung up.

I went back into my mother's room, still intent on changing her sheets. I planned to put our extra set on her bed. My mother and I took full advantage of Mac's washing machine and the large clothesline in his backyard, running piles of our laundry back and forth at odd hours of the day and night. My plan was to throw the dirty sheets into the bottom of the linen closet and wash them the coming week, after the waders had gone.

I tossed the pillows on the floor and jerked the sheets off the bed. Then I quickly made the bed with the clean sheets from the linen closet and snatched up the pillows to change them too. I pulled off one pillowcase and then picked up the other pillow to do the same. Pillowcases were the hardest part of changing a bed, on account of my hand.

Struggling with the pillowcase, I stopped suddenly, breathless again, from exertion or the cloying smell of the room, I wasn't sure which. I threw down the pillow and went into the bathroom. I opened the medicine cabinet Tony had put up and got out the inhaler my mother kept up to date, though I seldom had any use for it. I took two puffs, which made my heart lunge against my rib cage, as if it were banging on a closed door.

Back in my mother's room, I reached for the second pillow on her bed, then paused, still panting a little. Just then the sun topped Miss

Bess's house next door and flung a long shaft of light onto the bed, hard caught on the pillow I'd left lying there.

I looked down at the pillow, in that moment luminous as a poached egg, the case, yellowed and shiny, I now saw quite clearly, with hair oil.

I smelled the pillowcase.

And then I knew.

XIV.

———

I TOOK THE PILLOWCASE outside and dumped it in the trash. If I had to choose the moment I began to plot and plan, it was when I put the lid back on that trash can. This precarious balance, the pelican's perch on a lone piling, was not going to end in flight. Even then, I knew: we were not going to be left whole.

Standing in the hot sun, I began to think of certain possibilities. Ways of performing the task before me, which was to rid us all of Tony Amato.

Option A: Tell my mother to stop it—*it* being the unspeakable thing I envisioned but couldn't articulate at the time, even to myself. I discarded that idea the moment I thought of it. Nobody, least of all her daughter, could tell my mother what to do.

Option B: Tell Tony to stop it. I discarded this option as well. Tony was a weasel and weasels could squeeze out of anything. Not to speak of the fact that after the squirrel incident, I'd become afraid, deeply afraid, not just of Tony but of myself *with* Tony. If he could make me shoot an innocent creature who'd done me no harm, what else could he make me do?

Option C: Tell Mac, who loved them both. Not unless I wanted to break his heart. Not unless I wanted to cut the cord that bound the three of us.

Something more radical was required.

I carried the load of sheets and blankets over to Mac's, dropped them on the porch swing, then headed back home for some towels. Miss Bess was still standing on her porch, hanging on to the rail. She beckoned to me as I crossed her yard. I waved at her but didn't stop.

She beckoned again, more impatiently. "Memory Feather, are you sure you're all right?" she called out. "What did those awful women want with you?"

"They didn't want me going over to Mac's," I called back to her.

"Well, I hope you told them to mind their own beeswax. Judge not that ye be not judged. Each to his own taste, said the old woman when she kissed the cow."

"Mac doesn't kiss cows."

"It's just a saying, dear. Get that Mac McFadden to feed you a good supper. You looked peaked." She turned and hobbled back into the house, giving me a final wave.

Back inside, I gathered the remaining towels. Crossing Miss Bess's yard, I came to the conclusion that if there were going to be a villain in this story, it might as well be me.

By what means, though? That was the question I asked myself as I climbed the steps to Mac's porch.

He'd brought in the first load of linens. The door was ajar so I pushed it with my foot to let myself in.

Mac hurried into the living room. "Those are all towels?"

"Yes," I said.

"Go put them in the bathroom. Just stack them up on the floor. I don't know how many are going to want a bath."

"They're going to get wet tomorrow," I said, heading for the bathroom. "If they get that far."

I paused. "What do you mean? I thought this was a wade-in."

"They may be stopped."

"By who?"

"By whom." Mac could be tiresome about grammar.

"Whom, then?"

Mac waved his hand in the air, impatient at the question. "Oh, police, rednecks, who knows. Our job is to feed these people, make them comfortable. Try not to worry about the rest of it."

I put the towels down and came out of the bathroom. He was moving chairs around the living room, placing them in corners.

"Maybe we should go with them, wade in too," I ventured.

"Your mother would kill me if I dragged you into this."

"*You* could go."

"I don't know," he said, looking down at the floor. "I'll see."

"What's the matter? Are you afraid?"

"Of course not. Now come on into the kitchen. Aaron called this morning. There'll be twenty of them, counting him. They're coming in under the radar, just to boost the local numbers. We need to count out the bowls and spoons and napkins. Everyone will get one bowl and one spoon. Get them stacked up on the table. The bread pudding's done, but I want you to make some peanut butter cookies. Some people don't like bread pudding. Now hustle. They'll be here at first dark. If you're going to be here and help, I want you to go home and take a bath and wash that hair. I've been meaning to talk to you about your hygiene, Little. You've been letting yourself go lately. And you're thin as a rail. A girl needs to have pride in her person."

My hand flew to my hair, which was plastered to my head from an unhygienic combination of sweat and oil. Recently I hadn't been washing my hair as often as I should have because it had been falling out in the tub, clogging the drain. Between the constant walking and foregoing lunch and sometimes breakfast, I'd actually begun to feel exhilarated by a new feeling of lightness, the way my fingertips seemed closer to my heart when I touched my rib cage, as if my chest were a paper-thin membrane, the thrumming of my heart as resolute as the least terns that scurried back and forth at the shoreline, building their nests. When I washed my face at night, I would lean into the mirror and touch my neck, feeling the pulse surge and return, my neck as thin and elongated as any wading bird's, undulant and graceful, or so it seemed to me.

The expression on Mac's face, a mixture of alarm and distaste, told me otherwise. The look was familiar. The previous week Mr. Fann had given me the once-over at band practice. We were practicing for the spring band competition in Jackson. I'd put on my majorette uniform, which I hadn't worn since the Belle Cote Mardi Gras Parade the previous February. The only part that didn't hang on me was my tasseled hat, and even it sat lower on my head, resting on my eyebrows. Mr. Fann took me aside and whispered, as if he were saying something shameful, "Your mother needs to do some altering on your outfit. It's ill-fitting." Which was laughable since my mother had never picked up a needle and thread since she helped Mac make my ill-fated Halloween costume.

The afternoon Mr. Fann had talked to me about my uniform Tony was finishing a job in our kitchen. He'd replaced some pipes under the sink. He tended to go directly from one job at our house to the next. I was tired to the bone. There was nothing I'd have relished more than to come home to my very own place (such a cozy word, *place*, when it is one's own), grab a Nehi from the icebox, and settle in front of the television, maybe even doze off, the way regular girls did. Or at least, so I assumed. I didn't actually know what regular girls did, never having been one myself. Of late, I'd been given wide berth at school. I actually wasn't sure who was giving me wide berth; I only knew there'd been a subtle change over the past month or so. Never Miss Popularity, I'd nonetheless discerned of late that there was what I can only describe as a melting away. In the hallways, the other students looked studiously at the floor or somewhere to the right or left of me. It was as if I were the janitor pushing an oversized dust mop down the hall, everyone stepping aside to let me pass.

I opened my mouth to answer Mac, to tell him there was nothing wrong with me, nothing whatsoever. The words dissolved before I could speak them. "Where's the peanut butter?" I asked instead.

"Above the sink, where it always is. We'll talk about this later, Little. A girl needs to be neat and tidy with her person. And why you've gotten to be skin and bones I don't know. Your hair's thinning too. Maybe it's a thyroid condition. I'm taking you to the doctor for a checkup."

It hadn't occurred to me that something might have gone amiss deep within my cells, that I was ill. I didn't feel sick. I felt forever hungry. I yearned to make the long plunge-dive for the slippery fish that would fill me up and let me take my rest in the blessed shallows. But the fish was elusive and the water murky.

Back home, I drew a bath and lay down in the tub, submerging my head. I shampooed my wet hair and applied crème rinse, then put my head underwater again. Several years ago, a woman across town had been found by her daughter dead in the bathtub, her head underwater. It was a mystery how she got that way, though it was whispered that she and her husband were all the time arguing and that he might have had something to do with it. My thought, though, was that maybe the woman had just gotten sick and tired of life above water. Going under in a warm bath may have seemed like just the ticket.

My own water was getting cold. When I pulled out the plug, clumps of my hair circled the drain.

What I knew: One, that Tony and my mother were lying down on the bed together, which even I knew was wrong wrong wrong. Two, that Mac appeared blissfully ignorant of that fact. Until then, I'd admired my mother; I'd admired her in a way most girls did not admire their mothers. For one thing, my mother kept us both alive after my father absconded. A sterner person than I might say she should have swallowed her pride and taken me home to Belle Cote sooner. But I loved my mother for her pride, that toss of the head, the way her nostrils flared when she was angry. And there lay the rub. Mac let my mother keep her pride. He'd given her a way to make a decent living; he'd made it possible for her—and me—to have a *life*. He'd offered firm ground for us to stand on.

But Mac had his pride too, and unwittingly, he'd been robbed of it, the robber of our cozy nest none other than his best friend, Virginia

Feather. In fact, both of them seemed to have been struck blind by Tony, as if they'd looked too long into the sun. This I could not tolerate.

As I got out of the tub, I caught sight of myself in the mirror. I looked like a nestling bird, all bone and skin, featherless.

I pulled the comb through my wet hair slowly, but still the hair released. My hairline had receded like an old man's. I winced as I brushed my teeth. The canker sores in my mouth had multiplied in the last few weeks. I hurried into my room and put on some clean shorts and shirt, slipped my calloused feet into sandals. Minerva lay pancaked on the bed. She opened one eye and peered at me. *Care. Take care.*

By the time I got back to Mac's, it was three o'clock. The living room floor was strewn with sofa cushions, pillows, and bedding, a few inflated rafts. In the kitchen the gumbo was boiling hard. I turned it down. The spaghetti sauce was on a nice simmer. I turned it off. Mac drew the curtains, saying nobody needed to know what we were up to. Then there was nothing left to do. The rice was on, the gumbo simmering, and spaghetti sauce done. So Mac and I sat down in the darkened living room, he and I in opposite corners. If strangers had walked in, they would have wondered at the distance between us, the way we looked solemnly at each other across the room as if we were angry at each other in some quiet way.

RIGHT AFTER DUSK, THEY came, clutching their belongings in paper sacks and small suitcases. They came in like the tide in the Sound, quietly rippling through Mac's front door in one long thin line, settling themselves on the floor as soon as they could find a spot, their eyes large and round, following my every move as I pointed out the places to sleep, the location of the bathroom.

Outside, Mac directed the drivers to park in the backyard.

Once the waders situated themselves, taking their places as if they'd been assigned seats in school, they rose, one by one, and went into the bathroom.

While they finished, I passed out paper cups of water on the tray that Mac had put out on the kitchen table. Most of the demonstrators were about my age, their faces closed and afraid. I smiled down at them as I handed out water, trying to look reassuring. They took the cups, murmuring *much obliged*. The room hummed with their fear.

"Supper soon," I whispered as I moved about.

"Smells good," said one girl.

"Mac makes a fine gumbo," I said, and a smile played at her lips.

I went into the kitchen and got the seafood out of the icebox and put it into the gumbo. I turned up the heat, and the oysters began to curl at the edges.

About then, Mac and Aaron Henry and some other grown men, the drivers, came up the back steps and in through the kitchen, talking quietly.

"Smells like heaven in here," said Aaron Henry. "Thanks, man."

"I'm sorry I never had you down for supper," said Mac, then stopped, red-faced. "Someday we'll have a nice sit-down, a real meal."

Aaron Henry lifted the lid from the gumbo. "This looks real enough to me. You've outdone yourself, Mac. Sandwiches would have been fine."

Mac grinned, then turned to me. "Let's put the spaghetti on. These folks must be hungry."

"Spaghetti?" one of the men murmured, leaning in.

I took the lid off the sauce and the steam rose.

"Lord, I've died and gone to heaven," said one of the drivers. "We're going to be so full, we won't want to do nothing but sleep tomorrow."

Aaron Henry looked over at me. "And who is this young lady?"

"This is my daughter, Little Feather," said Mac.

Daughter.

"Didn't know you had a daughter, Mac," said Aaron Henry.

Mac put a hand on my shoulder. "Little and I adopted each other a long time ago."

"She's sure enough little," Aaron Henry said. "You need to fatten this girl up."

The men stood around me, smiling. One by one, they extended their hands and we shook. "Little Feather. What kind of name is that?" one asked. "You part Indian?"

"My regular name is Memory Feather," I said. "No Indian that I know of."

"Memory," said Aaron Henry. "You got a good one?"

No one had ever asked me that question. "I think I do."

"Well, remember this night. Remember tomorrow. This is history you're seeing, and you're part of it, Memory Feather." Aaron Henry said. "You're making a contribution. That's something to be proud of, tell your grandchildren about." He smiled, his eyes kind.

I hadn't thought of myself as being *in* history. History lived on Mac's bookshelves, its people larger than life and more heroic or villainous. Cleopatra and Queen Zenobia of Palmyra, Mary Queen of Scots, Joan of Arc, and the head-chopping Henry VIII. George Washington and Patrick Henry and Abraham Lincoln. History wasn't gumbo and spaghetti and pallets on Mac's splintery pine floor in Belle Cote, Mississippi.

Mac nudged me. "Let's make some history, Little, and get this meal on the table."

The water was boiling in the giant pot. I threw in handfuls of spaghetti.

"Five minutes," I said, the words loud against the soft talk in the kitchen, the uneasy silence in the living room.

I fluffed the rice and set it on the table. The butter and cornbread were already out. I peeled off the waxed paper covering the cornbread.

Mac went to turn on a few lamps in the living room, where it had grown dark.

Aaron Henry came up behind him. "Hey, Mac, let's keep it dark up here next to the street," he said and turned off the lamps. Then he looked out over the waders. Some were sitting on the sofa and in the chairs. "Let's everyone sit on the floor," he said. "Better safe than sorry."

There was a collective groan, then a quick shuffle, then silence.

"Almost there," I said to Mac. The waders rose and moved into the dining room, gathering around the table, their hungry eyes waiting for someone to tell them it was all right to eat.

I drained the spaghetti and threw it into the pot of sauce and tossed the mixture. Mac came over and lifted the gumbo pot off the stove and onto the table. Steam rose, and the waders drew closer.

In that instant, Minerva emerged from wherever she'd been hiding and jumped on top of the table, as if to take the first helping. We all broke into laughter, and it was as if the rope that had bound us to silence had been cut. "Whoa, horse, we better get in there before that big old thing eats it all up," said one girl. There was a another burst of laughter. Then everyone started talking at once, cutting up the way young people will do.

I wondered what it would be like to go to school with these girls and boys. Never once had they looked at my hand, never once had they snickered at me, called me the deformed majorette. I liked them immensely.

Aaron Henry cleared his throat, and everyone quieted. "Let's give thanks for our host and hostess and this good meal," he said. There were murmurs of appreciation and smiles. Then Aaron Henry got behind the table and began to talk to God as though he were right there in the room with us. It was a long conversation, so long that I worried the spaghetti would congeal. He began with Mac McFadden and Memory Feather— our kindness, our dedication to the cause of justice and fairness, our hard work to prepare this place of safety and sustain his people on their journey—and ended with a request to keep us all safe as we fought this battle together. Just when I'd given up on the state of the spaghetti, he arrived at amen and started ladling out the food, making a point to give everyone equal portions so that those at the end of the line wouldn't be cheated.

"There's bread pudding and cookies," I announced after everyone was done. There were groans all around, everyone stuffed to the gills. I'd put the cookies on Mac's silver platter in a pretty circular pattern, one cookie overlapping the other, pretty as the head of a giant sunflower.

"Little Feather's famous peanut butter cookies," Mac said, rising from where he and Aaron Henry had been sitting in a dark corner. "Better hurry. They go fast."

There was a scramble, and then one cookie was left. I took it, though I was no longer hungry.

Then I looked up and saw a girl emerge from the shadows. She looked at the cookie in my hand, then quickly sat down. I'd miscalculated.

"I was bringing this one to you," I said quickly and handed it over. When I bent down to give her the cookie, the streetlight outside came on and flashed across her face.

I wasn't surprised to see Leticia among the waders. Mac had told me she'd probably be coming. "That's all right," she said. "You take it."

"I was bringing it to you, Leticia," I said. "Didn't want anybody else to get it." I set it down in front of her. "I'd rather have some of Mac's bread pudding."

"Well then," she said, and took the cookie.

I settled down next to her, glad to see her. Truth was I'd missed her at the gallery, our little projects of arranging and rearranging, our small talk. "How're you liking it up in Clarksdale?" I asked.

"It's all right."

"Are you going to school up there?"

She took a bite of the cookie. "Of course I am, and Mac's been show-ing me some stuff I'll need next year when I get up to that college in Chicago. He wrote for me, got me a scholarship."

"University of Chicago?"

"Sounds right."

"He says you're smart as a whip. He says it would be a crime if you wasted that 'rare conceptual mind' of yours."

"He gave me that talking-to. I said to him, 'Mr. Mac, what do you think you doing, down there in podunk-ville with your little picture gallery?'"

"Bet he didn't like that."

"He said I ought to mind my own little red wagon, not his."

"Cold up there in Chicago. You're going to freeze half to death."

She shrugged. "I'll get me a coat."

"Boots too. They got snow up to your butt."

She smiled. "I love snow. You ever seen it?"

"Sure. I've lived all over.."

I scanned the room. Minerva was making her way through the bodies on the floor, heading for us. "I'm sorry it didn't work out at the gallery."

"Me too."

"My mother was sorry."

"Sorry about what?"

"Sorry you quit. So was I."

"Oh."

Minerva jumped onto Leticia's lap and situated herself, purring.

"She remembers you," I said. "Why did you quit?"

She flashed her eyes at me. "You know."

"*Him?*"

"He was bothering me. I'm not looking to be anybody's fancy girl."

"You got away?"

"This girl's nobody's fool."

"That's good."

She cut her eyes at me. "You could have given me a word of warning."

"I'm sorry. I should have."

She leaned forward, her eyes large and fierce. "You think sorry's good enough, white girl, you've got another think coming. Tell you what's better: justice, that's what's better. Putting cross-burning peckerwoods like that Tony in jail, that's what's better. Making them pay. That's what's better than cookies, or gumbo, or your fancy spaghetti."

I felt the push, the shove, of her words, as if they were a pair of hands on my shoulders.

We eyed each other for a moment. She was sitting directly under the portrait of Tony. It seemed to rise up between us, pushing us apart. Not only was I sorry not to have warned her, I was sorry not to have confronted my mother. Sorrier than sorry. Just a sorry piece of white girl.

In that moment of sorry and more sorry, there was a sudden flash of headlights across the darkened room, the close-up screech of a truck. Aaron Henry jumped to his feet. "Quiet! Everybody down."

A pause, then the burst of shattering glass. A bottle rolled out from under the front curtain and across the pine floor, then came to a slow stop. It had a fuse and the fuse was lit.

"Firebomb!" Aaron Henry shouted. "Run!"

The room froze. Then a girl screamed and everyone scattered, some running for the kitchen, some for the bedrooms. Someone ran to the front door, opened it, then slammed it shut, shouting, "Bunch of them, whole bunch of them!" and ran to the back of the house.

A few went to the back door. "Stay in the house!" Aaron Henry roared, freezing them in their tracks.

In the moment, despite all the commotion, I felt strangely tranquil, as if it were all a slow-motion dream in which Mac—I could tell it was Mac because he was the largest man in the room—dove for the bottle, opened the front door, and threw it back out into the yard, in the direction of a truck, which had parked in the front yard on an upward incline, with its lights pointed up onto the porch. The bottle landed in the back of the truck, shattered, and exploded. Smoke filled the yard, and the truck expelled the men in it.

One of them brandished a fist at Mac. "You'll pay for this, fag."

"Not if I see you first," Mac roared. He slammed the front door, locked it. He quickly scanned the living room and bolted in my direction. He grabbed my arm, half-dragging, half-carrying me to the bathroom. He dumped me into the tub. "Stay here, lock the door," he said. "Don't turn on the light." Then he was gone.

I crept out of the tub, locked the door, and got back into the cold porcelain. I could hear him in his bedroom, telling someone to get under the bed, then rummaging in his nightstand next to the bathroom wall. Then a metallic click.

"Minerva," I shouted through the wall. "Find Minerva."

Someone rattled the bathroom door, but I didn't move, wishing I had a bed to crawl under.

"Memory Feather," someone, a girl, whispered through the door.

I leapt up and opened it, and pulled Leticia in. "Get in the tub with me." I fumbled at her arm in the dark, then caught her hand with my good one. "Come on."

In the tub we clutched each other like each wanted to crawl up inside the other's skin. Leticia moaned and sprayed me with spit, pulled at my hair. Then quietly screamed when it came away in her hands.

When the gun went off, a single shot, we both jumped. "Peckerwoods!"

Leticia screamed. "Goddamn peckerwoods." Then we both broke out in one high-pitched wail that seemed to come, not from our own mouths, or even from the tub and room itself, but from somewhere under the house.

After what seemed like several hours, there was a voice at the bathroom door. "Let me in, Little."

I leapt up and unlocked the door. Mac came in and took us in his arms. "It's all right. I scared them off. They're gone now."

"Minerva?"

"Probably jumped out the kitchen window. She's fine. You know Minerva."

Leticia began to hum then. "Worrying about a silly old cat," she said, humming. "White girl worrying herself about a cat."

Then she pulled away from Mac and ran out of the bathroom, still humming.

Mac sat down on the toilet. He held on to both my arms now, looking at me in the moonlight.

"Do you think they'll be back?" I asked. "Do you think they'll be over in Biloxi tomorrow, waiting? How did those men know? How'd they find out?"

Mac shook his head. He slumped, let go of me, and put his head in his hands.

"It was *Tony*," I whispered.

"Don't be ridiculous."

"Yes it was. You know it was. My fault for telling. All my fault."

Mac stood up so suddenly I almost fell backward. "*Quit it*, Little. I'm going to walk you home now. Your mother should be home soon. We'll go out the back. I ought to check on Miss Bess too."

"Did you call the police?"

"That'd be jumping from the frying pan into the fire."

In the living room, Aaron Henry was taping a piece of cardboard to the broken front window. Beyond him, the damaged truck still sat in the yard with its lights on.

The police did not come. No one called them, it seemed. Perhaps the neighbors were used to strange goings-on at Mac's house; perhaps they thought he'd gotten his proper comeuppance. Perhaps they were simply afraid.

On the walk home, Mac and I skirted through Miss Bess's backyard, which had turned into a jungle. Mosquitoes buzzed around us; weeds caught at my bare legs. The lights blazed inside her house. Mac tapped at her back door. When she peered out from behind the curtain and saw him, she opened the door a crack. He had a few quiet words with her and we continued on our way.

When we reached my house, Mac came in with me. Minerva was sitting upright on the kitchen counter cleaning her belly. She'd polished off half the meatloaf my mother had made. Mac checked the house, then came into the kitchen, opened our junk drawer and pulled out a pen and a piece of scrap paper. He scribbled a name and phone number on it and handed it to me. "It's a lawyer," he said, "in case I get locked up tomorrow."

"I thought you weren't going."

"I wouldn't miss it for the world," he said.

AFTER MAC LEFT, MINERVA and I sat on the living room couch waiting for my mother to come home. Minerva groomed her tail, then all four paws. I simply sat, my heart still pounding.

When my mother came in, her hair was tousled, her face flushed, as if she'd been driving with the windows open.

I'd left one small lamp on. Her mouth dropped open when she saw me sitting there in partial darkness. "Mem. Oh. What are you doing up? It's late," she said, smoothing her hair. I rose and turned on the overhead light. She blinked.

I stood up, saw my face reflected in her eyes.

"I changed your sheets today," I said.

Then I began my song. Of betrayal, of disgust. I spit it all in her face, the sores in my mouth screaming, the acid from the spaghetti sauce stinging my unruly tongue.

She stood there through it all. When I finished, she went into the kitchen, and I followed. She drew herself a glass of water and drank it down. She put the glass in the sink, then stood looking out the window.

Finally, she turned to me."Sometimes I think you've lost your mind, Mem," she said. "Tony gets up at the crack of dawn and works hard on this house. I told him he could take a nap every now and then if he needed to. My goodness, that's the least we can do, after all he's done for us." Under the overhead fluorescent light, a glaze had folded over her eyes like a translucent cataract.

Minerva eyed us from under the kitchen table, her gold eyes lazy and hooded. She had caught a lizard. Minerva was fond of lizards. When she caught one, she would hold it in her mouth for a good long while before eating it, and that glazed, almost pleasant look—the same look that flickered across my mother's face—would belie her appetite, her pleasure, the fact that a small twitching tail was hanging out of the side of her mouth.

On monday night tony drifted back into Belle Cote. By then, Mac's household had returned to normal, the blasted-out truck towed away. The beach at Biloxi had exploded into a free-for-all, a bunch of white men with pistols and billy clubs attacking the waders and anyone in town who looked like them, while the police sat back and watched it happen. Several waders had been shot, and more beaten to a bloody pulp. Mac escaped with a few bruises and a chipped front tooth, which he said matched my mother's.

The Biloxi beaches wouldn't be open to everyone until seven years later, and that would be under court order.

XV.

———

ON TUESDAY I WALKED to the Harris County Library straight from school and studied up on rat poison, or rodenticide, which causes internal bleeding, resulting in death by anemia, and has the advantage of causing the subject to die calmly. It was also handy. Tony himself had used it to kill the rats in our shed, and my mother had stored a good-sized bottle of it under the kitchen cabinet. According to the dosage for rats (a large rat, I judged, weighed approximately two pounds) multiplied by eighty-five to equal Tony's 170 pounds, I estimated that there was enough left in the skull-and-crossbones-marked bottle to kill two or three Tonys if need be.

There was also strychnine, which, when inhaled, swallowed, or absorbed through the eyes or mouth, promised convulsions and eventually death through asphyxiation. The downsides of both rodenticide and strychnine, I suspected, were that both would taste terrible, and if not terrible, terribly odd, and therefore be readily discernible, even if cloaked in something tasty. There was also the autopsy to consider.

As serendipity would have it, the library shelf on run-of-the-mill poisons also contained a book on poisonous plants. There are more poisonous plants than I could have ever conjured in my wildest dreams:

hemlock and deadly nightshades like jimsonweed; white snakeroot and the rosary pea (as in, you better say the rosary loud and clear before even touching a tiny seed from one of those). On and on.

I narrowed it down to oleander, which grew in Mac's backyard, and angel's trumpet, which grew in the tangle of Miss Bess's. Both had the one critical advantage over rodenticide and strychnine of being impossible to trace back to the perpetrator. Tony might have walked by one of any number of oleander bushes, which bloomed to beat the band all over Belle Cote every summer; he might have absent-mindedly plucked a leaf to chew, the way men did back in those days. Or he could have been drawn, as I had been on occasion, to the heavenly scent in the early evening of an angel's trumpet and pulled one of the tulip-shaped flowers down to his face to smell more deeply, possibly tasting a bit of the pollen or tearing off a corner of the furled cone for a quick taste.

I didn't need to study up on oleander. Mac had a giant bush on his back fence line. In June, the blooms exploded in a spectacular fuchsia, which, when clustered among the oily green leaves, looked like flamboyant bridal bouquets. Last summer I'd asked Mac if I could cut some of the blossoms and float them in a glass bowl. He said absolutely not, warning me that they were lethal; even handling them might result in the gravest of effects.

"Like what?" I asked.

"Paralysis and death," he said. "Even the smoke from burning it can be fatal," he added. "*Nerium oleander*. It can stop the heart. *Zap, zap.*"

Angel's trumpet, of the genus *Brugmansia*, attracted me more. It was a softer, sweeter plant, more adapted to mixing; it also produced delirium and hallucinations leading to death. In the jungles of South America centuries ago, it was used to drug wives and slaves before they were buried alive with the head of the family. There were reports of men amputating parts of themselves, notably their penises (which seemed in Tony's case poetic justice), after eating the seeds or leaves of angel's trumpet. All this before tachycardia set in!

How much would be needed I didn't know, and one doesn't want to make many inquiries when planning on poisoning someone, even someone so richly deserving as Tony. I would need to make a dish, a stew or soup of some sort, in which the ingredients were well blended. I'd boil the angel's trumpet, taking care not to breathe the steam from the pot, and add it in. (I made a mental note to throw away the pot just to be on the safe side.) I suspected it would taste sweeter than oleander, since oleander, with little to no scent, wasn't even in the ballpark with the headiness of an angel's trumpet blossom.

But how to feed it to Tony without feeding it to my mother or Mac or myself? This seemed the hardest part. Maybe a lunch. Maybe I could just leave it out for him, forge a note from my mother saying, *Please eat this, Tony dear. I made it especially for you.*

There was also the technical problem of not being able to taste the concoction to check for bitterness. If he didn't like it, he might not eat it, or eat enough of it, unless she, or maybe I, were there. I'd need to arrange to be there at lunch and tell him *I* had made it. He couldn't refuse, and even if it tasted strange, he'd have to eat it to be polite. He wanted to get on my good side, I could tell. What he wanted from me, I wasn't sure (stupid of me not to think of the money, but money wasn't on my mind; I had bigger fish to fry).

Since I didn't know the quantity, I decided to err on the heavy side, to boil up more blossoms rather than fewer. (I'd have to remember to be careful about handling them and not be seduced by their innocent sweetness. Use tongs!) The recipe was still in the developmental stages, but it would need to involve robust flavors. Onion and garlic came to mind. Tony's favorite food, I'd learned from Mac, was lasagna. Maybe, instead of a soup or stew, a baked lasagna with lots of the *authentic* sauce he liked plus buckets of cheese to soak up any oddness of flavor. For an added kick, I could use the water I boiled the angel's trumpet blossoms in for the noodles.

The problem was that I'd have to wait until the angel's trumpet bloomed, which wouldn't be until early summer. What I didn't know then, and what I wish I had known, was that, in addition to their blossoms, the stems and roots of both plants are poisonous. I didn't have to wait for the angel's trumpet or the oleander to bloom. I could have gone ahead with my plan that April, which, had it been successful, would have made all the difference.

But I waited, knowing that in early summer the angel's trumpet bush in Miss Bess's back lot would swell to a delicate green and lift up its arms with its bulbous down-turned pods. One warm night they would open to the pale yellow flowers big as a man's hands. Then it would be time.

Meanwhile, Tony abruptly stopped working at our house. The shelves in my mother's closet were left unfinished, the ladder put away. Instead, he began to focus his energies on the gallery, displacing Minerva from her sunny front window. He whitewashed the dingy walls. He caulked all the windows and doors, and repaired a leak under the bathroom lavatory. My mother sang his praises every night, reciting long lists of Tony's latest accomplishments as if to chastise me.

For her part, my mother decided to become mother of the year. She came home from work in the evenings carrying a grocery sack, put on her apron with the monster crawfish on front that Mac had given her the previous Christmas, and miracle of all miracles, began to cook supper. All of this she did in good spirits, calling me into the kitchen to chat while she worked, speculating on the news of the day: the fate of Francis Gary Powers and the U-2 spy plane shot down by Russia, whether Woolworth's in Greensboro, North Carolina, would ever integrate its lunch counter, the rumors of college students called Freedom Riders preparing to head south come summer. In early May she clapped her hands and shouted out hallelujah when Walter Cronkite announced the legalization of a new pill to prevent pregnancy. After supper, the two of us would watch *Perry Mason* or play honeymoon bridge. It was as if my mother of our El Camino days had been plopped down safe and sound from a trip to the moon.

All of which vastly improved my everyday life. I came straight home after school and busied myself doing homework in peace at the kitchen table, knowing my El Camino mother would soon be home. My relief was so great I even considered aborting my plan. But the undeniable fact was that every Monday and Tuesday, my mother's days off, she and Tony would disappear into thin air and my stomach would do flip-flops all day. (Despite my mother's cooking, my appetite hadn't come out of hiding. I picked at food, made a show of eating.) Sometimes I'd see the two of them out in Mac's sailboat, small stick figures, tacking back and forth across the horizon. Sometimes they would take a picnic and sail over to Ship Island.

On Ship Island days, I would awake to my mother's hurried preparations of a picnic lunch. These lunches were extravagant affairs, with cheeses and salami and olive salad from Central Grocery in New Orleans, pralines from the Praline Connection in the Marigny, a bottle of chardonnay or a six-pack of Jax.

One morning, I tiptoed into the kitchen. I wanted to catch her in the midst of her anticipation, her plots and plans, thinking she might confess, offer some slight gesture connoting shame, some sense of wrongdoing.

She was standing on her left leg, her right foot planted at the side of her left knee, looking even more like an egret than usual. She had on a blue two-piece swimsuit, her hair pulled back from her face in a head-band like a young girl.

I was right up on her when she sensed my presence and whirled around, the knife she'd used to cut salami falling to the floor.

"Mem! You scared me. What's the matter with you? Why are you sneaking up on me like that?"

"Just seeing what you're making for your date with Tony."

Her hand flew to her hair. She pulled at it, as if she were about to tear it from her head. "Tony and I are *friends*, Mem. Get that into your head. *Friends.* Like Mac and I are friends."

"Why don't you take Mac to Ship Island?"

"Because he doesn't sail, you know that. And he has to be at the gallery when I'm off. I'm getting sick and tired of you questioning my every move. I work hard. I take care of you. I have a right to a little fun."

"More than a little," I muttered.

The slap took me by surprise. My mother had never hit me. The blow landed not on my cheek, where she'd probably aimed it, but on the side of my head. My ear rang with it.

"What the hell is wrong with you, Mem? Why are you intent on making everybody's life miserable? Have you gone mental?"

My ear pounded like a drum. Her voice seemed to come from a distance. "He's ruined everything, that's why. You've both ruined everything."

Something, a sadness, washed over her face. She closed her eyes, then opened them slowly, as if they had weights attached to them.

"Everything," she said. "What everything?"

"Me. Mac. Our *family*," I said. "Do I really need to remind you?"

She didn't answer, turning her back to me. She wrapped the food for Ship Island into waxed paper and put the packets of waxed paper into a paper sack. She walked around me, down the hall, and into the bathroom.

I went back into my room and shut the door. I heard the toilet flush, then her footsteps down the hall and into the kitchen. A pause. Then the front door clicked shut, and she was gone.

TUESDAYS THROUGH THURSDAYS, WHILE my mother and Tony occupied the gallery, Mac also managed to disappear. He spent more time now in Clarksdale helping Aaron Henry with plans for voter drives and demonstrations, sometimes coming home with furniture and paintings he'd picked up along the way, sometimes returning with nothing but a sheet-metal face and bloodshot eyes. The previous winter, he'd launched into building a finished room below his house, a large office for himself complete with a television, a leather sofa, a mahogany desk so dark it seemed almost black, a twin bed in a back corner behind a paper screen. In contrast to the sweep and light of the upstairs, the room was dark, with only two high windows on the side next to the driveway. The walls were lined with charcoal sketches of early sailboats, the kind that carried tea and sugar and millions of men, women, and children through the stormy seas of the Transatlantic trade routes. The sketches had been his father's. They seemed an odd choice of decoration since Mac himself hadn't set foot on a sailboat since his family drowned. After the storm passed, the boat had been retrieved undamaged with its sails up, though without its owners, whose bodies washed up several days later. Mac had taken his parents' deaths particularly hard, my mother said: He'd just told them some things about himself that upset them, had told them over spring break and then had gone back up to Harvard. They'd said they would never again be able to hold their heads up in Belle Cote, he needed to go and never come back. His sister said he'd ruined her life, that nobody would ever marry her now. So he felt responsible. Why were the sails up? His parents had been sailing since they were children. If they'd seen a storm coming, they should have taken them down.

Why Mac kept the sailboat I still don't know. My mother said he liked to offer it to friends. I sensed it was more than that. Maybe he wanted a tangible memory of his family, the way my hand reminded me of my father. Perhaps it was a puzzle he was still trying to work out, an unsolvable equation.

Mac took to his below-room the way a hermit crab takes to its shell. By late spring he appeared to have shrunk by several inches to accommodate the room's low ceiling. Outside, he walked with his head down, as if studying something interesting along the ground; the ebb and flow, the grand gesture of him, the man who gave shelter to the young demonstrators, who picked up Molotov cocktails in his bare hands, gone. His usual tan faded; even his golden hair dulled to a waxy yellow.

The morning my mother slapped me I decided to skip school and pay Mac a visit. I was hoping he'd take a walk with me along the Sound or maybe we'd go fishing in the Bay. *Wait,* Minerva called out from behind me, and I stopped to let her catch up. The Ranchero was in the driveway, looking more ramshackle than ever. First I went upstairs. The middle door was open so I called out, my nose plastered to the screen, which smelled of rust. When no one answered, I pulled open the screen. The living room was a mess from bottom to top, clothes strewn about, a trail of what looked like dried coffee crusted across one of the Oriental rugs, ashtrays overflowing, the smell of Tony's Brylcreem permeating everything. The curtains were drawn, giving the place a spooky look, as if I had come upon the scene of some long-ago crime, some floating sadness.

I backed out of the living room onto the porch. It was approaching midday, and the sudden burst of sunshine dizzying. I sat down in Mac's rocking chair right outside the front door. I had the jitters from the two cups of coffee I'd had in lieu of breakfast. A buzzing filled my ears as if a coven of crickets had taken up residence inside my head. I touched my ear, which still throbbed from my mother's hand. Some strands of my hair spun out onto a ray of light and floated to the porch floor. My hair was in a worse state than ever. Bare patches had opened up at the crown.

The air seemed too thick. A giant date palm scratched like sandpaper on the side of the porch. A ragtag squirrel appeared on the porch railing, its tail twitching fitfully. *Cheat cheat.*

When I felt better, I got up and went downstairs. I turned over an empty flowerpot to stand on and peered into Mac's below-room through the one of the high windows. He was asleep at his desk, his head down on one arm, the other hanging at his side like deadwood. A shipwreck dashed against rocks. Next to him an empty bottle of Seagram's.

Minerva, who'd followed me, stopped in her tracks at the sight of me standing on the pot, as if I were some exotic form of prey. *Why?*

I knocked on the windowpane, louder than intended. Mac jumped up and surveyed the room in one quick, darting motion, as if there were something in it that needed concealing.

I turned the doorknob. The door was locked. I knocked again, this time on the door.

The light hit Mac hard in the face when he opened the door. He blinked and glowered at me. No good morning, no hello, just a look that bespoke pure aggravation. His nose was red as a fire truck. He smelled of rotten apples.

"Don't you need to be at work?" I asked, attempting a smile. "Rise and shine!"

He scratched his head as if my question puzzled him, then said, "Why aren't you in school?"

"School's out," I lied. "Want to do something? We could go over to Granny's Kitchen for some coffee to wake you up, then take a walk." I took a step over the threshold, but he didn't move to let me in.

"Not today."

He tried to close the door. I put my foot in the space between us. "What's wrong with you, Mac? You're acting like a zombie."

Minerva slid between us, purring, rubbing Mac's ankle. *Father. Mother.*

"Little," he said, his voice tired, "you need to find some friends your own age."

I looked up at him, seeing what he didn't want me to see: that he was sad and he was afraid and he was exhausted. I should have reached out my hand then, I should have comforted him. Instead, I turned and walked away, following Minerva as she picked her way through the oak leaves in Mac's side yard.

The leaves on the ground were a moldy gray, just pushed out by the tree's new green growth. That spring Mac had let them have their way. Now they'd smothered the St. Augustine grass, which, as a consequence of his neglect, was dead underneath, the blades brown against the sandy ground.

As I rounded the corner of the house, Minerva stopped dead in her tracks, then made for the trunk of Mac's biggest oak tree. She scrambled up onto a huge twisted branch, disappearing behind a cluster of new leaves.

And there he was.

He was in a hurry, almost colliding with me. He was carrying a paper cup of coffee and a brown sack speckled in grease.

"Well, now, Birdy the busybody." He spit out the words, then grinned from ear to ear as if he hadn't said them. He had on a pair of shorts, his shirt unbuttoned, the cross tangled in the brush of his chest.

"I thought you were going to Ship Island," I said, then moved aside, up against the house, to let him pass.

"Right now I'm bringing Mac coffee and a biscuit," he said, leaning in so that I could feel the heat of his breath on my cheeks. Stale coffee cloaked in Beech-Nut gum.

He moved closer, then closer still, his arm now up against the wall, pinning me in, grinding his gum. "Busybodies ought to mind their own business." He glanced behind him; up in the tree where Minerva waited, only her ears comically visible. "That damn cat. Nothing but trouble with a tail."

He spoke so softly I almost didn't hear. It was in that moment, the sinister scurry of the phrasing, his lazy look at Minerva, that the heat of my anger at Tony turned to a block of ice in the dead center of my chest.

I began to wheeze, my breath squeaky as an old door handle. I glanced up at Minerva, but she'd disappeared behind the leaves. My breath came fast and shallow, fast and faster still.

He leaned in closer. "You like your cat?"

I tried to speak, but the words clotted in my throat. The blue, blue sky darkened to gray, as if a storm were coming in.

I WOKE UP PROPPED against the side of the house, one arm, skinned and flung outward against the downspout of a gutter, amuck with wet leaves. Minerva sat on my lap purring and kneading frantically, her claws bloodying my legs.

Mac was slapping my face.

"Quit it. How many people are going to slap me today?" I pushed away his hand.

"What on earth? Did you trip over the gutter? Are you hurt?"

I floated above him. "Inhaler. Get it."

He leapt to his feet. "Where?"

"Bath...room."

He left running. Then it began to snow. Snow in May?

When I awoke the second time, Mac was holding me in his lap on the ground and the inhaler was between my teeth. I pushed it away, my breath easier now. The sky was a deep blue. A white cloud drifted over. A mockingbird called out. *Spring spring.* Minerva rubbed my bare leg, purring. *Now then.* Mac rocked me back and forth, humming a little, as if I were a baby he was trying to get to sleep. "Skin and bones, nothing but skin and bones. How'd she get this way?" he said to Minerva. "What happened to my sweet girl? What happened to her?" His voice lifted off into the tree above, astonished, sorrowful, as though I'd just died in his arms.

"Let me up," I said.

He loosened his grip on me and I sat up, then got to my feet. The world spun for a moment and I staggered.

"Come inside and lie down," he said, leading me to the door of his below-room. "Come in and rest."

I went inside into the cool dark, Minerva trailing behind. He moved the paper screen aside and pushed me down on the twin bed. "Stay there," he said. "I'm getting some water and a wet cloth. I'll be back." He thrust my inhaler at me. "If you get woozy, take another puff."

The bed was softer than any I'd ever slept in, the pillow cool. Minerva situated herself in the crook of my arm.

I awoke with a washcloth clammy against my forehead, my inhaler in the palm of my good hand, a cotton blanket on top of me, tucked in on the sides. I pushed myself up on my elbows. A sliver of sun from one of the high windows spliced my mid-torso so that, when I looked down, it appeared I'd been cut in half. Minerva raised herself from the crook of my arm, yawned and stretched.

I sat up and let my legs dangle over the edge of the bed. When I stood, the dizziness returned and I sat back down. As I did, Mac came through the door, a ham sandwich in one hand and a Barq's Root Beer in the other. Eyeing the Barq's, I was instantly thirsty.

He kicked the door shut. "Here," he said. "Eat something."

He'd bathed and shaved. His shorts were neatly creased, and he had on a fresh shirt. His hair, still wet, was neatly combed back from his forehead. I'd never known anyone, I thought dreamily, with a nicer head of hair than Mac's.

I downed the Barq's, then took the sandwich. I hadn't eaten anything since the night before, but the ham tasted metallic. I let the sandwich slide into my lap.

Mac rolled his big office chair over to the bed and sat down. "Now," he said, "I'm not going to let you out of this room until you tell me what's the matter." He leaned over and brushed a bread crumb from my cheek. "Whatever this is, we're going to fix it."

It was the gesture, the brushing of the crumb from my cheek, so much a father's gesture, instinctive, gentle, without thought, that made me tell.

In the telling, Mac's lips disappeared even as his mouth opened slightly, showing the tips of his teeth, as if he were about to bite into something or someone. As the telling went on, he rolled his chair backward, away from me.

I stopped before the pillowcase, knowing it would be too much.

He sat there, his eyes shifting from object to object in the room. Finally he looked up. "Well, you've got yourself quite a story there, Little. Quite a story. Now let me tell you a story.

"Once there was a little orphan boy who lived by his wits on the streets. He tap-danced for pennies, wrapped himself in newspaper to stay warm, ate out of garbage cans. He posed for an artist over and over until he was sick to death of posing. Then he started shining shoes at a barbershop and learned to cut hair and make a living. And I'm not telling you the half of it. Tony's struggled tooth and nail his whole life. He doesn't know how to be anything other than what he is; he doesn't know how to act right because nobody ever taught him. He takes too much because he never had enough."

I said, "An orphan boy? So his father wasn't even alive when he came? Bet he wasn't even a barber. Tony lies. Bet he never rode an elephant either, the way he said he did."

"He can't bear to think of his father as being dead."

"And there's the sick mother. Remember the mother with shigella? Not to speak of him and *my* mother, and I haven't told *you* the half of it."

"Oh, Little, Tony flirts. He doesn't know how else to act. It's what he's done all his life. It's why he's still alive after the childhood he had. He loves us all, we're all he has."

"He lies."

"Of course he does. How else was he going to survive? Can't you be more charitable, Little? Haven't I taught you to be kind? Walk a mile in his shoes."

"He sent those rednecks the other night. He sent them, you know he did."

"He told me he didn't."

"He lies. You said it yourself."

"Not about this. Tony would never do anything to hurt me."

"Then who?"

"Anybody could have told them."

"Anybody?"

"Miss Bess. She could have. Or those awful women you dragged over here."

"Miss Bess would *never* do such a thing and you know it. She worships the ground you walk on. Look around you, look at *him*, Mac. You've been blind as a bat."

At that moment the one thin ray of sun from one of the high windows sliced his face. On one side, his mouth gave way ever so slightly, betraying an acknowledgment of what I was saying; on the other, there was a tightening, a hardening against my words.

"I think you should go now," he said. He went to the door and opened it.

That's when I almost said it: the pillowcase. The words surged up into my throat, squeezed through the spaces between my teeth, knocked on the door of my lips. Then I swallowed them. Bitter pills.

Instead I said, "They're at Ship Island right now. Right this very minute they're at Ship Island having a stinking picnic and a bottle of your good wine. Having themselves a fine old time at your expense."

"Don't you think I know that?" He motioned for me to go. "I hope they have a lovely time. I hope they have a marvelous time. I love them both."

"I hope he drowns on the way back," I said. "I hope they capsize and he drowns."

"He probably will if the boat goes down," said Mac. "Tony can't swim."

XVI.

───────

IT WAS TURNING DUSK as I walked home, the twisted limbs of the oaks in Mac's and Miss Bess's yards black against the setting sun. Minerva found a fallen nest of resurrection moss and pounced on it. Then she stopped what she was doing and looked up at me.

Things are going to get much worse.

It was the longest sequence of words I'd ever heard her utter. I stopped short, thinking I'd misunderstood.

"What?"

She pounced on the moss a second time.

Mac's story about Tony's boyhood had given me pause. I'd always taken what Mac told me as the gospel truth. Was there simply a spoiled part of Tony, like a swath of mold on a piece of cheese? Cut it off, and the cheese is fine again?

Or was he like curdled milk, sour through and through?

Now, the answer to these questions seems clear as day. Back then, though, I could only sense the web of deceit that was being spun.

What I didn't realize is that we were already caught.

Later, much later, the private detective I hired would find that Tony's mother, along with his father, had died when Tony was eight, both by a neat shot to the forehead in their small double shotgun in the Faubourg Marigny. The weapon was Tony's father's pistol. It might have gone down on the police blotter as a murder/suicide except for the fact that whoever had done the shooting had also set the place on fire, killing a family of eight living in the other side of the double, including a newborn baby and twin toddlers. Luckily, just minutes before, Tony's father had sent him down the street to the shoe-repair shop on the corner to pick up a pair of boots he'd had resoled. The police, said the report, surmised burglary— which was only a conjecture since the fire had destroyed everything. A Black man was picked up a half hour later walking up Esplanade, the pistol still warm in his jacket pocket. He claimed he'd found it in the weeds of the neutral ground that ran down the middle of the street. He said he was on his way to the police station on Lafayette to turn it in. Of course, no one believed a word of it. He died in the mercy seat at Angola.

Tony was taken to St. Vincent's Orphanage on Magazine. One night, when he was twelve, he escaped by sneaking out in the back of a milk truck and ended up in the Quarter, living by his wits. A street artist on Jackson Square, a woman of sixty, spotted him slumped on the steps in front of the Cabildo and saw that, under all that dirt and the permanent sneer on his face, he was a beautiful boy, so beautiful that she took him in, asking nothing of him but to model for her. The paintings of him sold like hotcakes; the artist, whose name was Frances Washburn, became famous for them. She rewarded Tony by offering him (for a substantial fee) to other painters or purported painters, some of whom used him as model and some for other purposes. He must have quickly become accustomed to thinking of himself as something of use, an aesthetic object to whom someone else's desires were attached. Once he came to this realization, he found he could make those desires move here and there at will because of what never changed, and that was his physical beauty. How easy it was, almost effortless, really. A smile, the downward turn of those impressive eyelashes, a gesture: how he could touch his own mouth and make your breath catch in your throat. It was seductive, this power of his, and once he realized he possessed it, he decided to make his way in the world easier. Simple.

And this was how Mac came to know him, through Frances Washburn's painting and then, later, through Frances Washburn herself, who by then had lost track of her protégé the way a spider may lose track of the fly who wriggles out of the web with nothing much left but its antennae, a scrap of brain cells, and a pair of eyes to see where it could next light.

THE LIGHTS WERE ON in my house, the windows open to the night. Minerva turned tail and disappeared into the shadows, a piece of moss trailing from her whiskers. As I drew closer, I heard my mother and Tony going at it. They weren't shouting the way my mother and father used to do, but rather hissing at each other like geese vying for territory. I peered through the front window. My mother was standing in the middle of the living room, her hair bedraggled, her arms crossed. Tony was slouched down on the couch, his feet on the coffee table. They still had on their swimsuits.

"It's not my money," said my mother. "It's Mem's."

Tony jumped up from the couch. "You mean to tell me that girl got *all* that stinking money and you can't get a thin dime? I don't believe it."

"Believe it or not, it's true."

"Why didn't you tell me?"

"Well, for one thing, it's none of your damn business," said my mother.

"I'll pay you back on time and you can put it back in the bank. She'll never know."

"There's no way you're able to pay back that kind of money, Tony."

"Sister, how the hell do *you* know what I can pay back and what I can't? You're saying I'm a slouch? You're saying I don't work hard? This damn house would be falling into the ground if it wasn't for me."

"Don't call me sister. I paid you for the work. Mac and I have both been paying you good money. Why'd you go and borrow five thousand dollars from a bunch of thugs? What do you need that kind of money for?"

"It was seed money. I thought I could turn it into something big."

My mother stamped her bare foot. A bowl on the coffee table quivered. "You *gambled* it away, that's what you did. How could you be so stupid?"

Tony rose from the sofa, kicking aside the coffee table. He lurched toward her, his hand raised. "You're calling me stupid?"

I ran for the front door and burst through. Tony froze, his hand still in the air.

"Don't you hit my mother," I said in a voice I didn't recognize, a voice that seemed to come from far behind me, deeper and more resonant than mine. "Don't you touch a hair on her head."

My mother walked to the screen door and opened it and looked at Tony. "Get out."

He dropped his arm, or rather he flung it down as if he wanted to rid himself of it. He walked toward the door, then paused in front of my mother. He tossed back a lock of hair that had fallen over his eyes. His eyes slid over me. "This girl of yours, she's a piece of work, a real piece of work."

"Don't you talk about Mem like that. Now get out of here." My mother held the door open.

"I'm gone," he said, glaring at me, then her. "I'm long gone."

And then he was.

My mother latched the screen, shut and locked the front door. "Are you hungry?" she asked brightly, as if nothing had happened. She glided into the kitchen, not lifting her eyes.

I followed her. After the dimly lit living room, the kitchen light made me squint. She was standing at the sink looking out the window.

"Mother," I said, the word strange and awkward. I never called her Mother, never called her anything when speaking to her. It would have been like addressing a piece of myself.

She didn't move for a while. Then she turned to look at me. "Oh, Mem, people make mistakes. People get angry. Nothing to worry yourself over. I don't know why I let Tony get under my skin so. He's nothing but a big baby." She reached for a dish towel on the kitchen counter and dabbed at her eyes. "Now then, what's to eat? How about eggs and grits? We'll have breakfast for supper. We can eat in front of the TV."

"He doesn't seem like a baby to me," I said.

She looked at me thoughtfully. "Well, I guess he wouldn't seem that way to you. You're still a baby yourself."

"You know that's not true," I said.

At that moment, there was a knock at the door. We both jumped.

"Stay here," said my mother and headed into the living room. I was right behind her. She turned on the porch light and opened the door a crack.

He was leaning against the door, his lips brushing the screen. "Listen, Virginia, I'm sorry. I'm just scared. I'm scared half to death." His voice broke.

My mother pulled me toward the screen. "She's the one you need to apologize to. She's the one you called a piece of work."

He mashed his whole face up against the screen, his lips two parallel slugs. "Look, Birdy, I was a jerk. I don't know what gets into me."

My mother poked me in the ribs. "Tell Tony you accept his apology."

"Well, I don't."

"Of course you do. Tony's sorry."

"You bet he is," I said under my breath.

She didn't hear me. She was too busy unlatching the screen. I snatched at her arm. She flung off my hand in one impatient motion. She stepped out into the busy night, then reached behind her to shut the inside door.

I headed back toward the kitchen and put my head down on the table, my breath coming hard. Minerva was scratching at the back door. When I went to let her in, I could hear my mother and Tony laughing softly on our front porch. The click of a lighter and cigarette smoke snaked its way around the corner of the house.

Minerva came in and said she was starving. I was opening a can of cat food when the phone rang.

It was Mac, who'd called to tell my mother I'd fainted dead away not once but twice outside his door. And by the way, he asked, where was Tony? He wasn't home yet and the boat was in the slip.

I told him my mother was busy talking to Tony; I'd relay that information myself when I could pry her away from him.

"Well, pry her away then. Have her call me. I think we need to take
you to a specialist in the City. They can do wonders with asthma these
days. Who knows? Maybe you're allergic to cats. I had a friend who had
to get rid of his."

"I'm not getting rid of Minerva."

As if summoned, Minerva began to gnaw at my toes.

"Well, have your mother call me, and tell Tony supper's ready," said
Mac, sounding brisk and energetic, as if my spells of breathlessness
earlier in the day had popped his bubble of lethargy.

I hung up and headed back into the living room. Minerva first tried
to trip me, and failing that, she let out a muted yowl and ran back into
the kitchen. I heard her jump onto the kitchen counter, then the can of
food hit the floor, then the soft thud as she jumped down.

I opened the door. My mother and Tony sat on the front steps
between the two giant pots of geraniums. They were smoking and staring out into the night. Lightning bugs twinkled across the yard like
low-slung stars. A bullfrog croaked *Come TO me, come TO me*, in his
hopeful monotone. The pines sighed as the breeze from the Sound
worried their branches.

"Mac called. He wants Tony to come home to supper, and he wants
you to call him back."

For a moment they didn't move. Then they gathered themselves
reluctantly, in slow motion, as if they were two very old people. They
parted without a word, my mother turning to come inside, Tony heading out of the yard, across Miss Bess's, toward Mac's.

In the doorway, my mother stopped to watch Tony go. A single tear
rolled down her cheek, and she wiped it away. That's when it occurred to
me that she might be in love. That she too might be trapped.

Inside, she went into the bathroom and began to run water for a bath.

I followed her and opened the bathroom door. She was peeling off
her swimsuit, her body plastered with sand. She tried to cover herself
with her hands.

"For god's sake, Mem," she said, "don't I have anywhere to go in this house to get away from you?"

"How about you and Tony run off together and be rid of me forever."

"Have you completely lost your mind? I'm really about ready to send you to Whitfield, Mem. I'm dead serious."

"Hey, that'll work too; that'll work just fine, so convenient. Declare me incompetent. Then you can steal my money and give it all to Tony. Perfect. Just perfect."

"Leave me alone," she said, stepping into the tub. "Get the hell out of here."

"Call Mac," I said and walked out, leaving the bathroom door open behind me.

I went into the kitchen. Minerva had smeared cat food all over the floor. I wiped it up with the kitchen sponge, taking pleasure in the fact that my mother would have a fit that I was using the sponge we washed dishes with to clean the floor. Then I took six eggs from the icebox to scramble and put on enough grits for the both of us. My mother was always famished when she came in from a day at Ship Island.

It seemed odd to be preparing food for her with the barbed wire of words between us. But I wanted her to remember the *me* of her, the Memory Feather of the El Camino, the small warm body against her own in the bed with the broken springs. We were a team, a tribe of two, she used to call us.

She was in the bathroom a good long time. Then she went straight into her room, shut the door, and popped the lock into place.

When the grits thickened, I put a lid on the pot and turned off the burner. I went and knocked on her door. There was no response. I knocked again, then said through the door, "The grits are done. Are you ready for me to start the eggs?'

"I'm not hungry," she said through the door. "I'm going to bed."

"I made grits for both of us."

"I'll eat them for breakfast," she said. The bed creaked and then the light went off under the door.

"What about Mac?"

"Oh hell," she said, and the light came back on.

When she emerged from her room, drawing her robe around her, her face looked stretched; there were two vertical slashes between her eyebrows as she squinted at me under the overhead hall light. Her shadow on the wall revealed the inherited curvature of the Feather spine. In that moment, I saw her as I imagined she'd look in old age. Chiseled, coiled in upon herself, a conch shell on the sand.

MINERVA FOLLOWED ME TO bed that night. She curled up on my shoulder, pawed my cheek, her claws retracted. I reached over and took her into my arms and held her. She wiggled free and climbed up onto my chest. *Things are going to get much worse.*

"I wish you'd stop saying that," I said.

When I woke the next morning, my mother was gone and so were the grits. The pot was soaking in the sink. She'd left a note thanking me for them. *Running late. Sorry but no time to make breakfast. Will wash pot tonight.*

I put on my swimsuit. As I pulled it up, I noticed my legs. They were ropey like an old woman's, the kneecaps prominent in comparison. I poured a cup of lukewarm coffee, washed the pot, and put it in the dish drain. There was a knock on the door, and when I opened it, Tony stood on the porch. I latched the screen.

He ran his hand through his hair. "Listen, Birdy, I'm sorry about yesterday. Guess I had too much of that wine your mother brought on the boat. Then here I go again, spoiling the whole shooting match, the four of us being friends." He shook his head. "Don't know what gets into me, playing the devil like that. I feel like a dipshit."

The word *dipshit* made me smile in spite of myself. Such a silly word. It made Tony seem boyish. Maybe my theory about mold on cheese hit the mark; maybe Tony's mold was drink. In the light of day, he seemed harmless enough; he seemed, well, *decent*.

"You called me a piece of work and a busybody. You *scared* me talking about Minerva like that, like you were going to hurt her."

"I was just talking, didn't mean anything by that. You know, Birdy, sometimes you hurt my feelings."

"Well, I don't mean to."

"Well, I don't mean to hurt yours either. I'm a pistol. Always have been. I'm trying to do better."

"It's all right," I said, wanting to be rid of this new, decent Tony. I didn't know what to make of him.

"Shake?" He held out his hand.

I unlatched the door and stuck out my good hand. He snatched it up, kissed it, then shook it.

He looked down at my swimsuit. "Taking a dip? Have a good one."

Then he grinned and did a little bow, and off he went.

As I watched him stride down the street, I began to pedal back my plans for poisoning him. The proof of one's good intentions is always in the pudding. I would watch and wait. You can't unpoison someone once it's done, and really, I thought then, what if I were wrong?

The next morning Mac called. He'd made an appointment for me with a pulmonologist at Ochsner Hospital in New Orleans for the following Friday. "Tony thinks we should make a weekend of it, the four of us. We could all use a little vacation. What do you say?"

"What about Beautiful Dreamer?"

"I'm the boss, I'll just close it."

I considered. This would be a good opportunity to reevaluate Tony, and there was safety in numbers. "Let me talk to my mother," I said, feeling suddenly breathless.

"I'll talk to her," said Mac.

An hour later I walked into the Sound with a light heart. The burden of poisoning a real flesh-and-blood human being, which I'd begun to realize was flagrantly extreme, had lifted, at least for the time being. The sun hot on my face, I waded in, then stood, the water up to my waist. A formation of pelicans skimmed the water's surface, each riding the wake of the one in front, the lead pelican calibrating the precise lift and thrust required to coast just above the swells. A riotous swarm of gulls hovered around a shrimp boat far out, frantically diving in and out of the water. *Mine, no mine.*

I cast out, swimming hard for a while, then flopping on my back, my arms outstretched, trusting the Sound to hold me up the way my mother had taught me. As I floated along, there was a sudden churning and I found myself in the midst of a school of porpoises. *Hip hip hurrah.* For a while I was swept along with the gang, clicking and buzzing and just generally having a marvelous time of it, reminding me of my classmates on football nights in the fall, when the team would win and everyone in the stands would cheer and leave the stadium arm in arm. The porpoises were more inclusive, welcoming me into their nosey clan, playfully poking me here and there. *Gotcha!*

There was only one other person in the water. A man, judging from the muscular arms, which rose and fell rhythmically as he swam back and forth about halfway between me and the shrimp boat.

I hit a cool undercurrent and began to swim again, heading out toward the shrimp boat, now a dot on the horizon. I always listed to the right, my good hand exerting more pull in the water. Every little bit, I corrected my route, swimming due left.

The swimming rested me, until it didn't. *Things are going to get much worse.* Minerva, I'd learned over the years, never erred in her predictions. She was a seer, a griot, a wise one. And no matter how much I may tell myself, in the shadow of years since she disappeared from my life as suddenly as she had appeared, that her predictions were something as glibly explainable as my own inner warning system, I will never believe this. She was a cat. She was warm, she had fur, she preferred bread over any fish you could throw at her. She had a voice and she spoke to me in words. On these points I am quite clear.

And, of course, she was right.

WHAT WAS SUDDENLY LESS clear was why I couldn't catch my breath when, a few seconds ago, I'd been swimming along quite nicely, feeling relieved that I didn't have to poison Tony, or at least poison him in the immediate future.

Now the shore seemed indistinct, as if some giant hand had dropped a piece of cheesecloth over it, rendering it a distant dream—the hazy silhouettes of giant prehistoric creatures, the woolly mammoths and mastodons, their tusks long and curved, foraging among the giant oaks. A saber-toothed tiger sharpening his claws on their trunks.

Now the shrimp boat seemed closer, but it too grew hazy. I felt as if someone had poked a sponge down my throat. I flipped onto my back, the way my mother had instructed me to do when I needed a break.

I opened my eyes against the sun and saw snow, closed them again. Then darkness and the sweet sway of the Sound under and above me. A little hummingbird darted about inside my chest, beating hard against my ribs, wanting out.

I could write a book on the variety of sensations associated with fainting.

I came to in the grasp of someone much larger than myself. He held me upright, his legs kicking hard to keep us both afloat.

I choked and coughed up water and fought against him.

"Stop it!" he yelled. "Don't fight me!"

The man's face was hazy, then it cleared. His hair was plastered to his forehead, his face red with exertion. He flipped me on my back and threw his left arm around my chest and under my arms, and began to swim with his right arm for shore, kicking and stroking, his breath purring like Minerva in my right ear.

I tried to push him away. "I'm all right now," I gasped.

"No," he said sternly, and I stopped pushing and let him take me in.

After what seemed like an eternity, he reached the shelf and stood up. I dangled in his arm as he trudged in a few more feet so that I could stand up too. Only then did he let me go.

He bent over and put his hands on his knees and panted. I moved farther into shore where I could sit down in the water. The force of gravity pushed me down like a giant thumb; I was so loggy and tired I could hardly keep my eyes from closing.

When he got his breath, he walked over to me. "Geez, Birdy, you scared the hell out of me."

I opened my mouth to answer but only a mouse's squeak came out.

"We need to get you home," he said. "Wait here. No, come on with me. I don't want you going out like a light again."

He took my arm, and I stood, weaving a bit. He pulled me to him and took my good hand and put it around his shoulder. "Walk," he commanded.

I staggered alongside him. When we reached the seawall, he pulled me up the steps and parked me on the grass. "Stay here," he said. Then he loped over to Pete's hot dog stand.

The St. Augustine grass was soft and inviting. I fell into a long dark tunnel.

I awoke to my mother slapping my face. Tony and Mac stood behind her, two bulky shadows blocking the sun.

My mother produced my inhaler and put it in my mouth. "Take a deep breath, Mem. Now!" Then she squeezed.

I breathed, then coughed up water.

Tony stepped closer. "It's a miracle I saw her," he said. "She was going down. Up and down, up and down. At first I thought she was a buoy."

I sat up and looked down at myself. My suit was covered in sand and small pebbles. A line of ants marched up my leg.

Mac got on one side and Tony on the other. They raised me up like a sheet they were about to fold.

As they guided me to the car, Mac said, "Little, you scared us half to death. You owe Tony your life." He looked across me at Tony, tears in his eyes.

Tony looked back at Mac, then at my mother, then back again at Mac. "Just glad I was out there," he said. There was pride in his voice but also something beyond pride, something quieter than pride.

"You saved my baby," said my mother, her breath ragged as torn fabric. She hugged all three of us.

"Stop," I said. "You're smothering me!"

"Let's get this girl home and into some dry things," said Mac.

"I'm freezing," I said, thinking I'd been wrong about everything. The devil I'd conjured up had transmogrified into an angel. Tony had saved me from being stone-cold dead at the bottom of the Sound, sloshing and swaying, an anonymous mass of gelatinous flesh, silent and cold and shark bait. He'd given me back my life just as I had been pondering how best to take his.

We walked to the car, Mac supporting me on one side, Tony on the other, my mother bringing up the rear.

Then Mac stopped short. He turned to Tony. "I thought you couldn't swim."

"Whatever made you think that?" my mother said to Mac. "Tony grew up on Lake Pontchartrain. His father took him out on the lake every weekend."

"Wasn't my daddy that took me out on the lake," Tony said to her, quickly. "It was a friend of my daddy's." He looked across me at Mac. "Just kidding about not being able to swim. Any fool can swim."

Then he squeezed my arm and winked.

XVII.

————

BY THE TIME WE got back to the house and my mother led me into the bathroom and peeled off my swimsuit and started the shower for me and I stood in the shower for a good long time scrubbing my body until it burned and I stepped out of the shower and rubbed myself raw with the bath towel my mother had laid out, I'd come to feel so thoroughly ashamed I couldn't bear to look at myself in the mirror of the medicine chest that Tony had put up for us.

What had I been thinking? I'd been on the brink of killing a man. Killing a human *being*.

I wrapped the towel around myself and headed for my bedroom. In the kitchen, my mother was standing at the counter crying hard, Tony and Mac hovering around her. Mac said, "Now Feather, don't worry. I already made the appointment for Friday. We just need to watch her like a hawk between now and then. Make sure she's got her inhaler. Keep her out of the water."

"Just glad I was there," said Tony, which made my mother cry harder.

In the bedroom, I put on my pajamas, collapsed on the bed, and tried to brush the tangles from what was left of my hair, a task I found exhausting.

Talk in the kitchen revved up again, plots and plans. Who would watch me when. My mother would sleep with me tonight. "Not a wink," she added. Tomorrow Mac would come by to watch me while my mother went to the gallery. Tony would get my grandparents' Plymouth tuned up for the trip. At five tomorrow afternoon, Thursday, my mother would close the gallery early for the long weekend and the four of us would head over to the City. And so it was settled. The front door shut and all was quiet. I crept into sleep, uncertain as to whether I'd ever wake up.

When I stirred again, it was dark. My mother was lying beside me, her hand on my chest. She smiled and rubbed my arm. "I was just about to wake you up. It's time to use your inhaler."

I sat up and groaned. Being saved from drowning hurt. I felt like someone had beaten me around the neck and shoulders.

She handed me the inhaler. "Are you sore? Tony said he had to get you in a stranglehold to get you in to shore."

A stranglehold. I touched my neck. It felt as insubstantial and fragile as the stem of a flower. How easily he could have snapped it! Was he tempted?

Better yet, he could have just let nature take its course. He could have let me drown.

There were at least two good reasons to put an end to me. First, I was aggravating, more than aggravating really, infuriatingly accusatory: a piece of work, a thorn in his side. Second, and more to the point, the money from my grandparents (I never thought of it as *my* money) would go to my mother (I'd made sure of that), whom he could easily bend to his will. If he were as rapacious as I'd imagined, my unfortunate demise would have been a stroke of luck for him. Oh, he would have said, there she was, going down, but I couldn't get to her in time. So sorry, I tried but she was too far away. Whatever possessed her to go out so far?

The facts led to an obvious conclusion: I'd been dead wrong about Tony. Yes, he had his flaws. Yes, he'd seduced both Mac and my mother in a way that was glaringly obvious to all but the two of them. Yes, he'd gambled away large sums of money. There was mold on the cheese.

But perhaps, I thought then, my near-drowning had washed it off.

Perhaps he'd saved not just me but himself, and now he stood before us, baptized by the Sound and his own good deed.

Sometimes now I wonder: Was Tony Amato ever the beautiful dreamer we saw him as? Was he ever a wistful flesh-and-blood boy who imagined himself as an artist, a writer, a mechanic, an astronaut? Even a fireman or barber? Was he ever innocent? Sometimes, now, I think Tony was more a figure of our imagination, the beautiful dreamer we all yearned to be and be loved by, the seductive villain of a story we were both drawn to and repelled by.

And isn't there a secret place in all of us, a vulnerability, that can, under the right circumstances, be defenseless against villainy and seduction? People want and want and want. The world is an endless desert; small wonder we are forever thirsty.

THE MORNING OF OUR leaving, my mother made bacon and pancakes. The *Betty Crocker Cookbook* was out on the counter, splattered in batter. Outside, a flock of parrots swarmed a date palm, screaming in delight. Minerva occupied her usual spot in the kitchen window over the sink, torn between the spectacle of the parrots drunk on dates and the bacon my mother had laid out on a paper towel on the counter. She settled on the bacon, it being more accessible, and made a dive for the paper towel.

My mother laughed and swatted at her. Then she picked up a piece of bacon and carried it over to Minerva's dish in a corner beside the icebox. "That cat!" She smiled at me, shyly, as if I were a houseguest she was entertaining.

"Who's going to feed her while we're gone?" I asked.

"I talked to Miss Bess. She'll feed her on her front porch. I already took over the food. It's going to be nice weather this weekend. Minerva will be fine outside. We'll leave the kitchen window open in case there's a storm."

"She's not going to be happy. When are we coming back?"

"Sunday afternoon."

"I'm going to go over and talk to Miss Bess. I want to make sure Minerva gets two meals a day."

My mother slid three pancakes and two pieces of bacon onto a plate and pushed it toward me. "Let's eat first, and then I'll go with you."

"I can go by myself." I intended to ask Miss Bess if she wouldn't mind getting Minerva in at night. I'd read somewhere that letting your cat roam at night was dangerous. There was a world of trouble out there in the dark. She could get into fights. Owls could swoop down. She could get run over or captured and sold to labs for animal testing. There were demonic cults that tortured black cats.

"All right, but eat your breakfast first—you're too thin—and take your inhaler. You should carry it on your person at all times. I'll watch you walk over," my mother said. "Don't stay long. We need to pack."

We ate in a companionable silence, sharing the *Times-Picayune*. Pancakes were clearly not my mother's forté; they were burnt on the outside and runny on the inside. Flawed as they were, they tasted good to me, the syrup covering the metallic taste of the food I'd been trying to get down lately.

"Thanks for breakfast," I said.

She smiled. My mother had many smiles. This one revealed more fear than joy. "You didn't get much to eat yesterday. I still can't believe what happened. If it weren't for Tony." She caught herself and didn't say it. Didn't say that today she could have been planning my funeral, that is if my body had washed into shore yet. The Sound was so calm; it was a miracle anything—or anybody—ever washed up.

"Don't worry about the dishes," she said, rising. "I'll do them. You run on over to Miss Bess's. No, don't run. Walk. And take this." She pointed to the inhaler on the table. "Go ahead. I'll watch you."

Miss Bess had already put two Wedgewood-blue bowls on her front porch, one filled with water, the other running over with enough kibble to last Minerva a week. And there Minerva was, parked in front of the food dish, looking up at me as if I were a complete stranger, as if she hadn't spoken to me, slept with me, been fed by me, day after day, year after year.

"Traitor," I said.

When I went in, Miss Bess was sitting in her chair at the window. She beckoned me to come closer.

After we said hello, she asked if I'd have a bite with her. I opened my mouth to say I'd just eaten a huge breakfast but then she gestured at the coffee table. There was a pot of tea there and under a damp dish towel a mound of sandwiches with the crust cut off the bread.

"How'd you know I'd be coming?"

"Have a sandwich, dear, and pour us some tea," she said. "I knew you'd want to talk to me about your cat."

The teapot was lukewarm. I brought her a cup and pulled up a chair.

"Bring us those little plates I laid out and some sandwiches, my dear," she said.

I brought the platter, and she made her selections. "The chicken salad is good," she said, pointing, "but I do prefer the egg and olive. Have some of both, Memory."

"Thank you, ma'am," I said and took one chicken salad.

"She who is hungry must be fed, as my dear granny used to say," she said. Miss Bess was the queen of the old saying. She had hundreds of them at her beck and call and would sprinkle them generously into any conversation. "You have to try the egg and olive. They're the best."

I took the egg and olive and nibbled politely, then, finding it astonishingly good, took another.

I drew my chair closer to hers. "Miss Bess, I was just wondering if it'd be too much trouble to try to get Minerva inside at night."

"Well dear, I can call her, but I can't go running around in the dark looking for her. You can lead a horse to water but you can't make it drink."

"Sometimes I open a can of tuna and call out 'tuna' and she comes."

"How ingenious. That's exactly what I'll do. Do you think she'd eat a tuna-salad sandwich?"

"I expect she would. She likes tuna and she loves bread. Thank you, ma'am. I appreciate this."

Miss Bess leaned over until her wrinkled, kind face was a few inches away. "I understand you almost drowned yesterday."

"But I didn't."

"That's obvious, my dear. And I understand that friend of Mac's saved you." Her eyes now grew hooded, hawklike. "I guess that's one good thing he's done in his life." She looked out of the window. "You know, I see more than you'd think from this perch. I see things others don't see."

"I expect so," I said.

She turned from the window to look at me straight on. "Best be on your guard, my dear. A tiger is known by his stripes."

"I'm not going looking for trouble," I said.

"Of course not," she said. "But sometimes a person can't see the forest for the trees. Now I expect you've got packing to do. Don't worry about your Minerva. I'll watch over her like she was my own."

"Thank you." I rose from my chair but found myself hesitant to leave Miss Bess's living room. There was a hazy tranquility that hovered about it, the faint smell of rose water and glycerin, her keepsakes arranged behind the leaded glass doors in a massive breakfront on the back wall: tiny demitasse cups, thin as paper; a green Depression-glass bowl filled with Mardi Gras beads, a red shot glass that said JANE, WORLD'S FAIR, CHICAGO, 1933. A porcelain figure of a girl reading a book, a piece of Indian pottery with lightning bolts running around the top. The detritus of a life lived large. I wanted to touch these objects, ask about them.

"Remember what I said, child. Be watchful. A stitch in time saves nine. Now off with you." She gave a little wave of the hand, dismissing me. Her eyelids fluttered and her chin met her collarbone.

By the time I got home, it was afternoon and Mac was pacing the living room floor. "I was just coming to check on you," he said. "I want you with me at all times, Little. Asthma's a wolf in sheep's clothing."

"You sound like Miss Bess. I need to pack," I said, heading for my room.

"I'll help," he said, hot on my heels.

I pulled down my suitcase from one of the shelves Tony had put up in my closet. So much of this house was his, if labor counted for anything. Hours and hours, days, weeks, months of labor.

Mac stood at the window looking out. "Little, I hope you've changed your attitude toward Tony."

"It's the least I can do," I said, grabbing a handful of underwear and throwing them into the suitcase. "Besides, he apologized to me. He said he was sorry."

"Sorry for what?"

"For calling me a piece of work. A busybody."

"Why would he call you that?"

"Because he and my mother had a fight and he raised his hand to her and I made him stop."

"He was going to strike her? I don't believe it."

"They were fighting about money."

"Money? What money?"

"He wanted to borrow some. She told him it was my money, not hers."

"How much did he want?"

The timbre of his voice, lower and more careful, gave me the feeling of swimming out beyond my depths, beyond the Sound and into the fathomless Gulf.

I rearranged my underwear. Why was I packing it first, on the bottom? Wouldn't it be the first thing I reached for after a bath, or in the morning?

"How much?" Mac asked again.

I laid the underwear on the bed. I refolded it.

"Don't remember," I lied. "Not much."

"I'd have given it to him. I'll ask him what he needs."

"Don't do that. Don't tell him I said anything." My throat suddenly a crumbling tunnel.

"You need to rest," Mac said. "Tell me what to pack."

So I lay down on the bed and called out the things to put in my suitcase, and Mac pulled them from my closet and drawers, all the while commenting on the decrepitude of my wardrobe, the need to shop for some new things for me, the need for me to put some flesh on my bones. The fact that I was in a dilapidated state.

"Don't you mean debilitated?" I asked.

"No. I meant *dilapidated*. Worse than debilitated."

As he clucked on about the state of my clothing, something important dawned on me: Three adults cared deeply for me. To each one, I owed my life: my mother, who bore me out of the razzmatazz of her own blood and flesh and bone; Mac, who'd woven for us the lively web of family life, unconventional though it was; Tony, who'd literally saved my life, even though I didn't deserve saving, would-be murderer that I was.

Add to that one cat: Minerva, who talked to me as if we were one species in this vast, lonesome, predatory world. Who'd told me the truth, at least as she knew it, even if she had her lapses of judgment, even if she was at times unduly pessimistic.

How I loved them all!

With that thought, I fell asleep.

I dreamed of travel. My suitcase being tied to the roof of Mac's Ranchero, then flying away, my underwear floating through the air, filling the sky, then drifting like great clumps of snow into the marshes, slowly sinking as a pair of bemused great blues looked on.

I woke as my mother and Tony came through the front door. My suitcase bulged on the bed beside me. My mother came into the bedroom, her eyes smudged with worry. "Time to get ready," she said. "Tony brought you something to eat."

"I'm not hungry."

Tony rounded the corner of my bedroom door. "Come on, Birdy," he said, bearing a sandwich. "Peanut butter and jelly. Everybody's got to eat."

He put the first half to my mouth, solemnly, as if he were offering Communion.

I took a bite.

"Look at you, eating out of my hand," he said.

I reached for the sandwich and our fingers brushed, his calloused and hard against mine, which surely must have felt like velvet to him.

Mac and Tony went home to dress for the trip. They returned with wet hair and clean shirts, Tony in blue, Mac in yellow pinstripes. They argued in a lighthearted way over who would drive, ending with Mac in the driver's seat of my grandparents' Plymouth, Tony riding shotgun. My mother sat beside me in the back. She reached over and pressed my thigh between her thumb and forefinger. "You're skin and bones. How'd this happen?" she murmured and looked out of her window for a good long time, her hand gradually sliding off my leg.

As we drove along, Tony produced a flask from his pocket and passed it to Mac.

Mac brushed it aside. "Precious cargo," he said.

"Give me some of that," said my mother.

Tony handed it back, and she took one swig, then another, then slumped against the door and went to sleep.

Highway 90 wove through the marshes where wading birds brooded over the murky water. Marsh grass shot up, green and new; dragonflies lit on its tips. Then the marsh gave way and there it was: the Rigolets as far and wide as the eye could see. As we crossed the bridge, the City came into view. The late-day sun splattered the buildings in gold, dazzling us.

When we stopped in front of the Monteleone, my mother woke up. "Let me help you out of the car," she murmured, rubbing her eyes.

I brushed her away. "I'm fine."

The corner of Royal and Iberville bustled and surged. Tourists jostled us as we stood in a clump while the porter took our bags and another man got behind the wheel. It was just past five o'clock. Men in suits and women in high heels and sleek dresses strode past tourists and street cleaners. A man in red Bermuda shorts crashed into Tony, sloshing his pink drink down the front of Tony's clean shirt. Tony cursed and shoved the man back, further sloshing the drink. Mac reached over and took Tony's arm.

"Let it go, Tony," said Mac.

The man spit on the sidewalk at Mac's feet. "This fucking place. Overrun with faggots."

Tony and Mac froze.

"Get the hell away from us, you idiot," said my mother, her voice deep as a man's.

"Shut up, bitch."

In one perfect motion, Tony took one of the man's arms and Mac the other. It was like a dance. They sat him down on the front steps of the Monteleone. When they got him settled, Mac said quietly—almost in a whisper—"Mister, we need you to apologize to the lady." Tony seemed in deep thought. He was toying with the man's thick forefinger, moving it up and down, examining the dirty fingernail.

The man's lips, red from the drink, twitched. He began to struggle to stand. People moved to the curb. The doorman conversed with a parking attendant, eyeing the three of them.

"Now Mac, now Tony," said my mother. She took my arm.

"Lemme up," said the man. "Somebody call the cops on these faggots. Town's full of fags and bitches."

No sooner than the sound of the *b* exploded from the man's lips, Tony and Mac were on him. Mac pushed him to the curb. He lay there, his legs in the street, his torso on the sidewalk. Tony landed on top of him.

The doorman blew his whistle, once, then again. A manager burst through the revolving doors, took one look, and ran back inside. A crowd had gathered. Tony began to pound the man, who was screaming.

Then we heard the sirens. Tony gave the man one final punch, got up, dusted himself off, and walked through the revolving doors, his shirt and pants streaked with the man's drink and his blood. Mac followed.

Blood surged from the man's nose, which was now located on the left side of his face rather than in the middle. A flock of pigeons landed at his feet and pecked at some cracks in the pavement, their plumage iridescent in the late-day sun.

My mother led me around the man. "The police will take care of him," she said disdainfully.

In the lobby, Tony and Mac were nowhere in sight. My mother went up to the desk, and someone handed her a key and told her that Tony and Mac had already checked in.

Mac had reserved the Queen's Room for my mother and me. He and Tony, Mac told us on the trip over, would be in the King's Room.

My mother unlocked the door to our room, then went over and banged on the door separating the two rooms. "You two should be ashamed," she called to them. "Acting like you're in a schoolyard brawl. I'm disgusted with you both." She turned to me. "Come on, Mem. Let's take a walk while it's still light. Get your inhaler."

Outside the wind had picked up. My mother pulled her green scarf from her purse and tied it around her head. She took my arm. "Let's go over to the river and watch the boats come in."

It was cozy, the way she held on to me, as if she were old and decrepit and I was leading her, though, in reality, I wouldn't have been able to take us to the river if my life depended on it.

But off we went, my mother directing: turn onto Royal, then Canal. Follow the streetcar lines to the levee.

From the top of the levee, we watched the freighters come in, their foreign flags whipping in the wind, flanked by the tugboats guiding the way through the channel. The wind whipped up off the water. Gulls swooped, then climbed, then swooped again.

As we stood watching, my mother put her arm around me. After a moment, she turned toward me, a few wisps of hair escaping from her scarf and catching on her eyelashes. "Mem, the world is bigger than you think. You need to find your own way," she said, the wind catching her breath. She waved her arm, a despairing gesture. "You need to leave all this behind."

"I don't want to leave," I said.

"But you must, and soon." As she uttered the words, a boy my age leaped up from where he'd been sitting on the seawall. He shouted at the top of his lungs and waved his jacket at a freighter from Hong Kong. A *whoof* of wind, and the jacket leapt from his arm and fluttered down toward the brown, roiling water. Then another *whoof* and it billowed and soared.

"Like that," said my mother, pointing. She reached over and brought my head toward hers, her skull touching mine, the ends of her scarf tickling my cheek. "Exactly like that." Then she laughed, and the gulls swooped and laughed too, and the echoes of their cries caught the river current and rode the river out to the sea.

XVIII.

THAT NIGHT WE ATE oysters at Felix's. Under the neon lights at the counter, Tony downed his Jax in one long swallow, his knuckles bruised and scraped from the fight. We were lined up at the bar like ducks in a row, Tony at the end, Mac between him and my mother and me, all of us watching the shuckers pry open the shells with a quick flip of the wrist that made their muscles strain the sleeves of their stained t-shirts.

Mac turned to my mother. "What time do you think we should head for the doctor? Appointment's at nine. He's over on Jefferson."

My mother groaned. "That's early."

"Lucky we got her in at all on such short notice. I said it was an emergency."

"Eight thirty?" said my mother.

"No later than that," Mac said. "I'll go down and have the car brought around." Mac was determinedly punctual. He always opened the gallery on the dot of ten o'clock. My mother, on the other hand, was lackadaisical about time. "What's a few minutes here or there in the great scheme of things?" she'd say when I'd tell her she was late for work. Mac pointedly gave her a watch last Christmas with an inscription on the back that read *10 a.m.*

After we polished off the oysters, Tony leaned behind Mac and said to my mother in a stage whisper. "Let's get out of here and go hear some music, head over to the Marigny and see what's cooking."

My mother perked up. "Sweet Lorraine's?"

Tony grinned. "Only if you're a good girl."

"I've been a good girl," I said.

"I don't think so, Little," said Mac, an edge to his voice. "You've got an early morning tomorrow, and it's already late. I'm tired, and I know you must be."

"I'm not," I said.

"Mac's right. You need to get to bed, Mem," said my mother. "Mac, honey, would you mind terribly if I went with Tony, just for a little while? It's been so long since I've heard some good music." She hopped down from her barstool and did a few dance steps across the tiled floor. My mother loved to dance. Sometimes, in our little room at the El Camino, we would rev up the radio and dance together out in the parking lot. She would take the man's part and twirl me until I grew too dizzy to stand up.

Mac shrugged, his mouth a knot.

"You're a real sweetheart." My mother leaned over and kissed him on the cheek. "We'll be back early. I promise."

But they weren't back early. Midnight came, then one o'clock. I lay in bed staring up at the gilded ceiling. Next door in the King's Room, the soft *slup* of Mac's bedroom shoes brushed the carpet as he paced. The clink of ice in a glass, the flush of the toilet.

At some point, my mother slid into the bed, a muddle in my dreams. She smelled salty like the Sound.

The next morning, Mac banged on our door. I sat straight up in bed, jolted by my mother's presence beside me into thinking I was at the El Camino. My mother turned over and groaned, her breath stale with beer. The heavy velvet drapes at the window made the room dark as pitch. I scrambled out of bed and opened the door a crack.

"You have an hour. Get your mother up," said Mac. He was freshly shaven, a bit of toilet paper on the dimple on his chin where he always cut himself. He'd opened his drapes and a weak sun illuminated his head. Beyond him, a lump in the bed, a patch of dark hair.

I nodded, shut the door, and padded over to my mother. I poked her and she didn't move. I poked her harder, and she told me to leave her alone. I pulled the covers off her, noting that she was wearing the dress she'd worn the previous night, a striped number with a flared skirt. She even had on her pinch earrings, which apparently troubled her not a bit as she slept the sleep of the dead.

"Mac says get up. We have to be out of here in a few minutes."

She lifted her head and glared at me. "Damn his hide."

"It's my doctor's appointment. You need to get up."

She sat up, looking down at the dress as if surprised by the fact that she was still wearing it.

"You smell. Take a shower," I said.

She peeled off her clothes and left them in a heap on the bathroom floor, forgetting to turn on the shower before she got in and shrieking when it came on cold.

"I'm going down to get something to eat," I said, shutting the door to the bathroom. "Do you want something?"

"Coffee," she called through the door.

In the dining room, I ordered a pot, two cups, feeling quite grown up. After a while, my mother rushed over to my table, her hair dripping wet, her buttons mismatched to the holes on her blouse. She snatched my half-empty cup and took a couple of swallows. "It's time, come on," she said, signing the check to our room.

Out front, Mac sat in the car, drumming on the steering wheel. "You're late," he snapped when we got in.

My mother looked at her watch. "It's only 8:35, Mac. We'll be fine. How's Tony this morning?"

"You tell me, Feather. You were the one out with him until two in the morning."

My mother didn't answer.

A man in the car behind us honked. Mac cursed and rolled down the window. My mother pulled at his arm. "Just move on."

Mac jerked his arm away.

"I'll be glad to get this over with so we can start having some fun," I said, leaning forward between them. "What are we going to do later?"

Neither of them spoke.

"A submarine is docking at the riverfront, and it's open to the public," Mac said finally. "We're lucky. It's only going to be here today."

"That sounds nice," my mother said unenthusiastically.

Mac let us out in front of the doctor's office. "We're ten minutes late," he said. "You two go on, and I'll find some parking."

In the waiting room, my mother said I should tell the doctor how it felt when the attacks came on. "You need to go through it with him, explain it. Take your time. Don't leave anything out."

Just as Mac came in, complaining that parking was impossible, a nurse opened the door and ushered us back.

The doctor was waiting for us. He was pink-faced and white-haired, on the pudgy side. He had a jolly way about him, tiny blue eyes that twinkled, a shiny bald head. Dr. Santa Claus.

"Well now, Miss Memory Feather, oh my, what a name, I understand you have a touch of asthma."

"More than a touch," Mac said. "One minute she's fine, the next she's out like a light. She almost drowned a couple of days ago."

The doctor motioned for me to sit on the examining table. He listened to my chest, then put the stethoscope to my back. He listened for longer than seemed necessary.

He frowned. "I'm not hearing any wheezing. Tell me what happens when you have one of these episodes, young lady."

"I can't catch my breath. I can't breathe."

"You mean you can't draw *in* the air?"

I nodded. "I can't get enough."

Mac leaned forward. "Then she starts panting. And then she faints dead away."

The doctor ignored him. "And what about pushing *out* the air?"

The question took me aback. "I don't think about pushing it out."

Dr. Santa Claus wrote down some notes on my chart, then turned to my mother and Mac. "Girls can get nervous at her age. Anything troubling going on in the household? School problems?"

My mother looked at the floor and said there was nothing she could think of. Mac shook his head.

"We can do some breathing tests to confirm, but panic attacks— moments of severe anxiety—can trigger breathing problems similar to those people experience during asthma attacks. The difference is that usually you can't breathe *in* during a panic attack, while you can't breathe *out* during an asthmatic episode. Females tend toward this kind of hysteria."

"I'm not hysterical," I said.

He smiled. "It's a medical term."

My mother said, "But she had asthma when she was little. I used to have to run the water in the tub so she could breathe."

"When did she start having these?"

"When she was nine."

"Did anything unusual happen then?"

"Well, yes, her father left us."

Dr. Santa turned to Mac. "So who are you? The stepfather?"

"In a manner of speaking," said Mac.

"Either you are or you aren't."

"I'm a friend."

"Boyfriend?"

"No, just a friend."

"Mac has been a friend of the family for many years," my mother said primly.

The doctor's almost invisible eyebrows shot up into his pink scalp. He turned back to me. "Tell us what's troubling you, my dear."

His whole demeanor was so pleasantly benign, so Santa-ish, I wanted to spill the whole can of worms. But where would I have begun? With my father flying off into the arms of the French hussy? Mac getting beaten up at halftime by a bunch of rednecks? The death-dealing virtues of oleander versus angel's trumpet? Eau de Tony in every nook and cranny of our house? Picnics on Ship Island? Minerva's dire prediction? And the coup de grace, getting unexpectedly saved by the villain in my story?

"Nothing," I said. "Nothing's bothering me."

He pointed at my hand. "Do you get trouble at school? Do the children make fun of you? We have people here at Ochsner who can fix that."

"No!" I jumped down from the table.

"Not so fast," he said. He pointed to the scales in the corner. "Let's get a height and weight on you, young lady."

I got on the scales. He pushed the first weight to one hundred, then sighed and moved it to fifty. The secondary weight toggled to forty-one.

He turned to my mother. "She's severely undernourished. Does she eat?"

"I eat," I said.

"What did you have for breakfast this morning?"

"We were running late," I said.

He turned back to my mother, ignoring Mac. "I want her on three full meals a day, and I mean full. Ice cream and cookies before bed. I want to see her back in a month. No swimming, no activities of any kind that could stress her either physically or emotionally. Oh, and make sure she takes a multivitamin with iron, good for the appetite. She looks anemic." He paused, looked at my mother, then said, almost under his breath: "And Mrs. Feather, if you think you can't handle this, perhaps social services can." Then he pointed at me. "Now Memory Feather, you come with me. We're going to do some breathing tests to make sure I'm right."

I looked back at my mother, who was stone-faced, her wet hair having dried around her face like a frowsy wreath of Spanish moss.

Mac scowled at the floor. Then he said to the doctor, "Just you hold up a minute. We love this child. She is well taken care of. Just tell us what to do and we'll do it."

Dr. Santa Claus paused on his way out the door. "Believe me, sir, I will," he said, then continued on his way.

The testing room was small and packed with machines. A nurse came in and put a measuring device in my mouth and told me to take deep breaths and blow them out slowly. As I breathed and exhaled, a chart showing a series of wavy lines emerged on a turning cylinder. After I completed the tests, the nurse left and the doctor came back into the room. He ripped the chart from the cylinder and looked it over. "It's as I thought. No asthma here."

"But the inhaler helps," I said.

"Of course it does," he said quietly. "It is reassuring, it's familiar. It makes you feel safe. I'm going to write you a prescription for some pills that'll have exactly the same effect—they'll calm you down, so you won't have to worry about anything. Anything at all. What you need to remember is that you'll always be able to get enough air. If the attack gets too bad, you'll pass out so the body can readjust. Your natural reflexes will kick in and your breathing will return to normal."

He scribbled on a piece of paper, then looked up from his writing. "Now, Memory, it's just us here. Whatever the trouble is, you can tell me. I can help you, you know. There are all sorts of ways I can help."

For a long moment, my mind held his words in a precarious suspension, the way the glass holds the water, wondering what would happen if I told him about Tony, how he'd upended everything, made pawns out of the two adults in my life. But Tony was impossible to explain; he'd become the oxygen the three of us breathed.

"I don't know what you're talking about," I said.

He sighed, then opened the door. "Let's you go sit in the lobby for a few minutes, Memory. I want to talk to your mother."

When the doctor beckoned my mother, Mac followed her back. I sat down and picked up an old copy of *Family Circle*. On the cover, a Norman Rockwell portrait of a mother, father, and their big cozy family sitting around a Thanksgiving turkey, their heads bowed. In that moment, the glass that held the doctor's words tipped over. I began to laugh. The laughter came hard and fast and loud. The receptionist looked up at me, alarmed. I waved the magazine at her, toppling over with hilarity, plunging into it, swimming hard. She smiled at me, thinking I'd read something funny, thinking I was a merry girl, a regular girl.

In that moment, my mother and Mac walked out, looking like a pair of whipped dogs. They went over to the desk and my mother wrote a check. Then they turned and looked at me, their faces a matching gray, their downward-tilted mouths at the same angle.

They headed for the door, and I followed. Outside the sun had come out. The heaviness of the air had lifted.

Mac put his hand on my shoulder. "The submarine? Or maybe there's something else you'd rather do? We just want you to be happy, Little. That's all we want."

"First Café de Monde," I said. I was enjoying the morning, the three of us making plans the way we used to do. I didn't much care what we did as long as we did it together.

"Yes, coffee," said my mother. "I need coffee. And *you*…you need beignets."

"Buckets of beignets," Mac said with a forced smile.

"And, before we go see the submarine, let's go by and get that lazy Tony out of bed," said my mother as she got into the car.

The crispness of the air evaporated. Sweat slid down the back of my neck and pooled up between my shoulder blades. I licked my lips, tasted salt.

"I don't think he's interested in submarines," said Mac.

"I need to go back by the hotel anyway. I want to change into pants," my mother said, shutting the car door. "I'm not going down that submarine rabbit hole in a skirt. You too, Mem. We girls need to get on proper submarine attire, right?" She turned to me in the back seat.

"It's called a hatch," Mac said. "You climb down a hatch. And if you're so bound and determined to rout Tony out, we ought to do it now so he can come along to Café du Monde. He's a bear in the morning until he gets his coffee."

My mother rolled down the car window. "Hope it's not going to rain."

"It always rains in New Orleans," Mac said.

As we trooped up to our rooms, Mac said he'd go in and wake up Tony if that were humanly possible. My mother and I would change. We'd all meet down in the lobby.

As my mother and I got into our pants, we heard voices in the next room, then running water.

"Come on," she said. "Let's go down to the lobby. Maybe I can snitch a cup of coffee before we go get coffee." She laughed at her own joke.

I didn't laugh. The revelation that I didn't have asthma but some stranger ailment called anxiety troubled me. The word itself grated on my nerves; a trickster word, the way the invisible *g* slipped in its center, the *x* disguising itself as *z*, the nervous tic of the ending. None of it straightforward, none of it reassuring in the least. I needed the Sound, the grit beneath my feet, the selfish shrieks of gulls (*mine, no mine*) to drown out the fearful noise of *anxiety*.

I glanced over at my mother. In the hotel lobby we sat across from each other in identical wingback chairs covered in striped satin. She took a sip of the coffee she'd gotten from the restaurant, leaned forward and put a hand on my knee, her eyes bottomless. "Mem, I'm sorry." She paused, her words hovering between us like flecks of dust. "I'm sorry you've been worried." She paused again, then opened her mouth as if to say something of utmost importance.

But here came Mac with Tony, who flashed a sheepish grin, his hand raised in greeting.

My mother set down her cup. "About time you rolled out of the sack, lazybones."

"Got to get my beauty sleep," Tony said. His hair was wet and slicked back. His eyes drooped lazily.

Tony's presence in our midst lent a sizzle, a pizzazz. My mother fell into step with him. Mac put a hand on my shoulder and pushed me forward. One by one we went through the revolving door and then out onto the street. Cars honked and a flood of people swept by, laughing and talking and smoking. I straightened myself as I walked along behind Tony and my mother, my hips taking on the sway of hers. Mac looked down at me in surprise.

Over coffee and beignets, Tony made us laugh. He had a repertoire of clever little vignettes about people he'd known—people who did silly things, said silly things. We laughed, then laughed at ourselves laughing. I inhaled the powdered sugar on my beignet and went into a coughing fit, which just made us all laugh harder. There was a lightheartedness to it all, as if nothing mattered but this day, beautiful and sun-struck as a picture postcard, the coffee slopping over into our saucers, our powdered-sugar mustaches, the way my mother's eyes glowed. Tony, I realized in the moment, wasn't just a pretty face. He was smarter than I'd given him credit for, a raconteur of no uncertain skill, his stories spinning us into the threads of our own cozy web.

After coffee, we went by K&B Drugstore and got my pills. My mother asked for some water at the lunch counter and gave me my first dose. Then we headed down to the pier where the sub was tethered. By the time we got there, the high from the sugar I'd both eaten and inhaled was beginning to wane, leaving me jittery and out of sorts.

The river was restless. *Hurry, hurry*, it said. There was another sound that churned and troubled below its surface busyness. One misstep and a person could be swept away. The sky had darkened; the wind whipped up.

Secured with several lines, the sub looked like a captive whale, still and watchful, an American flag harpooned to its back. A man in a sailor suit stood on top of it, helping people down the hatch. "Seventy percent of the earth's surface is ocean," he intoned. "Come see how we protect it from the Communists. Only two at a time."

Tony went first. He disappeared down the hatch; then his head popped up. "Come on, Birdy, it's really something to see."

I hesitated, but my mother and Mac clustered around me, urging me on. My mother gave me a little push, whispering not to be *anxious*.

I walked across the gangplank and took the hand of the man in the sailor uniform. He looked like a large child in his starched sailor collar and hat. Tony came up the ladder a bit more. There was a clumsy moment when he took hold of my paw but then realized his mistake and grasped the other hand.

He helped me down into the hatch, guiding my good hand to the ladder inside. "Careful now," he said. "Take it slow." He began to descend just below me.

I hesitated for a moment, trying to open my curled fingers to clutch the rung. Descending a ladder with one hand makes for a slow process. Tony saw my difficulty and steadied me with a reassuring fatherly hand on my hip.

Below, a countless number of instrument panels, busy and bright, confronted me out of the shadows of what appeared to be a narrow hallway. The result was claustrophobic and somehow disconcerting, as if the instruments were somehow measuring the two of us and might well reveal our secret selves on some baffling chart or graph.

A sailor led us through the crew's sleeping quarters, a dimly lit corridor lined with bunk beds so closely spaced one atop the other you couldn't sit up on them. The bottom bunks were equipped with short curtains so that, I imagined, a person lying in one would feel he was inside a closed coffin.

A small circular window looked out into brown river water. A monster catfish swam past, staring at us blankly with one eye. Then some debris carried by the current, a small branch with leaves and a piece of something that looked like a large pie plate.

Tony threw his arm around my shoulder. "Imagine that," he said, his voice reverential. "We're underwater, but still breathing."

At that moment, something strange drifted toward us, a figure of what appeared to be a woman. She had no arms, and her head was draped in something flimsy, a piece of fabric perhaps, or was it hair? For a moment Tony and I stared as the object bobbed and dipped in front of us, as if she had something she wanted to say.

Then Tony broke the silence. "It's a mannequin," he burst out. He slapped the wall beside the window. "Man, oh man, I thought it was a real woman, a dead woman."

The sailor moved closer. "You see some strange things down here," he said. "A river's a good place to cover your tracks."

"I thought somebody'd killed her and dumped her," Tony said.

I turned back to the window and she was gone.

I shivered. "This place is giving me the creeps. Let's get out of here."

Tony laughed, a short expulsion of breath, then, for a moment, a queer silence. "You first," he said after a moment, gesturing toward the ladder, "and, Birdy, don't be *anxious*. I'll catch you if you fall."

So Mac had told him what the doctor said.

I hesitated, searching out his face in the quiet dark. But I couldn't see him, not really, could only feel his breath on my cheek. I started up the ladder, Tony's hand now lightly touching my ankle, the instruments on the walls busily tracking and measuring my every move.

We emerged into a light rain. Mac and my mother stood on the wharf looking miserable.

"About time," Mac said. "We're getting soaked out here."

Tony looked up at the sky and then gestured at me. "I'll take her back to the hotel, no point in us standing around getting soaked."

My mother took Mac's hand. "Let's get this over with."

The rain began to pound the pavement. A cold wind had kicked up off the river. "Come on, Birdy," Tony yelled at me through the downpour, "let's go."

"No running," said my mother as she descended.

He took off without looking back. He crossed the train tracks and I ran behind him. He darted from overhang to overhang, his shirt flattening against his back.

After a few minutes of running through the pouring rain, I slowed down, out of breath. What difference did it make to run? We were both wet as drowned rats. But Tony kept darting here and there, as if the rain were an acid that burned. He looked like a boy, splashing in puddles. If Mac were right, he *had* been an orphan boy in the French Quarter, making his own way, outrunning the constant rain for whatever shelter he could find. My heart went out to him in that moment in a way it hadn't before. An orphan boy, just trying to stay warm and dry.

It was only when we reached the Monteleone that he stopped and looked back to see if I'd managed to keep up. When he spotted me, he grinned and waved, as if we were children together, as if we'd just had the time of our lives.

XIX.

———

IN THE HOTEL LOBBY Tony turned to me and asked if I had a key. I didn't, nor did he. We stood dripping onto the shiny black and white tiles, under the giant spider of a chandelier. I looked down at my wet blouse, unfortunately white and plastered to me. I pulled at it and pushed my hair back from my face.

"Go dry yourself off," said Tony, with a glance at my chest. "I'll be in the bar."

By the time I got back, he'd ordered two gin and tonics. He pushed one toward me. I took a couple of swallows, then a couple more, trying to finish the drink before my mother and Mac showed up.

The dark hairs on Tony's arm were still wet and plastered to his skin. He leaned over. "You and me, Birdy, we got a thing with water."

The bar rotated slightly. Everything smelled musty.

"Yep, you and me, we got a thing."

"With water," I added.

He reached over and tucked a piece of my hair behind my ear. "That day when you were drowning? A porpoise told me."

"It did?"

"It bumped right into me and said *look up*."

"Minerva tells me things like that," I said eagerly. "And birds. Sometimes plants."

"See? We got a thing, Birdy, something nobody else has."

I shivered.

"You cold?" He took my drink and handed it to me. "Drink. The liquor'll warm you up."

We sat in silence. In the time I'd known him, Tony had grown quieter. He could still talk your head off, the way he'd done that morning at Café du Monde, but then his talk would be followed by thick silences.

I gulped down the gin and tonic and began to chew on the lime.

The rotation of the bar was starting to trouble me. There were lights and mirrors everywhere. Tony looked like a grown man, I looked twelve years old. I hid my paw under the counter. My throat felt oily, my stomach churned. The chicoried coffee, the sugary beignets, the gin had drawn their swords and declared battle on one another.

The lime, which had turned the oily gin to acid at the back of my throat, bubbled up. I jumped off my barstool and launched into a run, over the spotless black and white tiles of the lobby, under the spidery chandelier, toward the revolving door. I barreled through the door, half-jumped, half-fell down the front steps of the Monteleone, and proceeded to vomit up coffee and donuts and shards of lime skin onto the feet of the astonished doorman.

As I lifted my head, my mother and Mac rounded the corner of Iberville and Royal. The rain had let up and they were strolling along, Mac with his hand on my mother's shoulder, deep in conversation.

Mac saw me first. "What on earth?" he roared. My mother stopped dead in her tracks.

The doorman's astonishment had turned to disgust. "Messing up my good shoes," he said. "People who can't hold their liquor ought to stay away from the stuff. The Monteleone's a nice hotel, a fine hotel."

"I'm sorry," I said. I bent over and heaved again.

"What the hell's wrong with you, girl? Can't you get your drunk self into the street to do that business?" the doorman said and stormed into the hotel, his soiled shoes making damp footsteps up the stairs.

Now Mac was on one side of me and my mother on the other. It was my mother who smelled it. "Memory Feather, you smell like gin," she thundered.

"My god, what's next with you, Little?" said Mac. "It's just one thing after another." He looked like he was going to cry.

"How'd you get alcohol?" demanded my mother, pulling at my sleeve. She looked around. "Where's Tony? Did he give you a drink?"

"No."

"Then who?"

"Somebody left one on the bar," I said. "I thought it was ginger ale."

"Ginger ale, my foot," said my mother. "And since when are you going around drinking people's leftover drinks? Here we are, trying to get you well. We turn our back for ten minutes, and you pull this." She took hold of my sleeve and jerked my arm up and down.

A man emerged with a bucket and mop. He gave us a dour look and began his task of cleaning up my mess. My mother pulled a dollar bill out of her purse. The man looked at it and kept on mopping.

"Oh good grief, Feather," Mac said. He pulled out a ten, snatched my mother's one, and gave both bills to the man. "Sorry about this."

The man put down his mop and took the bills. "Second time I have to do this in two days. Yesterday it was blood all over the place."

Mac and my mother looked at each other, then broke out laughing.

Inside the bar, there was no sign of Tony.

We took the elevator. Its mirrors seemed warped, elongating the lower halves of our faces as if we were in a fun house at the state fair, our mouths downturned, our chins resembling the Louisiana peninsula.

He was waiting for us in the hallway. He sat propped up against the door to the King's Room, the crown on the door situated directly above his head.

"Well, now, look what the dog dragged in," he said, not moving. He surveyed me. "You stopped upchucking?"

"Why didn't you help her?" said my mother. "There she was, vomiting all by herself out on the sidewalk."

"I don't do puke," Tony said.

"You let her pick up somebody else's drink?" Mac asked.

"What? What'd you do, Birdy?" Tony managed to look genuinely surprised.

"It was my own fault. I thought it was ginger ale."

"That's what you get for snitching other people's drinks," Tony said. He winked at me.

Mac reached over him and unlocked the door.

"Come on, you," said my mother, walking past them to the door of our room. "Mem, you're disgusting. Let's get you cleaned up for supper."

"I'm tired," I said.

"You don't want to go out?" she asked, her voice wistful.

I shook my head. "I want to go to bed. Stayed up half the night waiting for you to come in."

She sighed. "All right. Room service for us then. Now get yourself cleaned up. You stink to high heaven."

After I got out of the tub and we ate, she pushed me down into one of the satin-upholstered chairs, settled herself on the foot of the bed, and gave me a good talking-to. My mother's good talking-tos were long, tedious affairs. They were also infrequent, so they got my attention.

She took my good hand in hers and began: I'd always been an odd child, talking to animals, walking the shore for hours on end, refusing to get my hand fixed, becoming so anxious I couldn't breathe, et cetera, et cetera. Perhaps her fault, perhaps my father's, who knew? What was important is that we were turning over a new leaf. From here on out, I was under no circumstances to drink any form of alcohol whatsoever. I was to eat a balanced diet—more of everything and dessert every night. When school resumed in the fall, I would become involved in more extracurricular activities, something meaningful, something other than throwing a stick up in the air and catching it. We would give the pills time to do their work. Then we would *reassess*. There were places, nice places for *disturbed* girls; she hoped one of those places wouldn't be necessary. Meanwhile, I would put myself to use. Miss Bess was getting feebler. She needed companionship and help. The two of us would cook some extra meals every week and I would take them over to her. I would assist Miss Bess in writing her bills and carry her Social Security check to the bank each month. I would be *helpful to others*, which would make me feel good about myself. I would be useful in the world. That was the key, being useful and helpful.

She gazed into my eyes fiercely, as if she were trying to force open a closed door. "You can relax now, honey. You can *breathe*," she said. "You don't have to worry about a thing, not a single thing."

After the talking-to, she went into the bathroom and drew herself a bath. While she was bathing, I heard the water running next door, then Tony and Mac talking, then their door opening and clicking shut. They were off for a fabulous supper. There would be plates with crests on them, crystal goblets sparkling in the light from shining candelabras with thousands of prisms. There would be shrimp and oysters, crawfish remoulade, something tart and creamy for dessert. I dropped off to sleep, deeply envious of their supper but thankful for my plump pillow, the weight of the covers.

I woke up to loud knocking.

My mother sat straight up in bed, feeling around for my arm. "Who is it?" she called out, her voice full of sleep.

"Who wants doberge cake? Who wants Italian cookies?" The voice was Tony's, singsong, playful, slurred.

"Oh good grief," said my mother. She switched on the lamp beside the bed and peered at the clock on her nightstand. "One in the morning. You idiots."

She put on a robe and opened the door. Tony, who had apparently been leaning on the door, half-fell into the room, then stumbled into a chair. Mac came in behind him, a rakish grin on his face, bearing a box from Gambino's Bakery.

"You two are lunatics," my mother said.

Mac opened the box and waved it in front of me. "You get first dibs, Little."

"Where've you been?" I asked.

Mac said, "Commander's, then to Laffitte's up on Bourbon for a drink, then Gambino's, then the coup de grace, a visit to the fabulous Feathers."

"Had to drag him out of Laffitte's. Lots of pretty faces," said Tony with a grin.

I took a bite of cake. So many layers, so densely blended they appeared to be one solid piece.

"And the party continues," said Tony. He wobbled over to the King's Room and returned with a bottle of Seagram's in one hand and two glasses in the other.

"Haven't you had enough?" Mac said.

"You know I never get enough." He winked at Mac, then looked at my mother and me. "Need two more glasses."

"Just one," said my mother.

For once, I agreed with her. My head felt like someone had wadded up a piece of cheesecloth and poked it through a hole in my skull. My mouth was swollen and dry. Then, I blamed the gin, but over the coming days I'd realize it was the pills.

Mac filled up a glass of water in the bathroom and handed it to me. My mother and I sat on the bed, the Gambino's box at the foot, where Mac and Tony sat in the two chairs in the room. They both had gotten dressed up for their night on the town. Now that they'd shed their jackets and loosened their ties, they looked at once dapper and seedy. Tony was in his sock feet and propped them up on the bottom of the bed. Mac put his on the ottoman that matched his chair.

"A party," I said.

Tony leaned over and clinked his glass of whiskey on my glass of water. He cocked his head at Mac, who was dozing off. "He said to let you sleep, you two could eat cake tomorrow, but I said, 'Wake up those Feather girls, they're always up for a party.'"

Mac had begun to snore softly. When the three of us laughed, he coughed and choked and looked around in a daze, then fell back to sleep and began to snore in earnest.

"Old man needs his rest," Tony said. He clinked glasses with my mother again, then came over to her side of the bed. "Move over," he said and climbed onto the bed.

So there the three of us were, lined up like wooden ducks in a shooting gallery at the fair, my mother in the middle, holding the cake box. We were quiet for a while. Every now and then, one of us would take a cake or cookie. "Birdy," Tony said after a few minutes. "I'm glad you didn't drown."

My mother laughed a short little laugh that ended in a kind of muttering to herself. She put her head on his shoulder. In a few seconds she too was dead to the world, her mouth slightly open. Tony reached down and took the glass in her hand and put it on the nightstand on his side.

He asked whether I would like another cookie or cake, and I said no thank you.

"Ready to go to sleep now?"

Half-asleep already, I slid down on my pillow, opened my mouth to say something, but stopped in midsentence, dimly aware that Tony had turned out the light on his side of the bed. He got up and came around to my side and turned off the light on my nightstand.

"'Night, then," he murmured, and the dark rippled out and I heard the door click between the rooms. Mac's snores punctuated my mother's quiet breathing, and peace flowed out and covered me like a blanket.

It was several hours later, I judged, when I flung out my arm in my mother's direction and discovered she wasn't in the bed. Half-dreaming that we were at the El Camino and it was one of her nights to work, I didn't find this odd or alarming. Plus, Mac's snoring a few feet away reassured me that I was not alone.

When I awoke again, my mother was in the bathroom brushing her teeth. The only sign of Mac or Tony was the Gambino's box sitting on the nightstand.

She came over to the bed and peered at me. "I'm glad you're up. We all slept late. If we hurry home, I can open the gallery for the afternoon." She pulled open the drapes with a flourish, and the sun poured in, blinding me.

I sat up and groaned. "My head hurts."

"It's called a hangover," she said. "That plus the Valium. It's a wonder you're not in the morgue."

"I don't like those pills," I said. "They make me feel stupid."

"Better stupid than fainting at the drop of a hat. You need to take them until we get this anxiety under control." She reached into her purse and pulled out the bottle. "Here, it's time. Take one now. I mean it, Mem. Take it."

As I swallowed the pill, I wondered how one got one's anxiety *under control*. It's not even a thing you can see or hear. More a form of weather, present in the very air you breathe. What I didn't know then that I know now is how it hovers, always on the brink of arrival. How it begins, with a gentle arbitrariness, the way an afternoon shower in New Orleans begins with one big, slow drop on your nose, then becomes a deluge in a matter of seconds. One minute it's a boringly beautiful day, the next it's pouring cats and dogs; the streets have become rivers, the river itself rising and rising.

In the weeks ahead, I became accustomed to the pills. I looked forward to the way they settled me, their downward pull. When I didn't take them on time, my pulse scurried up and down my neck like a frantic mouse. I learned to keep a stash with me.

Sometimes, when the invisible hand touched my throat and threatened to squeeze, I took an extra one.

When school started again in September, I felt deeply calm, completely unflappable. I even began to hold scattered conversations with other girls, even a boy in my biology lab. As I calmed down, Minerva became stubbornly mute; a comment here or there about the weather was all I could get out of her. It was as if she'd given up on something.

At my mother's insistence, I became a joiner. I joined 4-H, where I met a pig whom I named Calliope after the muse of poetry, so called because of the harmony of her voice. Calliope complained incessantly of having to spend her time penned up, to the degree that I quit 4-H because her predicament made me sad. Then I decided to take my chances with the Latin Club, headed by Miss Oline Coffee, who had us practicing carols in Latin and French to sing for Belle Cote's shut-ins come Christmas.

Meanwhile, I wrote Miss Bess's bills, brought her supper several nights a week, and kept her company while she ate. I helped Mac make signs for the growing demonstrations: I AM A MAN and ONE MAN ONE VOTE. I made one that read I AM A WOMAN, but Mac said that's not the way the saying went, that "man" stood for men and women both. On the national news, I watched my signs being carried in the streets of Jackson and Canton and Memphis. I cried for the students from Tougaloo who got hosed and tear-gassed and stuffed into boiling-hot paddy wagons and locked up in the livestock pens at the state fairgrounds up in Jackson. I wondered whether Leticia was marching up in Chicago.

I had neither the time nor the inclination to walk along the shore. Since my near-drowning, the Sound had become strange to me, the way a familiar place will seem strange after a long absence.

SO TIME WENT ON, as time does. I breathed air without giving it a second thought. I was deemed cured from the mysterious ailment of anxiety.

The pills kept coming. We visited Dr. Santa Claus several more times. He said we needed to stay the course; my progress had been nothing short of a miracle.

My mother had taken to making complicated meals involving cream sauces and box cakes coated with thick sugary icings, Jell-O salads clotted with cottage cheese. In our pantry red-and-white cans of Campbell's cream of mushroom soup marched across the shelves, along with cans of fried onion rings, tuna, green beans, and asparagus. I gained weight, my face now lumpy as an old mattress. I found myself having trouble staying awake in my afternoon classes. I squeaked by geometry with a D. I stopped reading books, except for my necessary schoolwork, preferring instead to lie on the sofa in front of the TV, half-dozing.

I became an ordinary girl.

Our foursome seemed comfortable enough. Tony and Mac were in and out of the bungalow, troubling no one but Minerva, who retained her distaste for Tony and slipped out the kitchen window the moment he came through the door. Tony had his own brand of disappearing, but he always showed up again, acting as if he'd been there all the time. He and my mother had their picnics on Ship Island until it grew too cold, and when it did, they made day trips into the City together. Every so often a small spark flared into brush fire among the three of them, but someone would quickly blow it out and peace would again reign.

As the months went by, a silky tranquility settled over us.

Picture this: The four of us at Mac's gleaming dining room table, eating piles of shrimp, three heads turned toward Tony, listening, always listening, to one of his stories, laughing at the appropriate places. Before dessert, my head droops. *Oh she's working hard at school, put her on the couch, put a pillow under her head.*

Or this: The four of us, walking down a street, any street, in the Quarter, where we sometimes spend the weekend in my grandparents' apartment, Mac, my mother, and I following, always following, Tony. We are one multihinged appendage to his body.

Or: On a Sunday drive to my grandparents' beloved Boudreaux's Seafood, Tony always at the wheel, one or the other of us—the lucky one—in the passenger's seat next to him, the other two in the back seat, leaning forward so as not to miss a word.

I wander through my days, quiet, docile, willing. I want nothing except the rattle of my prescription bottle in my pocket. When Mac and my mother ask how I'm feeling, I tell them I'm fine, everything is fine. As they stand before me in memory (I picture them in Mac's kitchen, both leaning against the counter), they have indistinct shapes and features, like the fog that hovers over the Sound in early morning.

As THE FOUR OF us eased into fall, I found myself for the first time alone overnight, my mother and Mac having gone into the City on a holiday buying trip. I was old enough, my mother said, and more importantly well enough, to look out for myself for one night. Belle Cote in those days was probably the safest place in the entire universe; besides, Tony was in town and promised to look in on me.

It was past suppertime and full dark. I was heating up a leftover green bean casserole when Tony walked through the front door. This did not surprise or alarm me, though it did Minerva, who leapt to the kitchen counter and ducked out the window over the sink. I was, in fact, glad to see him, particularly since he was carrying a sack of oysters in one hand and two to three lemons in the other.

He made his way to the kitchen sink where he deposited the oysters. "Supper," he said and began to juggle the lemons, which made me laugh. "You've got saltines, right?"

I headed for the pantry and pulled out the crackers. Then I got some ketchup and horseradish from the icebox.

Tony meanwhile rummaged around in the cupboard and pulled out my mother's chipped platter. He opened the silverware drawer and pulled out our oyster knife, his movements smooth and knowing.

He filled up the kitchen, as if it were a pitcher and he the milk.

I turned off the stove. Like Mac, Tony wasn't a fan of my mother's casseroles.

He began to shuck the oysters, arranging them in their shells on the chipped platter.

I stood beside him, squeezing the ketchup into a dish. He smelled like he'd just stepped out of the shower, his hair still wet and combed back, his signature white t-shirt for once unspotted.

"How about a beer?" he said.

I went to the icebox and pulled out a Jax, got the church key and opened it, careful to open one side just a little before making the full *V* on the other. I handed it to him.

"Get yourself one," he said.

I hesitated. I hadn't had any alcohol since my unfortunate encounter with the gin and tonic at the Monteleone.

As I considered, a quiet settled over the kitchen, broken only by the *chuck, chuck* of the oyster knife.

"Oh live a little, Birdy. Who's going to know?" He didn't look up.

I pulled another Jax out of icebox. I would not overdo it, the way I surely had with the gin and tonic. The beer had a nice tickle to it. I took another sip, which caused me to sneeze.

"Don't guzzle it, and it won't make you sneeze," he said.

His unruly lock of hair had come loose from its comb-back and draped over one eye.

He glanced over at the bowl of ketchup. "Lots of Tabasco."

I nodded. My mother wasn't a big fan of Tabasco, always had to have her own dish of sauce.

But my mother wasn't there.

I reached up to get the Tabasco out of the top of the cabinet.

"I'll get it," Tony said and reached across me to retrieve the bottle.

I pulled back but not before his underarm brushed my shoulder.

He handed me the bottle of Tabasco, warm from his touch.

I added the sauce, then squeezed the lemons over it and stirred. The lemon always comes last.

I put the sauce and the box of saltines on the table and set out the plates and utensils, leaning over and around Tony, though never touching him. He moved when I moved, an elaborate dance.

As I put out some fresh napkins, he lifted the platter. "Ta da," he said, his t-shirt now dotted with gray spots.

We sat down and clinked beers like old drinking buddies and set to eating the oysters. Tony spooned on the sauce until it filled the shell, then brought the shell to his mouth and slurped the oyster, the sauce and liquor from the shell dribbling from the corner of his mouth. I was more dainty, stacking mine on top of the cracker with the sauce on top, the way Mac had taught me.

We ate along for a while.

I said it was good to have something besides casseroles for supper.

Tony laughed. "What's with Virginia and those casseroles of hers?"

Odd to hear my mother called by her first name.

"I think she's trying to fatten me up."

Tony surveyed me. "She's doing a good job." There was a pause, then he looked again. It was a slow lazy look. "I like my women with some flesh on their bones." He took an oyster shell, leaned over the table, and slipped the oyster into my mouth. The juice ran down my chin. I wiped it with the back of my hand.

For a moment, the old fear came flooding back.

But then he looked across the table at me and cocked his head. "You know, Birdy, you've got good hair."

Which distracted me. I'd never thought of myself as having good hair. Now that it had grown back in, it did hold a wave. It also was an unfortunate mousy brown, several shades lighter than my mother's.

His eyes narrowed and he cocked his head. He reached across the table and cupped my chin, turning my head to the left, then the right. "A French twist would be perfect. With that bone structure you'd look like Grace Kelly." His lips wet with oyster juice.

On my diet of Valium and casseroles, I'd come to love the movie stars. I bought all the magazines the minute they hit the drugstore shelves, finding them infinitely more interesting than Mac's dusty histories of mastodons and misplaced camels. Grace Kelly was at the top of my list of favorites. Plus, I thought, Tony must be dying to do somebody's hair, his ill-fated barbershop an unspoken failure.

When we finished supper and our beers, he pushed back from the table and said, "Let's try it. Let's make you into Grace Kelly. You've got hairpins?"

"I thought you only did men's hair."

"Hair's hair."

He stood up.

"I have to do the dishes."

"Forget the dishes. It's time to play. First more beer." He opened the icebox and pulled out two Jax, opened them, handed me one, and then headed in the direction of my mother's room. "Let's make you gorgeous. We need pins, hairspray, a brush, and a pick. Let's see what's in here."

I followed him, sipping my beer, caught up in the spirit. In the bedroom, he pushed me down on the bench in front of my mother's dressing table. He picked up her hairbrush and took the rubber band out of my ponytail. My hair fell to my shoulders. I'd always admired my mother's hair, which was a deep burgundy that burned with its own secret life. By contrast, mine seemed lackluster at best. Now, though, as I sat on that bench with Tony's hands drawing forth its threads of light, I saw how it leaped and rippled with its own peculiar beauty, the flick of a horse's tail in the sun.

Tony eyed it critically, running his fingers through it and letting it fall in clouds around my face. "How long since you washed it?"

"Four days," I said, suddenly embarrassed. "I was going to wash it tonight. Should I run do that first?"

He let it fall again, fluffing it. "No, no. A French twist holds better if the hair's dirty."

He brushed it out again, then started ratting it, snatching up some of my mother's hairspray every now and then and covering me in showers of aerosol until I began to wheeze, then proceeding to rat again until my hair stood out all over my head like a privet hedge, which made us both laugh.

"Once I get this done, you'll need to wrap it in toilet paper to sleep."

I nodded and slugged down my beer. He pushed his across the dressing table for me to share; then, as I drank, he took the pick and combed the privet hedge into a hornet's nest.

I want to say the story ends here, but it doesn't. After the French twist, out came my mother's red lipstick and mascara and rouge. Before I knew it, I'd been turned into Grace Kelly and Virginia Feather combined, and then the next thing was my mother's nightgown, all under careful directions from Tony, who turned his back while I changed. When I got my clothes off and the gown on, he showed me how to lean forward and push my girlish breasts together to make them appear fuller, like Liz Taylor, he said, and when that didn't work, he helped by pulling them up and closer to each other. He showed me how to stand with one hip jutted out, my hands on my waist. How to move against him, lightly at first, then locking in. He said one day I'd thank him; I'd know what a boy wanted.

"I'm getting dizzy," I said.

"Let's get you on the bed." He took my good hand.

Not once did he look at my paw.

THERE IS A CERTAIN exhilaration in surrendering to something you are afraid of.

He was gentle with every little thing. And I let him do those little things, which at the time seemed so insignificant, so *small*, because I felt drop-dead gorgeous and he had made me feel that way, he'd seen me that way.

It didn't occur to me that Tony was hungry in a way few people are, that Mac and my mother had not been enough, had never been enough; he just had to have me too. I was the sauce on the oyster.

MINERVA WAS A CAT who could move from room to room without a sound. She did not have large bones, but she was fleshy and carried more weight than you'd expect.

When she silently landed on Tony's head and dug in her claws, it was as if a saber-toothed tiger had risen from the ashes of history and caught up to the prey she'd been tracking for millennia.

He leapt up from the bed, screamed, tried to shake her off. She held on, gazing down at him tenderly, triumphantly. He let go of me and reached for her. She dug in, slid down to his forehead and onto his face, clawing her way.

He went wild, snatching at her. She took a bite out of his hand, slid to one shoulder, then lit into his ear, hanging on for dear life. He pulled her off, then threw her against the wall. She ran down the hall, zig-zagging like a rabbit in the field. He snatched on his pants, then charged after her, cursing and spitting.

"Don't hurt my cat!" I screamed as both of them disappeared.

A moment later, there was a crash in the kitchen. Then the front door slammed shut.

All was quiet for a moment. Then Minerva trotted back into the room, jumped onto the bed. She deposited what appeared to be what was left of Tony's bloody earlobe onto my pillow, and began to lick her paw. A claw dangled from it. She pulled at it and it came out, along with more blood. Then she looked up at me, her eyes slitted, as if she were pondering whether to jump me next. Then she began to purr.

"Look what you did," I said, pointing at the blood-flecked sheets.

No. You.

She limped out of the room, her tail high.

I woke up the next morning to the *tap tap* of Miss Bess's cane. "Yoo-hoo," she called out, making her way through the living room and into the kitchen. "Where are you, Memory? I called and you didn't answer the phone. Are you all right, dear?"

I leapt from the bed, catching a glimpse of myself in the mirror of my mother's dressing table. My hair a rat's nest. Lipstick and mascara train-tracked down my cheeks. I still had on my mother's nightgown. My head ached. My breath came hard. There was blood down the front of my mother's nightgown.

In the kitchen, the oyster shells reeked, the remains of the oysters dry-crusted. The dishes dirty in the kitchen sink, the casserole cold and still in the oven. Two plates, two beer cans.

Miss Bess was standing in the midst of it all, her hand on her cane. She looked at the beer cans and plates. Then she looked at me up and down, long and hard; and, for once, she didn't make a sound or breathe a word or even call up an old saying. She just shook her head sadly, so sadly that I began to cry. Then she turned and hobbled out of the kitchen and through the living room and out the door. I watched out the window as she struggled up the steps to her front porch, then turned and looked back at me. Her sorrowful gaze as deep and wide as the Gulf of Mexico, and as full of fearful currents.

I went into the bathroom and smeared cold cream on my stained face, popped one of my pills; then thinking of Miss Bess, took another. I drew some hot water and got into the tub and washed my hair, which, like the rest of me, was filthy. As I sloshed about in the tub, all that had happened the night before seemed to lose density and form and float away, the way a small wave dissolves back into the Sound and the Sound takes it back, then hands it on out to the Gulf like a gift.

The tub water turned murky, as if I were molting. When young herons molt, they hide themselves deep in the marshes and swamps, fearful of predators. I had not been so aware of my inability to fly.

XX.

———

EACH MOMENT IS TRUE unto itself but becomes something else in retrospect.

Later that morning I found a dead cat in the side yard. A calico with a creamy froth on its muzzle. Minerva sat upright beside it, as if she were guarding it. An empty sardine can lay on the ground between them.

"What?" I asked her.

You.

"*I* didn't do this," I said.

You.

I went to the shed and got out a shovel. I dug a hole in the back corner of the yard, my breath coming hard.

I went inside and got a dish towel. When I came back to get the cat, Minerva was still there.

"Don't say it," I told her.

I wrapped the cat in the dish towel and carried it out to the hole I'd dug. How light it seemed, its very bones turned to matchsticks.

Afterward, I put the shovel in the shed and the sardine can in the garbage can. The garbage had been collected that morning, but a white powder had stuck to the bottom of the can, like flour.

When I came into the kitchen, Minerva was on the counter licking an oyster shell.

"I suppose you're hungry." I got out a can of cat food. Then I began to clean up the mess from the night before, knowing my efforts were hopeless, that Miss Bess would tell my mother what she'd seen.

That afternoon around five my mother swept in like a victorious warrior queen with her loot, hundreds of crystal prisms she'd managed to snag at Keil's Antiques on Royal. They'd come from a damaged chandelier, a *huge* chandelier, and she'd gotten all of them, hundreds of them, for a song. What lovely Christmas ornaments they'd make. Meanwhile, a few would do nicely to hang in the front window of the gallery to catch the afternoon sun. She unwrapped one from her handkerchief and held it in the kitchen window against the last of the light. It cast a veil over the kitchen, coloring the countertop in green and yellow and blue.

"The perfect gift, don't you think?" She looked at me expectantly, her cheeks flushed, her eyes sparkling, the afternoon sun illuminating her face.

"It's pretty," I said.

She went on and on. Imagine! A whole Christmas tree covered in these! How they'd reflect the Christmas lights: what a spectacle, what a splash! They'd go like hotcakes when the season rolled around. She'd found them in some old boxes at the back of the shop. Except for the one she showed me, which she'd cleaned in the hotel bathroom, they were filthy, covered in dust and grime. It was a wonder she'd spotted them at all. Mac had taken the rest home to wash. Would I go over and help him? She and Mac wanted to have them hanging in the shop windows by tomorrow. She'd stopped by Central Grocery before she left the City and gotten us some French bread and olive salad and pastrami. She'd throw some supper together while I helped Mac. Oh, and how'd I get along overnight?

"Oh fine," I said. "Tony came by with some oysters. I washed your nightgown and the sheets on your bed, watched some TV. That's about it."

"Good, I knew you'd be fine, just fine," she said. "You've come a long way, Mem. I'm proud of you. Go along now. I'll see you back here when you and Mac finish up."

The phone rang as I walked out the door. I kept walking, knowing who it was. When I got to Mac's, I found him at the kitchen sink singing the old song "Beautiful Dreamer," the prisms soaking in his crab pot, starlight and dewdrops waiting just for him. He fished around among the soapsuds and pulled one out, scrubbing it with a toothbrush, then rinsing and placing it on some dish towels on the kitchen table.

"Oh good, Little, you're here," he said, half-turning. "Get a clean dish towel and start drying, would you? Aren't these prisms marvelous? Your mother's a genius. I never would have spotted them in a million years."

I pulled out a dish towel from a drawer and set to work. "Where's Tony?" I asked.

"The Mustang's gone, so no telling. He wasn't here when I got home, the scoundrel, always stealing my car. Did you get into any mischief while Feather and I were gone?"

"No."

He stopped his scrubbing and rinsing and turned his full attention to me, wiping his hands on the corner of the dish towel on the table. He sat down. "You look nice, Little. Fixing yourself up?"

"It's the hair. I washed it."

He looked me over. "It's more than that. You're fifteen now, getting to be a young woman, Little. The boys are going to be knocking on your door. I don't want you to have a boyfriend until you're at least thirty, but if you do, remember to make him use protection. A girlfriend would be better."

"You already gave me those pearls of wisdom, Mac."

Had Tony been planning to use protection, whatever that was? The word had a nice ring. I liked the idea of being protected. As to Tony, I knew only I'd been led, instructed. It was all a blur of color, a pheasant flushed from the brush.

"Well, somebody's got to tell you these things, Little. Don't shoot the messenger." Mac leaned on the table, ready to dig into the subject in earnest.

I ignored him, picked up a prism, and dried it. Mac got up and started in scrubbing again. He was handing me a prism when we heard the footsteps on the back porch steps. When Tony walked in the back door, we looked up at him, both of us frozen in place, the dripping prism making a puddle on the floor.

Tony walked over to Mac. "Hey, cowboy." He squeezed Mac's arm.

Mac took one step back. "What happened to your face?"

"Damn cat of yours. Took out after me for no good reason."

"Minerva? She must have had some reason."

"Sound asleep in bed and she jumps me like a damn wildcat. Tears off half my earlobe."

"How'd she get in?" asked Mac. "She's staying over at Little's now."

"Can't a guy leave his window open at night for a little fresh air?"

A quick glance at me.

At that moment the phone rang. I was expecting it and walked over and picked up the receiver.

"Come home," said my mother.

When I got home, I was expecting a talking-to about dressing up in her clothes, the messy kitchen that Miss Bess had seen and surely had told her about by now. The beers. Instead, my mother had laid out the meal. She sat at the table waiting.

She seemed preoccupied, as if she were trying to complete a mathematical equation. She didn't eat much, and then murmured that she was tired and was going to bed.

"Oh, by the way," she said, rising from the table. "I hope Tony didn't keep you up too late last night."

"He left right after supper," I said, too quickly.

She gave me a long cold look, then picked up her plate and took it to the sink. "Can you do the dishes tonight? I'm tired."

"Sure," I said.

And that was that.

OVER THE NEXT FEW days, I upped my dosage to two pills a day, one in the morning, one at night so I could sleep. The fingernails on my paw dug deeper into my palm, my jaw ached from clenching my teeth together. I found it impossible to swallow my mother's casseroles.

That week my mother hung the prisms in the gallery window. They went like hotcakes as she'd predicted. My mother was at the gallery dreaming of prisms, of color, of beauty. My mother was having her life.

Or so I thought.

She grew quieter, her eyes always fluttering away from my gaze. At night she went to bed earlier and earlier, but kept the light on. Once I woke up in the middle of the night and heard muffled sounds coming from her room, as if she were crying in her pillow. I took my pills and faked nonchalance. Everything felt honed to a razor's edge. I tasted metal again, ate less and less. Minerva walked through the house with a lizard tail hanging from the side of her mouth, reminding me of myself.

I took to walking along the Sound again. I went at sunset. Several nights passed. Then, one night, just as the sun slipped into the Sound, Tony came up behind me. "Let's get out of this podunk town, Birdy," he said, without preamble. "Let's travel the world. Just you and me."

A pod of pelicans flew by in an impossibly straight line.

"How?" I asked.

"On a ship," he said. "We'll be gone before anybody knows the difference. We just need to wait until you're old enough."

"Old enough for what?"

"You know," he said. "Eighteen, right?"

At that moment, did I think *oh*? Did I think *oh, that's it*?

But then he said, "We're going to have ourselves some kind of life, Birdy," and he flung open his arms so wide it seemed as if he were embracing the whole world—past, present, and future.

That night I dreamed of African safaris and the Amazon rain forest. I dreamed Tony and I climbed Mt. Everest and walked along the Great Wall of China.

I did not think of betrayal. I did not think of consequences. I did not think of Mac, or my mother.

SOME STORIES WALK RIGHT off the page. They meander down a dark street like drunken men. At the water's edge, they take off their clothes and fold them carefully. Then they walk into the water, wading out onto the long shelf as dawn breaks. When the shelf gives way, they begin to swim. Should you be walking along the shore, you can see them bobbing out there, riding the swells. You shade your eyes and watch as they disappear into the smear between land and sea.

Then all you have is a pile of old clothes and memory.

THAT LAST DAY WAS a Tuesday, my mother's day off. The weather had turned sour. It was blazing hot and muggy. A storm was moving into the Gulf. The southwest sky hung low and dark, a giant ledge pushing down on the waves far out at the horizon. Above the layer of clouds, a moving darkness grumbled like a wild animal.

Over breakfast my mother told me she was going to Ship Island with Tony—she wouldn't be home when I got in from school.

"You'll need to start the spaghetti sauce." Her voice quiet and steady.

She buttered our toast and put some scrambled eggs on my plate.

"Looks like it's going to storm," I said. I'd begun picking fights with Tony on the rare occasions when we were alone together, complaining about the Ship Island picnics with my mother. He'd said he didn't want to make anyone suspicious; we needed to be careful. He and my mother were friends, that was all.

And he and Mac? Were they friends too? The unspoken question I didn't ask.

"It'll pass over," my mother said. This struck me as strange. My mother had grown up on the Sound; she wasn't one to take storms lightly. She took four slices of bread from the bread box. Then she went to the icebox and pulled out some mustard and the remainder of the pastrami from Central Grocery. She made two pastrami sandwiches and put them, along with some saltines and cheese, into her beach bag. Each of those things she did slowly and carefully. Then she opened a drawer and pulled out the only sharp knife in the kitchen and put it in the sack too.

"When will you be back?" I asked.

"Before dark," she said.

"Obviously," I said.

As I left for school, she walked me to the front door. I paused on the threshold. Something in her face.

"Mother?" The word strange in my mouth.

"It's going to be all right, Mem. You don't have to worry about anything anymore," she said. "See you tonight."

She stood in the doorway as I walked down the street. I turned and waved. She waved back, her eyes dark and large against her white, white face.

I WAS AT BAND practice when it began to thunder. Sweat—salty and hot—rolled down my forehead, scalding my eyes. At the first flash of lightning, Mr. Fann told us to get off the field. On my way home, I decided to stop by the gallery. I found Mac balancing the books between customers. On a whim, I asked him to supper. A lock of his golden hair fell into his eyes when he looked up from his ledgers. He brushed it aside impatiently, his mouth zipped tight.

"Not tonight," he said.

"I'm making spaghetti, the way you like it."

"Where's Feather?" he asked.

"She and Tony went out sailing."

"Tell her to call me when she gets home," he said, frowning. "Tell her to call me here at the gallery. I'll be going over these accounts again. Things aren't adding up."

On the way home I walked along the Sound. The sky had ripened to plum with a smear of yellow. The wind was kicking up, the Sound choppy. A spasm of rain slashed at the date palms.

I scanned the horizon, hoping to catch sight of Mac's sailboat, but there were only a couple of shrimp boats heading into dock.

As I ran across the yard, Miss Bess's face loomed large in her front window. I pretended not to see.

When I got home, Minerva was sitting in the middle of the kitchen floor. I was glad to see her. Of late she'd been giving me wide berth. She would come inside to eat, but was soon gone. She'd been sleeping under the house.

I took a pinch of ground chuck my mother had left to thaw and tried to get Minerva interested. She walked over to her food bowl and gave me a pointed look. I fed her and walked away. She ate, then lifted her head, her eyes round as nickels.

"Yeah, I know," I said. "Things are about to get much worse."

She stared at me as if she'd seen a ghost, but she didn't leave my side.

I started chopping the onion and bell pepper, poured some olive oil in the skillet, and turned the burner on. I dumped in the ground chuck, onion, and pepper and stirred them as they cooked.

Minerva rubbed my leg.

"Well, thank you," I said. "It's been a while."

When everything had browned, I dumped in the tomato sauce and oregano. I took some recorked wine from the kitchen cabinet and had a sip from the bottle, then another. I went into the living room and turned on Channel 12 for the local news. The storm was kicking up the Gulf. We could expect seven inches of rain tonight, flash flooding, high winds. I walked outside onto the porch. My mother's geranium pots had been knocked over by the wind. I righted them and propped them up behind the rocking chairs. The sky, a sickly yellow by the time I'd gotten home, had gone gray, as if some giant pterodactyl were flying over. A gust of wind took my shirt and lifted it.

When I got back inside, the phone was ringing. It was Mac asking if my mother had gotten home yet; the boat was not in the sloop. "They're going to get caught out there," he said.

"Maybe they put in at Gulfport," I said.

"Call me if you hear anything," he said and hung up.

It was time to add the wine to my sauce, so I did, then took a couple of extra sips from the bottle. I sat back down to watch the local news. The newscaster looked stern, calling what was coming a tropical storm. We should batten down the hatches, stay home, get the pets inside.

I reached into my pocket and pulled out my pills and took one.

"You hear that?" I said to Minerva, who'd climbed onto the sofa beside me. "It's bad out there. You need to stay in."

At what point did I become uneasy? Not then. I knew my mother to be a good sailor. Tony too. Minerva tucked herself into my side as I watched the news, her warmth moving through my torso the way warm milk will soak a piece of toast. Milk toast, my mother called it. She made it for me when I was sick.

I grew sleepy, irresistibly sleepy.

I WOKE UP TO footsteps and something burning. Then Mac and Tony burst through the front door, Miss Bess behind them, hobbling in on her cane. Outside it was raining cats and dogs. They were all soaking wet and dripping onto the floor. Minerva spotted Tony, snaked her way down behind the sofa.

Miss Bess hobbled straight into the kitchen. I heard the skillet scrape as she pulled it off the eye of the stove.

"Is it burned?" I called out.

She didn't answer.

Mac sat down beside me and took my good hand. Tony stood in the middle of the floor, his arms wrapped around his middle. Of the three of them, he was the wettest. He had on swim trunks, red ones with a pattern of some kind, and a t-shirt plastered to his chest. The hair on his legs ran downward in streams. He was shivering. I went to the linen closet and took out a blanket and brought it to him.

That's when I saw that he was bleeding. There were long bloody scratches up and down his arms, as if Minerva had sharpened her claws on them. One long deep gash on his cheek, which looked like a wound made by something sharp. Another on his thigh.

He was also shivering. I went back to the linen closet and brought him a towel for the blood and another blanket to dry off. I sat back down on the sofa. Mac took my hand again.

I looked at the open door. "Where's Mama?" It was the first and last time I ever called her that.

Miss Bess tapped her way back into the living room and sat down on my other side.

She put her hand on my shoulder. That was when I noticed that she was crying, her pink cheeks red and splotched.

THERE ARE STORIES IN which the mother does not have to die. This is not one of those stories.

Mac tells it. The boat tipping in the wind, my mother losing her grip and being washed overboard, Tony throwing her a line, then jumping in with a life preserver. But gone, washed under. Coast Guard unable in this weather. Tomorrow, search.

Tony stood before me, wrapped in our blanket like a sheikh, his eyes downcast.

"You couldn't reach her?" I asked.

"I tried, Birdy. It was hard to see anything in that water. Waves up to here." He reached for the ceiling.

Something about his mouth, something still.

I grew cold. It started in my feet, swimming up my legs to my gut to my chest, then down my arms. My paw, usually so hot and clammy, the last to ice over.

"She's a good swimmer," I said.

There was a silence. Then Mac said, "Yes."

Miss Bess looked up at Tony. She pushed down on the arm of the sofa and lurched into a standing position, locking her knee against the coffee table. "Get thee behind me, Satan!" She spit the words up at him, a drop falling against my cheek.

Tony ignored her. He raised his head and looked at me, his eyes somehow unlatched from the here and now, as if there were nothing, nothing at all—not a man, not an animal, not a living creature on this doomed planet—behind them. Then he moved toward me, in slow motion, his arms outstretched. "*Birdy.*"

The sound of my name low in his throat, as if it came from a cave. Then he dropped the blanket I'd given him and began to moan and flail about, drops flying from his hair and swim trunks.

He might have been playing Lear on the London stage.

"Her name is *Memory*," Miss Bess thundered. "Charlatan!" She put her hand on the back of the sofa to balance herself and leaned out and slashed at his face with her cane. Tony jumped back, agile as a cat.

Mac had begun to sob, his head in his hands. Miss Bess poked him with her cane. "Get that devil from hell out of here. You brought him in, now get him out. *Virginia* knew what he was, I told her what he was." Miss Bess turned to me. "I told her what he'd done. I told her the whole long and short of it."

Mac raised his head. "Tony?"

Still, Tony came toward me. "Birdy," he said, pushing the coffee table to the side. Miss Bess staggered and fell back onto the arm of the sofa. He paid no attention but came on. Now reaching for me, even as I shuddered and pulled back.

The last thing I remember was the sound of claws coming up the back of the sofa, ripping and shredding, then Minerva on my shoulder, pushing off.

I WOKE UP IN a white, white room. Mac at my bedside, a nurse bustling about.

Mother.

Mac reached over and wrapped his hand around my paw like a mitten. I shot up in bed and looked at him. He looked back at me and I knew. He told it again. The sailboat and the storm and Tony trying, trying. Two days had passed and no sight of her. The Coast Guard. Everybody trying, trying to find her. But nobody, nobody.

I heard a sound I'd never heard before. It took some time before I realized it was coming from me.

While I was in the hospital, Mac showed my pills to the doctors, and they asked me too many questions and kept me in the hospital a good long time, giving me smaller and smaller doses until I was begging for a crumb, breathless and crying.

At first, I cried as much for those pills as I cried for my own mother.

Miss Bess and Mac came to the hospital one late afternoon and woke me up from my nap. In the hospital I slept most of the time.

They stood on opposite sides of my bed and leaned over me.

"Memory, dear, we're wondering about a service," said Miss Bess. Her voice cracked.

I squinted up at her, the waning sun bright on my face. "What service?" I asked. "What are you talking about?"

"For Feather," said Mac, "for your mother." He stroked my hair back from my forehead.

I squeezed my eyes shut against the harsh sun. "No," I said. That was all I said.

"'Though nothing can bring back the hour / Of splendour in the grass, of glory in the flower,'" Miss Bess murmured.

I opened my eyes. "Spare me the old sayings."

Miss Bess stepped back from my bed, her eyes flooding with tears. "It's Wordsworth," she whispered, turning away.

"Now, that's no way to talk, Little. We're just trying to help," said Mac. "Let's wait a while, then. Let's wait and see. You let us know."

I went back to sleep then, and I slept until morning.

MAC TOOK ME HOME from the hospital and put me up in his back bedroom, the one my mother and I had occupied when we'd first come to Belle Cote. I rued that day. I rued it bitterly. I would have gladly lived out my whole life in our one little room at the El Camino Motor Hotel. I would have gladly died there.

I did not return to school. I couldn't face being the one-handed majorette *and* the girl with the drowned mother, and anyhow what was that woman doing gallivanting around with a known house boy?

Mac worked at the gallery, and I spent my days with Miss Bess. I was now an orphan and supposed to be living with her, according to the social worker, not with Mac McFadden, a known decadent. Miss Bess instructed me on everything from the biology of the fetal pig to the function of the semicolon, peppering me with aphorisms like Rome wasn't built in a day and slow and steady wins the race. Minerva sat beside us as I did my lessons, purring. She never left my side. At night I went home to Mac.

Mr. Wadlington at the bank sold the bungalow to a couple from New Orleans, who planted oleander bushes in the planters on the porch. In the months that followed, the loss of my mother would wash me under again and again. "It's always darkest before the dawn," Miss Bess would say, stroking my hair. Each evening Mac and I went down to the water at dusk and waited in silence, like the egrets and herons.

I folded up Tony, making the edges meet just so. I placed him in a dark closet at the back of my mind and closed the door.

ONE LATE AFTERNOON, HE came. He came like rising water, silent but deadly. Mac was still at the gallery. I was taking a load of Miss Bess's clothes out of his washer. I planned to hang them up in the backyard overnight since no rain was forecast. Miss Bess liked the smell of fresh air in her clothes.

Minerva was outside waiting for me to bring the laundry. She enjoyed swatting at the sheets after I'd hung them out to dry.

The washing machine was in a corner of Mac's kitchen. He'd artfully placed a hanging lace curtain in front of it. Through the curtain I saw the familiar shape, a cutout of white, like the angels my mother made that one Christmas at the El Camino, outlined against the late afternoon sun.

He shut the door and came on into the kitchen. He had a jagged red scar down his face.

I stepped out from behind the curtain.

He said, "Well now. Look at you." His mouth twitched a little.

Then he said it: he had come—that afternoon, that very moment—to take me away; we didn't have to wait until I was eighteen. Best to do it now. I was almost sixteen, soon we could be legally married. He knew a judge. He told me to get my stuff. He told me to hurry.

Still, I must have appeared in some way unable to comprehend his meaning because then he started to explain. The coast was clear, my mother out of the picture. He said those very words, *out of the picture*. He said them confidently, stridently even, as if I would understand their import.

He cocked his head; he raised his eyebrows. He reached for me, smiling.

And that was when I knew, knew beyond a shadow of a doubt, what he'd done. What we'd done.

MAC'S SAILBOAT HAD BEEN found floating in the Gulf about a mile out. My mother had not washed up. Each afternoon, for months, I rose from my lessons at low tide and walked out onto the long shelf, the mud oozing up between my toes, the sun melting into the pools. With my good hand, I stroked the water, seining for a piece of her.

Sometimes, now, years later, I still do this.

MAC KEPT HIS KITCHEN well organized. The knives, of which there were several, were laid out neatly on the chopping block. He kept them sharpened.

The second largest of these caught my eye. It was long and slender. It would go deep.

I kept my eyes down. This, I knew from observation, was what animals do to appear submissive, to avoid danger. I moved toward the kitchen counter, the wet towel from the washer still in my hand.

In that moment of silence, broken only by the sudden rasp of my breath, there was a commotion outside: the *tap tap* of Miss Bess's cane. She seldom attempted Mac's steps, but it seemed she was doing so now.

"Memory," she called out as she tapped her way upward. "Memory Feather. You come out, right now. Come out of that house."

Miss Bess had a surprisingly loud voice for someone so small.

Tony took my paw and latched on. With my good hand I went for the knife.

Tony reached for it, trying to avoid the blade.

At that moment, Miss Bess burst through the front door and hobbled into the living room. She looked across the dining room and into the kitchen, the cataracts in her eyes as luminous and opaque as the inside of an oyster shell.

"Memory Feather," she said, her voice harsh and commanding. "Don't jump from the frying pan into the fire."

I tightened my grip on the knife. Tony froze.

Miss Bess tapped her cane on the floor, once, then again. "Put that thing down. There's more than one way to skin a cat, Memory Feather."

"First you have to kill it," I said.

Miss Bess looked at Tony. "You give cats a bad name."

Something akin to a laugh burbled up in my throat.

"I'm calling the police on you, Tony Amato," Miss Bess quavered, waving her cane at Tony. She took in a shaky breath.

He moved toward the back door, his eyes locked on mine. "I'll be back."

Then, almost before I could blink, he slipped out the door and was down the back steps. He went as silently as he'd come, leaving the door swinging open.

I began to shake. I held on to Miss Bess, and she held on to me. Together, with her cane between us, we moved like a single five-legged animal, a crippled one, over to the kitchen table. First she sat, then I did, landing squarely in her lap like a little child. I buried my face in the soft looseness of her neck.

She let out a little moan, and I jumped up, ashamed to have caused her pain. "How'd you know to come?"

"I told you before," she said. "I see more than most people do."

"What do you see now?"

"I see three good people hoodwinked by the devil himself. I see a tattletale old lady who's as much to blame as anybody. I see a crime, but no evidence," she said. "I see a girl who shouldn't blame herself. Hindsight is twenty-twenty."

As Miss Bess pronounced on hindsight, Minerva came through the kitchen door Tony had left ajar. She jumped up on the table and gently batted at my face.

Just then Mac burst through the door, his arms loaded with bags of groceries. "What's this?" he asked, peering over his bags. His face, I saw suddenly, had lost its color, his golden mane thinned at the temples.

"You girls having a party?" he asked, wistfully, hopefully.

"No," I said.

"We were waiting for you," said Miss Bess.

DECADES CAN PASS THE way the Sound passes into the Gulf, in secretive currents that dart like schools of mullet under the tidal back-and-forth. And what does time tell us but that we are made anew, cell by cell, thought by thought?

Memory, though, is a slow trickle.

That Tuesday morning before she sailed off with Tony to Ship Island, my mother left behind a second note about supper. She'd changed her mind about wanting spaghetti. She had a taste for shrimp. I should go down to Phillipe's and get a couple of pounds, boil them up. If it wasn't too much trouble, would I please peel them, maybe make some cocktail sauce? (*Not too much horseradish, smile!*) Would I check to see if we had enough ketchup? Be sure to remember to eat a good lunch.

See you before dark!

When I saw the second note on the kitchen table, I was tired from school and band practice. The wind had begun to kick up and the sky was already spitting rain. The ground chuck had been thawing all day. So I didn't go to Phillipe's. I didn't make the shrimp cocktail. As it turned out, it would have been wasted. Still, I wish I'd made what my mother wanted for the supper she would never eat.

I do wonder about the knife she slipped into the paper sack with those sandwiches. The only sharp knife in the kitchen. Did she plan on doing away with Tony and then sailing home to a macabrely fine supper of shrimp cocktail? Or was the knife for cutting pickles?

Some stories do not tie up their apron strings.

Looking back, though, I know she was planning *something*. There was a gravity to her manner that morning, in the solemn preparation of sandwiches, in the way she surveyed me across the kitchen table. It was as if she were carrying a pan of boiling water over a baby's face.

XXI.

———

LESS THAN A YEAR after my mother's disappearance, I'd been at
Newcomb two months, had just begun to settle in, make my way. The
call came at dawn one Sunday morning in mid-November. It was unseasonably cool, and I was sleeping under the wool afghan Miss Bess had
knitted for me as a graduation present. The hall telephone in the dorm
woke me from a dream of my mother and her prisms. She was rising
from the Sound covered in them. She blinded me.

When it rang, I got up and cocked the blinds to look out the window
at the quad below, which was blanketed in acorns from the overhanging
oaks. Dawn was breaking. The squirrels scurried about busily.

It was Miss Bess. She told me to come, come right then.

By the time I'd gotten a taxi to the Greyhound station and waited for
the one bus to Gulfport that ran on Sunday, then gotten another taxi to
the hospital, it was four o'clock that afternoon. Mac was sitting up in the
hospital bed looking dazed, one side of his mouth meandering down to
his chin, his right arm flaccid at his side.

He tried to speak, his eyes widening in horror when nothing came
out. Still, I heard his unspoken words: He hated for me to see him that
way. *Get out of here, Little; leave me alone.*

"Hogwash," I said to him, startling the nurse who was fussing with the lines that ran from various spots on his body to the humming machines. "I'm here and I'm staying." With that pronouncement, I curled up in the one chair in the room, the way Minerva would have curled up had she been allowed in the hospital.

As strokes went, it wasn't the worst in the world, said the doctor. Mac was a young man, just thirty-eight; there was an excellent possibility of complete recovery. It was odd that a man so young and vigorous had been laid so low.

But in the hospital and the little country rehab facility Mac insisted on going to afterward, he lay in bed and stared out the window, refusing to do much else. At Christmas, hoping to raise his spirits, I brought him home and hired a small army to take care of him. His legs were shriveled, one hand turned inward, reminding me of my own. In the spring he scribbled me a letter saying to leave him be, get on with my life, he was good for nothing.

Then one spring evening, Oliver returned. He drove up in a sputtering Chevy convertible, its top of shredded canvas tilted skyward. "The damn thing's stuck," he announced when I met him in the driveway. He unloaded an electric Smith Corona and several packs of typing paper from the seat beside him and handed them to me, then proceeded to wrestle two large suitcases from the back seat.

"Looks like you're here to stay," I said, peering over the typewriter.

He grinned that gummy grin of his. "Any objections?"

"What took you so long?"

The grin vanished. "Maybe a certain someone should have written me. Maybe then I wouldn't have heard it through the grapevine."

"Maybe a certain someone didn't know you cared."

"That someone would be incorrect in her assumption."

And that was the end of Mac's "silliness," as Oliver called it. In short order, Mac learned to walk again and regained the use of his damaged arm. The side of his mouth marched back up into its proper place. To my surprise and delight, he broke his silence one cold rainy May afternoon by crooning the old Billie Holiday tune "I'll Be Seeing You" and then started in on a rousing rendition of "There's No Business Like Show Business."

Minerva, who'd been living the high life with Miss Bess during Mac's time away, came home reluctantly. Miss Bess had gotten her second wind. She'd been cooking Minerva scrambled eggs for breakfast and opening cans of tuna for her supper. Minerva, according to Miss Bess, deserved this queenly fare. It was she who came over and bothered Miss Bess until she followed the cat into Mac's backyard and found him propped up like a bum against the trunk of one of the oaks. How long he'd been there no one, and especially not Mac, knew, though the doctor inelegantly surmised it wasn't long; "otherwise he'd have ended up a vegetable, or dead as meat."

By early summer, Oliver was ensconced at his Smith Corona in Mac's below-room during the day, cooking up a storm under Mac's watchful eye at nightfall, and traveling back and forth every other month to meet with his editor in New York. Minerva had returned to her resting place among the dead leaves under the front step. I'd completed my first year at Newcomb.

Despite the tranquil ebb and flow surrounding me, I began to watch for buds on the oleander and angel's trumpet. I was convinced Tony would come back, and if he did, he'd try to kill me too. But first he'd have to persuade me to marry him. He'd begin by telling me I was dead wrong; I'd misunderstood him. How could I imagine in a million years his saying he'd *killed* my mother? He'd been *fond* of Virginia. She'd been his *friend*. He'd plead guilty to just one thing: he wanted me. He'd do anything for his Birdy (no, not kill my mother, of course not; how could I think such a thing?).

Would that be the moment I'd begin to waver, begin to think I'd imagined his murmured confession? Would he sense my confusion, put his hands on my shoulders, turn me to face him, force me look into his eyes? Look at *me*, he'd say—and I might.

And, if I did, what would happen then? Would his hands slide down my back and draw me to him?

Even then, I didn't trust myself. I was barely seventeen, still a girl. I could be drawn to beauty like a moth to the flame. I was only beginning to learn what I know now: that beauty is not virtue; beauty is simply beauty.

There would have been no Miss Bess to barge in and spoil his scheme. She'd gone to bed the spring after Mac's stroke and drifted out to sea, gently, as was her nature. We buried her, Mac in his wheelchair, I standing silently at his side, in the cemetery behind the railroad tracks, near Miss Muldoon and Miss Madison's little house. I selected the stone, an angel with an impressive wingspan, and had *teacher, friend* carved on it. Mac and I realized we didn't even know her birth date.

By EARLY JUNE, THE oleander and angel's trumpet were blooming to beat the band all over Belle Cote. To kill Tony, the first items needed were a mortar and pestle, which I ordered from the Sears and Roebuck catalog, then tore up the receipt so as to leave behind no trace. The day after, I clipped the oleander blossoms from Mac's bush out back, and then one night I made off with a batch of angel's trumpets from Miss Bess's desolate backyard. The two poisons were overkill (literally), but I wanted to be sure. I laid out the flowers on newspaper, which I slid under my bed. Then I waited.

For the next three nights, I floated on the heady scent from the angel's trumpet blossoms that lay beneath me. I dreamed of strangely formed prehistoric animals, one with tusks on the sides of its head like giant handles, another a large feathered cat with the wingspan of the great horned owl, *Bubo virginianus.*

One afternoon while Mac was napping, I made the roux. I mashed up the blossoms from both plants and a few leaves for good measure with the mortar and pestle. I stirred them into the pot, my hands clammy in rubber dishwashing gloves, my nose covered by my mother's scarf, the only possession of hers Mac had asked for. When the roux was brown, I added water and, given that there was no turkey at the Piggly Wiggly in Biloxi, some pieces of chicken, thinking there was no point in wasting good seafood. The kitchen smelled heavenly, a combination of flowers and stewed chicken.

After the chicken fell off the bone, I set the pot aside to cool. I would need just one serving. I ladled out a portion of the stew into a small container. I grabbed the pot, headed out back, snatched a shovel from the shed and dug a shallow hole. I put the remainder of the stew—pot, lid, and all—into the hole and covered it up, then dragged some rocks over to cover the disturbed ground so that no animal, especially the intrepid Minerva, would dig up the poisoned leftovers.

Back in the kitchen, I snatched up the Pyrex dish with the still-steaming mixture and took it out to the freezer on Mac's back porch. I removed the contents of the freezer and placed it on the bottom. I wrote out a note saying, *Do not eat! Frozen dog feces for a science experiment!* I taped the note to the dish and piled the other frozen food on top.

Two years later, I would throw away the container, realizing by that time that Tony would never risk returning. Miss Bess did call the police because of what she'd overheard him say about my mother. But the police told her she might have been mistaken; perhaps her hearing wasn't what it used to be. Besides, they asked, what would have been the motive? Which was where I came in. But I didn't tell my own story of Tony. Mac wouldn't have been able to stand the sight of me, and Mac was all I had left.

Knowing Mac as she did, Miss Bess kept my secret.

Does Mac suspect that Tony killed my mother? We have never spoken of it. Over the years, a deep silence on the subject of my mother has rippled out between us.

Nor does he speak of the money stolen from the gallery. Did my mother take it to pay off Tony, or did Tony plan to use it to oil his hasty departure from us? Was it washed overboard, padding my mother's watery grave, or did it line Tony's pockets for months, even years, to come?

Sometimes, though, I can't help but think of Tony as the little boy he must have been. Did he play ball, ride a bike, learn his lessons, sleep through mass, shoot his own father and mother? All of the above? In zoology the question arises: How much behavior is learned? How much embedded in the DNA structures, the silent tick-tock that makes up the creature? When did the milk curdle, and why?

Mac, my mother, and I might also ask ourselves the same question.

In Mac's living room, there's a blank space on the back wall where Tony's portrait hung. After my mother was lost to us, I came home from the hospital to find the portrait gone, leaving an odd gray mold underneath. Mac scrubbed the wall clean, but every so often, even after all these years, the mold comes back and has to be scrubbed again. For this reason, we have never hung another painting in that spot for fear the mold might take hold of it too. Mac did place an antique mirror there. Each time I look into it, I see the darkness behind me. Never mind Mac's and my mother's transgressions. I'd betrayed them both, and, in my tally, the fact that I was just a girl doesn't matter one whit. I knew what I was doing.

Among us, Leticia was Tony's only innocent target, though she was nobody's fool, infinitely wiser in the ways of men like Tony, who played the rest of us like poker chips. Leticia was the one who came away whole.

AFTER MAC'S STROKE AND Miss Bess's death, time speeds up. I finish college; then I go to college again, this time down in Miami. I'm a girl, then a woman, my skin stained brown from waiting and watching at the shoreline, like the wading birds my students and I track, our binoculars swinging like heavy chains around our necks. I myself nest in my grandparents' apartment in the Quarter; I teach at Loyola and write papers on wading birds. There are more of them than you might think..

Each month now I drive in from the City to spend the weekend with Mac while Oliver is in New York helping nurse his editor, who is dying of the new virus. Now it is May, and Mac and I finish our simple supper to go sit on the porch and listen to the spring creeper frogs tune up. *Pseudacris crucifer.* I tell him their scientific name, showing off.

Tonight I am bearing news, my tongue thick with it.

He takes the rocking chair, groaning a little. I have the blanket ready for his legs. Since the stroke, they get cold and jumpy, even in the hottest weather.

I fuss over him, tucking the blanket around him. For a few moments, he doesn't say anything to me or I to him, but we are as companionable as any old couple who've lived a lifetime side by side. He breaks the chocolate bar he's carried out and hands me half. I take it without speaking.

It's an overcast night. I grope my way to the porch swing. He begins to rock; I push off the swing, which still creaks. We sit together, eating our chocolate, the moths bumping our faces.

He turns to me in the crowded dark. "You've got all the money in the world, Feather. You ought to travel." Over the years, he has taken to calling me Feather.

Since the stroke, Mac sings his words. Oliver and I are the only ones who can understand him. Others say he hums. Sometimes even Oliver can't make out what he's saying. To my ears, the words are quite clear.

"Go out to San Francisco and be a hippie. Stop in New Mexico and see Leticia. She's at Los Alamos Labs now, you know," he warbles in a melodic baritone. "Go to Rome and Florence and Venice and see the great art of the western world. No point sitting around here with an old man, wasting your life. *Tempus fugit.*" He ends on a trill.

He thinks of me as still young, though we marked my forty-second birthday last month.

"I love this place—the Sound, the birds. I love what I'm doing," I say, trying not to seem defensive. "Besides, I travel. I come to see you." There's I-10 now, but I drive old Highway 90, over the swamps and one-lane bridges, over the brackish still water where my birds, the great egrets and their cousins the great blue herons, hold vigil.

It is true: I think of them as my birds, the silent watchers: *Ardea alba* and *Ardea herodias.* I'm drawn by their attitude of waiting, their active stasis. I measure how long they stand motionless: not minutes but hours on end. How intentionally they study the water, watching for movement, for some sign of life.

Now Mac leans forward, then belts out in an operatic explosion, "Try the Amazon jungle. It's got birds galore, enough birds to last a whole boatload of wildlife biologists a lifetime. I'll be here when you get back, unless the next one takes me out to sea."

I do not like this kind of talk. I push the porch swing up, up, and away, the way Tony used to, as if I might lift off and fly, as if this dear sweet earth—its caves and grottoes, its mountains and rivers and blessed marshlands—were a much smaller place than I'd ever imagined, the great oceans mere ponds, the murmuring fascinations of a lost world barely a breath from here.

"Don't worry," he sings, "I'll keep a lookout."

We never talk about my mother being dead; we say she's gone, which of course leaves room for speculation as to when she'll return. Oliver told us we should have had a funeral, that we still needed what he called "closure." To that, Mac belted out, "Maybe we don't want your stupid 'closure.' What an idiotic term."

MY MOTHER LEFT US twenty-five years ago tonight.

I don't ask if Mac remembers. I know he does.

NOW, UNDER HIS WORDS and the squeak of the rocking chair, another voice, lower pitched: a buried sorrow. He begins his long song: He is sorry sorry sorry. He loved the man, but he should have known. He should have. He would have stopped it, if only. All his fault. Nothing he can do to make it up.

He sings and he sighs. It goes on and on.

I say I forgive him. I say we were all to blame; we beautiful dreamers are frail creatures. I don't tell him what part I played. I don't say I was a leading lady, not the hat-check girl, in our little drama, our domestic tragedy.

I touch my hand, the scar on the palm still tender from the long-ago surgery Mac insisted on before I went off to college. A fresh start, he'd said. Then Miss Bess had started in, tapping my hand lightly one morning while I was fumbling with a mayonnaise jar to dress our sandwiches. "Memory, dear," she said, "why are you hanging on to this? Let it go. Doors will open to you. 'Pretty is as pretty does' will take you only so far in this cold cruel world. You can take that to the bank, my dear."

The summer I graduated from the High School of Miss Bess, Mac took me to an orthopedic surgeon in the City, and two weeks later it was done. Presto, my paw was gone and I was an ordinary girl except for my two missing digits, which are barely noticeable. "See?" Mac said then, patting the hand the day he left me in my dorm room. "Everything worked out just fine."

"Not everything," I said.

After the surgery, doors did open in the you-come-you-go-you-wear-your-hat-just-so world of humans. But doors also closed. My nonhuman friends gave me the cold shoulder. Minerva meowed to be fed, the way ordinary cats do. She never spoke to me again. The palmettos outside my window at Mac's simply rustled at night, not urging me forward or pulling me back. Instead of words words words, the mourning dove's *coo*, the heron's *krack*, Minerva's purr. Commonplace sounds, ordinary as a loaf of bread half-gone.

I miss them all.

In fact, the sheer ordinariness of day-to-day existence without my paw and all the talk talk talk, without my mother, without Tony even, makes my life before the surgery seem deeply historical, even ephemeral: a lost world as ancient as the great Pleistocene creatures that once roamed these coastal lands.

Now, as if we'd planned it, Mac and I cease our rocking and swinging and are suddenly still, listening to the night. A cat—perhaps a descendant of Minerva—yowls in the distance. The frogs rock on; there are rustlings and murmurings. Under it all, the muffled slosh of the Sound.

By now the sky's black as pitch. Three feet of darkness separate us. For this I am grateful.

It is time to deliver my news.

I pick up the flashlight Mac keeps by the swing and pull the torn newspaper clipping from my pocket. I say an Antonio D'Amato aka Tony Sorrentino aka Tony Sorrentino Amato was found dead yesterday morning in New Orleans, his body tangled in a thicket of brush by the river, alongside the levee's curve on River Road above the train tracks. He died of what the *Times-Picayune* reporter called redundant stab wounds, about fifty in all. "Somebody must have been pretty mad at the old guy," the grifter who found him told the reporter. "He had a camp up here, ran hashish off the boats. Been in and out of the slammer more times than I can count."

As I read the clipping to Mac, I think about that last day in the kitchen with Tony. What is the consistency of human flesh when you sink the knife? Gristle? Butter? Gelatin? How many times would *I* have stabbed him if Miss Bess hadn't clumped her way up those three flights of stairs? Maybe more than fifty.

I ask Mac, "Do you think he's our Tony?"

"He's not *our* Tony."

"You know what I mean."

Then Mac nods: Yes. This is the Tony we knew. This is that Tony.

"How do you know?" I ask.

"I've heard things. I keep my ear to the ground."

It occurs to me that Mac has heard the news of Tony's death already, that he is merely humoring me.

"He's gone for good then."

Mac doesn't answer. He waves his hand in a hopeless way. His rocking chair hits hard against the back of the porch.

At that moment, there's a commotion in the oak leaves next to the porch. A cool breeze ruffles the hair off the back of my neck. A kick of salt in the air. The heat suddenly lifts. It is as if a door has been opened.

Now Mac sings that it's time to feed the ferals. I get up and retrieve a bag of cat food from the container on the porch. Mac throws his blanket onto the back of his rocking chair and rises. His knees are stiff, and I take his hand as we descend the front steps.

"You need to put in an elevator," I say.

He pushes my hand aside. He says he gets around just fine; last week he and Oliver walked an hour along the Sound. Have I read Ollie's latest? It's his best yet. Set right here in Belle Cote. Rave review in the *New York Times*.

In the yard, the mosquitoes buzz around us. I can see them up against the beam of my flashlight. I wish I'd had the foresight to wear long pants.

We stand in the center of the yard, my light shining on the spot where we buried Minerva. The ancient oaks brood above us. Does my cat sleep restlessly, the way I do, tossing and turning, wondering *what if?*

Of course not. She was the one who knew Tony for what he was. Minerva: goddess of wisdom and defensive warfare. Mac named her well.

And where is Tony now? In a pauper's grave, his beauty gone to rot? I would have killed him if he'd come back; truly I would have.

What I wouldn't do is tell the truth, establish motive. What I wouldn't do was risk losing Mac too.

`He leans down, fills the scoop from the bag of cat food. He begins to scatter the nuggets.

The cats come first. They are skittish but bold, bellies low to the ground, the mothers with their wiry kittens, the big toms on their long legs. The trees alive too as the raccoons shimmy down.

In the shadows, at the corner of the yard under a giant fern, a flash of black and white: a skunk, grateful beyond measure. She swishes toward the food. The cats and raccoons move to make a space for her.

There is plenty for everyone. No scarcity here.

Silent as ghosts, the animals feed, moving like water across the grass, nourishing themselves against whatever tomorrow may bring.

It is a pleasure to watch them.

Mother, I've made my way in this world of loss you left behind. I listen in new registers, studying cells and DNA, habitat and reproduction, beauty and its uses. I invite friends and lovers to my place in the Quarter. Sometimes I walk in the early morning hours, my hair now long and as speckled with silver as a fish's scales. The street people nod as I pass by: Jimmie with his lonely harmonica, the tarot card woman who snores softly by the river, Ruthie the Duck Girl with her faithful entourage of webbed friends.

I watch and wait at the place where the water meets the land.

What I've learned from the study of animals is that the unexpected can happen. Strange mutations, sudden extinctions, improbable returns. The whole thing is one big soup, Mother; so believe me when I say that, one day, when the mastodons walk again on this lost land and the saber-toothed tigers pace, you will cast off the veil of night and rise from the Sound in the red morning sun. You will burn away the dew from the leaves on the trees and skim the water like the ancient white pelican.

Then, at long last, in the space of a breath, you will shake the water from your hair and take to the shining shore, wet and glistening and new.

You will call out, *Memory*.

ACKNOWLEDGMENTS

———

C oming to the close of my pandemic project, *Beautiful Dreamers*, I had a beautiful dream. All of the lovely people who have helped me find the best in this book and then helped it find its way in the world were gathered around a large table. I was able to toast them, each one in turn. Everyone was wearing party hats; food and drink and flowers were in abundance. It was, for me, the party to end all parties.

On this earthly plane, my first toast goes to my brilliant agent and cherished friend, Jane von Mehren of Aevitas Creative Management, who read The Whole Thing several times and gently but firmly helped me separate the wheat from the chaff. The two of us met more than a decade ago when we ended up next to each other at a dinner in Taos, New Mexico. It was one of the luckiest breaks of my life, and I owe an enormous debt of gratitude to Jane, who has sent three of my novels out into the world and never wavered in her belief in my work. I also thank Maggie Cooper and Nicole Stockburger for their invaluable help.

I owe Meg Reid and Kate McMullen of Hub City Press a mastodon-sized debt of gratitude for offering *Beautiful Dreamers* a home with a big welcome mat, then taking on the editing of it with sharp eyes, open hearts, and a remarkable tolerance for my technical ineptitudes. I deeply appreciate your dedication and commitment to my work and to making Hub City Press a shining star among independent presses.

I'm also immensely grateful to Charles Frazier and his generosity in funding the Cold Mountain Series at Hub City. I'm honored that *Beautiful Dreamers* is now a part of this wonderful collection of fiction by writers from the American South.

Thank you also to Julie Jarema at Hub City and Kathy Daneman of Kathy Daneman Public Relations for their enthusiasm and expertise in helping *Beautiful Dreamers* find its way to readers, and to Luke Bird for his cover design featuring the stunning portrait by Irma Cook. I'm very grateful to the Johnson Collection in Spartanburg, South Carolina, for permission to use the painting by this remarkable woman portrait artist of the mid-twentieth century. And thanks to Iza Wojciechowska, whose eagle editorial eye sent errors scurrying, and to William E. "Eddie" Coleman at the Hancock Historical Society Library for invaluable help.

I offer a toast to Harry Thomas, author of the wonderful book *Sissy! The Effeminate Paradox in Postwar US Literature and Culture*, who helped tremendously with historical and cultural elements of the novel; and to Julie Mars, author and editor extraordinaire, who made it her business to show me the heart of the book and who has encouraged me in crucial ways over the years. Thanks also to John Howard, whose important book *Men Like That: A Southern Queer History* provided important information about the history of gay men in my home state of Mississippi.

I am deeply grateful to the late Kenneth Holditch and David Baker, gay men of my mother's generation who came of age in my hometown of Tupelo, Mississippi, and lived lives of courage and verve and style. Our roots go deep. Kenneth loved my schoolteacher grandmother, and in fact petitioned the Lee County School Board for (gasp!) a third year of Latin so that he could continue studying under her tutelage. As a professor and scholar, Kenneth published definitive studies on Tennessee Williams and adopted New Orleans as his home city, where in his later years I would find him giving French Quarter tours in his wheelchair. David was one of my mother's best high school buddies and rode out the historic 1936 Tupelo tornado with her after bringing her a stack of homework when she was grounded with a broken shoulder. Kenneth and David are gone now, but the example of their lives shaped this novel and my own life in crucial and unexpected ways. The youthful friendship between David and my mother was the catalyst for *Beautiful Dreamers*.

I'm also grateful for dear friends and family in Bay St. Louis, the town on which Belle Cote is based, and in Pass Christian next door, for their hospitality and love of the mysteries of the Mississippi Sound, especially my beloved cousin Lynn Kincannon Holland, the original Beautiful Dreamer, who drew so many of us there and to whose memory this book is dedicated. I also toast my fine friend Ellis Anderson. I wrote most of my first novel, *The Queen of Palmyra*, over the course of two summers in her beautiful Bay St. Louis home, which I recast as Mac McFadden's house in this novel.

To other members of my blood and chosen families far and wide who have supported me through thick and thin, I offer my heartfelt thanks. You have meant more to me than I can ever say.

Finally, a toast to my partner, now of thirty-four years, Ruth Salvaggio, who continues to be the smartest person and most discerning reader I know, and to the four-leggeds of our household who never cease to make me laugh.

Cheers!

The COLD MOUNTAIN *Fund*
S E R I E S

NATIONAL BOOK AWARD WINNER Charles Frazier generously supports
publication of a series of Hub City Press books through the Cold Mountain
Fund at the Community Foundation of Western North Carolina. The Cold
Mountain Series spotlights works of fiction by new and extraordinary writers
from the American South. Books published in this series have been reviewed
in outlets like the the *Boston Globe, Wall Street Journal, San Francisco Chronicle,
Garden & Gun, People* Magazine, and *Entertainment Weekly;* included on Best
Books lists from NPR, *Kirkus Reviews,* and the American Library Association;
and have won or been nominated for awards like the Southern Book Prize, the
Ohioana Book Award, Crooks Corner Book Prize, and the Langum Prize for
Historical Fiction.

PREVIOUS TITLES

Good Women • Halle Hill

The Say So • Julia Franks

The Crocodile Bride • Ashleigh Bell Pedersen

Child in the Valley • Gordy Sauer

The Parted Earth • Anjali Enjeti

*You Want More: The Selected Stories
of George Singleton*

The Prettiest Star • Carter Sickels

Watershed • Mark Barr

The Magnetic Girl • Jessica Handler

HUB CITY PRESS

PUBLISHING
New & Extraordinary
VOICES FROM THE
AMERICAN SOUTH

FOUNDED IN Spartanburg, South Carolina in 1995, Hub City Press has emerged as the South's premier independent literary press. Hub City is interested in books with a strong sense of place and is committed to finding and spotlighting extraordinary new and unsung writers from the American South. Our curated list champions diverse authors and books that don't fit into the commercial or academic publishing landscape.

Funded by the National Endowment for the Arts, Hub City Press books have been widely praised and featured in *the New York Times,* the *Los Angeles Times, NPR, the San Francisco Chronicle, the Wall Street Journal, Entertainment Weekly, the Los Angeles Review of Books,* and many other outlets.

HUB CITY PRESS books are made possible through the generous support of grants and donations from corporations, state and federal grant programs, family foundations, and the many individuals who support our mission of building a more inclusive literary arts culture in the South, in particular: Byron Morris and Deborah McAbee, Charles and Katherine Frazier, and Michel and Eliot Stone. Hub City Press gratefully acknowledges support from the National Endowment for the Arts, the Amazon Literary Partnership, the South Carolina Arts Commission, the Chapman Cultural Center, Spartanburg County Public Library, and the City of Spartanburg.